ASHES OF STONE

ALSO BY HALEY RYLANDER

LIFESTONE TRILOGY

Essence of Stone

Ashes of Stone

Shaping of Stone

LIFESTONE TRILOGY BOOK II

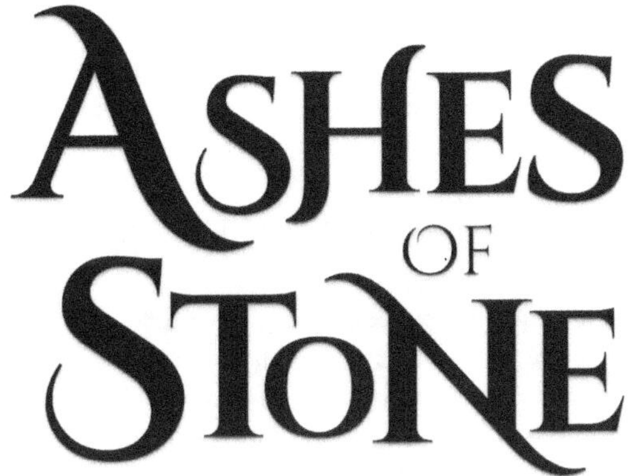

ASHES OF STONE

HALEY RYLANDER

Aspen Leaf
Press

Published in the United States by Aspen Leaf Press

Paperback ISBN 979-8-9856103-3-8
Hardback ISBN 979-8-9856103-4-5
eBook ISBN 979-8-9856103-5-2

Edited by Alfred Bagdonas
Cover art and illustration © Grace Crandall

Printed in the United States of America

First edition September 2022

Aspen Leaf
Press

CONTENTS

For Jake

Terulian Mountains
Ciel
Morcanan
Riverseep Forest
Yavran
The Wildwood
Lay Hills
Remsgraen
Lake Orhirion
Ard Gael
Maramor
Rone
Braided River
The Grasslands
Orhiri River
Telem Fier
Calafor
Tura
Semestrial Sea
Faeran

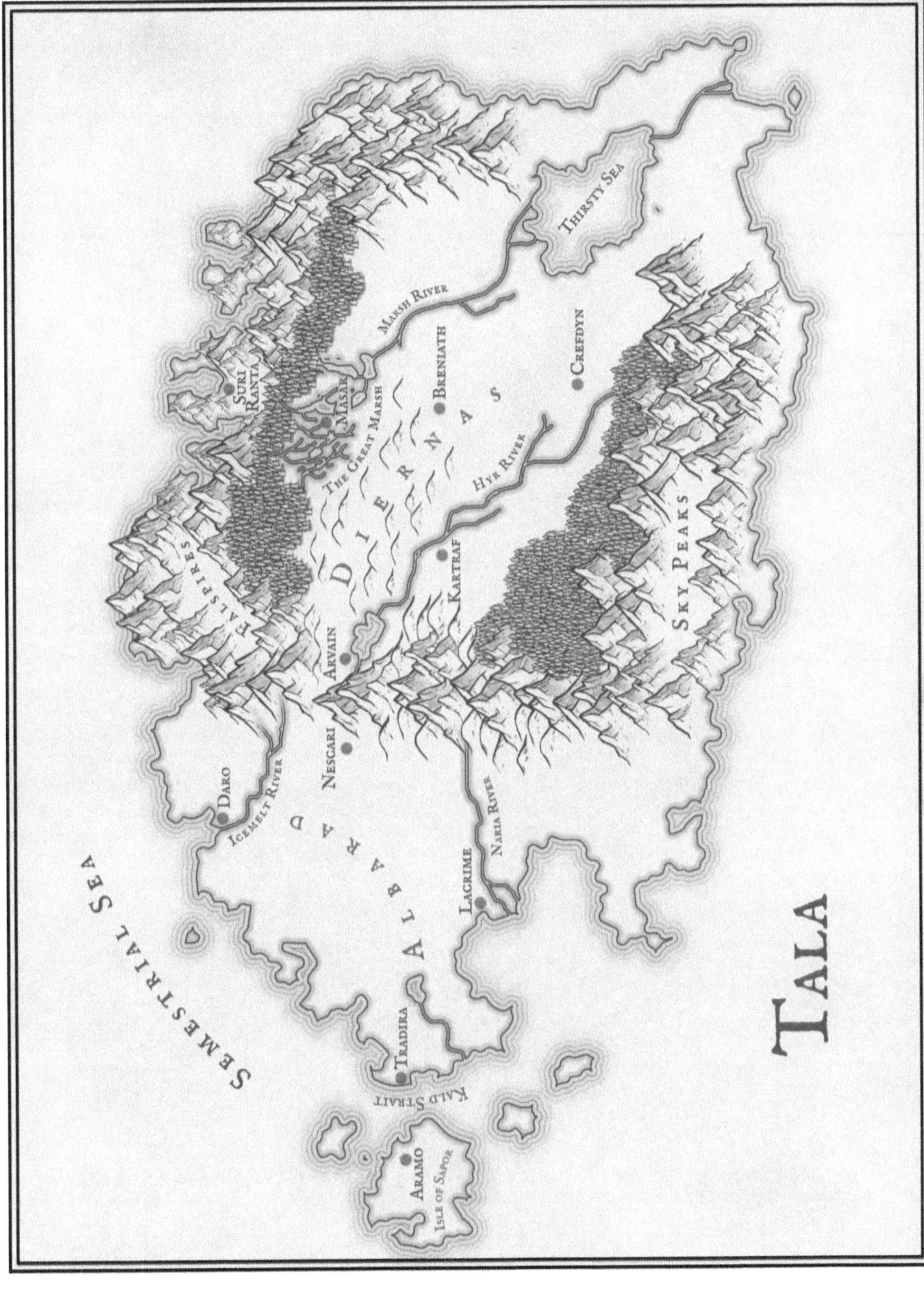

THIRSTY SEA
MARSH RIVER
BRENIATH
CREFDYN
SURI RANTA
MASAR
THE GREAT MARSH
D I E R N A S
HYR RIVER
BALSPIRES
ARVAIN
KARTRAF
SKY PEAKS
DARO
ICEMELT RIVER
NESCARI
A L B A R A D
NARIA RIVER
LACRIME
SEMESTRIAL SEA
TRADIRA
KALD STRAIT
ARAMO
ISLE OF SAPOR
TALA

CHARACTER LIST

Fieri

- Auralia (uh-rah-lee-uh): Kindom Council Member, Lady of Rone
- Caerlyn (kair-lihn): Sira performer, friend of Renyra and Firas
- Cuvan (koo-vahn): Kindom Council Member, Lord of Telem Fier
- Renyra (reh-neer-uh): Sira performer, hunter, Firas's wife, guest to Turi Council

Morcani

- Aryn (ahr-ihn): builder, vierstone master of Daro
- Dulon (doo-lon): Lord of Daro, host of the last Kindom Council
- Firas (feer-ahss): Renyra's husband, shipwright, Sira performer
- Miyela (mee-yel-uh): Kindom Council Member, Lady of Morcanan

Remsgri

- Rava (rah-vuh): Rale Master of Tura

- Rhosti (rah-stee): Kindom Council Member, Lord of Remsgraen
- Trali (trah-lee): Sira performer, friend of Renyra and Firas

Turi

- Alos (al-ohss): Turi Council Member, Master of Trade in Tura
- Alsena (al-sayn-uh): Turi Council Member, Master of Guilds in Tura
- Alura (uh-lurr-uh): Sira performer, Raren's sister, friend of Renyra and Firas
- Bredan (bray-dahn): stoneworker in Maramor
- Coren (korr-ihn): Master of Sport in Tura
- Dorian (dorr-ee-an): Turi Council Member from the southern Wildwood region
- Farra (fair-uh): Veldon's wife
- Gellion (gehl-ee-un): Kindom Council Member for Daro, metalworker
- Kaelo (kay-lo): metalworker exiled by the Turi before the Great War
- Kelia (kehl-ee-uh): gate guard in Tura
- Kyna (kihn-uh): visiting elf to Daro, guest to Turi Council
- Liera (lirr-uh): Kindom Council Member, Lady of Tura
- Maelom (may-luhm): jeweler, vierstone worker in Tura
- Raren (rahr-ihn): Sira performer, Alsena's brother, friend of Renyra and Firas
- Reanan (ray-uh-nahn): Turi Council Member, Master Builder of Tura
- Saethir (sayth-ihr): Turi Council member from eastern Ard Gael
- Tenille (tehn-ihl): Kindom Council Member, Lady of Maramor, Gellion's mother
- Tornac (tor-nak): Gellion's older brother, metalworker
- Valder (vahl-durr): Gellion's younger brother, shipwright

- Veldon (vehl-duhn): Gellion's youngest brother, stoneworker

HUMANS

Aektar

- Saladin: member of Aektar board of traders

Albaren

- Arceria, Chiara: wife of Marchon Arceria
- Arceria, Nicabar: head of wealthy trading family, Marchon
- Benta, Amadeo: Earl, messenger of King Naval
- Naval, Danelo: King of Albarad, based in Tradira
- Vensure, Justus: military commander of Tradira

Dierna

- Eira: trader from Arvain
- Eurig: Lawgiver of the Elder Clan
- Haf: trader from Arvain
- Talaith: trader from Arvain

Kayda

- Aku: husband of Ruta, son of Heleena
- Esteri: The Sovereign of the Kayda
- Isla: Heleena's aunt, taken in by a selkie, deceased
- Hakan: young son of Aku and Ruta
- Heleena: old woman from Suri Ranta, Aku's grandmother
- Ruta: spirit woman of Suri Ranta, wife of Aku

PART I

1

A TRAITOR

The doors before Gellion were simple, yet somehow elegant. Crisp paint lined a border that wandered over the top and sides of each panel. The doors were clean. Proud. At the prison guard's touch, they swung forward on silent hinges.

Gellion took a deep breath and let it out in a controlled stream. This was not the first time he had stood before a human leader to defend himself, nor was it the first time the safety and livelihood of the elves depended upon his amicable release from prison. How did this keep happening?

He limped slightly as he crossed polished wood to the man standing at the room's head. Except for this man, the hall was empty. Wide windows lined the back wall, looking over a lake that could have passed for the sea. Its surface, ruffled with waves, stretched to a distant haze.

Gellion's head and ribs still ached from the battle. Had it been only a few days since Gellion's world crashed around him? It could have been a week as far as he knew. Both Gellion and his brother had woken in their cell to the monotonous passing of the sun on an unknown day, and their human guards had not deigned to enlighten them on the happenings of the outside world. Part of Gellion didn't want to know. He didn't want to know if Valder were dead—or Firas, or Kyna, or any of the rest of his friends, family, or kin. For all Gellion knew, they were all back to Daro by now. Gellion's breath caught in his throat.

What was once Daro.

He blinked hard. No. He could not think about that now.

With a massive effort of will, Gellion anchored himself to the present. None of the rest of it mattered if he couldn't get out of this city, if he couldn't get back to Faeran before it was too late.

Gellion stopped several paces away from who he assumed was the leader of Arvain. The man stood with both feet firmly planted on the floor; there were no chairs in the room. His face was lined, and his hair was a matte of silver streaked with grey, but his eyes were bright and intelligent. They held Gellion's gaze.

"Your name?" He spoke in lightly accented Albaren, the trade language of the humans.

"Gellion."

The man nodded slowly. "I am Eurig."

Silence followed. Gellion shifted his weight, concentrating on keeping eye contact with Eurig. Was he supposed to acknowledge the man somehow? He inclined his head.

Eurig only looked at him.

"You are the—king?" Gellion said.

Eurig let out a puff of air. "We do not have kings. I am the head of the Elder Clan. The Lawgiver." His eyes continued to bore into Gellion, as though trying to read his soul. At last he spoke again. "Why did the elves ally with the Albaren?"

Gellion almost flinched. It was a question he had been expecting, and one that had haunted his waking hours for days. Why had the elves allied with the Albaren? If Gellion had voted 'no' that day—what now seemed years ago—would he be standing in Daro now? Would Daro itself still stand? Would Dulon—

No. Don't think about it.

"The elves are no friends of the Albaren," Gellion said.

"Yet you accompanied their army to our doorstep."

Gellion hesitated. "Yes."

Eurig raised his eyebrows.

"The elves have traded with the Albaren for centuries," Gellion said, "but we have had little contact with them otherwise. King Naval came to us, asking for our aid, claiming that the Dierna were raiding their villages, killing innocents, cheating them in trade, and encroaching upon their borders."

Eurig's face remained calm, but a fire burned deep in his eyes.

"Did he, now?" he said softly.

"We agreed to help the Albaren based upon their word." Gellion's nails bit into his palms. "Then they betrayed us."

Eurig's brows twitched upward again. He remained silent.

"They turned on us in the middle of the battle."

"Any who trust the Albaren are fools," Eurig said. "Yet ignorance is no excuse for your actions. The Dierna expected an army of two thousand Albaren. Instead we met nearly three thousand in addition to an army of elves. Still, we took the day because we planned for treachery, and we were not disappointed."

A shudder rippled down Gellion's spine. He could still hear the braying of horns just before the Dierna reinforcements had charged from the hills, scattering both the elves and the Albaren like a school of fish among sharks. Yet that memory alone was not what made his blood run cold. As the horns reverberated in his mind, a painfully sharp image of Dulon's face followed, blood streaked and staring, his easy smile lost to Riu forever. Gellion bit down on his tongue.

"All the same," Eurig continued. "I lost a quarter of my army in that battle. Men, women. Members of my clan and of Ash Clan. Fathers. Mothers. Sons. Daughters."

Gellion's heart was thudding against his chest. The Dierna had been the enemy. They had raided innocent villages. The elves had fought for what was right. They had fought for vierstone.

A vierstone quarry that never existed.

Gellion took a steadying breath. Not now. Not in front of the clan leader. He could not show weakness.

"The elves pose no further threat to the Dierna," Gellion said. "What remains of the army you saw is gone—returning to our lands. I am sorry for the death we have caused. Please—" Gellion paused, swallowing his anger and pride and guilt in a dry throat. "I humbly ask that you would allow us—my brother and me—to return to our people. We will bring no further harm to your clan."

Eurig raised an eyebrow. His eyes were an icy grey, somehow more disconcerting than the muddy depths of the Albaren's. With a last considering look, Eurig's gaze wandered to the side, sliding out of focus.

"The elves." He spoke as though to himself. "We have heard of the elves, though until recently, none of us had seen them. The Albaren traders wove tales—wild and colorful. Tales of the elves of the north—the faeries, the creatures whose faces do not grow old and whose powers transcend the will of the Almighty."

Gellion stiffened. How long had the humans brooded on these fanciful legends of the elves? His people had never paid much heed to the humans, content to politely ignore them in all matters beyond trade, yet somehow that passivity had bred tales of mystery, hostility, and fear. Gellion had been shocked by the attitude and accusations of the Albaren. The elves were not heathens or demons.

Eurig turned his head sharply back to Gellion. "Who are the elves? Where do you come from and what do you want in this land?"

Gellion did not answer at once, taken aback by the sudden change in Eurig's tactic.

"The elves come from a land far from here," he said slowly, choosing his words with care. "We built a city on the northern coast of Albarad for purposes of our own, but that purpose is now—"

That purpose is now destroyed.

"Now—fulfilled," he said. "The elves are leaving this land, never to return."

Eurig narrowed his eyes, clearly not appeased by Gellion's enigmatic answer.

"Why should I believe that? You come here with an army and no explanation, then claim that the elves are truly a peaceful folk, homebound, never to bother us again?"

Heat crept up Gellion's neck. "I told you, the Albaren—"

Eurig held up a hand to stop him. "I know what you told me." His eyes bored into Gellion. "Do you know why the Dierna were prepared for your attack?"

Gellion opened his mouth to answer, then closed it. The elves and the Albaren had emerged from the hills before the gates of Arvain to see a full army waiting for their surprise attack. Gellion had briefly wondered who had betrayed the Albaren, but the question had become lost in the midst of much more pressing matters.

Eurig scrutinized Gellion's face, as though watching for his reaction.

"Well?" he said.

"I—" Gellion shook his head. "I assumed it was an Albaren traitor, or a Dierna spy."

Eurig's eyes narrowed further. "It was neither."

Gellion looked at Eurig, trying to understand what the man was getting at.

"It was no Albaren, and it was no Dierna," Eurig repeated. "It was an elf."

Gellion stood stunned.

Every nerve in his body reacted to the word. A chill spread over his skin.

An elf? But why? *How?* In the two centuries of their time in Tala, the elves had never made contact with the Dierna. What possible motivation would have driven one of Gellion's own people to warn the Dierna of an Albaren attack? An attack that the elves were a part of? It had been no secret that many of the elves in Daro did not approve of the alliance with Albarad, but to sabotage a battle in which their own kin's lives were at stake?

Eurig watched him. "An elf comes to my people, warning us of an impending Albaren attack and passing us inside information, then an army of elves shows up on our doorstep standing beside the very enemy they had betrayed. An enemy you now claim betrayed you." A corner of his mouth twitched upward. "You see, then, why I am reluctant to believe the plausibility of your story."

At last Gellion found his voice, plucking a single question from the tangle in his mind.

"Who was the elf?"

"You claim that you did not know of this?"

"I didn't," Gellion growled, fighting to control the rising heat in his chest. "Who were they? When did they contact you? How did they contact you?"

"Enough." Eurig's voice echoed through the empty hall. The guards standing back from Gellion straightened, strengthening their grip on their swords.

"I did not bring you here to ask me questions," said Eurig. "How am I to trust the word of a race pleading innocence by ignorance and victimization by deceit when one of that race warned me of an attack they failed to mention they were a part of?" He chuckled without humor. "I cannot even phrase it in a way that does not sound ridiculous. What game are the elves playing?"

"I knew nothing of this. *We* knew nothing of this. I swear to you— I don't know who the elf was who contacted you, but they spoke with no authority for Daro. All that I told you is true. The elves acted as we thought was right. We placed our trust in the wrong people. Please. You must release us. Our people are in danger. We have to return to our home."

"Release you?" It was as close as Eurig had come to shouting. He took a breath and lowered his shoulders. "You give me no satisfactory answers and you expect me to trust your word that the elves are no threat to Diernas? I ask again. Where do you come from and why are you here?"

Gellion's head pounded, and a restless energy born of anger and fear clawed at his skin. He could not tell Eurig the truth. This entire disaster had sprung from a single human king learning about vierstone. To explain the elves' secrets to an equally powerful human leader would be madness.

But Gellion had to get back to Faeran.

Kaelo's face flashed before his eyes. Was the mentor of Gellion's youth still in Tala? Had he already secured passage to Faeran in whatever way he had come to this continent in the first place? Or was his revenge—or whatever motivation fueled his actions—complete at the destruction of Daro and its beloved vierstone?

"I cannot tell you," Gellion said. "I'm sorry, but I must protect my people."

Eurig's face was a mask of stoicism. "And I must protect mine," he said shortly. "I will not release traitors and secret keepers who threaten the safety and livelihood of the Dierna."

By unspoken order, the guards to either side of Gellion stepped forward and turned him back toward the entrance to the hall.

"Listen to me!" Gellion shouted, resisting the guards and facing Eurig again. "You have to let us go! You have to believe me! If we stay here even a week it will be too late!"

Eurig made no answer. The guards forcibly turned Gellion's shoulders and pushed him in front of them as they walked.

Gellion's heart beat to the time of his steps. Fighting would get him nowhere, but neither would sitting in a locked cell. He would find a way to get out of this city. He had to.

The prison was a short walk down the street. The road was wide and cobbled, with people and horses passing purposefully up and down its surface. Gellion watched them. Most wore plain clothes of simple wool or linen. All stared as he passed.

The guards stopped in front of a wide door with iron locks. At a hefty pull, the door swung outward with a groan.

Stale air hung like a moth ridden blanket inside the prison entrance. Within, sunlight faded, and the merry sounds of livelihood from the street muted to a distant memory. The guards pushed Gellion ahead of them and marched him through two gates of iron that separated the main doors from the prison halls beyond. Gellion glanced into a large common room to the left of the main entrance. Bars of sunlight striped across couches and game tables, and a great fireplace blazed on the far wall. Several men in crisp uniform lounged about the space and blew smoke from pipes.

"You are not here to sight see," one of Gellion's guards said gruffly, pushing him past the common room and toward the stairs at the end of the hallway.

Veldon's eyes flicked up as Gellion slipped through the door to their cell. A clang and catch behind him sealed their captivity. Gellion paced to the high window across from the door and huffed in frustration.

"Went well, did it?" Veldon said. He was leaning against a wall, fiddling with an earring of green stone between his fingers.

Gellion only clenched his jaw. The silhouette of a bird passed over the slice of sky beyond the window, letting out a joyful caw. Gellion thought of the soaring seabirds of Daro. His fists clenched.

"Well, what did he say?"

"We aren't going anywhere." Gellion sighed. "The clan leader fears the elves are a threat to Diernas and wants information on Faeran and the elves as a whole. I gave him nothing, and he did not like it."

Veldon nodded. "Fair enough."

Gellion rounded on Veldon. "Fair enough!?"

"What would you say if a mysterious nation of humans came to Faeran under banners of war, then ran back across the sea, pleading that they never meant any harm?"

"That's not what we did."

"It's a bit of what we did."

Gellion's stare was murderous.

"I'm not saying you should have told him anything more," Veldon said quickly. "I'm merely pointing out that his reaction is rational, given his understanding of the circumstances."

"I told him what happened. I told him about King Naval's accusations against the Dierna, of the alliance, of their betrayal. We were greater victims of this fight than the Dierna!"

"Did he believe you?"

"I don't know." Gellion ran a hand through his hair. "There was more to it than that."

Veldon's brows drew together. "What do you mean?"

"Eurig—that's the clan leader—says that someone gave the Dierna inside information about this Albaren attack, and it was no Albaren or Dierna."

Veldon's eyes widened. They were almost greener than the vierstone in his hand and matched their brother Valder's with shocking precision. Gellion turned away, pressing down the well of anxiety threatening to rise into his throat. If Valder was dead, it would be his fault. His mother would never forgive him. He would never forgive himself.

"An elf?" Veldon's voice was barely a whisper.

Gellion nodded.

"But who?"

"I don't know. Eurig would give no details."

Veldon shook his head. "I don't understand. Why would an elf betray the attack? And judging from the size of the Dierna army, they must have known weeks, maybe even months in advance. Do you think the elf may have tipped them off before we even accepted the alliance with Albarad?"

"Why? As an anonymous benefactor to a nation they had never even seen?"

Veldon rolled his vierstone earring between his fingers. Looking down at it, he said, "Could it have been the same elf who caused the earthquakes and destroyed Daro?"

Gellion stiffened. He himself had not known of Daro's destruction until just before the end of the battle days before. Renyra, a Fieri elf and the wife of one of Gellion's closest friends, had stayed behind in the city with a broken arm while most of the elves marched to battle. Mere days after their departure, the elf responsible for the last month of inexplicable earthquakes and dying vierstone had sent the city crumbling into the sea. Renyra had ridden across all of Albarad to bring the news of Daro's destruction to Gellion and Dulon, but she had arrived in the midst of battle. Gellion had told Veldon of Daro's fate, but had left out the detail that he knew who had caused all of it.

As soon as Renyra had described the man who sent Daro into the sea, Gellion had known who it was. He knew who had somehow acquired the ability to break stone and metal at a touch, render vierstone black and lifeless, and tear a city apart by its foundations. He should have realized it long before. The shocking reappearance of Gellion's past mentor still made his head spin and tied his stomach in knots. Kaelo had been banished centuries before the Great War for the unthinkable crime of murder, and had not been seen for over six hundred years.

"It could have been the same elf," Gellion said vaguely.

"I have been thinking about the elf. He must have known the city would be deserted. Maybe he had something to do with the alliance."

"The Albaren proposed that alliance to weaken the Dierna and to rid Tala of the elves in one fell swoop. It was entirely for their own purposes."

"But they knew about vierstone." Veldon held up his earring as illustration. "You said yourself that neither you nor Dulon ever told the Albaren about vierstone, yet they knew to use it as a bargaining chip. Only an elf could have told them that, and if it was neither of you, it must have been someone else."

Gellion frowned. Could Kaelo have told the Albaren about vierstone—orchestrated the battle just to empty Daro? The alliance had done more than present an abandoned city. The decision to join the alliance had caused a rift through the elves like Gellion had not seen since the Great War.

"But why would the same elf warn the Dierna of the alliance he had endorsed?" Gellion said.

"A penchant for mischief?" Veldon smiled weakly. "Alright, I don't know," he said to Gellion's sour expression.

Gellion put his back to the wall and slid down next to Veldon. The susurrus of conversation from the streets below carried through the thick glass of the window. Veldon tilted his head down and refastened his earring, then leaned back and stared at the ceiling.

"Do you think any of it was true?" he asked softly.

"Any of what?"

"The raids. The murder and the rape and everything else the Albaren accused the Dierna of committing."

"I don't know."

"The Dierna have not presented themselves as a barbarous race so far."

"No, they haven't. But they were no merciful servants of Riu in battle either. Vensure—" Gellion paused, a flare of hatred catching the name in his throat. He had never liked the Albaren commander, but now he hoped the man's soul would rot in hell for what he had done to Dulon.

"Vensure expected to see Dierna outposts in Restring Pass. He was a treacherous viper, but I don't think he fabricated the Albaren's grievances against the Dierna. The Albaren would have fought that battle without the elves, I'd wager. They just would have been denied the double victory they hoped for." He slammed a fist into the floor. "I really don't care a wit what the Dierna or Albaren have or haven't done or why they did it. I care about being free of them both and crossing the Semestrial Sea before Kae—" he caught himself. "before the elf works the same devilry in Faeran as he did in Daro. Before the last elven ships in Tala leave us here for lost."

Veldon hugged his knees to his chest. "They must think us dead." He turned his eyes on Gellion, pain and pleading in their depths. "What must Valder think? What if the elves send word to mother and Tornac when they get to Tura?"

Gellion's face softened. His brother's blind faith that Valder was still alive, mourning them for dead, wrenched his heart.

"All the more reason to get back to them soon."

Veldon did not look comforted. "When do you think the elves will leave Tala?"

"It took us about six days to get here from Daro on foot. But the elves won't be able to take the road back through Albarad, and some of them may be hurt. All the same, I expect they will set sail as soon as they get to Daro, so long as there are still ships in the harbor. In that case, we would have to travel fast to catch them now."

"And if it's too late?"

"We find another way." Gellion spoke the words with as much confidence as he could muster, but he had no idea what that other way would be. They needed to leave now. They needed to catch the elves before they took the last ships across the sea. Riu knew how long it would be before he and Veldon could find alternate passage, and come autumn, the Semestrial Sea would be impassable for half a year.

"Is there any reasoning with Eurig?" Veldon asked.

"Not without telling him everything about the elves and threatening the safety of Faeran further. Even then, I don't think he would release us in the next few days. He's sharp—shrewd. It will take some serious convincing to depart Arvain on amicable terms."

Veldon took a deep breath, releasing his knees and turning to face Gellion. A smile played at the corners of his mouth.

"Then we will have to escape."

2

SLIVER OF WOOD

Each day that passed doubled Gellion's anxiety and lessened the chances that he and Veldon would catch the elves before the last ships left Tala. But their plan had to be perfect. A failed escape attempt would utterly destroy what small chance they had. They had to account for every possibility, and they had to succeed on their first attempt. Getting out of the prison was the first priority, and Gellion and Veldon had agonized over the plan until they could recite it in their sleep, but what happened after that was much more difficult to anticipate.

From the small window in their cell, Gellion and Veldon could see little of the city, and their blindness to its layout was the greatest weakness in their scheme. The guards had walked Gellion through the streets near the prison to take him to Eurig. Gellion knew their cell was on the second of three floors of the prison, and he knew which way was north —the direction of the main city gates—but whether or not they could escape through the gates at night was a shot in the dark.

"We might be able to scale the walls to either side of the central gates." Veldon's voice was less than a whisper. They stood huddled in the back of their cell, gazing out the window at the winking lights of streets and distant buildings. Iron bars welded to metal sheets were bolted to the walls on either side of the window.

"Do you remember what the city walls looked like?" Gellion asked.

Veldon knit his brows in concentration. Moonlight reflected bluish silver off his face. His dark hair blended with the black of their cell.

"Not really. I can't see it from here. Most of the city is wood, and the gates were definitely wood, but the wall may be stone."

"Stone would be easier to climb if it is roughly built, but wood may have areas of weakness." Gellion shook his head. "The front gates would be our best bet if they're open, but we can't count on that in the middle of the night."

"There is always the lake."

Gellion sighed. "I know. But the city stretches along its shores for miles. We would have to get to the water at one of the edges and hope there's no current to swim against."

"It's not the direction they would expect us to go. If we slip out the western side we might be able to head straight for the mountains from the shore."

Gellion raked a hand through his hair. It fell to his shoulders in waves, seeming nearly as dark as Veldon's with its red hues sapped by the moonlight.

"It seems too easy. They must have defenses on the southern side of the city. Otherwise they would be vulnerable to attack."

Veldon shrugged. "They want to keep ships out, not keep individuals in."

So did their conversations go, hour after hour, day after night. Their plan for escape took every moment of Gellion's day, and every bit of his attention. He made sure of it. To think was to panic; to feel was to grieve. Gellion had no room for either just now.

After three days, Gellion and Veldon decided that the unknowns of their plan would become no less clear with more time, of which they were rapidly running out. They had to try to escape soon, for better or for worse, or else they would escape to an even worse situation than their current predicament. With the Albaren and the Dierna as enemies, the elves gone, and no way of building a ship that could cross the Semestrial Sea, Gellion had no idea what they would do if they arrived at Daro too late.

He blocked his mind against the possibility. He had enough to worry about tonight. He had to operate as though their escape meant certain passage to Tura. There would be no room for doubt and no mercy for mistakes.

The prison guards brought Gellion and Veldon's dinner just as the last light of day was sinking below the horizon. Gellion forced some bread, stringy meat, and root vegetables into his roiling stomach. The guards needed no reason to suspect anything was amiss.

Veldon grimaced over his mostly cleared plate, then held up his fork with a grin. The guards supplied them with wooden plates and utensils for each meal and took the cutlery away an hour afterward. They would notice a missing fork, but in the dim light of evening, none were likely to miss the single spoke of a fork. Veldon walked to the edge of a low bed and rested the fourth spoke of his fork against the wooden frame. His shoulders tensed as he carefully pushed down, bending the spoke backward until a *snap* rent the air. Gellion was sure it was his anxiety that made the sound seem like the splintering of a tree, but both he and Veldon froze and listened for several minutes before their shoulders sunk away from their ears.

Veldon handed the sliver of wood to Gellion, who carefully pocketed it. They placed their plates and forks in a neat stack by the door and waited. Oppressive silence pressed against Gellion's ears. Every step of the night's scheme ran on an endless loop in his mind. What if the guard patrol walked faster than usual? What if he had underestimated the number of guards? What if an alarm was raised before they got out of the city?

He bit his lip. Imagining the worst would not ease their task's difficulty, nor its consequences. Yet when Gellion tried to distract himself from the madness of the plan he and Veldon were attempting, still worse thoughts crawled into his mind.

Dulon's visage was a constant phantom in his musings, coming to him at unexpected moments and seeming to strangle Gellion's windpipe when it appeared. Gellion had known the Lord of Daro for nearly two hundred years and had considered him not only an able leader and partner in politics, but a friend. Dulon had not deserved to die as he did, not for a decision they had both made. Guilt writhed in Gellion's stomach. He pushed it away, but each time, another face took the place of Dulon's. Sometimes it was Valder, sometimes it was Firas, more often it was a woman with a straight nose and black hair.

Since their last parting, Gellion had tried to banish all memories and emotions associated with Kyna, but the feat was proving more difficult than he had imagined. Again and again he relived that night in Nescari: the flood of emotion he had glimpsed behind Kyna's stalwart walls for just a few moments, the fleeting tinge of pain in her cool gaze as she denied all of it with two words, her dark hair receding into the night. Heat burned in Gellion's chest. He did not know if he was more angry with Kyna or with himself. The woman had been aloof and baffling from the moment he had met her, and every instinct had warned him away, yet he had given in to foolish hope. The same foolish hope that had let him down in the Great War year after year, battle after battle, death after death. The same foolish hope that had fueled his admiration for a mentor disparaged by society and condemned before Riu.

Gellion jumped as a hand grabbed his shoulder. He rounded on Veldon, who quickly withdrew his hand.

"Are you alright?" Veldon asked.

The anger drained out of Gellion as quickly as it had come.

"Fine," he muttered.

"Footsteps."

Gellion tensed and listened. The heavy tap of boots on wood echoed down the hall, growing louder with each step. Veldon gave Gellion a significant look, and Gellion stood with a nod, moving toward the door and sticking his hand in his pocket.

There was a square window cut through the thick wood of the door, with thin bars running vertically across it and a sliding panel shut tight on the other side. With a metallic click, the panel opened to reveal a young man. His eyes widened in shock when he saw Gellion's face inches from his own, and he jumped back with a string of curses. Gellion slipped the wooden spoke past the bars and into the catch of the window panel in a fluid motion, then stepped back.

"Away from the door!" the young man barked, fear flavoring his words.

Gellion held up his hands innocently and stepped further back into the cell. A series of clicks and clangs, and the door opened a crack. A pale hand slipped into the gap to retrieve the empty plates, then the door slammed closed again.

The man peered through the window one last time, surveying the elves with suspicion, then slid the panel back and hurried away. A smile crept up Gellion's face. There had been no 'click' this time.

Veldon gave him an answering grin, eyes sparkling.

"Now we wait," he said.

The weak light in the room darkened and cooled until full night descended. Voices and footsteps outside became few and far between.

They heard a guard pass their cell. The night patrols had begun.

As far as Gellion and Veldon could tell, there was no stationed guard in any halls of the prison. Rather, a single guard, or possibly two spaced out, patrolled up and down the floors through the night. The guard always walked the same direction, indicating a regular path through the building.

They waited for two more passes. About fifteen minutes stretched between appearances. When the echoes of the third pass died away, Gellion jumped to the door. He reached a finger through the bars and securely pressed the sliver of wood against the catch. With his other hand, he eased his fingers between the panel and the edge of the window, and pushed.

It cracked open.

Heart beating fast, he slipped the wood sliver out of the window and back into his pocket, then slid the panel open as quietly as he could, pushing it back in segments with his fingers between the bars. When it was fully open, he turned and nodded to Veldon.

Veldon dropped to his knees next to the door. Rather than embarrassment at his role as a step stool, a jittering excitement emanated from him as he braced his hands on the ground. Gellion stepped on Veldon's back and bent his knees slightly so his shoulder was level with the bottom of the window. Retrieving the sliver of wood again with his left hand, he slid his arm through the bars and groped downward toward the lock until his fingers felt its impression on the far side of the door.

Pressing the sliver of wood firmly between his forefinger and thumb, Gellion placed the tips of his other three fingers against the lock and closed his eyes. It was simple iron. For that, Gellion was grateful. He knew iron better than the back of his hand.

The vierstone pierced through his ear warmed as he ran his fingers over the lock. He could sense the latticework of atoms—the lines they followed and the shape they took. Keeping his fingers on the lock, he slowly inserted the wood sliver into the keyhole. Tiny beads of sweat formed along his hairline as he concentrated. He moved the wood up, down, and sideways, twisting it as he deciphered the inner mechanism of the lock. It was not as simple as he had expected, and his pulse mounted with each passing moment, but after about a minute, a satisfying click sounded.

Reaching the sliver back through the bars, Gellion shook the burn from his arm and reached through again to disengage the lock and pull gently up on the door lever. The heavy door swung outward on greased hinges.

Gellion braced himself on the bars to keep from falling off Veldon, then stepped down and moved quickly through the opening, his brother on his heels. They closed the door, refastened the lock, and shut the window panel. Then they exchanged a look of triumph.

They were out of the cell. Now the real difficulty began.

They hurried on soft feet toward the door at the end of the hallway —the door through which the patrolling guard had passed five minutes before. There was little light in the passage, only dimmed lamps interspersed between every few cell doors. The floor was sealed wood, but blessedly made no creaks as they moved over its surface.

Veldon got to the door first and eased it open, holding it for Gellion to slip through before glancing once more down the hall and shutting it behind them. They were in a staircase. A barred window showed twinkling lights in the sky.

"Come on," Gellion whispered, moving down the stairs swiftly and silently.

On the landing of the ground floor, they paused. The stairs

continued down, presumably to more cells beneath the ground. Gellion pressed his ear to the door that led to the main floor. He heard nothing.

Cracking the door open as slowly as he could, he peered down the hallway. The first bit of the hall looked identical to the floor above, with cells to either side. On the right side, cells continued to the far end of the hall, but on the left, the walls opened a third of the way down. That was where the main entrance was, and beyond it the common room. There was no sign of the guard.

Given the time it took for the man to make his way back to the second floor, Veldon and Gellion assumed he did a snaking patrol from the top floor to the bottom floors, of which there were probably at least two, before climbing again to the top. They should have about ten minutes before he came back to this floor.

Nodding to Veldon, Gellion stepped into the hallway. They moved carefully past the cells, easing their weight into each step. They approached the opening ahead silently, but just before they reached it, Gellion shifted his weight into a bowed board that groaned like a creature disturbed from sleep. Immediately, Gellion stepped back, and his heart thudded against his ribs. Veldon stood motionless beside him. No further sounds disturbed the night. Maybe prisoners creaked boards in their cells regularly. Maybe there were no guards at the entrance, or they were distracted. Gellion shook his head. He could not dare to hope or assume anything. For all he knew, there were ten armed guards at the entrance, each facing inward and now on alert at the sound he had made.

At a nod from Veldon, Gellion stepped sideways and started to move forward again, more cautiously than before. After several more steps, they reached the edge of the windows that stretched before the main office. Crouching down, Gellion raised his eyes just above the bottom of the glass. Wooden desks lined the space, each piled with neat stacks of paper, scrolls, and quills. A single guard sat in a chair, facing the inside of the prison, but with his head down. He held a paper in one hand and a dark feather in the other. Absently, he brushed the tip of the feather against his cropped beard as his eyes moved back and forth across the page.

Gellion lowered onto his hands and knees and moved like a stalking cat beneath the window. He could feel Veldon behind him, but heard no sound. Straight ahead, he saw the object of their pursuit—the thick door leading to the common room. It was closed, and probably locked, but they had expected that. All that remained between them and the door was the expanse of the main entrance—two layers of bars before a set of doors that led to the street. There were sure to be guards at the door, but whether they would be inside or outside, one or six, Gellion could only guess.

A creak echoed through the hall from ahead. Gellion stiffened and sucked in a breath. Instinctually, he lowered himself so his belly was nearly against the floor. He could feel sweat slicking his sides and willed his heart to make less noise. Staring toward the far hallway, he waited for a guard to appear out of the shadows, sword in hand and ready to sound the alarm, but none came.

Maybe it was a prisoner creaking after all. No wonder no one came running before.

Gellion sent up a silent prayer and continued forward until he reached the first set of bars of the main entrance. Holding his breath, he eased his head forward. There were two guards, but they were clearly as bored as their friend in the office. They stood with lazy posture, their backs against the bars, and talked softly. Short clubs hung loose in their hands.

Gellion turned to Veldon and held up two fingers, then pointed toward the doors. Two guards, facing away.

They would have to take their chances. If they could get to the wall on the far side of the bars without catching any attention, they would be out of sight of both the main entrance and the office, and still have several minutes to get into the common room before the patrol came back.

Leaning against the wall, Gellion took deep, silent breaths, wishing he could talk to Veldon about the best course of action, but even the slightest whisper would be too risky with guards on two sides. Before Gellion could make any decisions, Veldon rose to his feet and pulled Gellion up next to him. With a grin and a wink, Veldon strolled casually past the bars with a straight back and an easy gait, as though he were on a morning turn about the garden. Gellion stared, his eyes darting to the guards, but they hadn't moved; they hadn't even lifted their heads. Veldon motioned to Gellion from the far side of the entrance.

With another breath, Gellion squared his shoulders and walked toward Veldon as calmly as he could, not daring to look toward the guards. He couldn't help matching Veldon's grin when he had moved safely past the bars. Engrossed in giddy relief, Gellion felt heat suffuse his face when Veldon raised an eyebrow and pointed meaningfully at the door handle to the common room. They were not out of this yet. Not even close.

Shaking himself, Gellion moved forward and placed his hand on the door handle. It was brass, tarnished on top from use. He slowly pulled it down, only to meet resistance. With an inward sigh, he reached back into his pocket for the wood sliver.

He felt nothing.

With a thrill of adrenaline, he reached into his other pocket, then into both.

It was gone.

Had he forgotten to replace it when he relocked the cell door? Had it fallen out as he crawled?

Veldon looked at him with wide eyes, immediately deducing their situation. He looked around frantically as though searching for a key. Gellion forced down the panic clawing at his gut and thought. He could not risk going back to search for the spoke, it could have fallen out anywhere. The light was dim, and the patrol guard would come any minute. Besides, it was far too risky to pass the main entrance and office again.

What else could they use to pick the lock?

His eyes scanned his surroundings, passing over the door, the walls, and the floor, searching for anything that might spark some sort of idea, anything that could slip into a lock. Anxiety clouded his mind until he could no longer focus his thoughts. He closed his eyes and shook his head, trying to clear it.

Then he felt a light hand on his shoulder and looked up to see Veldon moving past him into the hall beyond, where cells lined the far wall. Veldon moved in the shadows, not crossing to the far side until he was out of view from the guards at the entrance, then started to run his hands along the wooden doors of the cells. Gellion stood frozen, staring. He pressed himself against the door to the common room, alternately watching Veldon and glancing down the hall for any sign of a guard. What was Veldon doing?

At the third door, Veldon's hand stopped at the door's bottom edge. He crouched down and began fidgeting at the wood, pinching and pulling, then stood and hurried back toward Gellion with a corner of his mouth tugged up. Veldon held up a thin splinter, his eyes shining.

Relief flowed down Gellion's limbs. He fought the urge to laugh as he smiled and took the splinter from Veldon.

The lock was easy work compared to the cell door, and Gellion felt a soft 'click' just as another click echoed down the hall. He opened the common room door as quietly as he could and pulled Veldon in with him before easing the door closed again with the handle pulled down. Pressing his ear to the door, he held his breath and listened until steady footsteps neared and passed, then faded again. Gellion let out his breath and released the door handle, locking it again from the inside.

He stood straight and stretched the tension from his shoulders. Beside him, Veldon let out a long breath.

"Well that was close," he whispered. "We may actually do this." There was a mischievous glint in his eye.

"We may yet," Gellion said. "But we have a long way to go before we're safe. Quick thinking with that splinter," he added with a cocked brow.

Even in the slanting moonlight he could see Veldon's flush. Gellion grinned and walked into the room. The game tables were cleared and dusted, and each piece of furniture sat in neat lines pointing toward the dark fireplace. An iron grate sat in the mouth of the fireplace with two logs stacked in place on top of it.

Gellion stepped into the fireplace. He had to bend down, but the hearth was massive. Had he been on his knees, he could have straightened without hitting his head, and he could fully open his arms to either side. He craned his neck to look up the chimney. It was pitch black. Reaching a hand into the throat of the fireplace, he could feel that it sloped forward into a smoke shelf, but he thought there was still enough space between its lip and the facing to fit a body.

"We will fit, but it could take some maneuvering," he said. "Come help me up and I'll pull you after me."

"Why am I always the step stool?" Veldon looked much less enthusiastic to get on his knees in the black-smudged hearth.

"Because you maximize my height, and I can pull you up easier."

Veldon grimaced and crawled in behind the grate, straddling it with his arms and legs.

Gellion hoped the scene that followed never made it to Valder's ears, though he would have taken the humiliation gladly to know Valder was alive and well. He could practically hear his absent brother's sniggers as he clambered on top of Veldon in the tight space.

He stifled a curse as he rose too soon and bounced his head off the bricks. Veldon remained still and silent. Hands over his head this time, Gellion rose slowly, groping at the surfaces around him until he found the opening and squeezed his head and shoulders through it so his arms stretched forward over the smoke shelf. With a heave, he pulled himself upward, toes scrabbling at the slanting brick for purchase. He hit his head on the wall behind him twice before managing to crawl all the way onto the shelf.

After a moment to catch his breath, Gellion lowered onto his knees and reached one hand through the damper opening, bracing his other on the wall in front of him.

"Ok," he whispered. "Take my hand."

Veldon's slender fingers brushed his and then latched onto his wrist. Gellion held his breath as he pulled up with a steady strength until Veldon's hand reached the shelf. It was even more difficult for Veldon to pull himself up with Gellion taking up half the space, but eventually the two brothers stood nose to nose on the brick shelf.

Looking up, Gellion could see the glow of the moon at the chimney's opening.

"Well, no point waiting any longer." Gellion reached down and wrapped his arms around Veldon's waist, hoisting him up until he could pull himself up on the sides of the chimney and stand on Gellion's shoulders. Gellion stood blindly, trying to stay steady and make no noise as Veldon moved and pushed above him.

"Fun isn't it?" Gellion could hear the smile in Veldon's voice. Gellion grunted noncommittally.

Then the weight was gone. Soft scuffing sounds echoed down the flue while Veldon made his way toward the roof. Gellion listened hard for any sounds coming from the prison, but heard nothing.

"Alright, your turn." The distant whisper was eerie in the enclosed space. Gellion steeled himself and braced his back against the wall, putting one foot and then the other on the brick opposite him.

It was a painful climb, but the chimney opening grew rapidly nearer, and Gellion sighed in relief when Veldon pulled him up by the armpits into cool air. They each sat with their backs against the chimney, breathing deeply and rubbing the scrapes on their hands and arms. Gellion's minor injuries from the battle had mostly healed, but he could still feel the echo of their sting after this abuse.

The sky was clear black and the breeze light and drifting. Lights still glowed along main streets and in a few buildings, but mostly the city was dark and still. To the south, the black mirror of the lake extended to a distant shore.

Gellion could hardly believe they had done it. They were out of the prison with no alarm raised, and they had until morning before anyone would check their cell. As long as they remained cautious, they might just get out of this city.

Crouching low to the roof, they made their way to its southern edge and lay on their bellies, eyes scanning the streets.

"We're not far from the harbor," Gellion breathed.

"I do not see any guards in the streets, but a casual stroll would still seem suspicious this time of night. I think we should go straight to the western wall and follow it to the water."

Gellion turned his gaze to the wall running straight beyond the last buildings. He caught Veldon's eye and nodded, then grasped the edge of the roof and lowered himself over the side. They moved down the outer wall of the prison, landing softly on the cobbled street below. A pause and a glance assured their solitude, and they walked toward the narrowing streets to the west.

The night was cooled by the breeze off the lake, but still held a memory of the previous day's warmth. Distant notes of frog calls and water insects rose from the south, and the occasional dog bark bounced through the streets. Gellion saw no humans or horses. They passed rows of wooden buildings, most two stories high with windows looking onto the street. Arvain was far less extravagant than Tradira, the capital of Albarad, but held a clean dignity the latter utterly lacked.

Gellion sucked in a breath as Veldon's arm slapped across his chest. He tensed and bent his knees, looking for a guard ahead, but it was no guard who had caused Veldon to stop. A pile of wool blankets lay on a footpath off the street. Within its depths, Gellion could see a wrinkled face. A scraggly beard sprouted from the man's cheeks and chin, and his eyes were closed in sleep.

Relief dispelled the adrenaline in Gellion's veins. "Just walk on the other side of the street. We won't wake him," he said. But Veldon remained where he was, a line between his brows.

"Why is he sleeping on the path?" he asked.

"He probably can't afford a home, or has lost his." Gellion moved behind Veldon, who looked still more confused and troubled at this explanation, and pulled him to the side. "We have to keep moving, come on."

With a last look at the heap on the ground, Veldon followed. Gellion quickened his pace, eyes darting around him as they entered what appeared to be a neighborhood. He understood Veldon's confusion. Tradira was the only human city Gellion had seen until now, and it had shocked him to the core the first time he visited. In the outer districts of the city, he had witnessed robbery and assault, but what had truly disturbed him was the poverty. It had taken Gellion years to understand the complexity of the Albaren system of economics and life, and though seeing people like that man in the street still made his stomach turn, he knew it was a simple fact of life for the humans, and a problem that could not be solved as simply as he had first imagined. Veldon had never even seen humans prior to his visit for the Kindom Council months ago, and had certainly never seen one of their cities.

Gellion kept hearing scuffing behind or beside them, and jumped at every sound, but they encountered only one man on their way to the outer wall—a stooped figure with dragging steps who stopped at one of the neighborhood doorways. Gellion and Veldon melted into a side street before he noticed them, and thereafter kept to alleys and shadows as much as they could. Within ten minutes, they reached the outer wall. It was smooth stone and would have proven exceedingly difficult, if not impossible, to climb. Fortunately, they had decided on other plans. Gellion kept his gaze along the wall as they followed it toward the harbor, wary of watchtowers or guards, but the city seemed remarkably peaceful. Outside of the prison, he had seen no sign of guards or active fortifications.

The smell of ripe mud and fish wafted on the breeze as they neared the harbor. Gellion could hear the familiar slap of surf on boats and piers, and his heart ached for the wharf of Daro. With an angry shake of the head, Gellion forced his mind back to the present. No time for that. None of it mattered if he couldn't get out of Arvain.

"There," Veldon whispered, pointing ahead as the buildings thinned.

The city wall tapered down at the water's edge and submerged under its surface. There were no docks near the wall, just a few fishing boats gently bobbing in the tide. Gellion longed to take one of the boats, but they had no oars, and with the mountains looming on the horizon to the west, there was sure to be a current to the east. Besides, each little vessel was probably the livelihood of some fisherman and his family.

Sticking close to the wall, they made their way to the water's edge. Veldon stopped just short of the tide and turned to Gellion. A sudden gust of wind off the lake whipped his hair behind him and his eyes reflected the moonlight just as the lake did. A smile curved up his face.

"We made it, and not a single guard. We can walk half the night and be safely in the mountains by tomorrow."

Gellion tried to answer Veldon's smile, but his face stopped short at a grimace. It was too easy. The prison had been a slight challenge, but to meet no resistance throughout the city and escape by swimming around a wall? Eurig was a shrewd man, and from all Gellion had seen, Arvain was a well run and organized city. Was Eurig so comfortable in his security?

"Ready?" Veldon said.

With a sigh, Gellion nodded, and the brothers stepped softly into the tide. Cold water filled Gellion's shoes, and he held his breath as the lake bottom quickly dropped off. When the water was to his chest, he kicked out of the mud and swam with only his nose above the water as far as the wall stretched. He hovered next to the tapered drop. Turning to make sure Veldon was beside him, Gellion nodded to his brother and slipped beneath the water, swimming over the top of the wall and around the other side. When he was beyond the sight of the harbor, Gellion broke the water's surface with a deep breath. He nearly choked on it.

The shore was barely a stone's throw away, and standing next to the wall were half a dozen guards—two on horseback, and all armed with swords and bows. They raised their torches higher and pointed as Veldon's head appeared with a soft splash beside Gellion.

The lake water seemed to turn to ice around him. His chest tightened so he could hardly draw breath and he barely managed to hiss, "Go back. Go back," before ducking below the water again and dragging Veldon with him as he swam frantically back to the other side of the wall. Resurfacing on the other side, Gellion gasped and swam for the shore. He heard the thunder of hoofbeats on the other side of the wall, as well as splashing near at hand.

"Into the city," he gasped as he and Veldon scrambled up the muddy bank like beached whales, their sodden clothes dragging them down. They ran into the streets beyond the harbor, not caring which direction they went as long as they put as much distance between themselves and the guards as possible before their pursuers got out of the water.

"How did they know?" Veldon panted. "How could they have possibly known?"

Gellion paused, heart racing. His eyes darted down streets. "Go to the east side of the city." He broke into a run again. "They had horses and are probably to the main gates by now."

"What if they have guards on the east shore too?"

"They probably do."

"Then why are we going there?"

"Maybe there's a breach in the wall somewhere, a building or a tree close enough to climb over."

A low horn sounded from the north gates.

"Riu help us," Veldon muttered, doubling his pace and signing the star over his chest as he ran. Gellion lengthened his strides. The sound of hooves and feet clattered through the streets. None seemed close so far, but it was only a matter of time before they were over the whole city.

"We can't go to the east wall," Veldon said. "You saw how far the buildings were from the wall on the west side. It will take us too long to get across the whole city, and even longer to run along the wall, and we don't have any reason to believe we'll be able to get over it. The guards will catch us before we get the chance."

Gellion ducked into an ally as a horse cantered onto the street in front of them. He pressed his back to a wall and closed his eyes, trying to control his breathing.

"Then what do you suggest?" he said through gritted teeth.

Veldon made no immediate answer. Shouts now echoed off buildings, and flickering lights were coming on in the windows of houses.

"The main gates," Veldon said. "Unless we want to try and steal a boat without being seen, it's the only way out of the city."

"It's also the most heavily guarded part of the city and is sure to be locked against us."

"It might not be. They sent horses through it, and it is the last place fugitives are likely to go for."

"With good reason."

"We have to go somewhere. They probably have the harbor fully watched by now, and we can't get over the walls. Unless you want to find a place to hide and hope we can think of something better in broad daylight, the front gates are our only option."

"And if there are guards?"

Veldon hesitated. "We improvise."

Gellion looked hard at Veldon. He opened his mouth, closed it, and let out a snort of frustration.

"Ok," he said. "Lead the way."

They ran. Gellion cursed his sodden boots with every step, putting all his concentration into making as little noise as possible and not slipping on the cobbled stones. Twice they caught the attention of guards, but each time, Veldon managed to lose them by leaping nimbly over walls, under carts, or through yards and side streets. Gellion matched him step for step, leap for leap, and nearly ran into him when he skidded to a stop at the sudden end of a street. The main gates stood before them, wide open. Five guards stood at its mouth, all holding swords. Gellion and Veldon exchanged a look. They could hear shouts behind them, hooves clattering and echoing through the streets so it seemed they were all around. The city wall was sheer to either side of the gates.

Gellion took a breath. "Through them then?"

Veldon clenched his jaw, worry in his eyes, and nodded once.

They came at the guards from the side. The first to see them was a helmed man, and his eyes widened in shock to see two wet and weaponless elves running toward him. He raised his sword, but Gellion ducked beneath his arm and bucked backward, sending the guard's arm jerking across his body, weighed by his sword. Gellion drew a foot back behind the guard's ankle and spun around so the man staggered sideways. A quick elbow to his wrist, and Gellion had the sword in his hand. He shoved the man backward with a foot and whirled around to see Veldon moving smoothly around two blades as though he could see their movements before they came.

Gellion nearly laughed. These guards were no match for the A'vaeri; they merely presented a training exercise. He could see the empty gate beyond. He tensed. It was starting to close.

Turning to face two more guards, Gellion parried one strike and twisted out of the way of the other. With a quick upward thrust, he knocked the blade out of one guard's hand and sent him crashing into the other man with a well timed trip and push. Veldon appeared next to him with a sword in his own hand, and together they sprinted toward the closing gate. Angry shouts barked after them, and metal scraped against the cobbles as the guards scrambled for their dropped weapons. Gellion didn't care. Let them take up their swords again, they could not touch him.

The opening was narrowing, but they would be able to get through. His heart pounded in his throat, and he pushed his legs faster. Just a few more steps and they would be free.

Just as Veldon and Gellion reached the opening, a lone figure strode from behind the gates and barred their way. Gellion raised his sword, then recognized Eurig in the flickering lights of the gates. The gates halted in their tracks.

Sliding to a stop, Gellion stared at the man. Eurig stood straight with his hands clasped, wearing a blank expression with no weapons or armor.

Gellion's eyes darted from his sword to the man. Veldon had stopped beside him, seeming as confused by Eurig's sudden appearance as by Gellion's reaction to it. What was the Lawgiver doing? Gellion could cut him down in a moment and slip through the opening to freedom. He had little doubt that horses would pursue them once the gate was reopened, but amid the hills, the river, and the forest beyond, Gellion was reasonably confident of their successful escape.

If he could get past Eurig.

Footsteps came from behind Gellion. The guards were running at his back, and reinforcements grew closer by the moment. Gellion tightened his grip on his sword and took a step forward. Eurig did not move. Even his expression remained perfectly still. Blood rushed to Gellion's head so he could hardly think.

Just do it. You don't have to kill the man, just incapacitate him so you can get out.

Gellion's hand remained frozen in the air, the end of his sword pointed at Eurig's chest. It trembled slightly, then lowered.

Eurig watched the blade for a moment, then calmly held up a hand. Archers emerged from the gate's towers, all pointing arrows directly at Gellion and Veldon. A glance to the side revealed still more archers stepping out from trees, or from behind buildings. They had been surrounded the entire time.

"Please drop your weapons," Eurig said.

Gellion did not take his eyes off the man, but threw his sword to the stones with a clang. He heard an echoing sound next to him.

"You will kindly return to your cell now." The faintest smile flickered at Eurig's lips.

3

PROPHECY

Kyna scrutinized the handwritten words. Their ink was darker than that on the pages preceding them, but otherwise the prophecy matched the handwriting of the surrounding poems exactly. Kyna cocked her head, reading the words again. Why did prophecies always have to rhyme? Did Riu speak only in cadence, or did the elven prophets simply feel the need to make their work artistic? Kyna snorted. She read the prophecy again. It certainly sounded viable. It was just cryptic enough to be annoying, but obvious enough to point to their current predicament.

Kyna placed her hand on the page and turned back to the book's title: *Tellings of Trial and Tranquility.* A title as flowery as the book's contents. Kyna rolled her eyes. It would do.

The elven prophets of old had written accounts of visions and dreams, scribing words of inspiration and morality upon which the elven faith was based. Since the founding of vierstone nearly three thousand years ago, prophets had grown increasingly rare, but their writings remained, and not all of them were of dreams and existential musings. The shelf before Kyna was filled with advice and predictions—prophecies. Many of the prophecies referred to the Great War, many more to vierstone. Some were so confusing it was impossible to know if their object was in the past or future, or if they referred to the elves at all. But no one would be able to deny the relevance of this prophecy.

The refugees of Daro had been badly shaken by the events of the last months, but they seemed to think the worst was past. Their complacency incensed Kyna. How could they think that an elf who had sent an entire city into the sea after destroying all of its vierstone would stop there? Did they assume he had accomplished his goal and would now sit quietly in his satisfaction for the rest of his life, never revealing the purpose of his endeavor?

Fools.

If the elves would not face the truth of what was happening of their own volition, Kyna would bring them a reason they would listen to. She folded the corner of the page and closed the book, tucking it under her arm and walking through the stacks of the Archives of Tura. The shelves next to the prophetic writings contained histories—books on the Great War, the founding of vierstone, and the building of the Great Cities. They seemed to stretch endlessly. Why did the elves need so many books to recount a single history?

Kyna stepped into a glass lift and descended to the ground floor of the Archives. Her shoes tapped on the marble floor as she made her way to the main entrance.

A sickening wall of heat greeted her when she pushed through the front doors. She nearly groaned aloud. The heat in Tura was even worse than in Daro.

The Archives curved to either side of Kyna, their glass walls resplendent in the afternoon sun. Kyna looked around, at a loss of what to do now. It did not seem the right time to go to Liera with the prophecy. Kyna doubted the woman would take it seriously without due cause, and so far Tura had remained a peaceful oasis since the arrival of the elves of Daro.

The sun bore down on her, and Kyna twitched her fingers against the book in her hands. It was hours yet until darkness, and she had no desire to return to the East Neighborhoods where Liera was providing temporary housing for the Daro refugees. With a sigh, she began to walk toward the arching bridge that linked the Scholar Quarter to the Market Quarter. Upriver, she could see the great open air forges of the

Guild Quarter. The Turi were masters of crafting—metalwork, stonework, glass, architecture, and art. The Guild Quarter was larger than any other section of the City Center, and housed the finest workshops in Faeran.

Kyna rolled her eyes and continued across the bridge. She had never had interest in any of it. Where some elves saw through stone and metal at a touch, coaxing and working them to perfection through the channel of vierstone, Kyna saw only hunks of earth. She didn't see the point of the obsession and prestige the elves placed on creating beauty out of raw materials.

But images of Gellion's metal workshop in Daro swam before her eyes unbidden—the warm cast of lamps, the heat of the forge, racks of fine knives and lyres. Kyna squeezed her eyes shut, dispelling the memory.

She needed to find something to do. Quickly.

On the other side of the bridge, the markets of Tura stretched along the bank of the Orhiri River. They were wrought with ornate columns and spires and open to the air on all sides. A series of docks abutted the spectacle. Elves scurried between boats, carrying crates, barrels, and sacks. One elf leaped into a boat full of empty storage containers and shoved off from the docks. A gentle hum reached Kyna's ears as he switched on the motor and sliced through the water downriver.

The Orhiri River split the Great City of Tura in two, widening and winding beyond its walls into hills that swelled and grew into the mountains of Ard Gael, toward Maramor and Lake Orhirion. All the lands between were home to the Turi elves, one of the four elven Kindoms that inhabited Faeran. Kyna herself was Turi, though she had only been to Tura once before, and under very different circumstances.

Kyna stepped off the bridge and walked to the edge of the river. Along its banks, a black path snaked lazily to the north and south. Beside the path, three levit boards sat stacked and waiting. Kyna hesitated. She had never used the things. She had never had any desire to, but Tura was big. It took ages to walk across the city, and she had spent more than enough time in the summer sun. There was nothing to do around the markets, however. The gardens and sport arenas to the south would promise much more profitable distraction.

Kyna's eyes locked on the boats by the docks. Another one was about to pull out. A crooked smile stretched over her face. She ran to the docks, her sheet of black hair whipping behind her with each step. The boat was starting to drift away from the docks.

Kyna bounded down a dock and soared off its edge over the water, landing on light feet on the boat's deck. The elf at the motor stared at her open-mouthed.

"Mind if I catch a ride?" she said.

The elf closed his mouth, blinking. "Ye— alright."

Kyna flashed him a smile and moved to sit toward the craft's rail.

The day was much more pleasant on the water. Buildings, trees, and bridges shaded the boat as it moved down the river toward the southern docks. Across from the market, the most impressive buildings in the city sat in stately formation—the center of Tura's Public Quarter. Kyna had yet to darken the doors of the political buildings. Beyond them would be the homes of the Lady of Tura and her family, along with public buildings for meetings, gatherings, and visiting elves, the armory, and the bathhouses.

Kyna watched the public buildings shift to wineries and warehouses, then to gardens and houses. Trees, flowers, and shrubs interspersed buildings and paths, casting color and cool shade on the city. After living for months in a city crumbling from earthquakes, Tura seemed so pristine as to be fake. Not a line marred the walkways, streets, or Rale lines. Each building shone as though polished. Even the trees seemed sculpted from the landscape.

The boat's motor dropped to a lower frequency as they passed neighborhoods and drifted toward another set of docks, these much more extensive than those at the markets. At least a dozen boats were anchored in the river, elves transporting goods to and from the nearby lifts that sank over the edge of the sea cliffs to the wharf far below.

With a crooked smile at her flustered chauffeur, Kyna stepped onto the docks, then strode to another arching bridge. She could hear distant *pings* coming from the caesir courts, which sat on the southeast tip of Tura, balanced on the edge of a tall cliff that plummeted straight down to surging waves below. The Orhiri River plunged off the precipice with a wild joy, fresh water falling eagerly into the freedom of the ocean. The spray just reached the caesir courts, which were full of spectators.

Kyna found a vacant section of benches and sat down. Immediately her eyes locked onto the rapid progress of a metal ball as it bounced, soared, spun, changed direction, and bounced again, reflecting wild beams of light from the sun with each movement. Just smaller than her fist, the ball made a satisfying *ping* each time it made contact with a gleaming silver paddle or wall. Kyna's gaze transferred to the elves holding the paddles. Each wore soft pants that followed their movements and accommodated the heat of the day. The elves' backs lay bare to the sun. One bore a tattoo of elegantly flowing lines that wove together over his shoulders and down his arms. A trail of leaves fell down the other elf's spine, changing from green to red in a spectrum so perfect it looked painted. Kyna had never understood the appeal of the markings personally, though it was a rarity to find an elf of any Kindom without them.

If tattoos were an enigma to Kyna, the game before her was even less intelligible, though over the course of her few days in Tura, she had begun to unravel the mystery. The court was circular, with waist-high walls interspersed with taller panels. Hoops and targets made an obstacle course within the walls, and every surface was made of the same shining metal as the ball. The opponents ran, jumped, spun, and ducked in a dizzying dance, each trying to hit the ball in succession with his rival. Sometimes the ball would soar through one of the hoops before bouncing off a wall, or hit a target on its way to a paddle, and the spectators would cheer or sigh in accordance with their favorite player.

Kyna had never watched any elven sports until the Kindom Council in Daro, where she had seen several A'vaeri matches. That sport, at least, served a purpose. A line formed between her brows. The opponents before her laughed, even as they tried to dominate each other. Why anyone would choose to drench themselves in sweat while striving toward a goal they did not even care about achieving was beyond her, yet she kept coming back to the courts. The game focused her mind on something tangible. She needed that focus.

Most of her life, Kyna had relished solitude, far more content with her own thoughts than those of any other, but lately her solitary thoughts were taking her to places she would rather avoid.

The ship voyage from the ruins of Daro to Tura had only taken a few days, but it had seemed to stretch for weeks amid the monotony of silence and grief on board. The elves around Kyna had mourned, cried, and stared into space for hours on end. Kyna had stayed on deck as much as possible, watching the waves and the birds, but she hadn't been able to stem the flow of uncomfortable memories and thoughts.

Since arriving in Tura, she had done her best to keep busy, but the tightness in her chest returned at unexpected times. It made her angry. It was weakness. Who was she to feel guilty about what had happened in Tala? Dulon and Gellion had made the decision to accept the alliance with the Albaren. They, not her, had brought the elves to the battle from which only half an army had returned. How could she have known the Albaren would turn on the elves?

'Thank you for helping me bring the elves this far.' Dulon's last words to her hung in her mind like a persistent swarm of gnats. It wasn't her fault that he had died. It wasn't her fault that Gellion—

Kyna balled her fists until her nails bit into her palms. The twisting in her chest was worse this time. As though by instinct, she clasped a hand around the cuff on her left wrist, pressing the stone embedded within against her skin. With a sharp intake of breath, she clenched her teeth and focused again on the caesir match.

It doesn't matter. You did not really care for him, so there is no reason to grieve for him.

A cool prickle spread up Kyna's arm. She took a deep breath and felt her mind center again on the rapid *pings* of the caesir ball, on the feel of her skin, her breath, and her mind. Relief settled on her shoulders. It did not matter. She was in Tura, the elves had returned to Faeran, and Daro was a distant memory. Yet still, the sequence of events in the last month rankled her.

It was not supposed to have happened like that. She had thought her plans were unfolding perfectly, and then the Albaren had ruined everything.

Not everything.

She shook her head. Daro no longer mattered. Tura lay before her —an open book ready for the pen.

The book of prophecies sat heavy in Kyna's lap. Her hands tightened on its binding, and her heart gave a lurch. She could still fulfill her purpose.

The crowd cheered as one competitor sent the caesir ball through a series of complicated bounces that arched through two hoops and smashed into a raised target. The victorious elf raised his arms in the air and bowed to the spectators. His opponent lowered his paddle in defeat.

A corner of Kyna's mouth turned upward. Daro had not gone according to plan, but Tura would. She would make sure of it.

4

THE LADY OF TURA

Renyra stood before Liera, trying not to fidget. The Lady of Tura had a way of pinning souls to the ground with her gaze, which shone with bright fire. Though her eyes were sharp and her face was smooth, an essence of age clung to the woman. Despite the force of her presence, there seemed somehow less of her than of other elves. Based on what Renyra knew of the woman's past, she guessed Liera might be over two millennia old, an age surpassing that of most elves in Faeran. Renyra felt a child before Liera in more ways than one. She herself was not yet three centuries old, and the top of her hair would barely brush Liera's chin. Drawing herself up with as much confidence as she could muster, Renyra spoke.

"I am Renyra, one of the elves of Daro."

Liera's eyes moved over her in a rapid scan. "You were in the Sira show at the Kindom Council."

"I—yes, I was," Renyra said, taken aback. Liera's face did not change expression or acknowledge Renyra further, so she hurried on. "You may have already heard some account of all that happened since the Council left Daro, but—" Renyra paused. How could she put this?

I know more than them? I was at the forefront of it all?

"But I have information the Council needs to know."

Liera raised an eyebrow. "Go on."

Renyra had gone over what she would say to Liera the whole ship journey from Tala, but still she found herself grasping at words like leaves in the wind. So much had happened. So many things she wanted to push to the back of her mind and never acknowledge again. She sighed. No one else could tell this to Liera. She had to go on.

"I investigated the earthquakes in Daro from their onset. I discovered they were originating in the city itself and affecting only localized areas, and I worked with Dulon to discover their cause and relation to the blackened vierstone." It still hurt to say Dulon's name. Renyra had not known the man well, but he had been the leader of her city for so long, and he had always made her smile.

Liera's other eyebrow rose to join the first. "I have heard mention of this. You, too, claim that all the vierstone in Daro turned black and lifeless before the city's destruction?"

"Yes, it did." Indignation colored Renyra's words. "Dulon had a master of vierstone study the blackened stone. She obsessed over it for days before coming up with any theories, but just before she could tell us what they were, her workshop collapsed on her."

A touch of shock broke through Liera's stoic gaze. "She—died?"

Renyra was surprised this news had not reached Liera.

"Yes, she died. But it was no accident. She was unable to tell us what had happened to the vierstone, but she revealed that it was the work of an elf. It was an elf who destroyed the vierstone, and it was an elf who caused the earthquakes and destroyed the city. Dulon found proof, and I saw the elf responsible."

Liera's face was almost comical. She stared at Renyra as though she had just said an elf created the universe.

"This is madness," said Liera. "Had I not felt the first earthquakes for myself, I would say all of Daro had made this up as some bizarre ruse. No elf can cause earthquakes, and no elf can destroy vierstone."

"Why would I make this up?" Color rose to Renyra's cheeks. Of all the reactions she had imagined of Liera, denial was not one of them. "Your captains saw the destruction of Daro when they sailed to our rescue, and I told you, I have proof. I saw the elf responsible. I was there when Daro fell."

"I have spoken with other elves who stayed behind from the battle. They say how the city shook and broke, how it fell into the sea, but they give no witness to an elf causing any of it."

"Because they did not know! I knew it was an elf and I found him. I saw him lay his hands on the ground and split stone. I saw him bend metal with his fingers. I saw the streets laced with black and felt the current through the ground before he worked whatever magic he possesses."

Liera let out a humorless laugh. "Now you speak of magic?"

Renyra took a slow breath. "I don't know how he did it. But I saw him do it. I saw his face, and I know who it was."

The grimace fled Liera's face. Her eyes bore into Renyra's.

"You would accuse an elf of these crimes?" she said softly. "Of the desecration of our last vierstone reserves, of the destruction of a city, of murder?"

"I saw him," Renyra said again. The elf's hard eyes and sharp features had haunted her nightmares for days. She clenched her fists as she thought of his utter disdain for her, the way he had twisted her javelin in half and walked past her with a smirk, as though she were no threat worthy even of destruction. Renyra had not recognized him then —she had only heard Kaelo's story a few weeks before seeing his face— but looking now into Liera's face, she saw the same shape of nose, the same slant to the eyes. She suppressed a shudder.

"It was Kaelo."

All hint of color drained from Liera's face. For a moment, her eyes turned as hard as her son's.

"That is not possible."

"I have no explanation for why or how, but I know it was him."

"How can you know that? How could you have seen him before?"

Renyra ignored the scathing edge on the words. She could see the fear and pain in Liera's eyes.

"I had not seen him before, but Gellion had."

Liera almost flinched. Color began to creep up her face again.

"Then why does Gellion not tell me this himself?"

Renyra clenched her jaw and forced her voice to remain steady.

"He did not return from the battle," she said in barely a whisper.

Liera turned her eyes to the floor.

"I am sorry to hear that." Slowly, her eyes lifted again, the fire in their depths still simmering. "But how then did he see this elf destroy Daro if he was in a battle miles away?"

"He didn't see Kaelo destroy the city. Only I saw him then. But Gellion saw glimpses of Kaelo before the army left and identified him from my description before the battle ended."

"A description? This is no proof. It could have been any Turi elf based on description and glimpses alone."

"It was Kaelo," Renyra said, a touch of steel in her voice. She tried to soften it. "I am sorry. I understand this is—"

"Understand? You do not understand. Kaelo has been gone for nearly seven hundred years, banished for longer. He died in the Great War—fighting for the phoenix for all I know. Or care. How would he have gotten to Tala? Why would he destroy Daro? These accusations are ridiculous. I know you have been through a lot these past months, but you are wasting my time."

Renyra held Liera's gaze, willing herself not to look away under the heat of the woman's stare.

"I don't have the answers to your questions. I did not know Kaelo, and I know little of the circumstances surrounding his banishment and life, but I do know that I saw him in Daro less than three weeks ago."

"Based on stories and descriptions."

"No."

"How then?"

"Because I see his face before me now."

Liera froze. A muscle worked in her jaw.

"I do not tell you these things to hurt you," Renyra said. "I tell you to warn you."

"Warn me of what?" Liera's voice was like slivers of ice.

"We don't know what Kaelo wants. He will most likely come to Faeran, and Tura is the closest city to Daro. We need to warn the other Kindoms and prepare."

"Prepare how? How would this elf, whoever he is, get to Tura? Stow away on our own ships?"

"He got to Tala once. He can get back. All I ask is that you tell the leaders of the other Kindoms and set guards on the city. He possesses power none of us understand. We do not want a repeat of Daro."

"Tura is ten times the size of Daro with vierstone melted into its foundation. We have nothing to fear."

"Daro had vierstone in its foundations, too. That means little to an elf who can destroy it at a touch."

"No elf can destroy vierstone!"

Renyra took a step back. From her limited interaction with Liera, she thought of the severe woman as stone—cold and unyielding, but always level-headed. Now fire shone through the cracks, and the heat beneath was unsettling to say the least.

"I know this is hard to believe," Renyra said in a low voice. "I did not believe it myself until I saw it with my own eyes. But I did see it. I have told you things I know to be true in hopes that Faeran can defend itself against a threat that destroyed my home. My friends. Whether or not it was Kaelo who did these things, it was certainly an elf. That elf deserves justice for the lives he destroyed and must be stopped before his destruction spreads."

Liera stood perfectly still. The cracks slowly closed again until her face was a mask of dispassionate consideration. At last she spoke.

"Thank you for bringing your concerns to me. I will send messages to the other Kindom Council members with news of Daro's destruction and the nature by which it purportedly occurred. I do not believe that it was Kaelo you saw, nor do I see any reason that whatever elf destroyed Daro—if it was indeed, an elf," incredulity dripped from her words, "should bring his attacks to Faeran. All the same, I will remain alert to any suspicious activity within Tura and give your warning proper consideration."

Annoyance flickered in Renyra's chest.

As in, very little consideration.

Renyra forced a polite smile. "Thank you. If you or any other wish to know more about this, do not hesitate to ask."

Liera nodded once.

Renyra turned and walked out of the meeting hall with measured steps, her back burning with the force of Liera's gaze

Heat settled over Renyra like a blanket when she stepped out of the cool embrace of the Central Tower. A wide expanse of stone spread to the surrounding buildings in a fan, two fountains dotting the center. Renyra crossed to the edge of the court where the beginning of a Rale path shone black against the street.

Tura was a maze—a *huge* maze. Fortunately, Renyra had lived in Tura for a time before coming to Daro. It had been the last stop of her Sira troupe before she had uprooted her life to another continent. The familiarity was a comfort, but the reminder of her past life did nothing to console the loss of her most recent home.

A line of levit boards lay waiting along the Rale path. Renyra selected the nearest and stood sideways on its shining surface. She clicked a lever with her back heel and felt the familiar sensation of weightlessness spread up her limbs. The board hovered just above the metal sheet of ground and moved forward smoothly.

Levit boards had been a luxury in Daro, where one could walk across the city in half an hour, but in Tura they were essential for timely transport. Prior to the Remsgri's invention of the Rale system, Renyra imagined the river had served as the only means of efficient travel across the city.

The Rale path wound between buildings containing apartments, meeting halls, guest quarters, and centers of engineering and maintenance. Ahead the steaming glass of the bathhouses reflected the sun as it progressed toward the western horizon. Renyra coaxed her levit board to quicken its pace, moving toward the East Neighborhoods.

She took calming breaths. There was only so much she could do to convince Liera of the truth. If Kaelo did come to Tura, all the elves would know soon enough, and then Liera would have to believe her. Or maybe Gellion had been wrong. Maybe the elves had nothing else to fear from Kaelo.

The thought of Gellion made Renyra's throat constrict until she struggled to draw breath. Tears stung her eyes. The memory of her last moments with Gellion had run through her mind on an endless loop for weeks. She had been with him just before the elves reached the sanctuary of the mountains west of Arvain. It seemed impossible that his life could have ended mere minutes after their frantic conversation.

The wind whipped a tear from Renyra's eye. She forced a deep breath and concentrated on the street in front of her. Renyra could hardly remember crying through most of her life, yet in the past few weeks, she could not seem to stop the sudden onset of tears that seized her at random, day and night. She ran a hand forcefully across her eyes.

Houses now lined the winding road, each unique in its architecture and landscaping. Most were built of stone, though some glimmered varying shades of silver or copper. Renyra tried to remember which streets to turn down, gauging the familiarity of the houses she passed. Some were small, inhabited by one or two elves. Others sprawled along the road, probably housing whole families or split into multiple apartments. It was one of the latter buildings that Renyra approached. She stepped off her levit board and walked up the path toward a door of brushed brass. She blinked several times to ensure her eyes were dry before turning the handle and pushing the door inward.

Golden light reached through the western windows and spilled to every corner of the room, casting dark shadows as it met furniture. The room was empty. Renyra walked to the kitchen and splashed cool water on her face before setting a pot of water to boil. The apartment was small but cozy with simple furnishings. Renyra thought of the bright colors and splashes of Fieri design in her last home and felt a pang of grief. She imagined the woven rugs and carved furniture lying in rubble, saltwater stripping them of color and stain.

"How did it go?"

Renyra jumped at the voice, turning to find Firas standing behind her. She had to tilt her head back to look into his eyes—large and kind. Some of the grief bled away from her body. She moved forward and wrapped her arms around Firas's waist, pressing her head against his chest. He rested a hand on her hair and held her against him with the other.

"Not well." Renyra let out a long sigh. She pulled away from Firas and fished in a nearby cabinet for two cups. Firas stood quietly as she pulled a jar of dried herbs from another cabinet and scooped some into each cup. "Liera won't hear the possibility of Kaelo's involvement. I think part of her believes everything I said, but she doesn't *want* to believe it, and she won't take any action." Renyra stared into the pot of water. Thousands of tiny bubbles flocked together at the bottom, occasionally pushing one of their companions into a dizzying spiral to the water's surface.

"I've been wondering how Gellion identified Kaelo from my description," Renyra said. "I only said the elf was Turi—described his hair and face—but Gellion seemed absolutely certain, as though he had suspected it before I came to him."

"Gellion lived in Tura in his early life. He was probably here when Kaelo was exiled. I doubt the image of an elf that infamous would flee one's memory, even over centuries."

"I suppose." Renyra looked into her empty cup, thinking.

Renyra believed Gellion. Even if she hadn't, she would have honored his plea to warn the Council of his suspicion. But the conviction in his eyes had been so strong, so certain. He *knew* it was Kaelo, and somehow, it seemed to fit.

"Why did he do it, Firas?" Renyra said quietly.

Firas did not answer at once. Renyra looked up to see his eyes welled with sadness. She turned back to the water.

"The actions of others often seem incomprehensible when we cannot see the thoughts and motivation behind them," Firas said.

"You think he had a good reason for what he did?" Renyra could not keep the heat from her voice. Her eyes flashed as she turned to face him.

"I think he thought he had good reason," Firas answered calmly. "Though I can offer no suggestion as to what that reason may be."

Renyra took the pot and poured bubbling water into the mouth of each cup. Fragrant steam rose around her face.

"It is all I can think about," said Renyra. "Kaelo wanted the city to be empty—he *knew* it would be empty—but the earthquakes started before Dulon announced the alliance. What would have happened if there had been no alliance, or if we had refused to accept it?"

Firas raised an eyebrow at her.

"I know it is useless to wonder," she said, exasperated. "But my point is, did he intend for the elves to leave the city from the beginning, or did he adapt his plans as opportunities presented themselves?"

"Why does it matter?" Firas asked.

"If it was his intent from the beginning, he must have known about the alliance before the rest of us, and either bet we would accept, or orchestrated it." Renyra let out a long breath and sipped at her tea. "Do you think the centuries without vierstone drove him mad? Maybe there was no sense to his actions."

"It's possible," Firas said slowly. "Though the elves who originally left the Great Cities did not go mad, they lost their skill and connection with stone, metal, glass—turned inward and solitary. You saw him. Did he seem mad?"

Renyra closed her eyes. It was all too easy to bring Kaelo's face to the forefront of her mind. His eyes, so dark green as to be nearly black, had shone with triumph in his achievement, but so too had they been intelligent, and coldly sane.

"No. I think there was a purpose to what he did, and I do not think that purpose is done."

Renyra moved toward the small table in the kitchen, smoothing her skirt as she sat. The skirt was no more hers than the table or the apartment. She had sometimes worn Turi fashions or brought Turi decorations into her home in Daro, but it had always felt a bit like playing dress-up—stepping into an acted role. Now it was all she had. All that remained of Renyra's past life was the set of stained and torn wraps she had worn the evening Daro fell. She had washed the soiled clothes and folded them neatly, though they would never be fit to wear again.

"He will come to Tura, Firas, I know he will. We are not safe here."

Firas ran a hand over the stubble at the back of his head, then reached up to smooth the flaxen ponytail that sat on top of it like a cap.

"Some refugees have already left Tura," he said. "Gone to the lands of their Kindoms to start anew, or return to their lives before Daro. I cannot say my mind has not strayed to the same course of action."

Renyra bit her lip. She had been avoiding this subject ever since they left Tala. Daro had been a city of all Kindoms, as unique and diverse in its people as in its innovations and architecture. Fieri, Turi, Morcani, and Remsgri elves had woven a tapestry of colors through the fabric of

Daro, but in Faeran, most Kindoms kept to their own lands. Renyra had seen a handful of dark-skinned Fieri walking the streets of Daro, though few wore the brightly colored wraps of her people. Still fewer Remsgri dotted the population with their thick braids and cropped clothing. She knew Firas would want to return to the Morcani lands, far to the north in the Terulian Mountains, but she possessed little enthusiasm for the prospect. In fact, the thought of moving to Morcanan brought her about as much joy as the thought of Kaelo coming to Tura.

Only a few months before, a visiting Morcani elf had called Renyra 'Tathé'—a slang term and an insult for an elf not born and raised in one of the Great Cities. The Morcani were a strict and closely knit Kindom who preferred the company of their own. Renyra would stand out like a dark stain in the snow. She knew that not all Morcani would treat her as an outsider. Firas himself was proof of that, as had been Dulon. Renyra bit her lip harder. She tasted metal as she fought to retract the tears threatening to fill her eyes. Dulon had been Morcani, yet he had built Daro itself, instigating the melting pot of Kindoms and backgrounds that had made his Great City. But Dulon had been very much the exception, not the rule to his Kindom, and now he was gone.

A warm hand enveloped Renyra's shoulder and she sucked in a breath of air. The vierstone pierced through her ear warmed, and she felt a wave of solace. She looked up to see Firas sitting next to her, understanding in his eyes.

"We need not leave here right away," he said. "We have time to think, to discuss, and we will go nowhere you do not feel comfortable." He squeezed her shoulder. "I promise."

Renyra forced a weak smile and sipped more tea, leaning her head against his arm.

"Tura is an incredible city," she said. "It would break my heart to see it meet the same fate as Daro."

"We will not let it," said Firas. "The elves know what they're up against this time, even if some do not yet acknowledge it."

Renyra didn't answer. She knew Firas was trying to comfort her. None of them knew what they were up against. Seeing a threat clearly did not always make it easier to confront.

When the last dregs of tea were gone, Renyra washed the mugs and tidied the kitchen. The sun was low on the horizon, its light feebly fighting past buildings and trees as it was dragged to the other side of Riure.

Renyra and Firas took the Rale path to the City Center to find dinner. In the Market District, a vast array of taverns and stalls offered sea bird, venison, mushrooms, noodles, spiced sea weed, and fish of every species cooked in every sauce imaginable. Renyra found herself starting to relax as she settled to a plate of grilled dough with beans and vegetables, sipping at a glass of golden wine. Silvery lights lined the streets, and elves walked past in pairs and groups, laughter floating on the warm night air. If Renyra closed her eyes, she could almost imagine she was sitting at the Silver Swan in Daro with Firas and Caerlyn beside her. Dulon would be in the Domes of Rhelyon, whisking from room to room with a long stride and a smile. Gellion would be with Veldon and Valder at the table next to her, their sarcastic banter cutting the general hum of conversation with laughs.

Her eyes opened to a blurred cup and plate. She blinked quickly and concentrated on her fork as she waited for her eyes to dry. The tattoos on her hand caught her attention. The black ink shone against her chocolate skin, still as fresh as when she had first received the tattoo. Intertwining patterns wove up four fingers, each representing a different spirit of Riu—terra, water, ether, and flame. The patterns joined together on the back of her hand to form the three-pointed star. Her vision blurred anew. She could hear the voice of her mother at the back of her mind. She imagined the small woman gripping her hands and telling her to go to Riu for solace, but each time Renyra's thoughts strayed to Riu, something she couldn't identify whipped her attention back as though burned. Where once Riu had brought her nothing but hope, peace, and joy, now there was another emotion between them, one she did not want to go near just yet.

"Do you hear something?"

The strain in Firas's voice brought Renyra back to herself in an instant. His eyes were alert, and he looked toward the Public Quarter. Renyra followed his gaze and strained her ears. She heard nothing. But then—

No.

She barely picked up on the all too familiar rumble before a loud series of cracks split the night air and echoed across the river. Ripples chopped the surface of Renyra's wine, and her cutlery rattled as a tremor passed through the ground. A flutter of gasps and "ohs!" followed the progression of the shaking, then all was silent and still.

Firas turned slowly to look at Renyra, fear laid bare in the depths of his eyes.

Renyra's heart pounded. Her mouth was dry, and she could feel the blood draining from her face. They had hardly been here two days. How could he have gotten here in two days? But natural earthquakes didn't happen in Tura any more than they did in Daro.

By whatever means, Kaelo was in Tura, and his purpose was clearly not complete.

5

THE TURI COUNCIL

Kyna raised her eyebrows appreciatively at the damage in the square. Elves crowded the outskirts of the space, whispering and fidgeting. A few ventured into the square itself, either crossing quickly to get to a destination, or running a curious hand over the broken ground. The Central Tower of the Public Quarter rose at the head of the space, alabaster walls untouched and gleaming in the sunlight, but the expanse of stone before the tower resembled shattered pottery. Deep and jagged cracks raced and crossed through the rock, and a sheen of water reflected off of its surface. Kyna walked past a fountain, water bubbling feebly from its broken base, and her eyes tracked the black filaments that ran through the slick stone at her feet. Before, the stone had been white-grey, with the merest sheen of jade tracing its grain.

Liera's invitation had been a surprise, but not an unpleasant one. Kyna needed to talk to the Lady of Tura anyway, and this would present the perfect opportunity. Of slightly less surprise had been the earthquake. Kyna had known it would come, but she had not expected it so soon after their arrival, and was impressed by the grandeur of the first attack. In Daro, the first earthquake had been at the opening feast of the Kindom Council, hardly a small-scale event, but the implications of the occurrence had been entirely unknown. This time the elves knew better, or should have known better.

Attacking a public square of a Great City at the height of evening revelry was a bold and risky move. It was arrogant. And it had worked. No one had seen the culprit—no one but the refugees of Daro knew there was a culprit to be found. Yet the urgency of Liera's letter implied that she knew more than Tura's citizens did about the nature of the earthquake.

Every surface inside the Central Tower seemed to be rounded, from the walls to the furniture to the spiraling stairs. Kyna ignored the stairs and stepped onto a circular lift that rose to the upper floors. The back of the lift was clear glass that overlooked the river and the Market Quarter beyond. In the distance, the ocean glittered indigo against the horizon.

A soft click brought Kyna to her desired floor, and she slid the doors of the lift open. A long, arching hall stretched before her. She walked past doors, each a unique shape and color with carved frames and ornate door handles. Naturally, the building most frequented by visiting elves would have to show off the superior gifts of the Turi in every square inch. Kyna could see her reflection in the polished floors and fancied that she perceived a hint of lavender flavoring the air. She snorted.

The doors to Liera's primary meeting room were tall and slender with narrow panes of glass outlining their frames. Kyna paused before the doors, a slight flutter in her chest.

Stop being ridiculous.

Kyna had spoken with numerous Kindom leaders during the Council in Daro, but she had managed to avoid Liera throughout its duration. Obviously this avoidance would not be able to continue in Tura. Liera was necessary to Kyna's mission, but anxious as Kyna was to share the prophecy with the Lady of Tura, it was a meeting she anticipated with a mixture of dread and strange excitement.

Don't think about it.

Kyna had to keep her perspective narrow while she was in Tura, just as she had in Daro. It would not do to dwell on her higher purpose. She had to blend in with the elves of Tura as though she were an average citizen. It was a tedious task, but not without some intrigue.

Taking a deep breath, Kyna centered herself with closed eyes, focusing on her immediate surroundings and her body. She had scoffed at the A'vaeri when first she learned it, and still thought its methods erred on the side of sentimental, but she could not deny the art's usefulness when it came to refocusing her attention. It was easy enough to ignore the twinge in her chest each time she thought of who had taught it to her. She opened her eyes.

The doors rotated soundlessly as Kyna pushed through them. The room beyond was spacious but not large, with an oval table in the center and a curved window looking over the Guild Quarter and the West Neighborhoods of Tura.

At the head of the table sat Liera. She was bony, with sharp angles to her face and black hair that seemed faded, absorbing the light of the room rather than reflecting it. Her shoulders were squared, but her head was bent over a handful of papers in front of her. At Kyna's entrance, she glanced up distractedly and nodded in Kyna's general direction before turning back to her papers, but then she paused, her eyes moving back to Kyna. Liera straightened. Her eyes were matte green and bore a strange gleam as they flicked over Kyna's face before holding her gaze.

Kyna stared back and twitched an eyebrow up as the silence stretched. Then Liera blinked and looked away, gesturing to a chair two down from her own. She returned to her papers as though nothing had happened, but a small line creased her brow.

Kyna let out a breath, releasing the tension in her muscles. She closed the doors behind her and walked to her assigned seat, dropping into it with practiced indifference. She observed her colleagues with a shrewd glance. Two male elves sat on Liera's right, each with dark hair and fair skin—probably members of the city council of Tura. Both watched Kyna curiously. To Liera's left was a small Fieri elf. The emerald of her eyes shone against her dark skin, and she smiled hesitantly at Kyna. Kyna recognized her as the elf who had helped lead the survivors of the army back to Daro. She remembered seeing her in Daro with Dulon and Gellion. Kyna nodded to the woman. Had the Fieri elf been in Dulon's confidence as well?

No one spoke. After a few more minutes, another woman with sharp eyes and a silk dress swept into the room. She sat next to the other members of the Turi Council and brushed a tail of dark hair over her shoulder before turning expectantly to Liera.

Liera nodded and began to speak. "Thank you all for coming at such short notice. I have sent word to all the members of the Turi Council. They will be here tomorrow. However, given the immediate nature of our topic of conversation, I thought it would be prudent to meet with those elves who are most pertinent to my course of response." She looked around the table.

"Some of you know each other," Liera continued, "but for the benefit of those who do not, this is Reanan, the Master Builder of Tura and a member of the city's Council." She gestured at the tanned elf to her right. He straightened his broad shoulders and inclined his head toward Kyna and Renyra.

Liera moved her hand to the next elf. "Coren, the Master of Sport." A lithe and smiling elf raised his hand. "And Alsena, the Master of Guilds." Alsena lifted her head a bit higher, though it still barely topped Coren's shoulder.

"Joining us are Renyra and Kyna, two refugees from Daro who were involved in the—" Liera hesitated, "the events of the city. As it would seem the same events may unfold in Tura, their insight could be valuable as we move forward."

Kyna had assumed this was the purpose of her invitation. She looked at Renyra, who was glancing anxiously at the elves around the table.

"Last night there was an earthquake in the Public Quarter of Tura." Liera folded her hands in front of her and paused. "Some of you attended the Kindom Council in Daro three months ago and may have felt similar earthquakes prior to our departure. Based on these experiences, and the accounts I have heard regarding the destruction of Daro, we can assume that the same cause of those earthquakes is now afflicting Tura."

"Which is what?" Alsena said. "Did the elves of Daro discover the cause? I've heard rumors, but—" She shook her head incredulously, eyeing Renyra and Kyna.

Liera followed her gaze, looking thoughtful. "I will allow our guests from Daro to explain," she said.

Kyna and Renyra exchanged a glance. Kyna spoke.

"The earthquakes plagued Daro for two months, damaging buildings and streets until the foundations failed and destroying vierstone until none remained."

Several intakes of breath met these words.

"That is impossible." Alsena looked personally affronted at the claim. "Vierstone cannot be destroyed, least of all by earthquakes."

"They were not just earthquakes." Renyra's eyes were bright and fierce. "They happened in a grid pattern across the city, forming a network of weakened points in the foundations and the cliffside beneath until they were linked together, spelling Daro's destruction. This was no natural or random occurrence, it was an attack."

A hush fell over the room. Liera sat still, the knuckles of her clasped hands white.

"An attack by what?" Reanan said. The Master Builder watched Renyra carefully.

"You have heard the rumors as well as I," said Alsena before Renyra could answer. "Rumors I believe still less than those of dying vierstone."

"I have heard rumors, yes." Reanan did not take his eyes off Renyra. "But I have not heard a direct account. Please." He nodded to Renyra.

Renyra flicked an annoyed glance at Alsena, then said, "An attack by an elf. I saw him. He put his hand to the stone streets, and they cracked at his touch without a moment's hesitation. I saw him destroy the entire city. I still do not know how he did it, but I can tell you he did do it." She took a breath. "And I know who he—"

"We will discuss the possible identity and reasoning behind the attacks at a later date," Liera said, shooting a warning look at Renyra. "For now, I only want to impress upon you all the severity of our situation and give context for the measures I intend to enact."

Renyra slowly closed her mouth. She narrowed her eyes at Liera, but made no move to contradict her.

Kyna watched Renyra with a cocked head. Had the little Fieri truly seen him? Did she know who it was? Kyna moved her eyes to Liera. The Lady of Tura was tense, the skin of her knuckles now limned red around the white. Did Liera know as well? She was certainly acting as though she did, but if so, she was clearly in no hurry to make the knowledge public. Kyna was not the only one whose curiosity was sparked by Renyra and Liera's interaction, but no one pressed the matter as Liera began to outline her plans.

"There is panic in the city," she said. "But there is little we can do about that just now. I do not wish to make any public address until the Turi Council has met. What we can do now is begin to repair damages and set precautions against further attacks." She turned to the Master Builder. "Reanan, I want you to work with Alsena to form a team of Builders and stoneworkers to repair the damages in the square. Focus on the fountains first, then move to the cracked ground. Alsena, I want anyone with knowledge of vierstone to inspect the stone in the affected area." She sighed heavily. "There is black running through it, and I fear the accounts of Daro must be true."

The Master of Guilds' face drained of color. She nodded mutely.

"Coren," Liera turned to the Master of Sport. "We have not had guards in this city for a long time, and I hoped to never employ them again, but it seems that time has come. Choose a dozen elves and take them to the armory. I want guards throughout the Public Quarter tonight. Renyra and Kyna, I want you both at the Council meeting tomorrow. In the meantime, try to prevent the other refugees from spreading fear through the city."

Before anyone could comment on her orders, Liera dismissed the meeting, gathering her papers and standing as elves filed uncertainly out of the room. Renyra glanced at Kyna as she left, but Kyna was a long time pushing her chair in, and the Fieri elf disappeared into the hallway after the others.

Liera dropped her papers into a bag and straightened. Her eyes widened in surprise to see Kyna still in the room, but she quickly composed herself. "Yes?"

"I've been searching through the Archives," Kyna said, reaching into her pocket to withdraw a folded piece of paper. Liera's eyes narrowed as she looked at it. "I found something. Something I think might be important—in a book of prophecies."

Liera's eyebrows rose. "A book of prophecies?"

"Yes."

"Why were you reading through writings of the prophets?"

Kyna shrugged. "The prophets speak of momentous events. They foretold the founding of vierstone and the Great War. The elves just saw a city fall into the sea and were betrayed in a human war. An elf is causing earthquakes and destroying vierstone with his bare hands. Seems fairly momentous."

The merest flicker of suspicion flitted across Liera's eyes. "And you think you ... you found a prophecy that addresses this?" she asked in a voice of strained calm.

"Yes." Kyna unfolded the piece of paper and handed it to Liera. Words swirled across the page in her own writing:

The grounds will shake, the cities flood,
The stone stained redder than their blood.
From green to red, from red to black,
The life reversed will not come back.
The source of darkness, lone and kin,
Will bring the monsters up again.

The stone that dies will not return,
But safe from death is stone that burns.
From which he hates his doom shall rise,
A weapon forged from his despise.
The swords that shape and cool too late,
Will drown in ash, bereaved their fate.

Liera stared at the paper, her face as pale as its creamy surface. "In what book did you find this? What prophet wrote it?"

"Hirulan, a prophet from the early eras. I found it in *Tellings of Trial and Tranquility*. I have the book in my rooms if you want to see it."

Liera slowly dragged her gaze away from the paper and looked at Kyna with searching eyes. She blinked.

"That will not be necessary. I appreciate your concern over this matter, and the research you have done." She spoke in a measured tone, as though to a child who had drawn her a clumsy picture. "But this prophecy is grasping at straws. I find it highly unlikely that it refers to our present situation, and certainly do not think we should take any action based upon its words."

"But—"

"I am sorry, but I have already taken more time out of the day than I can afford. I really must go on to my next engagement."

Kyna stood her ground, watching Liera closely. The woman was afraid. She did not want the prophecy to be true, so she brushed it off as something foolish. Kyna chewed on her tongue. This might be harder than she had thought.

Liera gathered her bag and moved toward the doors.

"I will see you at the meeting tomorrow." She paused as she reached for the door handle. "Where are you from?" she asked.

Kyna hesitated, taken aback by the sudden change of subject.

"The hills north of Ard Gael," she said. "A village on the border of the mountains."

Liera nodded slowly.

"Why do you ask?" said Kyna.

"Oh, nothing," Liera said vaguely. "I was only curious." She shook her head. "I do not know my Kindom as I once did."

With that, she left the room.

Kyna stood still for a long time, listening to Liera's footsteps receding down the hallway. She carefully folded her paper and returned it to her pocket. She would need to find someone else to take stock in the prophecy. Liera would have to listen in the end. Kyna only hoped it would not be too late.

The next morning was grey and heavy. A thick fog rolled to the edge of the sea cliffs, spilling over the top to send wispy tendrils of smoke across the ground. Looking to the sea, it seemed as though the cliffs stopped at the edge of a frothy lake. Nonetheless, the morning was warm, and Kyna's clothes stuck to her in a damp caress. She walked through muggy streets toward the bathhouses. If she had to be wet, it may as well be with clean, saltless water.

There were not many elves at the bathhouses. Kyna found an unoccupied pool and hung her shirt and pants in a drying room. Returning to the pool, she slipped beneath the cool water with a sigh. Her hair slicked to her head and shoulders as she emerged, gleaming like the pelt of a seal. Leaning back in the water, Kyna watched the sky through the glass ceilings. The fog was thinning, burning away with the morning. By afternoon, it was likely to be another hot and sunny day. She closed her eyes and tried to absorb the cool water into her skin—a reserve for later.

Kyna looked forward to the Turi Council meeting. It was an exciting addition to an otherwise dull day, and given the reactions she had witnessed in the short meeting yesterday, there was bound to be some drama, especially if Renyra laid her accusation before the Council. A corner of Kyna's mouth drew upward. Yes, this would be a good meeting to attend. Of course, she also wanted to know how Liera intended to respond to the earthquake. Would she set guards about the city? Send elves to investigate like Dulon had? Those measures had not stopped Daro's destruction, and they wouldn't stop Tura's. If Liera was too stubborn and foolish to understand that, maybe the other Council Members would see reason.

The sun had burned away all the fog by the time any other elves came to Kyna's pool. She stepped out of the water as two women came from the drying room, laughing with their heads bent together. They had dark hair and matching noses. Probably sisters. Etched swallows flew up the bare arm of one and down the arm of the other. Kyna cocked an eyebrow. Sisters, or lovers.

She passed the two without a word and went to retrieve a towel and her clothes. She stayed in the drying room for a few minutes, relishing the feeling of dry clothes and skin, then sighed and left the bathhouses. At least it was slightly less humid without the fog. Slightly.

The morning and early afternoon dragged by. Kyna wandered the streets, observing the elves of the city. She ate a lazy and late lunch at the markets before crossing a bridge to the Public Quarter. The meeting would start soon enough, and she was curious to see the state of the square after yesterday's orders.

Sure enough, elves were stationed about the broken square, armed with spears and quarterstaves and looking around warily at the passersby. The night before had passed with no disturbance, and several of the guards looked bored with their task. Water no longer glistened on the stone of the square, and Builders clustered around the two fountains with tools. As Kyna neared the doors of the Central Tower, she saw a group of elves walking in a stately procession into the square, Liera at their head. Kyna stopped and watched them. Four elves trailed behind Liera, three males and one female.

As they approached, Kyna recognized the woman behind Liera with a lurch. Her auburn hair mirrored Gellion's to the strand, and dark circles hung from her eyes like bruises. Tenille, the Lady of Maramor. Gellion's mother. Of course she would be on the Turi Council. She was a Turi representative on the Kindom Council. Yet the possibility of her presence at the meeting had not occurred to Kyna.

Kyna gritted her teeth. Why should it have occurred to her? Tenille's presence meant the same as any other elf's. Just another Council Member. Kyna swallowed the tightness in her throat.

Just another Council Member.

Behind Tenille, an elf a head taller than her strode forward with his face set in stern determination. Dark brown hair fell in waves past his shoulders. He was handsome, if a little self important, and Kyna felt as though she knew him, or had seen him before. It was an uncomfortable feeling, and made her skin prickle. She shook her head and looked to the two elves at the rear of the group. They were of middling height and remarkably average appearance, with straight hair and practical traveling clothes.

Liera barely jerked her head to Kyna as she pushed through the doors to the Central Tower, her entourage trailing behind her. With a soft snort, Kyna walked in after them.

"Thank you to our representatives from the regions beyond Tura for their fast response in joining us." Liera nodded to the four elves Kyna had seen crossing the square. "It has been a long time since such urgency was necessary."

The two nondistinct visitors squared their shoulders at her words. Tenille just stared ahead blankly, and the handsome elf next to her all but scowled at Liera. A line formed between Kyna's brows. The impression that she knew the elf passed over her again, but the memory fled before she could grasp it.

The four visitors sat to Liera's left with Kyna and Renyra across from them. Two other elves sat beside Kyna, one of whom she recognized as Reanan from the day before. The Master Builder's shoulders sagged, but his eyes were alert. He must have been busy the last day trying to fix the damages in the square.

Alsena and Coren were not there. Kyna assumed they were a part of the city council of Tura, but not one of the chosen representatives for the full Turi Council that encompassed all regions inhabited by the Turi elves.

"We have two guests with us today," Liera said. "By now, you have all heard of the recent tragedy of Daro. Renyra and Kyna," she gestured to each in turn, "were involved in the investigation of the events that transpired there, and will give us a full account."

All eyes turned to Kyna and Renyra, some politely curious, others burning in their intensity. The handsome elf had turned his glare on Kyna. She twitched an eyebrow at him, and he looked away.

"You both know Reanan," Liera said. She pointed next to him. "This is Alos, Master of Trade in Tura." A slight elf with a high collar nodded to them. Liera faced the other side of the table. "Dorian and Saethir, representing the regions south of the Wildwood, and Tenille and Tornac, from Maramor."

Kyna's memory lurched. She had heard that name before. Tornac. From Maramor. Kyna looked hard from Tenille to Tornac, and with a jolt that went to her bones, Kyna realized who he was. She choked in a sharp breath. Concentrating on keeping her face carefully neutral, Kyna let the breath out slowly, dispelling the unexpected pain in her gut. Yet she couldn't take her eyes off of Tornac. The resemblance was striking.

How she hadn't realized it immediately was beyond her. Sitting across from her, next to his mother, was Gellion's older brother.

Kyna swallowed, looking down as Tornac noticed her stare. Shame and fury warred within her at the betrayal of her body. She was better than this. She was better than them. She would not succumb to this weakness of spirit. Pressing her wrist against her thigh, Kyna clenched her teeth as the stone in her cuff made contact with her skin. The pain lessened.

She glanced around. No one seemed to have noticed her reaction, except maybe Tornac, but all attention was now on Liera, who had begun speaking again.

"—elves of Daro now for their account."

Kyna relaxed her face and shoulders just in time as silence fell, and the Council turned to look at her again. She turned a controlled gaze on Renyra and nodded casually for her to begin.

Renyra outlined what had happened in Daro the last months, Kyna interjecting her perspective once she could trust her voice. They explained the earthquakes and the queer sensation of wrongness that accompanied each one. Renyra spoke of the strange and violent creatures that had begun to converge on the city as the earthquakes progressed, of the dying vierstone and the proclamation of Daro's vierstone master, Aryn, that an elf had been responsible before her untimely death. Kyna told of Dulon's plans to catch the culprit and of her own close encounter with the elf. When she spoke of the tunic he had worn—a tunic of woven metal crafted to reflect the lights and colors of its surroundings and render the wearer nearly invisible—Tenille looked up sharply.

"The elf had stolen the tunic from a competitor in the craftsman competition." Kyna hesitated. "From Gellion." She forced herself to say the name aloud, pleased by the lack of reaction it inspired in her this time. Tenille's reaction was not so subtle. She flinched visibly at Gellion's name, pain clouding her eyes. Next to her, Tornac's face was hard as stone.

Then Renyra described the departure of the elven army, and finally, the destruction of Daro. When she had completed the tale of her encounter with the mysterious elf, she glanced at Liera. The Lady of

Tura's face held no more color than the papers she clenched in her hands. A muscle twitched in her jaw, and she nodded to Renyra to continue.

"I did not recognize the elf when I saw him," Renyra said. "Only that he was Turi." Several gasps met these words. "But I rode to the elven armies. I was there, in the battle, and I found Gellion. I told him what I had seen. Gellion had seen a flash of the elf's face beneath his hood before, and when I described him, Gellion knew with no doubt who it was."

Kyna's heart was beating against her ribs, a steady rhythm, but quickened in pace. So Gellion had caught a glimpse of him. Why hadn't he said anything before? Kyna leaned forward as Renyra opened her mouth to name the accused.

"It was Kaelo."

Silence.

Not even gasps of shock broke the stillness.

Kyna's eyes darted to the faces of the Council, gauging their reactions. Liera's face had not changed, but she was nearly crumpling her papers. Most of the elves stared at Renyra, varying degrees of horror and bemusement on their faces. Some glanced almost fearfully at Liera. A blush of red was beginning to climb the Lady of Tura's throat, belying her stoic face.

The silence lingered, growing more tense with each passing breath.

"I have wondered if ... if he played some part in the alliance with the Albaren," Renyra said at last, shattering the fragile glass that had encased the room. "The city was nearly empty when he destroyed it. Had it been fully populated, he probably would have been caught once he began his full attack." She shook her head. "But the alliance was a ruse. The Albaren betrayed the elves—an attempted genocide of Daro. It seems unlikely Kaelo would have orchestrated that."

"Why?" Tornac said. "He has shown no concern for elven life before. Maybe it was simple revenge. Destroy a city and a population of elves cut off from help by the Semestrial Sea."

"Come now," said Alos, a half-hearted smile playing at his lips. "You cannot truly believe this elf is Kaelo. No one has seen him since before the Great War. And how, by Riu, would he have come upon such powers?"

"How would any elf?" Tornac said. "Kaelo is as likely to have done it as any."

"It is not possible," said Reanan. "He died in the war. How could any elf have survived those years, wandering the lands unprotected?"

"Unless he joined the enemy," muttered Dorian. "But in that case he would be just as dead now."

Several elves nodded.

Annoyance prickled at Kyna's skin. Kaelo had been exiled for murder by his own mother—a mother who had tried to sentence him to death the next time she saw him. He had been left for dead during the Great War. The Council was speaking as though it were only natural.

Hypocrites.

Renyra stepped in. "We don't know his purpose or how he came by these powers, but I know what I saw. I know *who* I saw. Whatever his reason, Kaelo destroyed Daro and its vierstone, and he is here now, in Tura. The earthquakes are beginning again. The vierstone is turning black again. It doesn't matter how or why, it matters that we stop it."

"Of course it matters how and why." Tenille's voice was soft, but it cut through the room like the edge of ice. Her bloodshot eyes remained fixed on the table as she spoke. "But we should try to stop the elf first, whether or not he is Kaelo. Capture him, and we can know how and why he has done what he has done."

"And how do we do that?" said Alos. "He can command the very foundations of the city to do his bidding if any of this is to be believed."

"There are ways." It was the first time Liera had spoken since Renyra had named Kaelo. "We can incapacitate the elf. Arrows from a distance. Nets."

Kyna searched Liera's eyes, looking for any trace of pain, any trace of fear, but if there was any, Liera hid it well. She looked for all the world as if she were talking about a stranger, not her son.

She doesn't believe it, Kyna realized. *She won't believe it is Kaelo until she's seen him.*

Did Liera think Gellion would not have recognized his own

mentor? Gellion had told Kyna of his past relationship with Kaelo before the elves left Daro, but Kyna wondered how many in this room knew Gellion had once studied under the purported traitor. Liera, Tenille, and Tornac would know, certainly, but perhaps not the others.

"Nets?" Alos looked as though he were about to laugh.

"Do you have a better suggestion, Alos?" Liera skewered him with her eyes, and his expression sobered at once. She looked away from him and continued as if he had not spoken. "I have already spoken with the Master of Sport, and he has begun to mobilize guards in the city. We will expand their number and their range to every quadrant of the City Center."

"How are they to see him?" Tenille asked.

"The tunic doesn't make him entirely invisible," Renyra said. "And it doesn't silence his steps. I could detect him well enough to aim. Though aim didn't do any good," she added resentfully.

"I will tell the guards all they need to know about the elf," said Liera. "Instruct them to incapacitate him and bind his hands. From Renyra's account, he must use his hands to affect his—abilities. If he is not caught within the week, we will further evaluate the situation."

Liera stood. A shadow fell over her face, her eyes burning embers within.

"We will not let this elf cause further damage to Tura, and we will not let him escape the city alive."

6

OUT OF THE SHADOWS

Eurig stood with his feet apart and shoulders square. The look of a disappointed father hung about his face.

Gellion's blood ran hot beneath his skin. There was an urgency to his anger and fear that made his skin itch, but he forced himself to remain still and staring. Veldon stood beside him, clearly making an effort not to let his eyes rove over the room in fascination. He looked almost pleased to be included this time, though he would not understand a word Eurig said without Gellion's interpretation.

Despite the skill and prowess he and Veldon had demonstrated during their escape attempt, Gellion stood before Eurig much the same as before, unbound with a few guards for company. In fact, very little had changed as a result of his and Veldon's failed scheme, save the two guards that now stood constant vigil outside their cell.

The prison guards had left Gellion and Veldon to themselves the days after their recapture. Gellion had spent most of the time in brooding silence, lying on his bed and staring at the ceiling. Even imagining the sequences of the A'vaeri did not settle his mind, and he had no motivation to practice the movements with his body.

Veldon had tried to make hushed conversation, but had soon given up the attempt against Gellion's morose and short responses. What was the point? They had no hope of escape now—not within the next few weeks at least—and by then it may as well be months, or years. How would they get across the sea without the ships of Daro? The only options remaining now were to tell Eurig everything he wanted to know about the elves and hope it was enough to buy their freedom without risking the security of the elven race, or stay in prison until another opportunity for escape revealed itself.

Or until Eurig or his successor puts us to death rather than deal with our eternal imprisonment.

As hope bled from Gellion's heart, a black stain took its place. He thought constantly of his friends and family, picturing the faces of Valder, Firas, Renyra, and Kyna as clearly as he could. He told himself they were dead. All of them. He pushed the knife of grief as far into his heart as possible, but no matter how hard he tried, he could not give in to the pain. He could not eradicate the foolish glimmer of hope that stubbornly remained in the recesses of his mind: that they lived, that he would see them again.

So instead he turned at last to the one death he could latch onto with certainty. He recalled the scene as often as he could—Dulon fighting through a dozen guards, the sound of his cry upon Maranyl's death, the look on his once laughing face as he fell to Vensure's knife. At least he had taken the treacherous captain down with him. It gave Gellion little satisfaction.

Gellion was no stranger to death. In the Great War, it had haunted him to the core. So many elves had died over the course of those two hundred years that it should have become commonplace by all rationale. Each death should have been easier to bear than the last as hope and grief in turn eroded away to numbness, yet Gellion had felt every one. After the war, he had buried his memories in the cold depths of his conscience, but now they returned with a heat so powerful it seared his soul. Those deaths in the war had been tragedies forced upon him by the power of an evil created by Olcon himself. Dulon's death had been a meaningless slaughter for a betrayal neither of them had seen coming. A betrayal either of them could have prevented.

Gellion had never wanted to accept the alliance with the Albaren. He had always thought the humans were less than genuine in their cause. It was Dulon who had given in to the draw of vierstone, to the bribe of a quarry that had never existed. Why hadn't Dulon listened to him? Why hadn't he listened to Miyela, or Tenille, or any of the other elves who had spoken against the alliance? Gellion held on to these thoughts like logs in a river. It had been Dulon's fault. He should have backed out of the alliance when Daro began to fall apart. They had fought two enemies at once, and lost to both. Dulon should have known. He should have chosen differently.

Yet no matter how many times Gellion repeated this to himself, he could find no conviction in his anger. Through its haze, Gellion's stomach knotted with the knowledge that his had been the deciding vote. He had given in to the opinions of the masses and voted against his instincts to represent the elves of Daro. He had voted in favor of the alliance, and his had been the vote to change history. Again.

Gellion's memories of the Turi Council were so sharp they could have happened a week ago, yet it had been seven centuries since he sat on the Turi Council. Then, he had done the opposite; then, he had ignored the pressure of his peers and voted upon his own beliefs, but clearly that choice had been wrong too.

Gellion tried to block his mind from these thoughts as he stared defiantly at Eurig. Whoever's decision had brought him here, he was the only one who could get himself out now. The hopelessness that had possessed Gellion the days before had been replaced this morning by a final resolve. He would try one more time. He would make Eurig understand. He would get back to the elves and fix the consequences of his mistakes.

Eurig stood in silence for a long time. Clearly, he wanted Gellion to speak first, to lower his eyes in shame and beg forgiveness. Gellion would not do it. He felt no shame for what he and Veldon had done, only that they had not succeeded.

Finally, Eurig spoke.

"You tried to escape." It was a simple statement.

"Yes," Gellion said, face still composed.

Eurig raised an eyebrow. "How did you get out of the cell?"

Gellion just looked at him.

Eurig sighed. "I had been expecting your attempted escape, but I must admit myself curious as to the manner in which you achieved it."

"Is that why you waited so long to speak with us?"

All trace of amusement left Eurig's face. Gellion could see a dark anger behind his eyes. Veldon shifted uncomfortably, glancing between Eurig and Gellion.

"I have had other affairs to deal with," said Eurig. "Your escape was not my highest priority. My guards saw you on the prison roof and tailed you through the city, sending word back to me of your direction." Eurig took a breath and straightened. He seemed to grow larger. "How did you escape the prison? Did you use magic?"

"Whatever faerie stories you have heard about the elves, we do not wield unholy magic. We are not heathens and we do not pose any threat to the humans." Gellion's voice rose as he spoke.

"Then how did you escape?"

"We picked the lock!" Gellion said impulsively. It was not as though they could escape by the same means again with guards outside their door. Veldon had started slightly at Gellion's shout. Through his rising anger, Gellion took a breath and quickly translated Eurig's questions for his brother.

Eurig's brows were drawn together. "With what?"

"It doesn't matter with what!" Gellion said, turning back to face the man. "We picked the lock with what we could find and we escaped because we had to escape. We had no choice. You will not listen to or believe us and we have to get back to our kin. We have to. Our families are in danger, can't you understand that? They do not know their peril, but we do, and it has nothing to do with the Dierna, or with the Albaren or with Tala. We are only trying to get back to our home."

Eurig considered him, eyes narrowed. "Your people killed hundreds of my own."

"And your people killed mine."

"We did not start this fight."

"Nor did we."

"No? I have a hard time believing that. And yet—" He trailed off, eyes boring into Gellion as though trying to read his conscience. He cocked his head. "You ran from my guards. Even those few you fought you did not kill, and when your last barrier to escape was the life of your captor, you lowered your blade."

"I am no murderer," Gellion said.

Eurig's mouth twitched; he let out a snort of amusement. The heat in Gellion's chest swelled and spread to his limbs.

"I am no murderer!" he shouted, ignoring the raised weapons of the guards to either side. "Do you think I enjoyed the slaughter on that battlefield? Do you think any of the elves did—relished in the pointless death we caused? The elves fought for a cause we deemed just. We fought to help relieve a nation of suffering. We fought because we thought the Dierna an oppressive foe. And we fought because we were desperate. Instead, we lost everything." Gellion's hands were shaking. He thought again of Dulon, of Daro, of the broken remains of his life. "Everything," he repeated. Tears stung his eyes and he bit hard on the inside of his mouth to stop them.

The first shadow of uncertainty Gellion had yet seen flickered behind Eurig's eyes. He did not take his gaze off of Gellion, but seemed to be absorbed in his own thoughts.

"You ask me who the elves are," Gellion continued. "The elves are a people who love, fear, suffer, laugh, cry, and bleed just as you do. And now they are a people threatened from within. We have to get back." He glanced at Veldon, who stood pale and uncomprehending, but with his face set in a determined calm. "We have to help them, though it is probably too late already." He turned back to Eurig with his chin up and fire in his eyes. "I will not tell you where the elves are. My people have enough danger among them without a human threat besides, but I will tell you that they are far from here, and we have no hope of returning without a ship, the last of which has probably left without us by now."

Gellion stood then as one defeated. The heat of his anger cooled to tired hopelessness. Eurig made no answer. He watched Gellion, then shifted his eyes to Veldon. His expression was unreadable.

"Take them back to their cell," Eurig said.

Gellion held Eurig's stare until the guards turned him away.

***

"What did you say?" Veldon asked when they were back in prison.

Gellion leaned against the wall and slid to the floor with his head in his hands.

"I told him why we tried to escape. I told him why we have to get back. Don't look at me like that. I gave no details." He sighed. "I just tried to make him understand one last time that we are not monsters, spies, or any threat to his people. Clearly I was unsuccessful. Nothing new there." He ran a hand over the side of his head, pausing over the vierstone in his ear. It was warm with the fire of his emotions.

"Keep talking to him," said Veldon. "He can't keep us here forever. He has to let us go eventually."

Gellion didn't have the heart to contradict him. "Maybe."

The rest of the day passed with little excitement. They ate their food, watched the streets outside, and at Veldon's insistence, Gellion started teaching him some Albaren words and phrases.

It was a misty day, and night fell early.

Gellion lay awake for a long time, imagining every possible way to proceed from here. What more could he say to Eurig? How else could they get out of this cursed city? He thought of his mother. She would be back in Maramor, walking the floating platforms and bridges, the Orhiri River gushing beneath. Tornac would be there with her, her one dependable son. Gellion grimaced and turned on his side. Did she now believe Tornac was her only son?

He fell into a fitful sleep, interspersed with dreams of Councils and eyes under a hood in the night.

Weak light had barely reached the corners of the cell when Gellion woke to the soft sliding of metal on metal. He sat upright, only to see Veldon already standing and watching the door. The latch clicked, and the door swung slowly forward. Veldon glanced at Gellion and moved further away from the door, backing into the light from the window. Gellion stood.

A dark shape moved into the cell. Gellion tensed, automatically searching his surroundings for some kind of weapon. Had Eurig sent someone to dispose of his uncooperative prisoners already?

The figure straightened and turned to face them.

Gellion's tension did not lessen, but a flash of impossible familiarity made him step back with a pounding heart.

It can't be.

He was imagining it. Any moment the figure would reveal himself to be the assassin Gellion suspected.

The figure stepped forward into the early dawn light, and Gellion sucked in a breath, shock freezing his limbs even as cautious hope flooded his core. He heard a similar gasp beside him.

Standing before them, was Valder. He was grinning.

Veldon recovered from his shock faster than Gellion. In two steps he was in front of Valder. The brothers clasped hands and slapped backs while they laughed. Gellion took a step forward, barely believing his eyes, but immediately stepped back again as a second figure came in behind Valder. The figure shut the cell door behind him.

"Valder—" Gellion began, but the man pushed back his hood to reveal another familiar face, and one nearly as surprising.

Eurig. An odd smile touched his lips at the scene before him.

Veldon drew back from Valder, watching Eurig warily.

The man did not move, but gestured at the thin beds on the back wall.

"Sit," he said.

Gellion did not move. He could hardly interpret the strong and confused emotions warring within him. Intense relief and joy that his brother was alive was foremost, but it seemed too good to be true. What role did Eurig have in this? Veldon glanced at Gellion and kept his own ground. But the smile had not faded from Valder's face. He stood next to Eurig and nodded encouragingly, and Gellion and Veldon slowly backed into the nearest bed and sat.

"I will get straight to the point." Eurig stepped deeper into the cell. His voice was pitched not to carry beyond its walls. "I do not have any ships. Diernas borders no oceans and has no use for them."

Gellion stared at Eurig. A shock of adrenaline ran through his body as the roiling confusion of emotions within him turned to cautious hope at the man's words. Gellion sat perfectly still, afraid to shatter the moment, to somehow change the course of Eurig's next words.

Was it possible? Was the man toying with them? And why and how in all of Riu's creation was Valder here?

"I have no ships," Eurig repeated. "But I know someone who does."

7

A TROUPE UNITED

Renyra sat on a bench with her knees drawn to her chest. Above, the sky was a brilliant blue dotted with puffs of white, but over the sea, a dark mass of angry greys charged toward land, pushing the stray white wisps ahead of them. The rain would be welcome if it came, but Renyra had lived against the ocean long enough to know the storms did not always make it to shore. The breeze that blew from the south was cool and wet, however, and growing stronger by the hour. If the clouds drew much closer they would need to take shelter.

A series of colored stones and cards littered the table in front of Renyra. Next to her, Firas sat upright, a slight frown on his gentle face as he scrutinized the cards in his hand. Renyra watched him. He had shown little outward grief at the loss of his two best friends, but Renyra knew he was devastated by their loss.

His pain added further to the agony that continued to tear through Renyra's gut at regular intervals. She bit down on her tongue as tears threatened to betray her. Looking at Firas's face, a slow anger boiled in her veins. How could Riu allow such things to happen? She thought of Veldon's kind eyes, Valder's mischievous grin, Gellion's sideways smile —all gone. All wasted. And all leaving behind torn hearts and relationships. Tenille had been a mess at the Turi Council, and Tornac had looked as angry as Renyra now felt. She clenched her fists so her veins stood out against the tattoos on her hand. She looked away from them.

Across the table from Firas sat Caerlyn, a tall and straight backed Fieri. Caerlyn analyzed the board in front of her with the intensity of a hunting cat. Firas took two long fingers and drew a card from his deck, laying it on the table and moving two blue stones diagonally toward Caerlyn. She observed the move, then looked to her own cards.

Spyre was a game of strategy that was engaging to play, but rather dull to watch. Her mind wandered to less pleasant matters. It had been four days since the Turi Council, and thus far little fruition had come from Liera's plans.

"How goes the search?" Caerlyn asked, seeming to read Renyra's mind. Her voice was light, as though asking about the search for a missing shoe.

"Not well." Renyra cleared her throat to hide all trace of the emotion that had afflicted her moments before. "In four days, no elf has gotten near Kaelo, not even glimpsed him, and though there has been no more shaking, the entire Public Quarter is laced with black, and it's beginning to spread to the Scholar Quarter."

Caerlyn let out a low whistle. "That's moving a fair bit faster than in Daro. And without the earthquakes?"

"There has been no shaking, but still reports of the air seeming to shiver, a current in the ground, queer energy—the usual attempts to describe what we all felt when an earthquake came, only this time there's no shaking. The vierstone just dies."

Firas drew his brows together. He had gone back to the game, but was listening intently.

"Before, the earthquakes were a beacon to where Kaelo was," Renyra said. "And a means of finding him once we knew what to look for, but now it's harder. You have to be exactly where he is to sense what he is doing, and with the tunic and a much larger city to hide in, I don't see how the guards have a chance." Renyra let out a puff of air in frustration. "The guards are making a point of advertising their presence, marching boldly through the streets and carrying spears for all to see. Of course Kaelo won't reveal himself around them, and he clearly doesn't need to reveal himself to continue his work. What they need to do is catch him by stealth. Move about unseen and unheard, as he does, and track him."

Caerlyn raised a sardonic eyebrow. "Elves who are light on their feet, you mean. Masters of movement and adept at climbing and jumping. Hunting even?"

"Well, yes," Renyra said.

Firas's mouth twitched upward. "Don't give her ideas, Caerlyn."

Caerlyn scoffed. "I gave her no ideas. It was plain on her face long before I voiced it."

Renyra could feel heat rising in her cheeks. "Well, why not? I saw him before, didn't I?"

Firas's eyes darkened. "Yes, and he could have killed you."

"I didn't know what to expect then. Now I do."

"How would you approach differently this time?"

"Don't let him see me. Use roofs, walls, shadows. I could carry arrows rather than a javelin—they shoot faster and if I nock more than one he can't possibly stop them all."

"And to track him in the first place?"

"Every living thing leaves signs of its passage—follows patterns in its movements and habits. I have learned them for a dozen animals, and I will learn his."

Firas gave her a long look. Caerlyn glanced between them with a raised eyebrow.

"Would you at least let me come with you?" Firas said at last.

Renyra opened her mouth in surprise. She had expected more of a fight from him than this. Considering the offer for a moment, she said, "Yes."

Firas seemed almost as surprised by her quick acceptance as she had been by his.

"You're as light on your feet as me," Renyra said. "Certainly as able to jump, climb, and balance, and your height could be useful."

Firas chuckled. "I am flattered to be of such convenience."

Renyra blew a kiss at him, and Caerlyn groaned. She had always feigned disgust at Renyra's relationship with Firas, though Renyra knew better than to take her seriously. Caerlyn may seem haughty and coarse on the outside, but she was Renyra's best friend, and fiercely loyal.

A rumble of thunder made them all look up. Renyra had hardly noticed the shadow descending over the city as they spoke. Dark clouds covered half the sky now, blotting out the sun and visibly moving north. Over the sea, she could see a curtain of blue moving toward them.

They packed up their game of spyre and walked through the gardens to the neighborhoods beyond. Caerlyn parted company with them at her own temporary home, muttering her goodbyes and keeping her head down as fat drops of water began to fall around them. Renyra took Firas's hand as they jogged to the safety of their apartment.

The storm broke.

Late afternoon brought clear skies again, the clouds having dropped their load and moved on. The air was thick with moisture, even inside the cooled rooms of her house, and Renyra was restless. In Daro, there had always been something for her to do. She missed tending the greenhouses and hunting in the dry hills east of Daro, but more than anything, she missed Sira. In the madness that had consumed Daro since the Kindom Council, she had not trained or performed in months. The beautiful sport had brought joy and purpose to her life, it had brought her to Firas, and it had brought her to Daro.

Renyra's mind strayed to the tall training halls and stages in the Scholar Quarter of Tura. She had thought of the familiar spaces often since her arrival in the Great City, but something had stopped her from going there. The memories were too fond, too pure. It had been there, in the training halls, here in this city, that she had first heard the call for Sira performers, musicians, and craftsmen to go to Daro—the newest Great City across the sea. It had seemed a grand adventure. It had been a grand adventure.

Renyra's eyes roamed over the apartment. There was not much space in the little living room that also served as dining room and kitchen, but Renyra positioned herself in a square of emptiness between the table and the door. With a calming breath, she bent forward until her palms lay flat on the ground, then stacked her shoulders over her hands and brought her feet to her wrists, rising onto her toes. With another breath, she curled her belly inward and lifted through her shoulders and hips, bringing her legs straight into the air with pointed feet. She almost laughed at the joy of being upside down again, and let her back arch as one foot came to the ground behind her, the other still extended straight above.

Her muscles were stiff, and the exertion was more difficult than it should have been, but her body remembered the motions and settled into them with cautious acceptance. Kicking off the ground with her foot, Renyra brought her legs in a scissored arc back to the ground and rose again to her feet, smiling.

Firas was watching her over the top of his book.

"Don't you miss it?" Renyra asked with a sigh.

"Yes." Firas closed his book.

"It was something separate from the rest of the world," said Renyra. "Something one could lose themselves in for just a while before coming out again refreshed and reminded of how simple joy can be." Renyra walked to the couch on the balls of her feet and sat next to Firas. "They were good years, weren't they? Performing, training, traveling. The world seemed open and eager, the years endless."

Firas smiled. "You had never seen more of the world than the villages surrounding your own. I never knew an elf's eyes could grow so big when you first saw Tura."

"Almost as big as when you first saw me," Renyra said, smirking.

Firas laughed aloud.

Renyra collapsed against Firas, and he took her in his arms, kissing her hair. She remained nestled against him for several minutes, enjoying the comfort of his companionship, but her mind would not let her relax entirely.

"Do you think they're still here? Alura and Raren?" she asked, her voice soft. "With Caerlyn and the two of us that would be five of the six. I know it seems ridiculous, given all that's just happened, and with Kaelo in the city—" She paused, biting her lip. "But it would be nice to see them again."

She felt Firas nod. "It is not ridiculous," he said, moving his hand along her back. "Rekindling old friendships would be a comfort after losing others." Renyra felt him tense. Waves of his grief seemed to radiate into her where their skin touched. He sighed. "I cannot say I haven't thought of Raren and Alura myself. They did return to Tura after leaving Daro, and it is possible they are still here. We could go to the training halls and ask after them."

Renyra sat up, a thrill of excitement coursing through her, but she immediately checked herself.

They may not even be here, and what do you expect if they are? To reform your troupe of old and return to the life you led before Daro, as if none of it happened? As if it all meant nothing?

Shame quenched the excitement in her stomach. What right had she to hope for such things when the city around her was facing the same threat as her last home? There was no normal to return to now, not unless Kaelo was stopped.

"I don't know," Renyra said, her shoulders slumping. "I should focus on tracking Kaelo, on doing something—" She trailed off, trying to grasp the right word. "Useful."

"You cannot fill your days tracking Kaelo, and the running of Tura is not within your power. Seeking some companionship and joy will not take away from your responsibility." Firas's voice softened. "Nor your grief."

Renyra looked at Firas sharply. His hand still lay against her bare skin, and she could feel his understanding flowing into her. The vierstone in her ear warmed. She drew back, annoyed at Firas's acuity.

"I'm not worried about that," she lied. "I just—" She let out a sharp breath through her nose. "Fine, we will try to find them," she said, as though the whole thing had been Firas's idea of which he had finally convinced her. She stood.

"Now?" Firas said.

"Now."

Outside, the streets gleamed in the watery sunlight as heat again suffused the day. Renyra and Firas took a levit board each and glided down the winding Rale path through the streets. More elves began to dot the pathways as they progressed into the Public Quarter.

Try as she might, Renyra could not quite keep her eyes from the latticework of black that spread through the stone of the street and the buildings around her. Aside from the stains, the stone was whole and smooth.

Why did Kaelo leave the city unharmed now, even as he destroyed its vierstone? But there had been the one earthquake.

Maybe he wanted to get everyone's attention. There is no possibility of secrecy now. But what point is he trying to prove?

The sprawling square before the Central Tower looked nearly as good as new now; only the fountains sat dry and misshapen. Renyra narrowed her eyes at the Central Tower. She knew Liera and the Council were responding to the situation as well as they could, but their stubborn denial that Kaelo was behind it all rankled her. The Council treated her as though she were young and naive, making up stories out of old legends in her overexcitement. They treated her as though she were a tathé.

The Rale path wound around two more buildings before opening onto the main street that led to the eastern gates of Tura. Across the street, Taeva Hall, home to the main stage of Tura, rose majestically next to the Archives. The training halls were attached on one side.

Renyra stepped off her levit board and followed Firas to the northern side of the building, where another fanned courtyard sat between the buildings of the Scholar Quarter. The front of Taeva Hall was a work of art. Marble of every hue and grain formed a strip of color at the base of the domed roof, and intricate stonework lined every column, arch, and door. Just above the main doors, the three-pointed star seemed to rise from the stone as if it had always been a part of it, embossed against the smooth wall in sharp relief. Each point of the star was taller than Firas and carved in intricate detail—leaves, flowers, patterns, lines, all coming together to form pictures that the eye saw one minute but not the next.

The first time Renyra had seen that star, she had stood staring at it in awe, so reluctant to take her eyes away that a laughing Raren and Alura had taken her by the arms and led her into the training halls beyond. Now, the star set a weight on her chest, and she drew her eyes away quickly, digging her nails into her palms.

The training halls were nearly as tall as the ancient building next to them, but the stone walls were simple white, with oval windows outlined in copper. Firas strode to the doors as though they opened into any normal building, but Renyra paused on the threshold, the familiarity so sweet and so sad she could barely bring herself to step into the halls. Taking a breath, she walked inside.

The air was cool and dry. The smell struck Renyra as no sight could have—clean sweat, ropes, and dusty cotton. Renyra took in a deep breath through her nose, her mind overwhelmed with memories flashing by so quickly she could only grasp the feel of them. The same smell had permeated the practice areas of Daro, but this one was subtly different, unique to the place, to the elves that used the space. Lifting her eyes, Renyra looked through a jungle. Ropes, cotton straps, shining sheets of fabric, and chains hung from the ceiling, some cascading all the way to the floor, others suspending trapezes or hoops. Thick shelves lined the wall nearest the door, holding buckets of multicolored balls, rings, and clubs, swords engineered to set on fire, staffs, giant metal wheels, small metal wheels, tufted sticks, and objects for which even Renyra did not know the purpose, all in every color imaginable.

Elves were scattered throughout the space, some suspended in the air, others climbing on top of each other or throwing a dizzying mess of rings between them. Many of the elves were Turi, but there was more diversity here than on the streets. There appeared to be at least one elf from each Kindom—a full spectrum of heights, hair, skin, muscles, and bodies. Almost all of them were smiling, and some waved to Renyra and Firas, who returned the gestures, but walked past them all, eyes scanning for a familiar face.

Renyra's heart sank as each elf proved to be a stranger, or only vaguely familiar. She did not see Raren or Alura.

"They're not here," Renyra said, trying to keep the sullenness from her voice.

Firas did not answer, but put a hand on her shoulder. She looked up to see a grin spreading over his face. He pointed.

Heart lurching, Renyra followed his gesture to the back corner of the room. Among a sea of thick cushions sat a giant metal seesaw, an elf perched on each end, though rarely at the same time. One was male, of middling height with dark hair pulled back in a bun. He was falling in a straight line toward his end of the board and pushed down on powerful legs as he landed. The much smaller elf across from him soared into the air, tucking her body into a series of flips and twists before landing with a puff of air on one of the cushions to the side.

Raren stepped off the seesaw and walked toward his sister, saying a few muffled words to her. He grinned, then lifted his eyes to see Firas and Renyra staring at him. His grin faltered, shock clear in his eyes even from a distance, but then his face split in a smile more radiant than before, and he turned Alura to face them.

Under a short crop of brown hair, Alura's eyes widened to saucers, and though she did not smile, her hug was more than enough welcome as she closed the distance between them in several bounding strides and threw her arms around Renyra.

"I still can't believe it," Renyra said, stirring a cup of tea so vigorously she sloshed some onto the table. "I don't know where else they would have gone, I suppose, but I never thought I would see them within the next century at least. I was crushed when they left Daro. We have to tell Caerlyn."

Renyra knew she was repeating herself, and saw the patient tolerance on Firas's face, but she could not rid herself of the giddy delight that the reunion with her old friends had brought her. Such was her enthusiasm, Renyra had dragged Firas to Caerlyn's apartment on the way home from the training hall, and then again fifteen minutes later. Caerlyn had been out both times.

"Only now I feel terrible for not finding them immediately," Renyra said. "I didn't even think that they might worry over us with the news of Daro. Alura was nearly in tears."

"They know now." Firas put an arm around Renyra's shoulders.

She tried to calm her racing heart. It was a wonder to feel her pulse quickened due to something good for once.

"Kaelo could be caught and brought to justice in the next week for all we know. Then we would be free. We could all go to Remsgraen together and convince Trali to join us again. It would be like old times, traveling to cities and towns, staying in the Great Cities for months.

Alura and Raren said they've been in Tura the better part of the last century. Surely they would be excited to leave again, just for a while. Or maybe we could stay here. I like Tura."

Better than Morcanan.

"Maybe we will." Firas smiled, but the expression did not reach his eyes. Renyra could tell he thought her as naive as the Turi Council did, but she didn't care. What was the harm in dreaming? If one could not imagine a future beyond the current darkness, what hope was there in the present?

"Well, we will at least start with lunch tomorrow," Renyra said. "And a few hours of training together again." Her eyes darted to the window. "I wonder if—"

A soft knock sounded at the door. For a moment, Renyra's heart jumped with excitement, thinking it must surely be Caerlyn, but how would she have known that Renyra was looking for her? Renyra exchanged a glance with Firas, lifting an eyebrow, and walked to the door. Renyra nearly drew back in surprise when she opened it.

It was not Caerlyn standing at the threshold, but Kyna.

8

CONFRONTATIONS

"Can we talk?" Kyna asked.

Renyra's eyebrows had shot up as soon as she saw Kyna, but she quickly covered her surprise and wrestled her features into an uncertain smile.

"Of course," said Renyra, stepping back to allow Kyna inside.

The apartment was small, but orderly, much like Kyna's own housing in design and feel. After a cursory glance of her surroundings, Kyan's eyes immediately locked on a willowy elf leaning against a wall and watching her with a queer expression. Kyna recognized his short tail of fair hair.

"This is Firas," Renyra said. "My husband."

A corner of Kyna's mouth curved up and she nodded to Firas. "We have met before."

Firas blinked slowly. "A meeting with Dulon and Gellion," he said to Renyra, his face sober. Then he looked away from Kyna as though the sight of her brought him pain.

"Right," Renyra said awkwardly, glancing between the two. After a beat of silence, she said, "Would you like something to drink?"

"I will leave you two," Firas said before Kyna could answer. He reached for a book lying on the table and turned toward the back room.

"You can stay," said Kyna. "I won't be long, nor do I require any refreshments. I only wanted to show you something." She looked at Renyra.

"Have a seat." Renyra walked to the small table in the center of the room, still eyeing Kyna uncertainly. Firas hovered for a moment, as though unsure what to do with himself, then slowly put his book down and drew out a chair.

"I will get straight to the point," Kyna said. "The moment we arrived in Tura, I went to the Archives. Blackened vierstone, elf-made earthquakes, battles—it was all too significant, and our understanding too little. In Daro, speculation got us nowhere, and I knew the forces we faced there would follow us here. And so they have."

"I searched the prophecies—dozens of books containing writings from millennia before the founding of vierstone and centuries after. I thought *something* must mention our present circumstance. Nothing of this magnitude has occurred since the Great War. I thought there might be warnings, insights, words unheeded and long forgotten." She drew the folded sheet of paper from her pocket and laid it flat on the table in front of her. "I found something—something I think is important. I brought it before Liera, but she took no more heed of it than if I had brought her a human faerie rhyme."

Renyra looked at the paper warily. Her brows had drawn together at the first mention of prophecies.

"I fear Liera is blinded by the past," Kyna continued. "Afraid and unwilling to accept the full importance of what's happening." Kyna turned the paper to face Renyra and Firas. "I would like you to read this. See if you agree with me that this is something we should not ignore."

Renyra and Firas both leaned toward the paper and read the prophecy.

The grounds will shake, the cities flood,
The stone stained redder than their blood.
From green to red, from red to black,
The life reversed will not come back.

The source of darkness, lone and kin,
Will bring the monsters up again.

The stone that dies will not return,
But safe from death is stone that burns.
From which he hates his doom shall rise,
A weapon forged from his despise.
The swords that shape and cool too late,
Will drown in ash, bereaved their fate.

Kyna watched their faces with tense anticipation.

Firas's expression did not change, but his face paled as his eyes moved down the paper.

Renyra clenched her jaw, looking sick. "Will bring the monsters up again," she muttered.

They both sat in silence for several moments, scanning the words again.

"Where did you find this?" Firas asked, staring at the prophecy as though willing it to answer his question.

"The Archives." Kyna tried to keep the sarcasm from her voice.

"In what book?" Firas asked calmly.

"*Tellings of Trial and Tranquility*, written by Hirulan."

Firas's eyebrows raised, and he nodded, as though he knew the book.

Renyra dragged her eyes from the page, fear plain in her eyes. "And Liera thought nothing of this?"

Kyna smirked. "She did not think it relevant—said I was grasping at straws in a frightening situation."

"But it has to be relevant." Renyra's voice grew more excited as she spoke. "The grounds will shake, the stone that dies." Her eyes traveled over the words again. "The monsters in Daro." She turned to Firas. "You said they were like the creatures that came from the forests and waters in the Great War. They're being brought up *again*."

Firas nodded slowly, a line creasing his brow.

"But what does the last part mean?" Renyra said, looking back at the writing. "'From which he hates his doom shall rise, a weapon forged from his despise.' A weapon?" Doubt flickered across her face. "But—" She looked from Firas to Kyna. "But, we just have to capture Kaelo, bind his hands as Liera said. If we can discover his purpose, perhaps we can reason with him, or at most imprison him."

Kyna snorted. "Liera's 'capture' method is not working any better than our past attempts so far."

"She is going about it the wrong way." Renyra's eyes were burning. "I know he can be found, can be stopped, we just have to use a different method. Intimidation and force will not work."

"If you ask me," said Kyna. "None of it will work. Every attempt to catch Kaelo in Daro failed utterly, and that was in a much smaller city."

Renyra opened her mouth, clearly ready to further defend herself, but she stopped and cocked her head.

"You believe me then, that it is Kaelo?"

"Of course," Kyna said. "You said Gellion identified him. That can leave little doubt."

Renyra nodded, though a trace of confusion remained in her eyes at Kyna's confidence. Kyna hesitated. These were Gellion's friends, but something told her Gellion did not readily share his history with Kaelo to any elf. Her gut twisted as she thought back to a hot afternoon in the warehouses, packing food with Gellion. He had opened himself to her completely that day, laid his feelings bare before her. He had been a fool to confide in her. She who would never confide in him. She did not know why he had told her about Kaelo, but for some reason she was reluctant to repeat his words to others.

Don't be ridiculous. Gellion is gone. Sharing his secrets means nothing.

"Kaelo was Gellion's mentor when he was young," Kyna said, almost defiantly. "If any elf could recognize him, it would be Gellion."

Looks of shock crossed Renyra and Firas's faces. Firas was staring at Kyna as though seeing her clearly for the first time.

"He told you this?" he asked softly.

Kyna nodded.

Firas drew his brows together and looked down.

Renyra's eyes were wide. "Do you think he suspected it was Kaelo before?"

"I don't know," said Kyna. "If he did, he never said anything to me. But that doesn't matter now. What matters is there is an elf with hence unheard of power who can move about unseen and destroy vierstone, and Liera is not taking it as the threat that it is. What if he destroys all the vierstone in Tura, then moves on to other cities? This could become something huge and irreversible if we don't act soon."

"What are you suggesting?" Firas was still staring at the table.

"That we take measures beyond simply capturing Kaelo and accept that this could be bigger than any of us realize." Kyna laid a hand on the piece of paper on the table. "The end of this prophecy could hold the answers to our next actions. 'Stone that burns—a weapon forged.'"

"It could," Renyra said, eyeing the paper one last time as Kyna took it to fold into her pocket. "I still have hope that we can catch him in the coming weeks." Renyra sighed and shook her head. "But it fits too well. I think to ignore it entirely would be foolish."

She stood. "Liera should be calling another meeting in the next few days, whether or not Kaelo is captured. We can see what happens—see what the Council Members have to say. I think we should give our own methods another chance, but if nothing is progressing in the coming weeks, we should bring this before the Council."

Kyna smiled and pushed back her chair.

"I am glad you see it so." She glanced at Firas. He still sat staring at the table, eyes glazed in deep thought.

Renyra followed Kyna to the door. She paused at the threshold, looking down and shifting her weight before saying in a quiet voice, "You are ... you are doing alright?"

Confused, Kyna slowed to a stop and turned to face Renyra. The small woman was watching her, eyes impossibly green against the dark hue of her skin. They were laced with sympathy, almost pleading. Kyna's face warmed as she realized what Renyra meant by the question.

"I—Of course." Kyna cleared her throat. "There is certainly enough to keep busy here." She fought to keep a pleasant expression on her face as unease prickled along her spine. She hated when elves did this. Renyra didn't even know Kyna. Why should she ask awkward questions about her emotional well-being? Why should she care what the answer was? It was not her concern.

"It all just seems so impossible—all that's happened, all that's been lost," Renyra said. She looked away at last, eyes glistening.

"Yes," Kyna said awkwardly, relieved to be free of Renyra's prying and empathetic gaze. She longed to close the door and walk into the solitude of the darkening evening. Clearing her throat again, Kyna tried to put determination into her next words.

"Well, we will stop it. One way or another. And with this," she pressed her hand against her pocket, "we will find answers."

Renyra nodded, but there was doubt in her eyes.

Kyna sighed. Glancing around, she flattened her wrist against her thigh, a shiver spreading up her arm from the stone strapped to it. Renyra was more receptive than Liera, but she still doubted the prophecy. Doubt was something Kyna could not risk.

I may as well do the thing right.

She reached for Renyra's hand and gave it a squeeze, grimacing inwardly.

"We will find the answer," she said, forcing a confident smile onto her face.

Renyra's eyes widened in surprise at the gesture, but then she returned the smile, a flicker of hope and determination crossing her eyes.

"Yes, I'm sure we will." She glanced toward Kyna's pocket. "I'm sure we will."

It was another two days before Kyna received a notice from Liera. As she had expected, there had been no word of any elf seeing, let alone catching Kaelo in that time, and still the blackened vierstone spread. There had been no further earthquakes, and Kyna was growing bored. With no meetings or drama to fill her time, she had taken to wandering the streets in the mornings and nights, before the sun grew too warm for comfort and after its heat had drained from the day.

Tura was always in motion, but never in a hurry. Between dawn and midnight, one could see another elf on the streets almost anywhere in the city, but each moved with leisurely rhythm, walking, working, talking, laughing. Often, passing elves would acknowledge Kyna with a smile, a nod, or even a wave. Kyna would scrutinize these elves to see if she knew them, but she never did.

She was not used to so many elves. Even Daro had been too populous for her, and Tura's outgoing friendliness made her feel constantly surrounded and watched. At least Tura's size made it easier to blend with a crowd.

Sometimes Kyna regretted her part in all of this, wishing she could be a passive observer, bound to no place or cause. It would certainly be easier, but if she was bored in the midst of chaos, how much more so would she be outside of it? It was like an itch she could not scratch, no matter how she tried.

The morning after Liera's summons finally came, Kyna found herself walking to another Turi Council meeting, possessed again of a sense of purpose and excitement for events moving forward. The fountains in front of the Central Tower bubbled merrily once more, and the cracks in the stone were filled and smoothed. Only the black lines in the stone and the reluctance elves showed to walk through the space now hinted that anything unusual had happened there. Kyna felt no such reluctance and strode through the main doors of the tower with force to her step.

She walked into a half-filled room charged with energy and conversation. Liera sat straight and silent, her eyes moving between those around her.

"It is not a question of area covered," Alos said, looking between Reanan and Coren. Kyna was surprised to see the Master of Sport at a full Turi Council meeting, but then Liera had placed him in charge of the guards, which were clearly not working.

"Tura is large, yes," Alos continued. "But the attacks are all happening in the City Center. If no guards have even *seen* anything unusual in a week, we either do not have enough of them employed, or we need more motivated guards."

"The guards are not the problem," Coren said with barely concealed anger. "I have had ten guards per quarter nearly every night, but constant night shifts are difficult to fill. The reports are always the same: no shaking, no sightings, but claims of a current in the air, hair raising on arms, dizziness—the list goes on. If they were not different elves over different days I would think they were taking me for the fool, but with so many reports—"

"That does not explain how no one has seen the elf, nor why we wake up each morning to more destruction."

"Enough." Liera's voice was soft, but it silenced every voice like a smothering wind. "We will wait until the full Council has arrived before discussing this further, and then we will do so in a civilized manner."

Alos and Coren looked away, only slightly abashed, and a heavy silence settled until more Council Members started to file in. Caught by the tense atmosphere, the newcomers kept their mouths shut and sat with folded hands and downturned eyes waiting for Liera to begin the meeting.

"Now that we are all here," Liera said once Tenille and Tornac took their seats, "I," she emphasized the word, "will give a brief report before moving on to our next course of action. Coren has posted armed guards throughout the City Center every night for a week. Not one has seen or heard the passage of any elf he or she could not identify. Yet half of the City Center shows signs of blackened vierstone in the foundations and buildings. The guards report experiencing a current in the ground and the air, but this is not as easily tracked as an earthquake, and there have been no further earthquakes. We must change tactics."

Liera sat back in her chair. To Kyna's surprise, Renyra beat all others to the first word.

"We cannot wait for him to come to us," she said. "Liera is right, without the earthquakes for warning, we will never find him by simply standing guard. Instead of sentinels, we need trackers—elves to actively hunt down his trail at night."

"How do we know this is all happening at night?" Tornac asked. Though he still looked distinctly unrested, his scowl was replaced by a look of determination this morning. "Hundreds, even thousands of elves may pass through any given street of the City Center in a day. Would any notice the presence of one more? Especially if he is Turi."

"If it is happening during the day, it must be in areas where there are no elves," Renyra said. "Even if there is no shaking to notice, it is impossible to ignore the side effects of the attacks. It is as Liera said. The very ground and air seem to change when Kaelo does—whatever it is he does."

Though Liera did not flinch at the name this time, the air of the room immediately tensed.

"Besides," Renyra continued, "he couldn't very well walk the streets in that tunic in broad daylight. Someone would notice it, and if he went without concealment someone would be bound to recognize him."

"If we are assuming it is Kaelo," said Dorian, sounding very much as though he did not assume this in the least.

Tornac, however, nodded, sitting back and clasping his hands.

"Alright, I agree, he is likely attacking at night then. Night is the only time we could feasibly track him anyway."

Renyra looked vaguely surprised by Tornac's support, but seized it with gusto.

"I don't think we should take out the guards, but we could spread them out further and add stealth to the equation. The trackers should remain hidden as much as possible."

Liera watched Renyra shrewdly, betraying no hint of her opinion. Several heads nodded, but other elves looked skeptical, Reanan and Alos chief among them.

"I appreciate the idea," Reanan said. "But every day passed is another section of vierstone gone forever. We do not have time with which to experiment. How will the guards differentiate between the trackers and the tracked? The tracking itself may take weeks—if it works at all—and how much of the city's vierstone will be affected by then? At this rate, most of it. I say we cannot rely on the luck of capture."

Kyna's heart lurched at his words. She had been waiting for the opportunity to bring up the prophecy, and she saw her opening. Hand moving to the page in her pocket, she opened her mouth to interject, but Reanan spoke first.

"We must make him come to us."

Kyna paused, then closed her mouth. Interested, she listened.

"We do not know what this elf—Kaelo or otherwise—wants, and I do not think we will find out by discussion among ourselves. One of us needs to talk to him. Meet him face to face under parley."

"Why would he agree to that?" asked Tenille.

"If he wants something, he could ask for it then," Reanan said.

"We could threaten him," Saethir said.

"With what?" Tenille said. "If we could pose any serious threat to him, we would have done so by now."

"He doesn't have to know that." Excitement glinted in Coren's eyes. "I like the idea. Offer terms of parley under threat that drastic measures will be taken if he does not consent to meet with us."

Kyna raised an eyebrow. An interesting idea, and one she would like to witness. She took her hand away from her pocket.

"Who will meet him?" she asked. "And under what conditions?"

No one spoke at first. Eyes moved around the table, assessing those around them while avoiding eye contact.

"I think it should be Liera."

Everyone turned to Renyra. Her words were soft, but there was conviction in her eyes as Liera looked at her with a face of stone. Kyna just managed to catch a spark of fear before it vanished from Liera's eyes.

"If it is Kaelo," Renyra said. "Liera could identify him better than any elf here, and ..." she hesitated. "And might be able to speak with him, even reason with him, as none of us could. I think he would be more likely to come if he knew it was with her he would meet."

The silence was heavy and charged. Liera looked as though she would like nothing more than to throw Renyra from the room, but her voice was steady when she responded.

"I still cannot believe this is Kaelo, and if it were, I disagree that he would be more likely to meet with me than with any other." She looked away from Renyra, regarding the room at large. "However, the running of this city falls to me, and it is only appropriate that I personally address any threat within its walls."

She sighed. "I agree that it would be wise to attempt contact with this elf, if only for our own information. He may not come, but then at least we may rest easy that we did all we could before taking more drastic measures. I will meet with him—or try to. I do not wish to employ any trackers until the parley has occurred." She shot a hard look at Renyra.

"Coren." She turned to the Master of Sport. "I want the guards to remain, but take them out of affected areas and try to cover more space. Tell them to announce my message of the parley tonight, once an hour. If the elf is out, he will be sure to hear it at least once. I will meet him tomorrow night, at midnight, behind my family's house."

"My Lady, no!" Reanan said, eyes wide with horror. "Meet him in a public space—well lit."

"You think he would come then?" Liera raised an eyebrow. "Perhaps I should simply meet him at high noon in the markets?"

Color crept up Reanan's face. "It is not safe. He could do anything —kill you, capture you."

"I daresay he could do any of those things at any time given his power," Liera said. "It is a risk worth taking."

"At least let me have elves waiting hidden," Coren said. "A party armed with bows and arrows in case things turn for the worse."

"If he suspects an ambush, he will not come," said Liera.

"Then we will not allow him to suspect it. This is no time to value honor over safety. We are talking about the well-being of all the elves in Tura, the livelihood of our entire city. This elf is a threat we cannot allow to continue by any means."

Liera's eyes bore into Coren's until he sat back in his chair, silent.

"I appreciate your concern for my safety, but if I am to do this, it must be done in a way that works. If I bring a score of guards and the whole Turi Council with me, we will be standing alone in the dark all night. No. I will meet him alone."

There was a glint of steel in Coren's eyes, and Kyna could practically hear the ideas and counterarguments whirring through his mind.

"Am I understood?" Liera's look dared opposition.

Slowly, every elf in the room gave his or her assent.

"Good. Then let us reconvene when this is over, for better or for worse."

Kyna's heart fluttered as she watched Liera's face. A reunion of mother and son after all this time—assuming Kaelo agreed. Would he?

Kyna honestly did not know, but she knew, one way or another, she would be there to witness it if he did.

***

The next two days brought an undercurrent of excitement to the city. Though the guards announced Liera's offer at night in abandoned streets, elves could not help but hear the message from their rooms, and word quickly spread. Kyna now saw the wisdom of Liera's choice of location. Random elves would be much less likely to show up to the Lady of Tura's private residence uninvited. Kyna would, of course, but she did not intend to get caught.

Chest tight with anticipation, Kyna resumed her morning and evening strolls to expel the energy building in her muscles. To her consternation, she found herself missing Daro. She missed sleuthing through the city on Dulon's orders. She missed discussing politics and tactics. More than any of it, she missed—

No.

Kyna recoiled from her own thoughts. She had to be more careful with her musings. Gellion had been part of her mission, nothing more. Daro was nothing. Tura was now.

On the evening of Liera's parley, Kyna waited anxiously in her apartment until the moon had progressed above the trees. Wearing dark colors and soft shoes, she took to the streets, moving like a shadow to the Public Quarter. It was over an hour until midnight, and Kyna heard no sounds except the shuffle of guards, but she kept well out of their sight.

Liera's home was one street over from the public square. It was built of the same stone as the Central Tower and glowed silver in the lights that strung through the streets. There was a courtyard behind the house, filled with summer flowers and vegetables. Two cypress trees marked the exit to the gardens, each pruned at the base to reveal twisting trunks. Kyna eyed the trees. Did she dare hide so close to the meeting point? It was early enough that no one would likely see her, but she would have to be utterly silent when Liera came out and hope the the woman did not look up.

Kyna turned a scrutinizing eye on the surrounding buildings. Most had sheer walls, and though she might be able to scale them with the aid of window ledges and shrubbery, it would be quite an effort, and may wake those inside. She would hardly be able to hear or see anything from the roofs anyway.

Glancing around, Kyna ran to the base of one of the cypress trees and climbed. The tree's bark was smooth, but its gnarls and twists made for easy foot and handholds, and she reached the tree's canopy without breaking a sweat. Safely concealed by leaves and darkness, Kyna lay flat on her belly along a branch.

She settled to wait.

As the branch under her became distinctly uncomfortable, Kyna started to think she had misjudged the time. Surely it had been an hour by now? She fidgeted and shifted against the hard wood, wincing when sharp needles bit into her hands. She began to hear shuffling around her —muffled footfalls and the scrape of skin on stone, but she saw no elves on the streets. Were the guards congregating near the area? Were other elves trying to watch as she was?

Come on, hurry.

Finally, after what felt like hours, the door leading into the courtyard opened, and a dark shape emerged, walking with stiff steps through the flowers and shrubs.

Liera wore a simply cut dress of indigo silk, her hair wound into a tight bun. Against the dark fabric and black hair, Liera's face seemed to glow white. She bore no weapons and walked with her hands to her sides.

Kyna's eyes scanned what she could see of the surrounding streets. No Kaelo. Not yet.

Liera walked to the back of the courtyard, between the trees, and onto the street. She looked to either side, then clasped her hands and stared straight ahead, waiting.

Each moment seemed a day, each minute a lifetime.

Kyna jerked her head toward several sounds, but each turned out to be more muffled scuffs similar to what she had heard before. How many elves were here? Liera's ears twitched at the sounds as well, but she did not look toward them. If there were elves around, none of them were Kaelo.

Liera stood alone.

He's not coming.

Kyna's heart sank. She really had thought he would come, despite her misgivings. She had hoped he would come.

Then she saw Liera stiffen. It was a subtle motion, and barely detectable from Kyna's vantage point, but it contrasted with Liera's previous stillness enough to catch Kyna's eye. She gripped the branch with her fingertips, straining her eyes in the direction Liera was looking.

An elf had stepped out from between two building across the street. Shrouded by shadow, he could have been any elf, but there was purpose in his stance and confidence in his shoulders.

He stood facing Liera.

All sound seemed to bleed from the air. Even the night insects muted their calls.

The elf stepped into the light of the street. Kyna heard a sharp intake of breath from below her, and Kyna's skin prickled as she looked between the two elves standing a street apart—dark hair, pale faces, and slanted eyes a mirror across the distance.

Kyna'a pulse mounted. She looked down, trying to see Liera's face from the side, but she could not read her expression. The woman had unclasped her hands and taken a step back, and the hand Kyna could see shook visibly against Liera's dress.

Kaelo did not wear Gellion's tunic. He stood clearly visible with his head bare and hands empty. What he did wear bore a subtle resemblance to the tunic, however. The material was crimson and black. It gleamed in the light and moved more like metal than cloth. Even so, it matched and followed Kaelo's every movement and did not appear to give any weight to his shoulders.

His eyes were hard and bore a cold satisfaction as he watched his mother.

Liera opened and closed her mouth several times, but seemed to be at a complete loss of words.

Kyna had the wild urge to speak, to say something, anything, just to break the unbearable silence. She almost jumped as Liera's hoarse voice at last pierced the stillness.

"Kaelo," The word was barely loud enough for Kyna to make out. Liera stood with her mouth open, as though his name had been the only word able to escape her throat. "How?" she said after several more moments. "How are—" She trailed away, her eyes darting to either side of the street.

Kaelo made no move to answer. He just watched her with that same cold gaze.

Liera shook her head, staring at him as though he were a specter come to haunt her. Clearly trying to compose herself, she took a breath and raised her chin. A measure of steel returned to her voice when she spoke again.

"You did this? All of this? Daro? The vierstone?"

Kaelo's silence was answer enough.

"*Why?*" Liera hissed. Kyna had never known a word could carry so many emotions.

Kaelo seemed almost surprised by the question. A queer half smile spread up his face, and he tilted his head to the side.

"Why," he said softly, as if to himself. "You never cared about the answer to that question before."

"You never answered it." Liera's hands closed into fists. They were still trembling.

"You never asked it."

"There can be no answer—no reason to justify what you have done." Liera released her fists and took a step forward. "How many elves' lives weigh on your conscience now? An entire city?" She shook her head again, disgust in her eyes. "For centuries I have disowned you, exiled you from the Turi and the elves at large, but if there was yet more I could do to extricate my blood from yours, I would do it gladly."

Kaelo's face did not change during his mother's speech. Only the twitch of his jaw revealed that he had reacted to it at all.

"But then, I should not be surprised," Liera said, acid in her voice. "A single city's destruction could hardly compare to what you must have done in the war."

The impassivity in Kaelo's face transformed. Kyna was surprised that Liera did not step backward again, held under the cold anger that simmered in Kaelo's eyes now. He drew his lip up in a snarl.

"The war?"

"Your soul was blackened already. What else would you have done? With powers like this, you must have been high in the phoenix's ranks. But how did you escape the final destruction?"

Kaelo's eyes seemed to glint red.

"This is what you think of me?" he whispered. "That I joined the forces of Olcon? That I draw my power from corrupted spirits and demons?" He let out a stream of air from his nose and lifted his upper lip in a humorless smile. "You know nothing, mother." He spoke the last word in a way that made Liera flinch. "You never have." He shook his head, looking his mother up and down. "Seeing your face was reward enough for this meeting, but any further words are clearly wasted on you. No matter what my cause, you would never heed it coming from me. I should not have come." He turned his back to her.

Anger sparked in Liera's face. "Why?" she shouted to his back. "Why are you doing this? Revenge? Hate? What do you want?"

Kaelo paused, slowly turning his head over his shoulder.

"You will thank me one day," he said softly. "All of you. I only regret that *you* will benefit along with the others."

He turned away again, making for the shadows.

Drawing her brows together, Liera opened her mouth and took a step forward.

Then everything happened at once.

Elves flooded out of the alley from whence Kaelo had come. More leaped from rooftops and came running down the streets. All were armed.

Kaelo froze.

"Stop!" a voice said needlessly from the roof above where Kaelo stood. It sounded familiar.

Kyna craned her head around the cypress's branches to see the source of the sound, but she could not see the elf's face in the darkness.

"Surrender," he called. "And you will not be harmed. A hundred arrows are pointed at you as I speak."

Kaelo slowly turned around. The look of hatred in his eyes as he looked at Liera made Kyna's throat constrict.

But there was only shock in Liera's face. She looked around at the armed elves and shook her head. "I—"

"I hoped you would not do this," Kaelo said.

"Raise your hands!"

Kyna at last recognized the voice as Coren's. Based on Liera's reaction, he had taken matters into his own hands tonight.

Liera glanced at the roof, then back at Kaelo. Her eyes moved quickly, as though she were thinking fast, then they steadied on Kaelo. She took a breath, resolve flowing down her face even as the blood drained from it.

"Do as he says," she said.

Kaelo held Liera's gaze for a moment longer, disgust glimmering in the black depths of his eyes, then, slowly and deliberately, he raised his hands behind his head.

Kyna's mouth fell open.

Liera's shoulders relaxed for a fraction of a second. The elves closest to Kaelo lowered their bows and took a step toward him.

Then Kaelo brought his hands forward in a fluid motion, flipping up a hood of the same shining make as his shirt. As the hood fell over his head, he dropped into a crouch, flattening his palms on the ground.

"Shoot! Throw the ropes and bind his hands!" Coren screamed from the rooftop.

The twang of bowstrings sang in the air, but as the onslaught reached Kaelo, each arrow bounced off of him as though hitting stone. Ropes and nets flew through the air, but before they could reach their target, the street split apart.

Cries filled the night as elves were thrown backward. Another chorus of released arrows cut the noise, but these did as much good as the first volley, and the ground began to shake violently, felling those archers who had not been pitched backward.

"No!" Liera cried, leaping toward her son with a hand outstretched. Kaelo looked up from where he crouched and clenched his fists against the street. A pillar of stone broke away from the ground under Liera's feet and threw her into the air.

Kyna clung desperately to the cypress tree as it pitched back and forth, a terrible splintering sound beginning in its trunk. Even as she tried to keep herself from falling, Kyna kept her head wrenched upward, watching the events unfolding before her.

"Get off the roofs!" Coren's voice was barely audible above the shuddering and fracturing stone and the shouts of fear and pain from the elves on the street.

The buildings were beginning to tremble. A deep rumbling grew louder and louder.

The elves on the roofs threw down their weapons and ran. Some leaped to neighboring roofs, others began climbing down the walls, a few jumped straight into the chaos below.

A deafening series of cracks rent the air. In an instant, the smooth walls of the buildings closest to Kaelo split into millions of pieces, then, in what seemed slow motion, the pieces fell.

The buildings collapsed in a heap of rubble and struggling elves. A cloud of stone and dust billowed from the destruction and obscured half the street.

Kyna tightened her grip on the tree as it tipped closer to the ground. Abandoning her perch, she slid off the branch so she hung from her arms, then jumped, landing with bent knees on the broken ground below.

Liera was slowly pushing herself up nearby. Glancing at her warily, Kyna stood and ran into the street before Liera could see her in the courtyard. Almost immediately, Kyna's vision seemed to turn white. She stood stock still in the cloud of debris. Elves still shouted, but the sound was strangely muted by the stone particles suspended in the air. The street lights had gone out, and silvery moonlight illuminated the haze.

Kyna found herself smiling at the ethereal effect, the chaos around her a distant thing observed from without. The ground had stopped shaking. It now seemed unnaturally still.

Then Kyna felt the hair on her arms stand on end. A current of energy ran through the ground, seeming to vibrate up her legs. Her head swam with the waves, and gasps and cries sounded all around her. Then everything was quiet again.

The dust slowly settled.

Kyna moved to the side of the street, joining the throng of elves who had flocked to see what was happening. The air cleared to reveal a dozen guards running back and forth over the area where Kaelo had been. Others sprinted down the streets in all directions.

Drawing in a shaky breath, Kyna melted into the shadows.

Kaelo had escaped again, and none could now doubt his identity, or the threat of his power. Kyna thought of the prophecy that lay folded in her rooms. Perhaps the Council would be ready to listen to her now.

9

A BROTHER'S TALE

"Probably another week," Eurig said. "There will be a stop in Masar —the chief city of the marshlands. At least a few days. With that, I would anticipate a total of seventeen or eighteen days if all goes smoothly. Progress will slow once you reach the Falspires. There may even be remnants of snow if you are forced higher up, but it has usually melted from the trading passes by now."

"Is the road dangerous?" Veldon asked. He had picked up an impressive bit of Albaren in the last week. Though he could not understand when anyone spoke the language at a normal pace, he could pick out words and was able to formulate short sentences.

"You should meet no trouble from men," Eurig said. "The lands north of here are settled pastureland, all of the Elder Clan. The marshes are unpleasant and home to some dangerous wildlife, but most leave the path well alone. As for the mountains, you will walk by day and set watches at night—with fire."

A line creased Gellion's forehead. He did not like the sound of that.

Eurig waved a hand dismissively. "My traders know how to handle themselves. It is the Kayda with whom you should concern yourselves."

Valder looked up sharply. "I thought you said the mountain folk were trustworthy."

"They are. But they are also a superstitious folk, and no wonder considering the things they live with. Just be cautious how you present yourselves. I do not know how they will react to elves. If they even know of your existence."

"What do you mean 'the things they live with?'" Gellion asked warily. "Why do we need armed watches at night?"

Eurig's eyes darkened. "The mountains are a strange place. Creatures out of stories. Frightening things that should not exist. Great cats with long fangs nearly as dark as their fur, wild dogs with glowing eyes and twisted claws, birds with wicked beaks who follow travelers through the forest. The list goes on." He shook his head. "My grandfather used to tell stories of his own grandfather's days, when the mountains held no more than clean, white wolves and the occasional bear. I do not know what happened in the Falspires, but we have not let it stop our trade with the Kayda. Do not worry over it."

Gellion was not worried, but Eurig's descriptions struck an uncomfortable chord in him. He looked to his brothers to see if they shared his thoughts, but neither seemed particularly disturbed by Eurig's words.

Valder and Veldon had been giddy as young goats since being reunited and looked forward to the upcoming journey with anticipation and grins. Gellion had been as relieved as Veldon to see their brother alive and well, but Valder's presence did not lessen the danger of the rest of the elves. It was still imperative that they get across the sea before autumn, and it was a long journey to Suri Ranta. Even their arrival in the mountain city would not mark the end of their uncertainty. Eurig claimed he held close ties with the Kayda, but he could hardly order them to provide a boat for Gellion and his brothers. And if the Kayda were as superstitious as Eurig said—

"How many traders will we accompany?" Gellion asked.

"Three."

Gellion raised his eyebrows. "So few?"

"No need for more. We sent a large trading party a month ago and will again in the autumn."

A smaller party would make for much faster traveling, but Gellion hoped the three traders would not mind as many elves coming with them. Thus far, the brothers' reception by the citizens of Arvain had not been warm.

Eurig had released Gellion and Veldon from prison quietly, telling only those humans most involved to treat his 'guests' with respect. With the recent battle fresh in their minds, however, the rest of the Dierna held no great love of elves, and Gellion and his brothers did not walk the streets of Arvain without guards—this time for their own protection. Mostly they stayed in the quarters Eurig had set aside for them and met with him in his own home.

This was their second meeting with Eurig. Sometimes the man would interrupt their meetings to consult with other people, settling disputes and answering questions about city decisions. Gellion found it curious that Eurig conducted much of his business from his home. Eurig behaved as though he were a common citizen and spoke to those with whom he dealt with respect, even if his orders were harsh to Gellion's ears.

Once a man had come complaining of his neighbor's dogs killing his chickens. Eurig had calmly ordered the dog put out of the city to fend for itself and the neighbor fined the price of the chickens. Hardly fifteen minutes later, a woman had come accusing a young man of cheating her on a horse sale. She gave proof that the horse had been painted a darker shade and drugged prior to the sale, and Eurig had ordered the seller publicly lashed in addition to repaying the woman's money. She had gotten to keep the horse.

Gellion could see why the Albaren thought the Dierna barbarians. They wore simple clothing, built simple houses, and had no distinguished classes or showy society like the Albaren, but they also kept their city remarkably clean, seemed to hold women in as high esteem as the men, and kept firm order, even if it was by means that Gellion found unnecessary and harsh. Eurig's leadership was strangely comforting to Gellion, if only for its sharp contrast with the Albaren customs of title, power, and show.

"I will tell you when I have a date for departure," Eurig said. "In the meantime, stay out of the way and don't cause any trouble." He looked at them like a grandfather suspecting his grandchildren of naughty behavior. He stood to dismiss them.

Gellion's chest lurched.

"Wait," he said quickly. "I have a question."

"What is it?" Eurig said.

Gellion paused. Eurig had been shockingly cooperative since their release—almost suspiciously so. Gellion did not want to push the man for more help, but he had to know.

"You mentioned, before, that ... that an elf came to you, warning you about the Albaren attack and giving you inside information."

Eurig's eyes narrowed.

Veldon and Valder had gone still and were watching Eurig out the corners of their eyes.

"I did," Eurig said.

Gellion took a breath. "Will you tell us about them?"

Eurig considered Gellion, then let his gaze pass to Veldon and Valder before meeting Gellion's eyes once more.

"They gave no name. I saw them only once in person, and they wore a hood. Thereafter all correspondence was through birds, and no name was signed on the notes."

Disappointment filled Gellion. He saw the sentiment echoed in Veldon and Valder's faces.

"But I can tell you that it was a woman."

Gellion's eyes locked on Eurig's. "A woman? You are sure?"

"Of course I am sure. I heard her voice."

"Can you remember anything else about her?" Gellion tried to keep his voice steady.

"She was of average height, pale skin. I know no more than that."

Gellion's mind was racing. Veldon and Valder looked as flabbergasted as he felt. A woman? Then it had not been Kaelo. But who had it been?

"A woman," Valder lounged back in his chair, running a hand over his chin.

Valder and Veldon both stared at the table between them with identical expressions of deep thought. A corner of Gellion's mouth turned up. Loath though he was to be stranded a sea apart from his kin, surrounded by hostility and desperate to return, at least he was with these two. There was no one else he would have chosen.

Gellion was still shocked by Valder's story. He had always known his brother was intelligent, but somehow Gellion had never thought him one to come up with wild and brave schemes involving trickery and persuasion.

There had been no time for explanations when Eurig and Valder had come to release Gellion and Veldon. Before the sun rose, Eurig had led them out of the prison to the top rooms of a building two down from his own home. There he had left them, not returning for nearly two days. Naturally, Gellion and Veldon had demanded answers from Valder as soon as they were alone, and with a grin, Valder had told his story.

"I was behind you as we were running to the mountains," he had begun. "I was running to you, but it was all madness. The moment I gained ground, a man or horse would cut me off. I was ducking and weaving, trying to keep you in sight. Then I saw the horses ride up behind you—two Dierna riders. They were carrying cudgels and hit each of you in the back of the head. I was horrified. You dropped like stones, and I thought they had killed you, but they stopped their horses and dismounted. I was still running toward you, but then even more horses were galloping past, and it was nearly impossible to keep a straight course."

"They picked each of you up and slung you over their horses. I didn't know what was happening, but I had hope that you were still alive if the soldiers were taking the trouble to bring you with them. Most of the elves were to the mountains by then. I couldn't just leave you to the Dierna, and there was no question of coming back for you with a force of elves, so I just dropped where I stood. I sheltered against the belly of a fallen horse and lay as though dead until it was all over."

Veldon and Gellion had stared at Valder then, imagining what it must have been like to lie perfectly conscious on a battlefield for hours while the rest of your kin escaped into the mountains.

"I stayed like that until night fell. The Dierna had begun to take their dead back to the city, but they did not get far before dark, and they hadn't touched the enemy soldiers yet. When it was dark, I took off my armor and stole clothes from some of the remaining Dierna casualties," he grimaced, "tearing fabric to create a hood. Then I went near the gates and waited until sunrise. Getting through the gates was easy once they were open. People were streaming in and out from the battlefield, and no one questioned a stooped man in rags limping past." The conspiratorial gleam in his eye had made Gellion bark a laugh, shaking his head at the image in his mind.

Valder had spent the next week acting as a beggar in the city. With his clothing, hood, and dirt-smeared face, no one had ever suspected an elf beneath his disguise, and he had subsisted on stolen food and charity, while secretly ferreting information about Gellion and Veldon. By watching the prison and making subtle inquiries in the trade language, Valder had deduced that Gellion and Veldon were very much alive, and were being questioned by the Lawgiver of the clan.

"I heard the alarm sound when you escaped and tried to find you, but now I think it better that I did not. We would have all been imprisoned then. I feared you would be put to death after that, or at least be more heavily guarded."

"They did put more guards outside our cell," Gellion said. "I thought we would never have the opportunity to escape again."

"Anyway," Valder continued. "I caught a glimpse of you," he nodded to Gellion, "when they led you back from Eurig two days later. That's when I went to find Eurig. I followed him home and hid beneath his window once it grew dark. I listened to him talking to his wife, then to himself after she had gone to bed. He spoke Dierna, of course, but I caught your name in the mix. From what I had seen of him, he seemed a reasonable man. So I knocked on his door."

Gellion's jaw dropped. Veldon's eyes widened to saucers.

"You what?" Gellion said.

Valder shrugged. "I knocked on his door and took off my hood. He was shocked, but he stood his ground. I spoke to him in Albaren. I knew he must understand the language to some degree if he had communicated with you, though my mastery of the tongue has never been equal to yours. Anyway, I made myself understood well enough. I told him who I was and asked if he would speak with me. I carried no weapons. He let me in. And we talked."

"You talked," Gellion repeated, dumbfounded.

"It was not difficult to convince him," Valder said. "He had already made up his mind for the most part. I told him who I was. I told him our story—most of it. I didn't mentioned vierstone. Anyway, he listened to it all, then asked me about the elf who had passed him information about the Albaren. I think he could read my shock at the news as real, and finally believed that we had been betrayed twice—that we had not played games with the Dierna. I could tell he still didn't trust the elves, or like them at any rate, but he seemed to accept that we would pose no further threat. I thought he would release you, then. Just set you quietly outside the walls with orders never to come back. I haven't a clue what made him decide to help us like this. He's a decent man, Eurig."

Gellion had wanted to agree. The man had commanded an army against him, imprisoned him, tricked him, and kept him from returning to Daro in time to sail home with his kin, but Gellion could not help respecting him. Eurig had been acting in the best interest of his people, and had still been willing to listen to the elves' side of the story. But Gellion had been betrayed by seemingly cooperative humans before and could not help questioning Eurig's generosity. To turn away any chance to get back to Faeran would be foolish in the extreme, but Gellion planned to keep his eyes open and his guard up until he was safely on elven soil once more.

But you cannot let your guard down among the elves, either.

The question of who had betrayed the elves nagged at Gellion. It had not been Kaelo. Had there been *two* enemies within Daro? Were both elves now a threat back in Faeran?

"I still think it must have been the same elf who caused the earthquakes," Veldon said. "The same elf who destroyed Daro."

Gellion sighed and leaned his elbows against the table.

"I know we have discussed this," Veldon said patiently. "But it could make sense. The elf wanted to destroy Daro. He—*she* that is—needed Daro empty to accomplish her task, and wanted the elves' attention set on something else, so she sowed the seeds of the alliance with the Albaren."

"Then tipped off the Dierna?" Valder said. "Unless she knew the Albaren would betray us."

"This is all very well," Gellion interrupted. "But the elf who caused the earthquakes was not a woman."

"But none of you saw the elf's face," Veldon said. "It could have been a woman."

Valder's eyes sparkled. "Perhaps a very masculine woman."

"Renyra saw his face," Gellion said seriously. "It was a man."

"What?" Valder's eyebrows rose. "She saw his face? Did she recognize him?"

Heat rose to Gellion's face.

"No," he said a little too quickly.

And she hadn't. Not on her own.

Gellion did not know why he didn't tell his brothers about Kaelo. If he told them who Renyra had seen, he would have to tell them that he had been the one to recognize Kaelo, both from Renyra's description and from the signs and suspicion that had been growing within him all the time, though he had not recognized it. He would have to tell them everything—his entire history with Kaelo. Anything less would be lying to them.

But are you not lying to them now, keeping secrets?

Gellion clenched a fist under the table. Knowing about Kaelo would change nothing in their speculations just now. He would tell his brothers eventually, but now he wanted to find out what elf had betrayed them to the Dierna.

Valder eyed Gellion, but then sighed. "Ok, so—what? There were two elves? One who caused earthquakes and destroyed Daro, and one who contacted the Dierna—either of which may or may not have worked with the Albaren as well. One was a man and one a woman. Well. That narrows things down immensely."

Gellion ignored Valder's sarcasm. "It narrows it down some. The woman was either Turi or Morcani if she was pale skinned, and she could clearly speak some Albaren or Dierna, or she would not have been able to contact Eurig."

"So she was a citizen of Daro," Veldon said. "There are no resources to learn human languages in Faeran."

"You have learned almost enough Albaren in a week to make effective communication," Gellion pointed out. "I do not think we should narrow this to long-term citizens of Daro. We had a lot of visiting elves for the Kindom Council."

"Some of which were clearly not rooting for Daro's success," Valder added.

Gellion looked at him. "Miyela?"

Over the months in which Gellion and Dulon had tried to uncover the mystery of the earthquakes, Dulon had insisted that Miyela had a part in it. The strict and powerful leader of the Morcani had made no secret that she strongly disapproved of Dulon and all he had done in creating Daro, and had sparked a veritable uprising of elves to oppose the Albaren alliance.

"She put on quite the show," Valder said. "It could have all been a part of this. Spark an alliance of war with the Albaren, oppose the alliance to turn the elves against Dulon, then sabotage its success by tipping off the Dierna."

"Miyela may not have liked Dulon," Veldon said. "But to take such extreme measures? To sacrifice the lives of elves to prove a point?"

Gellion ran a hand through his hair. "Dulon thought she was involved with the earthquakes. I could not believe it at the time. I said the same thing as you, Veldon, but now I am beginning to wonder if I was mistaken."

Could Miyela have been working with Kaelo? The thought seemed absurd. Maybe Kaelo had used Miyela's plot as an opportunity to take his chances with Daro. The two would not have had to be related. Maybe Dulon had been more right than Gellion had given him credit for. A soft stab of pain accompanied the thought as Gellion remembered the fire in Dulon's eyes when he had talked about Miyela. Dulon had been a cheerful and capable leader, but something about Miyela had always seemed to get under his skin.

"But she would have had to come to Tala before the Kindom Council," Veldon said. "The Albaren messenger came to Daro the day after the ship's arrival. Miyela wouldn't have had time to arrange anything with the Albaren."

Another thought occurred to Gellion. "If she came early, she is a braver elf and a better seafarer than any of us could guess. The Semestrial Sea would have been nearly impassable even a few weeks before the visitors arrived. Besides, she came in on the same ship as the rest of the visitors."

"She may have met the ship just off the coast as it came in," said Valder. "Or maybe she only contacted the Dierna, after the Albaren man proposed the alliance."

"I don't know if there would be any way to prove anything unless she confessed," said Gellion.

"I think we should focus on stopping the other elf first, the one who destroyed Daro," said Veldon.

Gellion nodded reluctantly.

The one who is a threat because of me. The one who might go on to destroy far more.

"And none of this matters if we cannot get to Faeran," Valder said.

"We will." Gellion tried to put as much confidence in his voice as he could. He did have hope that they would find a way to Tura before autumn. A boat was not so much to ask, even from strangers, and Eurig's backing increased the chances that the people of Suri Ranta would cooperate. But whatever he said to his brothers, Gellion was disturbed by the prospect of a second elf traitor to contend with. Had the two worked together? What if it wasn't Miyela? What if it was?

Urgency and impatience burned in Gellion's chest. He wanted to be with the elves *now*. Waiting weeks or months to get to Tura was more than he could bear. They would get to Tura. Gellion was sure of that. He just hoped it would not be too late. What 'too late' would mean, he did not know. He did not want to know.

10

THE GATES CLOSE

Renyra's breath came in spurts. She tucked her chin to her chest, relaxing her back for a moment and taking in a lungful of air. She had always found it difficult to breathe in a backbend. While it rarely presented a problem in a fast-paced performance, practicing moves for extended periods of time could become distinctly uncomfortable. She bent backward again, pulling down on the rope that wound around her body and her leg so that it brought her right foot to her head.

Her eyes glanced toward the entrance to the training hall far below her. They should be here soon. A wave caught her eye, and she spotted Alura moving toward her, with Raren, Caerlyn, and Firas trailing behind her. Renyra returned the gesture and untwisted herself in a rapid flourish, climbing down the rope hand under hand. A subtle regret filled her when she touched back to the ground, but her arms were more than happy for the break. She walked to an open space and sat with a glass of water. Alura followed and dropped down next to her. The others followed suit.

"Tell us everything," Alura said, eyes wide.

Raren and Caerlyn leaned forward, awaiting Renyra's reply.

A smile played at Renyra's lips. It was strange, being one of the elves most involved in momentous events. Renyra did not feel she had done anything worthy of such involvement. She had merely done what she had to in extreme circumstances, and those circumstances had somehow placed her in the center of events, in a battle, and at Turi Council meetings.

"It was a tense meeting," Renyra said. She glanced at Firas. She had told him everything already—every word she could remember of the two-hour Turi Council meeting that morning. She was not sure how much she should say to the others, though she trusted her friends with her life.

"Liera was bruised and scraped and clearly shaken to the core despite her outward attempts to hide it. I don't blame her. She wouldn't let herself believe it was Kaelo before. It must have been a terrible shock to see him again after all this time and to realize what he had done."

Renyra had already told her reunited troupe about Kaelo. Upon their first full reunion two days before, Renyra and Firas had recounted the entire story of Daro. Caerlyn had been through most of it with them, of course, but even she did not know about Kaelo. Alura and Raren had listened to the tale with wide eyes, expressing amazement, shock, and sorrow in all the right places.

"Does the Council believe it is Kaelo now?" asked Caerlyn. She sat on the floor, leaned back against a tightwire pole. A sheen of sweat glossed her dark skin, and she was smoothing her hair into a braid that went to her waist. It was another hot day. The cooling system in the training halls struggled against the outside air.

"Yes," Renyra said. "They would have believed Liera alone, I think, but a few of the guards recognized Kaelo too." Renyra shook her head. "Liera was furious about Coren's surprise attack. She did not invite him to the meeting and subtly abused him through most of the first part."

"What do you think would have happened if the guards didn't attack?" Raren was stretching his shoulders as he spoke. Hard lines of muscle showed through his skin.

"I don't know," Renyra said with a sigh. "Liera said very little about what actually happened between her and Kaelo. The only words she repeated were 'You will thank me in the end. All of you.'"

"Well that's sinister." Caerlyn snorted, but there was little humor in her eyes.

"What could he mean?" said Alura. Though half the size of her brother, she was his female mirror. "Did he say what he intends to do? Why on Riure would any elf thank him for destroying all the vierstone in Tura?"

Renyra just shook her head. The elves had woken that morning to find the entire City Center devoid of living vierstone. As little as Liera had liked Coren's organized attack, it seemed Kaelo had liked it still less and had made his feelings known.

All of Tura now knew the threat they were facing, and word of Kaelo's involvement would spread to every elf by tonight, yet still no elf knew Kaelo's purpose. This had been the subject that dominated the Turi Council Meeting that morning, and no one had developed a satisfactory answer.

"He came to Tura before the war asking for vierstone," Tenille had said. "And he was refused." The look she shot at Liera was almost accusatory. "Does he wish to acquire vierstone for himself now?"

"That makes no sense," Alos said. "He could steal vierstone without destroying it. And that does not justify the destruction of Daro."

"We are making too much of this," said Tornac. "It is simple revenge. Hate. He feels wronged by the elves and is retaliating by destroying that which he was denied."

"You think, then, he only wishes to destroy all the vierstone and all the Great Cities he can out of spite?" Reanan shook his head. "It is madness. He cannot possibly go to every city in Faeran and work his devilry without being stopped."

"Can he not?" Tornac lifted an eyebrow. "He escaped from an ambush of sixty armed elves last night with nothing but his bare hands."

Renyra had spoken up then. "It's impossible to prepare against attacks like Kaelo's until you have seen them with your own eyes. Now Tura knows what Kaelo can do and can plan accordingly. The more the elves learn about Kaelo, the less likely he will be able to spread his attacks further."

"How can we prepare against an elf who can destroy an entire street in a few minutes while under fire?" Alos said, turning to Liera. "We must know what he wants. Otherwise we are chasing an unpredictable target. He must have hinted at something?"

Liera's stare was withering. Her eyes were bloodshot, and her face utterly devoid of color.

"No," she said. "Kaelo's purpose remains his own."

"Does he wish to gain power?" Reanan said. "Hold some kind of dominion over the elves?" He said the words as though they were strange on his tongue.

"He could never achieve such power," said Tornac. "No elves would follow him after what he has done. He has no army, no way of enforcing control."

"He could use vierstone as a bargaining chip," Alos said. "Use its destruction as a threat to keep his power."

"No." Liera stared straight ahead, her eyes burning. "Kaelo could never hope to maintain power over all the elves and he knows it. I do not know what he has become, but he has not lost his wits. It does not matter why he has done these things, so long as he is stopped."

"Trackers," Renyra said.

Liera slowly turned to look at her.

"The only way to keep him from using his powers is by sneaking up on him," Renyra said. "By incapacitating him before he knows his danger."

"It will take more than that." All looked at Kyna. She had not yet spoken in the meeting, her eyes merely moving silently from elf to elf, narrowed in thought. Now, she gave Renyra a significant look. "Tracking may be worth trying, but all of this is bigger than we yet perceive. It took months for all of Daro's vierstone to turn black, yet only a week for half the City Center of Tura. Last night, the other half was destroyed in a matter of hours. Either Kaelo is growing more powerful, or had reason behind his gradual moves until now. We tried to track him in Daro. We tried to overpower him here. Both failed. He can move about unseen, deflect arrows as though made of stone, and can send the very stones of the street against any who oppose him. We must take this for the threat that it can become, not that which it is now."

"What is it you suggest?" Liera asked cooly, eyeing Kyna as though certain what she were about to say.

Renyra held her breath, heart beating faster as she waited for Kyna to speak. With a final glance at Renyra, Kyna began.

She told of her search in the Archives and of the prophecy she had found. No one spoke through her tale, and as she read the prophecy word for word, Renyra watched their faces. Liera was still, but a grudging worry was now in her face as she listened to Kyna. Tenille watched Kyna as though she were a prophet reborn. The rest seemed to be warring with skepticism and fear as Kyna read the last lines of the prophecy.

Everyone stared at her when she finished, no one eager to respond first.

"I think," Renyra said slowly. "It has merit."

Tenille was nodding, but most of the elves still stared, dumbstruck.

"Why has no one seen this prophecy before?" asked Liera.

"Clearly someone has," Kyna replied. "If it was in a book. But among the hundreds of prophecies in the Archives, it would be easily lost to memory over the centuries—millennia even. Some may have thought it referred to the Great War and passed it off as irrelevant."

"Some of this fits," Tornac said. "But the cities have not flooded, and what is this about a red stone?"

Renyra's chest lurched suddenly. "But the cities have flooded!" she said excitedly. "Daro is in the sea. A city cannot flood worse than being underwater. I don't know what the red stone means, but the rest of it makes sense. None of us can deny the grounds are shaking, we told you about the monsters in Daro," she looked to Kyna, who nodded. "'The stone that dies'—it all fits."

Tenille had reached for the page bearing the prophecy and was reading over it with a creased brow.

"The source of darkness, lone and kin." She looked to Liera.

A flush began at Liera's neck. "Maybe this prophecy refers to what is happening now, maybe it does not," she said in clipped tones. "But what are we to do with it if it does?"

"Use it," Kyna said. She extended her hand toward Tenille, who reluctantly gave the page back to her. "'Safe from death is stone that burns—a weapon forged from his despise.' We find out what this means and we use it to defeat Kaelo before it is too late."

"Too late for what?" Liera said, her eyes turning warily to the interest of the other Council Members.

Kyna shrugged. "Drown in ash? We could puzzle over what that means, but I think our time would be better spent trying to prevent it."

Liera's eyes hardened. "Thank you for bringing this to our attention, Kyna. I am sure it will give all of us a lot to think about. But I do not think it wise to spend all of our time chasing after rhymes while our true threat stalks the streets around us."

A few elves seemed taken aback by Liera's dismissal of the prophecy. Tenille's brows drew over her eyes.

"I am not saying the prophecy is nonsense," Liera said quickly. "We can think over it in the coming days and weeks, but right now, we should do all in our power to stop Kaelo by any means possible. He shows no interest in talking or being reasoned with. He will not be intimidated by forces of armed elves. We must catch him by surprise—corner him and end this once and for all. I want him captured." She turned a cold stare on all of them. "Alive or dead."

The meeting had ended shortly after that. The Council had discussed new measures to enact: guard placement, weapons and restraints to carry, and trackers.

Renyra did not want to bring up the prophecy to Caerlyn, Alura, and Raren—not yet—but there was something else she needed to discuss with them.

"Liera does not seem interested in what Kaelo's purpose is," Renyra said to her friends. "Only that we stop him by any means possible." She shivered at the remembered coldness of Liera's voice as she had said those words which Renyra would not repeat: 'alive or dead.' "She wants elves to start tracking him at night—elves who are light on their feet, quiet, and experienced moving about difficult terrain and obstacles." She raised her eyebrows.

Raren let out a laugh. "Is this your way of asking us?"

Heat touched Renyra's face. "You do not have to agree. This is dangerous work, and if you succeed in finding him, the real danger begins."

"I'll do it," Alura said, fire in her usually placid eyes. "Any elf who takes it upon himself to destroy my city will have to answer to me first." She ran a hand through her short crop of hair, leaving it standing on end.

"Of course we'll help." Raren said. A smile still lingered about his lips, but his eyes were serious.

Caerlyn nodded. "One elf doesn't scare me, even if it is Kaelo. He should pay for what he did to Daro."

Renyra's heart swelled with affection for her friends. Getting back into Sira training the last few days had done wonders for Renyra's mood —and soreness—but it was nothing compared to the renewed companionship that came with it. Stepping back into life with her old troupe had been easier than she could have imagined. In a matter of days, they had all caught up on each other's lives and moved forward as though no time had passed. She looked from one face to another, expressions of determination on each.

A warm pressure on her wrist let her know Firas gave his support as well. A grin stretched over Renyra's face.

"Good," she said. "We should patrol in pairs for safety. Switch off nights and tell each other what we learn each night."

"Where should we start?" asked Caerlyn.

"That's a good question, and one I do not have an answer to," said Renyra. "Kaelo has affected the entire City Center now, and it is anyone's guess where he will go next."

"Are other elves tracking him as well?" said Alura.

"Yes, but I don't know how many. I will ask Liera, find out where the others will be, and Firas and I will start tonight. We will tell you where to search tomorrow."

"Fair enough," Raren said. "And what do we do when we catch him?"

Some of the excitement faded from Renyra's face. "Incapacitate him. Don't let him use his hands. Liera says ... she says capture him by any means necessary. Any at all."

A flicker of understanding passed over Raren's face. Horror lit in his eyes.

"I think the best thing would be to knock him out," Renyra said quickly. "Tie his hands and shout for the nearest guards."

Raren nodded slowly. So did the others.

"Makes sense to me," said Caerlyn. She stood, sweeping her braid over her shoulder. "Well, now that's settled, let's get to it." She folded at the waist and clasped her arms about her calves.

The tension dissipated in an instant. Renyra sighed with relief as everyone began talking about lighter matters. Tonight, she and Firas would begin the difficult and risky feat of tracking Kaelo, but there was no need to let that interfere with this afternoon.

Renyra collapsed into bed next to Firas early that evening. After a grueling and exhilarating afternoon balancing on, twisting around, and leaping over the other members of her troupe, Renyra had taken the Rale to the bathhouses with Firas and Caerlyn to soak away the sweat and aches of the day. Alura and Raren had gone the opposite direction to their homes in the West Neighborhood.

Clean, relaxed, and exhausted, Renyra and Firas had shoveled down an early dinner in the markets, stopped by the Central Tower to get instructions from Liera, and retired to their home. If they were to wake before midnight and spend the deepest hours of night running about the city, they needed to regain some strength.

Renyra pressed her back against Firas's. Though the heat of the day still lingered outside, the apartment was cool, and Renyra relished the feeling of Firas's warmth against her skin. For a moment, she was utterly happy. For just a moment, it was like she was back in Tura before news of Daro had ever reached her ears. Her world was joyful and peaceful, and there was no Kaelo, no grief.

As Renyra balanced between sleep and wakefulness, her tired mind took her to her bed in Daro. She opened her eyes a crack, expecting to see the carved dresser that had always sat against the wall on her side of the bed, but instead she saw an unfamiliar door. She blinked, closed her eyes again, and drifted further toward sleep.

Images of waves and rubble crashed through her mind, filling all that had been warm and safe with cold fear. Without warning, the gate Renyra had temporarily sealed against sorrow opened in full force. She was assaulted by the memories of Daro. The faces of Gellion, Dulon, Valder, and Veldon were as clear against her eyelids as they had ever been in life. Clashing weapons, cries of death and pain, blood, and fear pressed upon her from all sides in a waking dream of battle. She saw Kaelo's face among the friends she had lost, a crooked smile on his face.

She opened her eyes with a gasp, and tears spilled down her face. Guilt wove through her pain and grief. How could she have been so happy just moments before when she had lost so much, when Firas had lost his best friends, and so many of the elves of her home lay dead half a world away.

Renyra stifled a sob and felt Firas move beside her. She held her breath, trying not to let him hear, but her body shook with the effort. Firas said nothing, but turned her to face him and wrapped his arms around her, bringing her head to his chest. Renyra cried. As she did, the guilt in her chest was slowly replaced by anger.

"How could he?" she said into Firas's chest, now slick with her tears. "How could he let this happen?"

Running a hand down her back, Firas said, "Kaelo—"

"Not Kaelo!" Renyra closed her eyes, squeezing two more tears onto her cheeks. "I don't care about Kaelo."

Firas grew still. Renyra's vierstone earring warmed against her skin. She felt Firas's pain—his own and that which he felt for her—and she felt his understanding of her words. It was a comfort, and it made her still more angry. She longed to rip the vierstone from her ear and throw it across the room. It wasn't worth it. She wanted it all to go away.

"They were *good* Firas. All of them. It is cruel. And Riu must be cruel to allow it."

"I am sorry," Firas whispered into her hair.

"It's not fair."

"I know."

Renyra could hear the tears in Firas's voice and hated herself all the more for causing him pain. He had lost as much if not more than she. Yet she was angry with him. He was supposed to tell her things would be fine—to keep hope. It's what her mother would have said.

"Tell me it's alright," she said when Firas spoke no more. "Tell me everything will be alright."

She felt Firas's head shake slowly. "I cannot tell you that."

Renyra drew away from him. He reached a hand to her face.

"What happened was not alright," he said. "And what will happen may not be either. I cannot promise you our life will always be peaceful or joyful."

"It's supposed to be," Renyra said, clenching her jaw against the trembling of her lip. "What did they do wrong, Firas?" she asked in barely a whisper.

"Oh my love," Firas said softly. "I do not think that Gellion, or Dulon, or any of the others who died did anything to cause their deaths. What happened in Tala was nothing more or less than the consequences of choices made by elves and men."

"They were lousy choices," Renyra said bitterly.

Firas gave a humorless chuckle and moved closer to Renyra. "Our choices may cause suffering , but they also give worth to our joy. We can allow suffering to defeat us, or we can use it to create opportunity for good."

Renyra pressed her head against Firas.

"Alright, you win," she said. "Your ability to form words will forever surpass my own."

"And your ability to perform the standing splits on someone's shoulder will forever surpass my own," he said seriously.

Renyra laughed—a deep laugh that loosened the tension within her muscles and heart alike. Scrubbing the tears from her face, she took a shuddering breath and curled tighter into Firas, closing her eyes and focusing on the rise and fall of his chest.

A dreamless sleep carried midnight to hand with surprising rapidity. Renyra woke to a black night and scratchy eyes. Firas made no mention of her earlier breakdown as they dressed and prepared for the night. Renyra was grateful. She splashed cold water on her face and set determination to her step. This was something she could do. She had no control over what had happened in Daro or before the gates of Arvain, but she could put an end to what had caused it—who had caused it—and prevent it from happening again.

The night was pleasant, with a cool breeze blowing in from the sea. Liera had told them to patrol the section of the city north of the Scholar Quarter—the streets and buildings that lay between the two main gates of the city.

Excitement fluttered in Renyra's chest as she and Firas began their watch. She missed hunting and could not deny the exhilaration that sneaking through the dark streets brought.

As the hours passed, she and Firas moved through alleys and over roof tops, tuned to any sounds or queer feelings in the air. They searched for signs of fresh passage: footprints in the dew forming on the streets or in the grassy walkways, any streaks of black in the stone of walls and pavement. But as night dragged toward dawn, they found nothing. No sign of Kaelo. No sign of blackened vierstone.

Just as the eastern horizon was beginning to turn blue, and Renyra's hope of progress was petering out, she heard footsteps slapping on stone. They were coming closer. She grabbed Firas's wrist, but he had already heard and flattened himself against the roof on which they were perched.

"Should we get off the roof?" Renyra whispered.

"No. If it is Kaelo, we should be able to tell as well from here as on the street and can follow him from above. But those steps seem too obvious to be an elf who wishes to remain hidden."

Renyra had thought the same thing, but stubbornly held on to the excitement in her veins. Unknown footsteps were a lot more promising than anything else they had experienced that night.

Renyra moved along her belly until she could see onto the street. An elf was moving toward them, walking quickly and periodically looking over their shoulder.

Whoever they are, they seem nervous, or watchful at any rate. It could be Kaelo. Or just a guard afraid of being ambushed by him.

Upon closer inspection, however, Renyra saw that the elf was a woman, and she looked more than a little nervous. The woman held a dagger in one hand, and Renyra could hear the speed of her breathing as she drew nearer.

"Not Kaelo," Renyra said to Firas. "Should we ask if she's seen anything? She certainly looks as though she has."

Firas nodded and moved away from the roof's edge. Renyra followed him and climbed down the side of the building with nimble movements, landing on the ground in a graceful role as she jumped from the last window ledge.

When they stepped onto the street, the woman was two buildings ahead of them.

"We don't want to scare her," Renyra said. "She has a weapon and looks more than willing to use it."

"Right. Perhaps you should speak first."

Renyra nodded and jogged forward until she was within speaking distance of the elf.

"Is everything alright?" she said in the friendliest voice she could muster.

The woman wheeled around, dagger raised, but lowered it when she saw Renyra and Firas. She glanced behind them with wide eyes, as though searching the street.

"Who are you?" she asked.

"We're patrolling this area under Liera's orders," Renyra said.

The woman nodded. "I am Kelia. I was on guard at the western gate. I closed and locked it. There was—" She looked beyond them, worry in her eyes, then shook her head. "I need to get to the eastern gate."

A cold shiver passed along Renyra's spine, memories of Daro's sealed gates coming to her mind.

"What did you see?" she asked.

"Walk with me." Kelia set a brisk pace in the direction of the eastern gate. "I was watching inside the walls mostly. More concerned about stopping Kaelo from escaping than letting anything in. I can't imagine he goes in and out of the city every night, and we never have problems with wild animals, or late night travelers. But I kept hearing things from the outside. Rustles, and ... and growls." She glanced behind them again. "And then I saw eyes, glowing from the shadows, and a shape I couldn't make out, but something about it turned my blood to ice—made the hair on my neck stand up."

Renyra exchanged a look with Firas. This sounded all too familiar.

"More eyes appeared near the first and were moving closer. I closed the gate. It sounds foolish. Probably just wolves or cats from the mountains, but there was something not right about them, whatever they were, and I didn't want them in the city."

"No," Renyra said to herself. "No you don't."

Light was beginning to suffuse the sky.

"Go on to the east gates," Renyra said. "We'll keep watch in this area for another half hour."

Kelia nodded and continued on.

"Bring the monsters up again," Renyra said when the woman had gone.

"It was a familiar description." Firas looked worried. "Should we go to the gate?"

They hurried back to the western gate, climbing to a vantage point that allowed them to see outside the city walls. To the left, the Orhiri River gushed into the city, and a road ran along its banks into the distance. To the right, soft hills stretched to copses of trees, still shapeless lumps in the dawn. Renyra listened and looked hard into the shadows, but whatever Kelia had seen seemed to be gone now.

A slow fear made its way into Renyra's blood. Her confidence in tracking Kaelo was fading, and now a new threat was stalking the city from the outside. It was all happening again, and she did not know if any of them could stop it. She thought warily of Kyna's insistence on the prophecy.

Maybe she is right.

A sudden movement caught Renyra's attention, and she thought she saw the glimmer of an eye in the receding shadows. Before she could look closer, it winked out again.

Riu help us.

She laid her head against Firas's arm.

11

LAWGIVER'S FAREWELL

Gellion pressed his forehead against the window. It was warm and breezy outside, with ample sunshine. The citizens of Arvain strolled along the streets, enjoying the weather. Their images blurred and refocused as Gellion's steady breath fogged the glass. It was dark in their tiny apartment, and the cool from the night still lingered without the sun and breeze to warm the space. Gellion longed to go outside, even just to sit on the street a step away from these cursed rooms. He wanted something to *do*.

Boredom had once again become Gellion's constant companion. The excitement of Valder's appearance, speculations about the elf traitor, and planning for the upcoming trip to Suri Ranta had been a blessed relief, but now the trip plans were set. Gellion and his brothers had spoken circles around the identity of the elf who had contacted the Dierna. There seemed to be nothing more to discuss. Now the apartment felt as much a cell as the prison.

Valder was lying on his back on the couch, softly singing songs to himself and to Veldon, who grinned at the witty tunes while whittling a stick he had picked up on one of their rare outings.

Gellion's hands itched to pick up a similar task. His mind turned invariably to his workshop in Daro, now gone forever. He could not seem to make the concept real in his mind. Unlike the rest of the surviving elves, Gellion would never see the proof of Daro's demise. Every day he seemed to think of something new to mourn—the Performance Hall, Master's Street, the Domes of Rhelyon. He could not fathom the complete destruction of them all in a single day.

Even these thoughts would have been a preferable alternative to contemplating Kaelo's return and what he might be doing in Tura, but thoughts of Daro always brought memories of those elves who had lived there.

Gellion pressed his head harder against the glass as the now familiar knot in his stomach tightened.

Stop thinking about it.

But as time passed, he found it harder and harder to turn away from what had happened. Gellion couldn't help but think Dulon would have known how to appeal to Eurig from the very beginning. Dulon had dripped charisma with elves and humans alike and probably would have had them on an escorted march back to Daro the day after the battle.

Why didn't you just run like the rest of us you valorous dolt? You couldn't have waited another five minutes for the Dierna reinforcements?

Gellion couldn't summon the energy to be angry. He turned away from the window with a sigh. He was sick of watching people going about their normal lives on a beautiful day.

After pacing the room several times, Gellion retired to the cramped back room he and his brothers used as a bedroom. Despite having nothing better to do, Gellion had not been sleeping well the last week. Each night he tossed and turned and worried and could not seem to turn his mind off. When he did sleep, he dreamed. The good dreams were worse than the bad.

Gellion dropped into the tangle of blankets that served as his bed and closed his eyes, trying to empty his mind, but ordering his mind not to think usually had the effect of bringing forward the thoughts he most wanted to put away. Kyna's face insisted on flashing against his eyelids, her lopsided smile mocking him as he tried to fall asleep.

Kyna's refusal had been largely swallowed by the death and fear that came after, but now that Gellion was beginning to come to terms with the worst of his problems, Kyna's face haunted him more and more.

Was she even alive? Heat of shame and betrayal rose to his face every time he thought of the infuriating woman, but the thought of her lying dead on a battlefield was more than he could bear.

"Leave me alone." Gellion muttered, turning over and squeezing his eyes shut harder.

Pestering thoughts turned to fitful dreams, mingled memories and invention forming places he had been and places that did not exist.

He poured molten metal in his shop; he ran from a misty figure in dark streets—Daro one moment, Arvain the next. Then his surroundings clarified. He stood in a bowl shaped room in the Central Tower of Tura. Around him were the members of the Turi Council as he remembered them. All were staring to Gellion's right. He turned and stumbled backward. Kaelo stood next to him, every detail of his face clear and real. He watched Gellion's reaction with expressionless eyes.

Gellion closed his hands into fists and cried out as a sharp pain laced his fingers. Looking down, he saw two hunks of raw vierstone, broken to jagged, sharp edges. Where the blood from his fingers touched the stone, the stone turned red. The stains spread until both rocks were deep crimson. Horrified, Gellion looked up to see Kaelo smiling at him. His mentor extended a hand for the stones. Gellion drew them against himself and took a step back, but Kaelo's gaze seemed to hold him under a trance.

Reluctantly, Gellion began to loosen his grip on the vierstone. The members of the Turi Council shouted at Gellion, telling him not to release the stones, but Kaelo drew Gellion like a flame on a cold night. The vierstone was growing hot in Gellion's hands. The cuts on his fingers stung. He wanted to be rid of it.

"That is not for you," Kaelo said gently, hand still extended. "Let me take it."

Gellion wanted to shake his head. He meant to shake his head. Instead, he saw his hands reaching toward Kaelo. The vierstone was glowing now, and so hot Gellion feared it would burst into flame, consuming his hands with it.

"Quickly now, you will burn yourself," Kaelo said, his eyes locked on the stones.

Panic rose in Gellion's chest. He wanted to drop the stones, to throw them away from himself. Finally, he released his grip. The vierstone fell into Kaelo's palms and engulfed them both in flame.

Gellion drew in a sharp breath of air as his eyes flew open. Valder was kneeling over him.

"Finally," Valder said. "I thought I would have to pour water over you. If you slept half so well at night you wouldn't keep me up."

Gellion blinked several times. His heart was pounding. It had felt so real.

"Eurig called for us," Valder said, leaning back on his heels. "We are leaving tomorrow."

Gellion tried to focus on what Valder was saying. Arvain. They were in Arvain, and they were going to Suri Ranta. He raked a hand through his hair and almost gasped as his fingers brushed his vierstone earring. The memory of his dream washed over him anew.

A sudden panic seizing him, Gellion fumbled at the clasp of his earring and brought the stone before him. It was green and cool.

"What is it?" Valder was staring at Gellion now, a flicker of worry in his eyes.

"Nothing." Gellion reclasped the earring, feeling foolish. "Just a dream."

Untangling himself from his blankets, Gellion stood and followed Valder into the main room, where a guard stood waiting at the door.

***

"The horses' saddles are packed with supplies," Eurig said. "You will restock in Masar."

Gellion stiffened. "We're riding horses?"

"Of course."

A quick glance at his brothers told Gellion they shared his enthusiasm for large and sweaty animals with a mind of their own.

"I appreciate your offer of tack and horses," Gellion said carefully. "But we would prefer to walk."

"Nonsense," said Eurig. "You would slow the journey by days. I have informed my traders that you will accompany them, and they have agreed." Something in Eurig's face told Gellion it had not been a fully willing agreement. "Treat them with respect and they will guide you well. They are honorable men and women."

Gellion supposed 'honorable' was the best they could hope for. He could not expect any of the Dierna to be friendly to the elves, with or without Eurig's support.

"I am sending a note with you, explaining to Sovereign Esteri who you are and what you need. I signed and sealed the missive. The Kayda are a proud and independent people, but they are peaceful and willing to give chances. Humility will win their favor more than charisma or confidence."

Gellion was finding it difficult to get a clear picture of the Kayda from Eurig's passing descriptions. They were superstitious but proud, peaceful but suspicious. Anxiety prickled at Gellion's skin. He had been an emissary to the Albaren and sat on every level of the elven Council. Dealing with groups of people was something at which Gellion was usually adept to say the least, but among the elves, he knew who he was dealing with. With the Albaren, Dulon had set most of the precedent for their relations, and Gellion had followed suit and slowly taken over. Gellion had often rolled his eyes at Dulon's antics, but he had seen how capable the man was. Dulon had had a way of approaching the most serious matters with a smile and a wink, but he did so in a way that solved the problem every time.

Almost every time.

Gellion swallowed against his restricting throat. He would not approach the Kayda with a smile and a wink, but he would convince them to listen. He had to.

"You will leave at first light tomorrow."

Gellion pulled his focus back to Eurig.

"A guard will come for you in the morning."

Gellion almost flinched at the statement. Memories of being led from a cell to a crowd of Albaren shoved their way to the forefront of his mind. That had been a trap—a way to disparage the elves in front of an entire city to further justify betraying them in battle.

This isn't a trap. What would Eurig have to gain?

But what was Eurig gaining from the help he offered? Selflessness was not a quality Gellion had come to expect from humans of any nationality. Still, if this was a trap, Gellion had no good way of avoiding it, and if Eurig's help was genuine—

"Thank you." Gellion hesitated. "You have proven beyond doubt the treachery and lies of King Naval."

"There is some truth to all tales," Eurig said. "But the Dierna did not attack and pillage Albaren villages to merit any war. Not in recent years at any rate."

"The Albaren should not bring you further trouble after that battle," Valder said.

"Oh rest assured they will," Eurig said. "It may take ten or twenty years, but they will soon forget their defeat, or else use it to fuel their next crusade. It has been so for centuries, and it will remain so."

"All the same," Gellion said. "I am sorry for what happened and for the part we played in it."

Eurig set his piercing eyes on Gellion. "The Albaren can poison the minds of the best of us. I think the elves suffered consequence enough for their blindness."

Gellion did his best to ignore the flash of heat that moved through his body at the words. Blind they may have been, but it had been seeded in good intention. That had to count for something. Gellion swallowed the words.

He stood to leave and extended a hand to Eurig.

"Let us hope to never meet again." He smirked.

Eurig snorted and shook Gellion's hand.

***

Gellion woke to a dawn soaked by fine mist and resigned himself to a highly unpleasant day. He donned the clothes Eurig had provided them —plain but well woven linen with leather shoes and a wool cloak. The cloak and the boots would keep off most of the mist, anyway. Gellion was grateful for the warmth of summer that still clung to the air despite the rain.

The three brothers walked through Arvain with nothing but the clothes on their backs. The guard who led them kept looking at them suspiciously over his shoulder, as though expecting them to make a run for it at any moment, or attack him with their bare hands. Gellion did his best to ignore the man. He was tired of being treated like a dangerous animal.

They met no other humans on the streets. Light had barely begun to illuminate the clouds when they reached the stables. The guard opened the door, and the smell of musty hay and sweat assaulted Gellion's nose.

"Mmm, just think, we will get to enjoy this floral fragrance for at least two weeks," Valder said cheerily as he stepped inside.

"It's not so bad." Veldon's wrinkled nose belied his words.

Gellion sighed, resigning himself to the weeks of discomfort he was about to endure, and strode past stalls of horses, stepping sideways as some of the animals swung their big heads over their doors to investigate the newcomers.

Eight beasts were tied in the aisle near the back doors of the stables. Two of the animals sagged under large packs that draped over their sides. The other six bore high backed saddles with bags bundled behind them. The horses stood with bowed heads, clearly as thrilled as Gellion to be starting a long journey this dreary morning.

"These are the elves?"

A woman stepped out from behind one of the horses. Fair hair twisted in a plait over her shoulder, and pants tucked into her boots just below the knee. She was eyeing Gellion and his brothers with the look of one presented with unsatisfactory livestock.

The guard nodded. "Is everything prepared?"

"Yes," she said. "We have tacked and packed *all* the horses, though I assure you it will be the last time." She narrowed her eyes at Gellion, leaving no room for discussion that Gellion would be responsible for his own horse from now on.

Already off to a great start.

Gellion flashed a smile. "Of course. And thank you—?" He lifted an eyebrow.

The woman gave him an appraising look, then snorted. "Eira. And these two are Haf and Talaith." She jerked her head behind her, where a tanned man and a slight woman stared over the backs of their horses. Unlike her companions, a reluctant interest shone in Talaith's eyes.

"I am Gellion, and these are my brothers, Valder and Veldon."

Each nodded in turn. Valder was grinning. A flush was beginning to creep up Veldon's face. He looked away from Talaith, who had set her gaze on him.

"There is food in the packs," Eira said. "You can eat while we ride."

With that, she turned her back to the elves and began to untie her horse, a palomino with long legs and a thin face. Grabbing the lead rope of a bay next to her, she led the two horses into the misty dawn without a backward glance. Haf and Talaith followed her example, but with many a furtive glance at the elves.

Gellion found himself standing alone with his brothers and the remaining three horses: a stocky chestnut, a lanky bay, and a roan with the whites of her eyes showing so she looked permanently surprised.

Gellion heard the receding steps of the guard and the opening and closing of the front doors of the stable.

"Well, I suppose we just pick one." Valder eyed the horses with distaste. "You take the red one," he said to Gellion. "It matches your hair."

"You take the thick one, it matches your wit," Gellion replied pleasantly.

Valder laughed and shouldered past Gellion to take the reins of the chestnut with a look of pride and solemnity. Veldon smiled and rolled his eyes, moving to the bay.

Gellion walked to the roan's head. Her surprised expression did not change as he approached, but she bobbed her head and snorted in his chest when he reached for her reins.

"Thanks," Gellion muttered, brushing off the front of his shirt. With a sigh, he pulled her reins free and turned to walk toward the misty morning, hoping the animal would follow him.

Outside, the three traders had mounted their horses, Eira and Haf each holding the lead of a pack horse. All heads, human and horse alike, turned to watch the elves emerge from the stables.

"Hurry, or you'll have to catch up with us," said Eira. "We will not slow our pace for you."

Gellion awkwardly looped the reins over his horse's head and pulled himself into the saddle. The roan's muscles immediately tensed under him, and she took a bouncing step forward.

"Not yet," Gellion said through clenched teeth. He gathered her reins to pull back. It worked too well. The mare took several steps backward and ran into Valder's horse, who whinnied reproachfully and stepped sideways. Valder cursed and stumbled forward with one foot in the stirrup and one still on the ground.

Gellion looked up to see Haf staring at them from his dusty brown steed, clearly dismayed by the quality of company he was being forced to escort. Next to him, Talaith was trying to hide a smile. Heat suffused Gellion's face.

Talaith nodded to Gellion's horse. "That is Synabra. And there is Bresgian and Fane." She indicated Valder's and Veldon's horses. "You will come to know them in time."

Gellion very much doubted that, but he sat up straight in his saddle, trying to look at ease. Valder had managed to mount his horse now, and sat with the reins in one fist and the pommel of the saddle in the other. Only Veldon looked like he had ever ridden a horse in his life, and his eyes sparkled in amusement as he watched his brothers.

Eira was not amused. "If you fall, we will not stop. Come on." She turned her horse toward the gates of Arvain and clicked it to a brisk walk.

"I think she likes us," said Valder.

12

FROM GREEN TO BLACK

"I think he will be in this area tonight." Renyra pointed to the East Neighborhoods of Tura. A map of the city was sprawled on the kitchen table, with marks coloring any area now devoid of vierstone. Marks covered more of the map than not.

"He doesn't move randomly," she said. "After he finished with the City Center, he has been moving counterclockwise around the rest of the city." She moved her finger from the West Neighborhood along the cliffs, past the South Neighborhood, and to the docks. Her finger stopped where they now stood.

"I think we can find him." She looked around at those gathered close to her table: Firas, Caerlyn, Alura, and Raren. "I say we all go out tonight. Cover the area from the river to this house."

The others nodded. All were tired, but each night of evaded capture put more determination in their bones, not less. Over the last week, a slow but perceptible pattern had arisen around Kaelo's passage, and as the area of the city still unaffected by Kaelo's magic shrank, his risk of capture grew. Kaelo did not seem concerned about being caught, however. He continued on his course as though no elf knew who he was or what he was doing. Renyra didn't blame him for his confidence. The Council was growing increasingly desperate, sending out absurd numbers of guards at night and sealing and watching every entrance to and exit from the city, but no one saw Kaelo.

Renyra and Firas had gone out two more nights since the first, sliding silently through streets, over buildings, up trees, between walls—anywhere their minds could think of and their bodies could accommodate. Since Kaelo was affecting such large areas, it was easy to tell when they were in the same area as Kaelo, but Renyra was beginning to wonder how far Kaelo's power could reach from where he stood. Whenever Renyra and Firas felt the familiar current in the air, they quickened their pace, splitting up to cover more ground and searching for any sign of movement or indication of a stronger current that may lead to its source. There did seem to be an increase in the effect's strength when Renyra moved in certain directions, but she never managed to catch a glimpse of Kaelo.

Two-thirds of the city was now devoid of vierstone. It was happening so fast. Not a single earthquake had shaken the foundations of the city since Liera's fateful meeting with Kaelo a week before. He did his work quietly but thoroughly.

What does he want? To destroy all vierstone? But why?

As though the vierstone was not concern enough, sightings of glowing eyes and dark shapes had become increasingly common. Both city gates now remained firmly shut at night, and elves stood along the wall that bordered the northern edge of Tura. Renyra was grateful for the sheer cliffs that fell away on the other three sides of the city. At least anything lurking in the waters below would not be able to threaten the city above.

Renyra shook her head and looked up from the map. Liera was right. Kaelo's purpose didn't matter so long as they stopped him.

"I can start near the caesir courts," Raren said. "Alura and Caerlyn can watch the southern half of the neighborhoods, and Renyra and Firas take the northern half near their house."

"You should not be alone," Alura said, looking at her brother with her brows drawn together.

"We're going to split up anyway once we find any signs," Raren pointed out.

Alura opened her mouth as if to argue, then shut it again in resignation.

"If things go as planned, none of us will need to face Kaelo," said Renyra. "If it comes to that—run. He doesn't seem inclined to give chase or attack needlessly."

Caerlyn snorted. "Unless it's to destroy a city."

"Every elf has his code of honor." A half-hearted smile tugged at Raren's lips, but he gave up the effort and sighed. "I hope we catch him tonight, but at this point, we've already lost enough vierstone that it hardly seems worth defending the rest."

"And then what?" Firas's voice was soft. "He moves on to the next city, and it begins again. We do not only fight for Tura."

Raren turned his eyes down.

Renyra did not feel much more hope than Raren showed. With each passing day, she wished Liera would call another Turi Council meeting. More and more, the prophecy tugged at Renyra's mind. '*This could be bigger than any of us yet realize,*' Kyna had said. Renyra was starting to believe her. She thought over the words that plagued her day and night.

Safe from death is stone that burns.

Stone did not burn. What could it mean? Should they set a fire in the city? She almost laughed aloud. Just what Tura needed.

From which he hates his doom shall rise.

What did Kaelo hate? The elves? That was unhelpful.

A weapon forged from his despise.

A weapon forged by the elves? They had weapons already. None of them were working.

"Are we done here?" Caerlyn stretched her arms up and backward. At her full height, she was a head taller than both Renyra and Alura and had curves that turned the eye of any elf she passed. Today, her hair hung loose, in shimmering glory, to her waist.

"I would say so," Raren said.

"Then I say we go have some fun," Caerlyn said.

Renyra smiled and nodded, but stayed where she was as her friends stood. Something told her that exercise would not be able to work the stress from her muscles or turn her mind away from worry today.

Firas remained next to her and trailed a hand over her back. She leaned against him and tried not to think about what the night would bring.

No moon or stars lent their illumination to the streets when Renyra followed Firas out of the apartment. Strings of glowing lights lit their surroundings just well enough to walk through the deserted neighborhood.

Renyra's hands strayed to the dagger at one hip, the rope wrapped around her body, and the javelin at her back. It felt good to carry a javelin again. She had no intention of throwing the weapon at Kaelo—not this time—but it was as good a weapon as any to smash over his head, and would allow her to attack from a distance. The knife was probably useless against Kaelo, but it gave her comfort.

As they neared their destination, they took to deeper shadows beyond the streets, moving under trees and against buildings, all the while listening and watching, feeling the air around them and the stone at their feet.

All was quiet.

They chose the roof of a house slightly taller than those around it to climb and make their watch post. From their perch, they could see for several blocks and would be able to hear any commotion throughout the entire neighborhood, though they hoped there would be none. If one of the others found Kaelo and succeeded in his capture, it should be a quick and silent affair. Renyra and Firas would not know until he was brought before them, securely restrained with his hands tucked away from any nearby stone.

They waited.

Every once in a while, a breeze blew past, tickling Renyra's face with her hair. She wrinkled her nose and smoothed her hair back again. She wished she could at least talk to Firas to pass the time. Keeping utter silence and focus was as boring as it was exhausting. Even letting her mind wander could compromise her ability to see and hear the cues she anticipated. She tried to clear her mind, to focus only on the outlines of roofs and trees, to feel the breeze on her skin and the roof under her belly, and nothing more.

The clouds began to break up as the night wore on, revealing slices of starry sky and the occasional brighter piece of moon as they moved overhead. As the third hour after midnight approached, Renyra began to think that tonight would be even more dull than those preceding it. At least there had been a trail of current to follow then.

"Maybe we should move to the southern half of the neighborhood," Renyra whispered to Firas. "He probably won't start on this end anyway."

"Caerlyn and Alura have that area covered," Firas said patiently. He did not seem the least affected by doing nothing for hours.

Renyra fidgeted again. Her skin was practically crawling with anticipation and impatience.

No. It was something else. Renyra sat up.

"Firas," she said.

"I know." He was alert now, scanning the streets below.

The feeling grew stronger, bringing the familiar vertigo. It was coming from the southwest.

"Come on." Renyra climbed down the side of the building.

She paused when her feet hit the street. A vague curiosity seized her as she looked down at its surface. She could feel the current running through the stone beneath her shoes. It was distant, like looking through a fogged window. What if she removed the barrier?

Bending down, Renyra placed her bare palm against the street.

She gasped audibly, barely managing to suppress a louder cry. Firas was at her side in an instant.

"What is it?" he said, worry in his voice.

Renyra had snatched her hand away from the street, but now cautiously touched it again. She winced and recoiled from the power of the current that flowed up her arm. Shaking her head, she stood and rubbed her palm.

"It ... I felt ... It was so much stronger—the current. I could feel it in my bones. It was moving, clashing." She shook her head again, unable to come up with words to describe the horrible sensation. But amid the sensation she had felt something else. Direction.

"It came from there." She pointed down a side street, now eerily sure of where Kaelo was.

She ran down the street until she knew they were closer to Kaelo, then stopped, gritted her teeth, and put her hand on the street again. The current was even stronger now, and it seemed all she could do to keep herself together in the dizzying waves that came over her. Pulling her hand away, she moved off the street and between two buildings to her left.

He was one street over, around this building. She had felt it.

"Go that way, to the street over," she breathed, hardly daring to put any air behind the words. "I will come from this alley and try to get at him, but you go a building down in case I miss."

Firas did not look thrilled by this arrangement, but he did as she said.

Renyra took a deep breath. She was alone in the dark, stalking a predator far more dangerous than herself. The current had stopped now, but Renyra kept to her path. She had to get to that street before he passed it. She ran quietly down the alley.

The opening to the street came closer. She tried to slow the pounding of her heart, to think clearly. She had one chance.

When she reached the end of the alley, she flattened herself against the side of the building nearest where she had sensed Kaelo. She wished he would start the current again so she could at least know his concentration was on something else.

Slowly, so slowly she could hardly bear it, she moved her face past the edge of the building to peer down the road. It was a narrow street, winding, with trees to either side. Lights were strung in the trees, and stark shadows fell on the path in blotches of leaves and branches.

He wasn't here yet.

Before she could fully formulate her plan, she leaped to the trunk of a tree two steps beyond the alley and climbed to the lowest branch as smoothly and silently as she could. If the leaves rustled or the branch moved, it would have been masked by the breeze that blew just as she had left the ground. Renyra sent up a silent prayer.

Pressing herself against the trunk, she reached behind her back and took the javelin, holding it in tightly gripped fists while she balanced herself. She watched the shadows beneath the trees.

They flickered.

Renyra held her breath. She had never been more still in her life. She saw the shadows move again, but did not pick out any feet disturbing them. She strained her ears. Yes. There. So soft she would not have heard it if the breeze had blown again. She made out the fall of footsteps.

She looked hard, willing herself to see Kaelo's shape, to make out the shimmering outline of Gellion's tunic, and then, at last, she did see it. The shadows beneath the trees moved and shook, but there was one place they transformed and flickered, as though reflected in a many sided mirror.

She kept her eyes locked on the trick of light, watching Kaelo come nearer. He moved beneath the trees, but did not seem to be in a hurry. His steps were even.

When he came under Renyra's tree, the lights strung through its branches reflected off his hood, giving a clear target.

A grim determination seized Renyra. This was the elf who had destroyed her home, who had killed Aryn, and who had thought Renyra no threat worth quenching. How wrong he had been.

Renyra bent her knees, raised the javelin, and dropped from the tree without a sound, bringing her weapon down where she had seen Kaelo's head.

What happened next, Renyra never knew, nor even remembered clearly. One moment, Kaelo had been beneath her, the next, she had dropped through empty air to the ground. Her javelin smashed onto the stone street, sending reverberations up her arms and throwing her off balance as she landed on her feet. She staggered sideways, automatically raising her javelin again and looking around wildly to see where Kaelo had gone. Then she saw the gleam of his eyes. A cold, steady gleam that held neither surprise nor fear.

She swung her javelin at the eyes as hard as she could.

Her hands stopped mid swing, as though they had struck stone. She felt warm skin touch her own, the grip of a hand around her wrist, and then her body seized up as though electrocuted.

Whatever she had felt when she touched the street had been a gentle spark; this was a bolt of lightning. She couldn't scream, she couldn't even breathe as mind-numbing, senseless fear and panic seized every neuron in her brain. She had to let go of the javelin. It was the only feasible action.

Let it go. Drop it. You can't stop him.

The current had stopped, but the waves of terror kept coming. She wanted to scream, to cry, to vent her fear in some tangible way, anything to make it ease, but even those simple actions were too much. She fell to the ground, shaking so violently, the clashing of her teeth was all she could hear. She curled into a ball.

Renyra did not know when she had dropped her javelin, or when Kaelo had let go of her wrist. She did not know where he was, and she did not care, so long as he was far from here.

There had never been any point. She had been foolish to try to stop him—he who possessed more power than she could fathom. She curled tighter.

She heard footsteps coming toward her, increasing their pace.

"Renyra!"

The name brought her back to herself slightly. She loosened her grip on her knees.

"Renyra!" The name came again, and hands lay on her shoulder and thigh. She jerked away in panic, but nothing happened when these hands touched her.

"Are you hurt? What happened?"

Slowly, Renyra opened her eyes. Her mind cleared as though emerging from honey, and the fear she had felt moments before seemed a faraway dream. She drew her brows together. Why had she been so terrified? She couldn't remember now.

She pushed herself up with one hand. Firas helped, for which she was grateful. Her arms felt like jelly.

"Are you hurt?" he asked again.

She shook her head.

Never in her life had she felt any emotion like that. Just the memory of it was enough to make her heart pound again. She signed the three-pointed star over herself and reached for her vierstone earring before she knew what she was doing.

Her hand froze. Her heart seemed to skip two beats.

"What?" Firas's voice held a panic Renyra had never heard in it. "What is it?"

Renyra brought her other hand to her earring and carefully unfastened it. She had not felt the usual surge of *something* when she touched it. She had not felt it warm at her emotion or Firas's touch.

A strange numbness had settled over Renyra. She held the earring in a fist. She felt that she should have been afraid, but it seemed all propensity for that emotion had temporarily bled out of her. Opening her hand, she tilted her palm so the lights still shining from the tree above reflected off the surface of the earring.

It was black.

PART II

13

AROUND A FIRE

Gellion cursed as a set of square teeth snapped at his hand. He glared at the wild-eyed roan.

"Just a moment ago you were trying to nuzzle me so hard I couldn't get at your tack, now you bite me when I try to loosen your saddle? What do you want from me?"

"She was only trying to scratch her head on you before, and you pulled up too hard on the girth before you loosened it just now, so it pinched her side."

Gellion did not turn to the voice. His temper was in rare form after three days of saddle sores and condescension, and he did not want to snap at the one human member of their company who tolerated the elves' presence reasonably well.

Although Talaith displayed no bitterness toward the elves, she found endless amusement in their lack of natural horsemanship, which Gellion found almost as annoying as Eira's snide comments and Haf's narrowed eyes. Fortunately, the four-legged beasts had been mostly placid throughout the journey thus far, plodding obediently behind the horse in front of them so that Gellion doubted whether they would turn from the path if Gellion or his brothers asked them to. That was just as well to Gellion.

"Do it in a controlled way, like this." Talaith nudged him aside and took the dangling leather strap that Gellion had dropped. With both hands on the strap, she crouched down, positioned the strap over her shoulder, and slowly rose upward until the buckle fastening the girth slipped out of its hole. As Talaith released the strap and pulled it loose, Synabra let out a breath that sent her nostrils flapping. Talaith patted the mare's neck, then stiffened as a polite cough sounded behind them.

"The elves are responsible for their own mounts," Eira said in a clipped tone.

"I was only helping," Talaith said calmly.

"We are giving them help enough dragging them to Suri Ranta. Come help with the fire."

"Why don't you ask one of the elves to help?"

"They are busy with their horses."

Gellion looked between the two women. Talaith, a head shorter than Eira, exuded an impressive force of will, her dark eyes meeting Eira's gaze unflinchingly. Gellion got the sense that a silent battle beyond his comprehension was at play between them. After several tense moments of glares, Talaith blinked, then shrugged and walked toward the packs of supplies with squared shoulders, as though tending the fire had been her intention all along.

Eira watched Talaith until she was kneeling beside Haf, then turned her steely eyes on Gellion. Gellion wrestled his features into a somber expression and began to dutifully pull the saddle from his horse. Despite the cool regard of Eira and Haf, Gellion and his brothers had met the humans' every scoff with polite gestures and only slightly sarcastic solemnity. Gellion could hardly blame the traders for their dislike of elves, nor for their annoyance at having to escort three strangers across Tala. He had hoped, however, that they may show a little more tact.

At least the humans were limiting their sentiments to attitude and remarks. Never once had Gellion felt any true threat from the traders. Even his suspicions of an impending trap had lessened as the days of dull travel progressed.

"You sure you can handle that mare all on your own?" Valder dropped his own saddle on the ground next to Gellion's.

"You would not be any help," Gellion said. "I saw you trying to wrestle the bit into that hairy tub's mouth this morning."

Valder raised his eyebrows. "Oh I see, now we are talking about the horses."

Gellion closed his eyes as he realized Valder's quip and ran a hand through his hair, shaking his head.

"Very funny."

"Ah, I'm only joking." Valder tilted his head toward Veldon, who was quietly brushing Fane's gleaming coat. "It's Veldon she bats her eyelashes at over meals and campfires. She only likes besting you."

"Do you ever stop?" Veldon said over his shoulder. His voice was uncaring, but Gellion could see the beginnings of a flush on his neck.

"Alright, alright," said Valder. "Keep your blushes to yourself."

The red on Veldon's neck deepened. Valder grinned.

Gellion watched his brothers' easy smiles with a weight in his stomach. No matter what was happening around them, they always seemed so carefree, so in control. It had always been so in the Great War, but then they had been young. Now, centuries later, they still handled trial and uncertainty with a grace Gellion could never hope to match. He had rarely seen either of them truly angry.

They acted as though this were all an amusing adventure—that everything would work out in the end. But Gellion could not believe it would be so simple. Hardly a moment went by in the endless hours of riding when he did not worry over what he was riding to, what would happen once they arrived in Suri Ranta, and what could be happening in Faeran as he watched the rolling hills pass under him.

The same anxiety did not seem to touch his brothers, but then, there was no Kaelo in their world, and no Kyna. They held no responsibility for all that had happened since leaving Daro. To them, Dulon was only the leader of Daro who had met an untimely and sad end, but not through any fault of their own.

Gellion blinked himself out of his thoughts to see Veldon watching him. There was no smile on his face now. A line formed between his brows.

Trying to paste a pleasant expression on his face, Gellion turned away from Veldon and walked to the smoking pile of twigs Talaith had helped Haf assemble from the scattered trees and shrubs that dotted the landscape. The traders had packed enough food to make hunting unnecessary. Time taken to hunt or trap was time away from their journey, and the humans rose at dawn and did not stop to make camp until an hour before dusk. The time between was monotonous and painful, but Eira set an easy pace for the horses and broke for lunch at middays.

Gellion had traveled worse, but he still preferred the soreness of tired feet to a painful backside. Nor did the constant awareness of a living yet unreadable creature beneath him help him to relax.

Haf sat a pot over the fire. It was filled with water from a stream that ran near the road. Streams laced the Dierna landscape like veins under skin. Water was everywhere. The contrast with Albarad and the coastal lands of Daro was astounding.

Wariness touched Haf's eyes as Gellion approached. The burly man hardly spoke when the elves were around.

"May I help?" Gellion said.

Haf nodded to the packs, set neatly in a row a few paces from the fire.

Gellion fished through the bags until he held a pouch of tea, a bag of cornmeal, and a slab of salted beef. Gellion eyed the soft meat with some distaste. The Turi did not farm cattle for meat, and hunting game was a pastime more popular among the other three Kindoms. Gellion preferred fish and bird to the richness of red meat, and he always preferred it cooked.

Soon the smell of boiling cornmeal permeated the air, and the six members of the company gathered around the fire to assemble their dinner. Eira had found some herbs and wild onions nearby and added them to the cornmeal along with some salt.

The first dinner of their journey had been an uncomfortable affair. It was easy enough to hold silence or break into groups of conversation on the road, but when sitting around a common fire, the quiet that stretched between the group was an itch that all longed to scratch, but none dared be the first. To Gellion's surprise, it had been Veldon who spoke first that night.

"Are there no other cities between Arvain and the marsh?" he had asked in improving Albaren.

"Not large ones," Talaith had answered. "The main trading routes are between the chief cities of the clans. You'll find larger towns along those routes, and along the Hyr River. The road to the marshes is not often used."

Eira had glared at Talaith then, as though she were revealing precious secrets to the enemy. But Veldon had set a precedent for conversation, and since then, Talaith, at least, had become increasingly open in her interactions. Even Eira had grudgingly told Gellion about the five Dierna clans when he asked: Elder, Ash, Rowan, Oak, and Aspen. The clans were reminiscent of the elven Kindoms, except each clan occasionally went to war with one or several others over land, resources, or hurt feelings. Currently, the Elder Clan was on good terms with the Ash Clan, which bordered its lands to the east, but not so keen on the Aspen Clan to the south. This was unfortunate, because Kartraf, the Aspen Clan's biggest city, sat between Arvain and Crefdyn along the Hyr River and made trade with the Oak Clan awkward, if not dangerous.

Gellion tried to wrap his head around these new politics, but could not find the focus or the motivation to set them to memory.

Instead, Gellion tried to learn about the people they were going to meet.

He picked at the spongy salt beef in his bowl as the company sat down to their dinner.

"Do you know the Kayda well?" he asked.

"Well enough to trade with them," Eira said.

"Eurig says they are superstitious."

"Yes."

She makes Kyna seem like a fountain of loquaciousness.

"Do you know any of their legends?" Valder cut in eagerly.

"They believe in all sorts of creatures and spirits," Talaith said. "Beasts possessed of burning eyes and evil spirits, men that turn into seals, ancestors speaking through animals and fire. Their entire society is littered with rules based on the legends: when to go outside, when to hunt, when to travel. There are rituals you must perform every day or once a year or whenever you say a certain word."

Gellion's fascination was tempered with anxiety. What would such a people think of another race of beings? Had they heard the same stories about the elves as the Dierna? Had the Albaren's malice spread so far?

A simmering heat began in Gellion's chest. He could hardly remember the list of transgressions for which he hated the Albaren now. Their plan to drive the elves from Tala had clearly been a long time in the making, and he was as ashamed as he was furious that neither he nor Dulon had seen it coming.

"Are the Kayda on good terms with the Albaren?" Veldon said, his thoughts clearly in the same direction as Gellion's.

"How should I know?" Eira said. "We trade with them, we don't talk politics with them."

"Mountain tea is prized in Albarad." Haf did not take his eyes from his food. "Their trade relations are good I imagine, though I cannot speak to their politics."

"Somehow I can't see the Kayda getting along with King Naval," said Talaith. There was satisfaction in her face, as though anyone who did not get along with King Naval was another victory over the foul man and his country. Gellion couldn't help but agree.

"I can't see the Albaren holding a truly favorable relationship with anyone," Gellion muttered.

Eira watched him shrewdly, but said nothing.

They finished their dinner and cleaned their bowls, refilling the pot over the fire to make tea. Talaith pulled a small flute from her pocket and began to play a lilting tune. The music lifted Gellion's mood, even as it made him heartsick for Daro. He stared into the embers of the fire and followed the notes, trying not to think of a sunny afternoon of music with Kyna, looking over the sea.

"May I?" he asked when Talaith paused.

She raised an eyebrow at him, then shrugged and tossed him the flute. The look on her face told him she expected his skill with a flute to match his skill with a horse.

Gellion examined the little instrument. It was made of wood. He knit his brows. He had never seen an instrument made of wood. After wiping the mouthpiece, he set his fingers over the flute's holes and played a few test notes. Simple flutes may differ in their pitch, but all had similar fingerings, and soon Gellion was playing a haunting Morcani melody he had learned from Firas. His own skin rose in goosebumps as he played, memories washing over him like waves of cold water.

The notes slipped and flowed over one another, their minor resonance seeming to darken the dying sun.

Everyone around the fire had gone very still, and when Gellion finished the song, only the soft pop of embers permeated the camp. The humans were staring at him. Valder and Veldon no longer wore easy smiles, but sat with faraway looks.

Gellion looked at the flute again, impressed with its acoustics despite its rustic appearance. He wiped the mouthpiece again and then tossed the flute back to Talaith, who raised her hands just in time to catch it.

"It is a nice instrument," Gellion said. "You play well."

Talaith stared at him a moment longer before turning her eyes away in embarrassment.

"What was that song about?" she said.

"About? I'm not sure. It is a mountain song, probably written during times of war."

Talaith nodded, her eyes glazed in distant thought.

Haf was watching Gellion. "Your people like music?"

"I have never met a people who do not," Gellion said.

Haf grunted, then turned his attention back to the tack he had been cleaning, as though ashamed to find himself talking to an elf.

Gellion hid a smile and stood, walking to the stream to clean his empty cup of tea.

As dusk faded to night, Gellion found himself growing bored and restless. He knew he should be exhausted, but his mind did not seem to be in tune with his body. He sat a ways away from the fire—now a grey, smoking heap—and watched the stars begin to wink into existence in the east.

Valder lay wrapped in a blanket a stone's throw away with his back to Gellion. His exposed shoulder rose and fell with the rhythm of sleep. Valder could sleep anywhere, under any circumstances.

Gellion sighed with envy.

To his other side, Veldon sat bent over with his hands clasped and his eyes closed. Gellion watched him curiously. Was he praying? Running through the A'vaeri in his head? Whatever he was doing, he did not appear to be relaxed. Lines creased his brow and his hands were clasped tightly. Gellion moved closer.

"What are you doing?" he said.

Veldon's eyes flew open and he jerked his head up. His eyes met Gellion's with an expression that was almost dazed.

"Veldon?" Gellion said, slightly alarmed.

Veldon shook his head as if to clear it and opened his hands. His vierstone earring lay centered in one palm.

"What were you doing?" Gellion said again. It was not the first time he had seen his brother holding the earring, but he had assumed Veldon had simply taken to fidgeting with it in his boredom. This did not seem to be mere fidgeting.

Veldon let out a breath and closed his palm on the stone, a slight shudder shaking his shoulders.

"I have been trying to discern what the elf in Daro could have done to it."

"The blackened vierstone?"

Veldon nodded. "I am trying, but it is a difficult substance to analyze for prolonged periods of time."

Gellion could imagine. He used the channel of his vierstone to work metal, but he had never attempted to work the stone itself. Few elves did. It took incredible focus, self-control, and as far as Gellion could tell, an affinity for the stone itself that not all elves possessed. Their father had been such an elf, and now it seemed Veldon had inherited the talent. Gellion remembered the crafting competition in Daro, what seemed like years before. There had been a reason the elves were astounded by Veldon's vierstone lamp. Not only had he worked the stone like glass, he had used its properties to enhance the lamp's function.

"Have you found anything?" Gellion said.

"No." Veldon sighed and looked out over the hills. "Not really. I—" He hesitated. "I mean, I can sense its current. I cannot understand it, but I can feel it. But then I have always felt that, at least in the last few years. I think it must have had something to do with the current, whatever the elf did." He looked at Gellion. "I spoke with Dulon, after the crafting competition."

"I know. He asked you to examine the vierstone, to pick up where Aryn left off."

Where Aryn was cut off.

Veldon nodded. "And I did. Dulon said that Aryn had said something *stopped* the current in the dead vierstone. I agree with her. What I cannot discover is how it could possibly be stopped."

Gellion thought hard. Veldon's description did strike a chord in him. Gellion had never examined vierstone seriously and had never thought of its essence as a current, but when he used the stone to 'see' into metal, there was almost a rhythm to the work, like a heartbeat that extended into the metal he was working.

"I have never felt a current like it anywhere else," Veldon continued. "And I cannot touch, let alone alter, the current in the stone on my own."

Gellion closed his eyes, trying to summon the memory of metalworking. It was like grasping at smoke.

A sudden idea sparked in his mind. He felt around him for a stone. When he found one the size of his palm, he held it in his hands and closed his eyes. Though Gellion was not a stoneworker by trade, he could feel the vierstone in his ear warming as he concentrated on the rock in his hands. He ran his fingers over it, trying to discern its structure, its properties. It was almost as if he were reaching into the stone. He could sense its atoms, its makeup, and knew how he could have used the knowledge to cut and carve the stone in just the right way to make it into something useful or beautiful.

"The current goes out from the vierstone," he whispered, his eyes still closed. "I can feel it. I use it, though I hardly notice that I am doing it." He opened his eyes and shook his head. "But even then, I cannot *change* the stone I am touching, only see it and understand it. How does he break and move stone at a touch? It is as though he forces it to do his bidding."

"The current goes out of the vierstone." Veldon frowned in thought. "Could he be somehow using the current of the vierstone to manipulate rock and metal? Using it so forcefully that it takes the current out of the vierstone entirely?"

Gellion opened his mouth, then closed it. "I suppose it is possible, though I cannot imagine how."

"You could try."

Gellion hesitated. If Veldon's theory was true, Gellion would be risking the destruction of his own vierstone earring. He was not sure that was a risk he wanted to take.

Veldon seemed to read his hesitation. "Maybe once we are back in Faeran. Then you can use another vierstone source."

Gellion clenched his fists. No. This was too important. If they could use this time in Tala to discover what exactly Kaelo had done, and how he had done it, they might be able to stop him.

"No." He sighed. "I will try."

Wrapping his hands around the rock again, Gellion closed his eyes and concentrated with all his might. He could feel the crystalline structure of the rock—mostly quartz and feldspar.

He felt the bonds between the atoms, between the different elements, and he tried to cleave across the bonds—to force the stone to break. He pictured it happening, imagined using a hammer and chisel to exploit the areas of weakness. The vierstone's current seemed to be almost flowing out of his fingers. He tried to direct it to the points of cleavage in the rock and force them apart.

Nothing happened.

"Maybe it just takes practice?" Veldon said.

"Maybe."

Somehow Gellion didn't think so. Over thousands of years, he could not imagine that no elf but Kaelo would have discovered how to direct vierstone's current fully out of itself to manipulate other substances, even if by accident.

Unless another elf did discover it, but was so horrified by the consequences that they buried the knowledge.

Still, it did not seem likely.

"I will keep working at it," Veldon said. "What you said about the current's flow is helpful."

A well of frustration rose in Gellion's chest.

"It is clearly possible to figure out," he said. "Aryn knew—or thought she knew—before she died, and that was after only a few days of trying, according to Dulon."

"Aryn was a master of vierstone," Veldon said.

Gellion raised his eyebrows. "And what do you call an elf who can mold vierstone like glass and sense its life as few others can?"

Veldon looked away. "I am no master." He sighed. "But I will keep trying."

The brothers sat in companionable silence for a while, watching the moon rise above the mountains in the distant east. Could Gellion learn to do what Kaelo had done? He tried to imagine himself shaking the ground with a touch, bleeding the life out of vierstone. He shuddered, and images of red hot vierstone in Kaelo's palms flashed before his eyes. *'That is not for you,'* Kaelo had said. *'You will burn yourself.'*

Gellion was not one to set stock in dreams, but he could not shake the frightening realism of Kaelo's face, nor the burning pain in his palms as he had held the crimson vierstone.

The dream had brought back the memory of another dream, several months old, in which Gellion had stood amid the burning remains of Maramor with vierstone melting in his hands. Kaelo had been in that dream too.

The back of Gellion's neck started to prickle, and he looked over to see Veldon watching him.

"Admiring the view?" Gellion smirked.

Veldon's eyes remained serious. He did not answer at once, yet he seemed to hold words poised on his lips, unsure whether or not to say them. Finally, he spoke.

"Are you alright?"

Heat spread through Gellion's core. He berated himself for allowing his thoughts to color his face.

"I do not relish sitting on a horse all day and would rather be on a boat to Faeran tomorrow." He tried to keep his voice light.

Veldon was not fooled. "I know it was not an easy decision for you," he said quietly. "Taking the elves to battle."

Gellion bit down on his tongue. The heat had spread to the rest of his body now. He did not want to talk about this now. He never wanted to talk about this.

"It was not my decision alone," he said flatly.

"No," said Veldon. "Nor were its consequences your fault."

Gellion fought back the emotion threatening to rise from the place he kept it firmly suppressed. It had not been his fault. Not his alone. But he could have stopped it. Did that make it his fault?

Veldon let a long breath out his nose and rested his chin on his arms, which were folded over his knees. He looked away from Gellion.

"I know you do not like talking about these things," he said. "I don't want to cause you more pain by bringing it up, but I have watched you struggling for weeks. I feel guilty."

Gellion looked up at that. Veldon's kind eyes were laced with pain.

"What are you talking about?" Gellion said.

"My home stands waiting for me in Maramor, my life exactly as it was when I left for Daro. You lost everything. Your home, your workshop, your community. Dulon." He spoke the name in barely a whisper.

Gellion ran a hand through his hair. "Veldon, I would never forgive myself if you lost Farra or your home because of me. That you have it all to go back to after this is one of the few things that still gives me hope. You should not feel guilty for that. And Dulon—" He winced at the shock of pain that always accompanied the name. "Dulon was not the first elf I have seen fall in battle."

"That does not make it easier."

"It should," Gellion muttered. He shook his head against the pinpricks in his eyes that threatened to betray him. "He was a good leader, and many will mourn his loss, but—"

"He was also your friend."

Gellion went still. Another stab of pain.

"You built Daro together," Veldon said.

"And I wanted to bash his head against a wall half the time." Gellion let out a low snort, then squeezed his eyes closed as they welled with tears.

He suddenly wished he were talking to Kyna. The sympathy swimming in Veldon's eyes was hardly bearable. He wanted someone to make him laugh, to turn his mind away from the pain that constantly dragged at him. He could imagine Kyna making a snide remark about Dulon's notorious hair flipping and steering the conversation to the annoying insects buzzing in the stream nearby.

The pain in Gellion's chest worsened. Kyna was probably gone too. Even if she weren't, she had made it more than clear that Gellion was wasting his feelings on her. He dug his nails into his palms.

He wished the Kindom Council had never happened. He wished Amadeo Benta had never come to Daro. And he tried to wish he had condemned Kaelo to death when he had the chance, but even after all the elf had done, Gellion could not bring himself to truly regret his vote for Kaelo's release all those centuries ago.

Gellion opened his eyes, and a single tear rolled down his face, hot as molten stone.

1 4

STRANDED

Being involved in the action of Daro had been much more exciting than this. In Tura, all it seemed Kyna ever did was sit in pristine rooms and listen to pointless debates between elves Kyna was quickly growing to dislike, each in their own way. Liera was stubborn as diamond, Tenille morose and righteous, and Alos an arrogant fop. Reanan, at least, was intelligent, but he was too ponderous, and Kyna still couldn't tell Saethir and Dorian apart. Even Tornac's good looks were spoiled by the pang that assaulted Kyna's stomach every time she looked at his face.

Then there was Renyra. The little Fieri perplexed Kyna. She was earnest to a fault and annoyingly sociable, but Kyna found that she didn't dislike the woman as much as the rest, hard though she tried. A good deal of Kyna's regard for Renyra came from the woman's distinct lack of intimidation against Liera. Renyra was not afraid to stand up to the all powerful Lady of Tura, and Kyna couldn't help but respect her for it.

Just now, Kyna was thoroughly enjoying the look on Liera's face as Renyra stood with her chin lifted and her eyes possessed of an expression that would melt stone.

"He must have touched it," Liera said. Her eyes were fixed on

Renyra in a way that showed how little she wanted to look at the black earring on the table.

"He didn't touch it," Renyra said in a flat voice. "He touched me. He destroyed it *through me*." She emphasized the last words with gritted teeth. "And he ..." her look of indignant determination faltered slightly. "He did something to me. Incapacitated me." A hint of fear flickered behind her eyes before she squeezed her fists and pointed to the earring. "This is more than simple destruction. Kyna was right from the beginning. This is something larger than any of us realized, and we must do more than set guards and patrols."

Kyna smiled. No, the Fieri elf wasn't so bad.

Half the Council Members in the room were watching Liera, waiting to see what she would do. The others were still staring in horror at the earring on the table.

Renyra's story had caused quite a stir when it became public knowledge. An elf that could not only destroy the vierstone of the city's foundations, but physically stop an elf in her tracks with a touch and blacken her earring through her body? That was more frightening. Would Liera finally realize the insufficiency of her measures? Would she finally give stock to the prophecy?

Liera's jaw was working frantically. If Renyra's expression could have melted stone, Liera's would have exploded it, yet within her angry exterior, Kyna could see discomfort. Would it be enough?

But Liera held her silence.

Kyna was starting to get desperate. The elves had to follow the prophecy. Everything depended on it. If she could not unite this Council, she would fail, utterly this time.

No. Don't think about that. You can't think about that.

She would not fail. She could not fail.

"What harm can it do?" Kyna said. "We are running out of options. Soon we will have no vierstone left in the city. Kaelo might move on to other cities, or he might go further in Tura. So far there has been little physical damage to the city, but do we want to risk the possibility of another Daro?" Kyna looked away from Liera to appeal to the rest of the Council. "We should at least try to discern the meaning of this prophecy. Then we can decide whether or not to act on it. What other options do we have?"

Tenille and Reanan were nodding. Everyone except Liera appeared open to the idea, but Liera had the bearing of a wild animal backed into a corner.

Kyna narrowed her eyes at the woman. What was she so afraid of?

"I already said any elf could take as much time as he or she wants with that prophecy," said Liera. "No one has come forward with any suggestions. If someone has made sense of it, they are welcome to bring it to the Council. Otherwise, this Council is to discuss practical and actionable plans."

"And what do you suggest now?" asked Reanan. His voice was polite, but clearly laced with skepticism.

Liera stiffened.

Kyna cocked her head. Was the Lady of Tura beginning to lose her hold on the Council? It may not be the worst development. If Liera's stubborn refusal to accept the prophecy was not shared by those around her, Kyna may be able to appeal to the Council in spite of its leader.

Liera paused for a moment, as though trying to think of a new plan on the spot. She kept glancing at the piece of paper on the table containing the prophecy. Kyna now brought the not so subtle reminder to meetings regularly.

"I will send for the full Kindom Council to reconvene in Tura as soon as possible," Liera said at last. "We will ask for the aid of the other Kindoms."

"We should have told the other Kindoms what was happening long before now," Tenille said. "Does no one outside of Tura know our threat?"

Liera ground her jaw. "I sent messages to all Kindoms with the news of Daro's destruction."

"But not our suspicions at the time as to how it occurred, nor that the attacks had extended to Tura?" The sparks in Tenille's eyes reminded Kyna forcibly of Gellion. She fixed her gaze on Liera.

"It did not seem necessary at the time," said Liera, but some of the confidence had bled from her words. "Things escalated quickly. There was little time. And there were many actions for Tura to take against ...

Kaelo," she still hesitated each time she said the name, "before going to the other Kindoms."

"Or did you not want the other Kindoms to know who was threatening the elves?" Renyra said.

Kyna raised an eyebrow at the boldness of the words. Liera flinched.

"They need to know," Renyra continued. "If this," she picked up the useless earring, "happens to more elves—to all the elves—and if this," she swept an arm in a broad circle to indicate the city beyond the room, "happens to the other Great Cities? What then? Do you know what that could mean?"

Anxious muttering broke out in the room.

"He cannot get that far," Liera said, almost desperately. "We will stop him from leaving the city. We have guards posted night and day. We will mount ambushes—attacks. We have just been unlucky. There is a way to stop him, and we will find it before his threat can extend beyond the Turi."

"And what if there isn't a way?" said Reanan. "What if we don't stop him and are responsible for the further destruction of other cities and vierstone? What if the only way to stop Kaelo is hidden in this prophecy that you refuse to acknowledge?"

The corners of Kyna's mouth turned upward.

Liera looked like she was about to shout, but instead took a deep breath and closed her eyes before she spoke.

"I will send for the Kindom Council immediately, through our messenger birds. The Council Members should all be able to arrive within the week by Rale or ship, and then," she sighed. "Then we can show them the prophecy and see what they think of it. But in the meantime, we double our guards and we continue patrols and tracking *from a distance,*" she shot a look at Renyra, as though it were her own fault for letting Kaelo touch her.

Renyra held Liera's gaze steadily, then turned to Kyna.

"Kyna?" she asked in a pleasant voice. "Would you make copies of that prophecy to send home with the Council Members? I think it would be prudent to do all we can to interpret its words for ourselves before bringing it before the Kindom Council."

"Certainly," said Kyna. It was an effort not to smirk at Liera. "The printers are in the same building as the messenger birds?"

Liera nodded slowly.

"I would be happy to send off your letters while I am there."

A subtle flush crept up Liera's face. Kyna's offer implied her lack of trust that Liera would follow through on her promise. It also transferred some of the woman's power to a nameless Turi on no Council but her own. Kyna smiled.

"Thank you, Kyna," Liera said in an obvious effort at calm. "But I will bring the letters myself."

Kyna bowed her head and took the folded prophecy from the table.

"Perhaps I will see you there," she said, and stood to leave the meeting.

The building that housed all aspects of Turi communications sat near the Rale station on the far northeastern side of the city. One floor contained printing presses, another was dedicated to their design and assembly. All the paper in the city was made here, and anything to do with the Rale system, both internal and external, happened in the upper floors that looked out over the city and the giant Rale line that stretched into the distance.

Kyna took her time getting to the printers. She wandered through rooms of glossy machinery and stacks of paper so fresh they still smelled of wood pulp. It was difficult not to be impressed by the technology the elves had invented over the last several centuries. While Kyna found the grandeur of Turi architecture and crafting a waste of time and effort, she held more respect for the feats of engineering and chemistry accomplished by the elves at large.

Though the Rale system made Kyna distinctly uncomfortable in its foreign and seemingly magic design, she had to admit it was a work of genius that made travel and communication incredibly efficient. And printing was a good sight easier than writing. Kyna made her way to the printing rooms of the building. The metallic scent of ink and metal mixed with the earthiness of paper, and a gentle hum hung in the air from the purr of the machines.

"There you are!"

Kyna jerked toward the voice, nearly dropping the paper she had pulled from her pocket.

What in Riure is she doing here?

Renyra was walking toward Kyna. She looked pleased to see Kyna, but her smile did not reach her eyes as it normally did.

"I was waiting for you here," she said. "I tried to catch you after the meeting but you disappeared."

Precisely so I wouldn't have to talk to anyone.

Kyna pulled up a corner of her mouth in what she hoped was an accommodating smile.

"Did you need something?" she said.

"I just wanted to talk to you, and I thought I would get a copy of the prophecy while I was at it." When Renyra mentioned the prophecy, her face sobered at once. "I was hoping we could think over it together. Multiple opinions are better than one when it comes to these things, and as we are not making the prophecy public knowledge yet, there are not many elves with whom to discuss it." She cocked her head at Kyna.

Kyna's immediate reaction was to say no. She had little desire to sit with Renyra and play detective over tea, but she forced herself to pause and consider the offer. It was vital that the Council come to the right conclusions about the prophecy. A misinterpretation could have disastrous consequences, and her trust in the mental capacity of the other Council Members was not high, nor was her confidence that they would all take the necessary time to think over the words before their next meeting. If she and Renyra brought their combined interpretations of the prophecy to the Council, it would have more clout than one elf alone.

Kyna smiled again, more genuinely this time.

"Yes, I think that would be a good idea. I'll just make these copies now." She looked down at the handwritten lines on the paper in her hands and glanced at the mystifying machines before her. Heat rose in her skin. "You can wait outside if you want."

The gentle acuity of Renyra's look made Kyna look away.

"Have you used the printers here?" Renyra asked. Before Kyna could lie or shame herself, Renyra continued. "We used to use them years ago to print fliers for our Sira shows when we performed in Tura. They're pretty simple, but I had never seen anything like them before I came here. It took me a while to get it down." She extended a hand to take the paper from Kyna.

With some reluctance, Kyna let her take it, and watched her move gracefully to the nearest machine. The woman moved like a cat—her small feet barely seeming to bear any weight when they touched the ground, and her limbs moving with a fluidity reminiscent of dancing. With skin like smooth chocolate and eyes a brighter green than Kyna had ever seen, the little Fieri held a fascinating beauty. A spark of jealousy awoke in Kyna's chest, and she tried to focus on the levers and moving parts Renyra was pulling and pushing to encase the piece of paper in machinery.

Within minutes, Kyna held ten copies of the cryptic prophecy.

"You can come to dinner tonight," Renrya said. "And we can talk over the prophecy after. Firas and I will not be going on any more stakeouts." A shadow fell over her features and she paused briefly, as though remembering again the trauma of her last night of tracking. Then she blinked and pasted a smile on her face.

"So our evenings are free again."

Kyna's stomach squirmed. She would much rather meet Renyra in the Archives. She had agreed to discuss the prophecy, not to socialize over dinner.

"Come on," Renyra said with a disarming smile. "You have to eat dinner anyway, and Firas is a great cook."

Kyna let out a soft snort, annoyed that Renyra had picked up on her reluctance so easily.

"Ok," she said.

Renyra beamed, and the discomfort in Kyna's stomach intensified.

A loud bang made both elves jump and wheel around to face the door leading from the printing room.

The door swung on its hinges away from the wall, and Liera stood on the threshold, ashen faced. She was clutching three letters in one hand.

"They're dead," Liera said without preamble.

Kyna raised a brow. Renyra's eyes widened in horror.

"Dead?" Renyra's voice was hoarse. "Who?"

"The messenger birds. All of them. Their throats are slit."

"Liera!" a voice echoed down the hall.

Liera's head snapped to the side. Her nostrils flared.

"Rava? What's wrong?"

"I have been trying to find you for hours." A tall Remsgri elf appeared in the doorway, concern in her eyes. "The Rale line out of Tura has been disabled," she said. "We have been trying to fix it, but we don't know what went wrong. It just won't run."

There was no color left in Liera's face to drain, but her skin turned a sort of green as the meaning of the elf's words sank in.

"No Rale lines can get out of the city?" she said in a quiet voice. "Or in?"

Rava shook her head. "The entire system has just failed and won't respond to any stimulus. We have elves out now trying to see how far down the Rale line the failure extends."

Liera nodded slowly, then turned to look at Renyra and Kyna. Her gaze was almost accusatory as she glanced at the copies of the prophecy in Kyna's hands.

"It would appear," she said. "We will not have the help of the other Kindoms after all."

15

EYES IN THE MARSH

Gellion decided that he would never particularly *like* horses, but was pleased to notice that he no longer climbed out of the saddle at the end of each day in pain. Synabra's mind was still a hidden mystery to him, but he was growing more comfortable reacting to her unexpected movements.

If only the humans were so easy.

Haf briefly met Gellion's eye as he passed him an oatcake. The man's gaze held less fear and accusation than it once had, but he was still unwilling to make prolonged eye contact, let alone conversation, with the elves. All the same, Gellion preferred Haf's wariness to Eira's haughty disdain, and even to Talaith's teasing. It did not really matter whether the traders liked Gellion or his brothers. If things went to plan in Suri Ranta, he would never see any of them again. All the same, keeping constant company with dislike, suspicion, and hostility grew wearisome.

"Thank you." Gellion nodded to Haf and took the oatcake—bland, but filling. Breakfast was a meal eaten in the saddle, and Gellion reluctantly placed a foot in a stirrup and climbed onto Synabra's back. The mare jumped and took a step forward as she always did, but Gellion held the reins tight in one hand this time and managed to keep her standing in one place until the rest of the company was ready to move forward.

The morning was warm and muggy. After several days of rolling hills and grassland, torn by winds and dotted with horses and cattle, the land had begun to flatten. Shrubs and scattered trees turned to patchy woods, the golden grass of pastureland to thick greenery and saturated soils. They still passed the occasional farmhouse, but dwellings became fewer and further between, and the air grew heavy with moisture.

"I cannot say I look forward to a week in a marsh," Valder said. "But I welcome the change in scenery. Pastureland is picturesque in its way, but forty hours of riding across it takes away the appeal." He still held tightly to his saddle as his stocky chestnut plodded forward.

"I would look forward to it a lot more if we didn't have to go through a human city," Gellion said. "Tradira and Arvain are as much human society as I need in a lifetime. I do not relish seeing the inside of a third prison."

"Perhaps if you behaved yourself you would not be imprisoned so often." Valder's tone was light, but his words held no humor for Gellion. Of the two times Gellion had been imprisoned by humans, each had been the consequence of his causing the death of a human, directly or otherwise. A cold chill spread through his body, and Gellion fought the anxiety in his chest. Neither occurrence had been his fault, not entirely. Besides, it was the past. There was nothing he could do about it.

Valder seemed to realize the effect of his comment, and the smile slid from his face.

"I'm sorry," he said. "I didn't—"

"If we are imprisoned this time it will be because you said something inappropriate to a nobleman or a king." Gellion raised an eyebrow and let a corner of his mouth curl upward. "You do have a way with words."

Valder laughed, a touch of relief in his eyes. "I did well enough with Eurig. You would still be in Arvain if it weren't for my 'inappropriate' words."

Gellion chuckled.

"I am not so concerned with saying something wrong as with our very presence causing a disturbance," Veldon said. He had ridden up beside Valder. "We have not asked much about the marsh people."

Gellion frowned, realizing Veldon was right. They had used whatever conversation they could drag out of the traders to learn about the Kayda—a much more important subject given their ultimate goal—but they were all but blind entering the marsh. Anxiety crawled under Gellion's skin. He had all but forgotten his fears of treachery by the Dierna, but what better place to close a trap than an unknown and foreign city surrounded by impassable marshland? He shook away his paranoia. Their traveling companions may not be warm and trusting, but somehow Gellion could not picture any of them stooping to a betrayal worthy of Vensure—not even Eira.

"We will ask the traders about Masar tonight," he said. "We still have a few days until we arrive."

Eira had said that Masar was in the exact center of the Great Marsh. The last hours of riding the day before had brought edges of the marshland encroaching upon the land, and Gellion expected the company would be well into its embrace before nightfall, but he doubted they would come across any marsh villages in that time.

"Do you think the marsh people know of the elves?" Veldon said.

"I think it is safest to assume all the humans know about elves at this point," Gellion said darkly. "And that their impression is not favorable."

Anger flashed in Valder's eyes. "This is ridiculous! We have never once given a single human reason to mistrust us, let alone condemn us as unnatural and evil."

"It does seem strange," said Veldon. "Had you never had trouble with Albarad before?"

"No," Gellion said. "It took a while for the humans to get over the shock of our appearance in Tala—it took a while for the elves to get over the same shock—but we have held stable, if not openly friendly, relations ever since." He shook his head. "We never gave much thought to the Albaren. They had their land and we had our corner of unused coast. We both benefited from the trade, and no Albaren king before Naval ever gave us reason to mistrust him."

"What changed?" Valder said.

"I don't know." Gellion had asked himself the same question for weeks and could find no satisfactory answer. As far as he could remember, the elves had offered no insult to the Albaren—no suggestion of threat or ambition, not even an unfavorable trade agreement.

"That is why we never suspected treachery," Gellion said, tightening his hands on the reins. Synabra flicked her ears back. "I should have known when I went to Tradira. Those who weren't using my novelty for political gain looked on me with fear and suspicion—if not loathing. Some were in Naval's pocket from the beginning. It was all a setup to give the humans tangible reason to mistrust the elves, and I never suspected it was more than a terrible accident."

Gellion thought of what Nicabar Arceria had said before he attacked Gellion. *'Demon. Incubus.'* The man had accused Gellion of corrupting the Albaren with faerie magic before coming at him with a dagger. Gellion had assumed the man was mad in his drunken fit, coming up with accusations to fit his fury at finding Gellion alone with his unfaithful wife. He had been wrong.

"No one would have seen that coming," Veldon said gently. "And you said the betrayal was planned long before your trip to Tradira." He frowned. "We think that an elf approached the Albaren—told them about vierstone. Could they have had something to do with Naval's sudden change in loyalties?"

Gellion raised his eyebrows. "Convinced the Albaren that the elves were a threat you mean?"

"Why though?" Valder shook his head. "What elf would betray their own kin like that?"

"What elf would destroy an entire city and its vierstone?" Veldon said reasonably. "If this was the same elf, I think it quite possible they would have done anything to achieve their ends, whatever those may be."

Gellion shifted uncomfortably in his saddle.

To what end? To seek revenge on an entire race that had disowned him—denied him vierstone and tried to sentence him to death? But why Daro? Tura was where Kaelo should have centered his vengeance if that was the case.

"It is safe to assume we have been betrayed at least twice, if not more," Gellion said. "In that case, the reasoning behind the Albaren's betrayal is moot. All of this happened because it was meant to happen. Someone—or multiple someones—fixed events to suit their purpose, and that purpose is likely continuing on in Faeran while we slog across this marsh countless miles and a sea away."

Synabra snorted and tossed her head, flashing her wild eyes back at Gellion. He loosened his grip on the reins guiltily and tried to focus on the path ahead of him. It was long, and the end seemed too distant to exist, but it was his only way back. He pressed his heels to Synabra's sides.

By midday, a myriad of still, reflective pools had begun to weave through the landscape, creating misshapen islands of knee high grass. Any trees or shrubs had dwindled to reeds and rushes, and the low hum of insects hung in the air.

Gellion had just begun to wonder how the ever softening road would navigate the marsh, when he saw a raised structure above the water coming nearer with each step. He squinted, trying to decipher the shape.

"What is that?" he said. The elves rode close to the traders now that the road had narrowed and begun to twist around the pools.

"The Marsh Road," said Talaith.

"How does it work?" said Veldon.

Talaith flashed him a smile. "It is made of wood—great, thick beams that float. Each set is lashed loosely to a post so that the road can rise and fall, bend and tilt, to accommodate the changing waters."

"Impressive," Valder said.

As they neared the start of the path, Gellion had to agree with Valder. He had expected the wooden 'road' to be thick with algae, rotting away in places and stained or broken in others. Instead, the beams were a dark wood—nearly black—that was smooth and cut with precision. Each plank fit snuggly next to its neighbors and seemed to be in excellent repair. A soft creaking mingled with the buzzing insects.

The first of their horses was approaching the wooden platform now

—Eira's palomino. The animal did not seem fazed by its surroundings at all and made for the step up with a bored expression. Gellion expected these horses had made this journey many times before.

The palomino had just raised its mud caked foot to step onto the wooden beams when it shied back suddenly. Gellion took in a sharp breath.

A man had appeared next to the path—no, two men. Gellion looked around, trying to see where they could have hidden, when a third and a fourth man stood, emerging from the marsh grass like water snakes. Two of them carried slender bows. Another a spear. The man nearest the path stood unarmed, but a knife hung at his belt.

All had red-brown skin and hair so black it seemed to absorb the weak sunlight that had managed to penetrate through the wispy clouds. The men were slight of build, but muscle showed beneath the skin of their bare arms.

"What business do you have in the marsh?" the man with the dagger said, looking at Eira with a blank expression. He stood with his feet in the water, the edges of boots visible above its surface. Light linen hung from his shoulders with a sash tied at his waist, and the same material came over his head like a tight hood.

Eira had quickly calmed her horse and sat with a straight back.

"We are traders from the Elder Clan of Diernas. We have business in Masar." She produced a rolled piece of paper from her saddle bags and extended it toward them.

The man stepped forward warily to take the paper. His dark eyes scanned the page, then moved over the company of riders, first taking in the three humans and their pack horses, clearly laden with trade goods. Gellion tightened his grip on the reins, his fingers twitching to grab the hunting knife tied to his saddle. Were these people official guardsmen of the marsh people, or a band hoping to rob the unwary at the borders of their territory? The other three men had not lowered their weapons.

"You are all traders?" The man's gaze rested on Gellion, his eyes narrowed in suspicion.

A muscle twitched in Eira's jaw, but her expression remained steady.

"Not all. These three are going to Suri Ranta and are accompanying us for the journey."

"Who are they?"

"Guests of Lawgiver Eurig," Eira said.

"They do not look Dierna."

"They aren't."

"We do not allow strangers to enter our lands."

Eira let out an impatient breath. "They are emissaries of a foreign nation. We are escorting them to Suri Ranta. They are under our protection," she paused, as though the words caused her pain. "And they are our responsibility. They will not cause trouble in Masar."

Gellion tried to look unassuming, turning his eyes down, but to the side he could see Veldon staring at the man with wide eyes. The marsh man looked from Gellion to Valder to Veldon.

"What foreign nation?" he said.

Gellion clenched his teeth, his pulse quickening.

Just let us through.

Eira looked as uncomfortable as Gellion felt. She looked to the side, as though trying to think of a better answer, then said, "They are elves."

Grips on bows and spears tightened. The head interrogator's gaze sharpened on the elves.

"Elves?" he said slowly. "Is this a joke?" He whipped his head back to Eira, uncertainty and anger in his face.

"It is not a joke," Gellion said. All eyes turned to him. "We are elves from Daro—a city north of Albarad. We have peaceful business with the Kayda, and Lawgiver Eurig was kind enough to send us an escort. We do not know these lands. We mean no harm to the people of the marsh and are only passing through."

The man did not answer, but looked at Eira, awaiting her confirmation of Gellion's words.

"We will not let them out of our sight," she said.

All four marsh men exchanged looks. One or two made gestures Gellion could not interpret, then the leader spoke again.

"They will carry no weapons. They will stay with you at all times."

Eira nodded and looked to the elves. Reluctantly, Gellion untied the hunting knife and sheath from his saddle and moved Synabra forward to hand the weapon to Eira. Valder and Veldon did likewise.

"Enter then," the marsh man said, assuming a formal stance. "And may the truth be in your hand."

"In our hearts and minds," Eira answered.

Some of the hesitance left the man's face at her words, and he stepped back to allow them passage.

Gellion could feel the eyes of the marsh men boring into his back as he coaxed his mare onto the wooden planks of the marsh road. The men had lowered their weapons, but had not released their grips on them.

"Pleasant folk," Valder said when they had put some distance between themselves and the marsh guards.

"Shh," Eira hissed. She stopped her horse and turned to face the elves. "Cover your heads. There is material in your bags. You should have done it before we entered the marsh, but I did not think the guards would stop us so far from Masar."

"They do not seem keen on strangers," Veldon said, more quietly this time. He opened his saddle bag and began to look through it.

"Will there be trouble?" Gellion cursed himself for not asking about the marsh people sooner. They had walked into a new nation with no knowledge of its people or its customs. But Eira should have warned them without provocation. It was her job to guide them, after all.

A job she hardly relishes.

He needed to be more careful.

"Not if you keep your heads down," Eira said. "The Aektar are trustworthy in their way, but they are strict and proud. They keep to themselves and are wary of outsiders. But Masar is a big place, and our business is with traders, not high ranking officials."

"Do they know of the elves?" Veldon asked as he wrapped a linen sheet over his head.

Eira shrugged. "Probably. Everyone on Tala has heard of the elves by now, though the further you get from Albarad, the more the stories become faerie tales. Many may not believe you exist at all."

"That would be preferable to believing the Albaren's tales," Gellion muttered.

Eira gave him a considering look, but said nothing.

"Why do they wear these?" Valder asked, struggling to wrap his head as gracefully as Veldon had.

"Insects," Haf said.

Gellion raised an eyebrow.

"You will see soon," Eira said.

Gellion did see. As the afternoon wore on, the constant buzzing of the marsh increased in pitch, and insects ranging in size from tiny gnats to lanky flies the size of his palm started flying around his head. He snorted as a gnat tried to fly up his nose, and pulled the fabric up to cover his face.

"Most of them thin out in the evening," Talaith said. "They like the heat." Her brown eyes shone through the slit in her own head covering, and her voice was muffled through the fabric so Gellion had to strain to hear her.

Gellion found himself acutely missing the solid road and open air of Diernas. The wooden path beneath them swayed and bobbed under the horses' feet in dizzying monotony, yet it had a lulling effect that made Gellion hard-pressed to keep a sharp focus on his surroundings. It did not help that he had to keep his eyes constantly squinted to avoid flinching at the flying insects. All the same, he tried to observe the marsh around him. He saw no signs of other people, though once or twice he thought he saw the outline of a building or an animal in the distance. Twice he saw what appeared to be logs sticking out of the water, but when the horses neared, they sank below the water with a subtle splash. Gellion thought he saw the gleam of eyes.

"There are a few villages throughout the marsh," Talaith said when Gellion asked about the emptiness. "But most of the people are centered in Masar, or the area directly surrounding it. You'll find the odd house out here, though. Farmers and trappers."

"Farmers?" Valder said, surprised. "What do they farm in this?"

"The Aektar call them cultivators," Talaith said. "They tend patches of wild rice and encourage its growth in other areas. Then there are the herders of water buffalo and ducks. Some people follow their charges around the marsh, though others live in the outer circles of Masar. The fishermen and herbalists live in the outer circles as well, and go out into the marsh during the day to do their work."

Gellion listened with fascination. It was a life so vastly different than any he had ever seen that he could hardly fathom it. The land did have a sort of beauty to it. The patches of grass cut off evenly into the pools of water to form a perfect, globular patchwork. The water was so still that it reflected every cloud in the sky, taking on hues of purple and pink when the sun began to set. Gellion sighed in relief as the number of insects lessened to the point that he could pull the linen from his mouth and nose.

"Where do we stop for the night?" Veldon asked uncertainly. The road had wound through the marsh uninterrupted since they set foot on it hours before. They could not very well stop in the middle of the path. Gellion had wondered the same thing himself, but assumed they would just have to make camp in one of the soggy patches of grass.

"There is a waypoint up ahead," said Eira.

"The waypoints are mostly for the nomadic herders," Talaith explained. "Or for those whose fishing or hunting keep them in the marshes past dark."

"Will there be others there?" Gellion asked, suddenly wary.

Talaith just shrugged. "They won't bother us."

They arrived at the waypoint just before dark. The floating logs extended to either side of the road into a vast square platform. Raised pits of stone were scattered over the space, and a series of wooden lean-tos lined the furthest sides. A flickering glow emitted from one of the stone pits in the far left corner.

"There is dry wood in the lean-tos," Eira said. "Make a fire for dinner, then choose a shelter for the night." She eyed the elves. "Stay on the platform until morning." Dismounting, she led her palomino and the grey packhorse to one of the shelters.

Spending the night under a lean-to on a dry platform was better than Gellion's expectation of lying in tall, wet grass, but sleep was still difficult to come by. Though the buzzing of insects had died down, the sound was now replaced with the much louder voices of frogs. By midnight, Gellion was cursing every one of them and wished he could shout them into silence. There was only one other person using the platform, and they had made their camp on the opposite side from Gellion's company, but Gellion still thought his own companions would not take kindly to his shouting.

After another hour of fitful half dreams, Gellion rose with an urge he suddenly realized was rather problematic. He was surrounded by water, yet the thought of standing on the edge of a public platform to relieve himself was distasteful even in the middle of the night.

With a sigh, Gellion walked onto the platform and looked for a place to cross into a patch of grass. He found one quickly enough and leaped from the platform onto soggy ground, then waded into the grass. Within moments, the vegetation had soaked his pants past the knee.

Just when Gellion was about to return to the platform, he heard a faint rustling in the grass to his right.

Probably more frogs.

He wished he had a weapon. A few less frogs was better than nothing.

The dock was in sight, and Gellion took a few more steps toward it, but then froze, the hair on his arms standing up. The rustling had come again, and he had the distinct feeling of being watched.

His moment of hesitation saved him.

Right where he had been about to stop and leap to the platform, a huge and glistening shape exploded into existence. Gellion cried out and jumped backward, but the soft ground slowed his force, and he felt the heavy impact of something alive slap into his legs. His knees buckled, and he fought to keep his feet, scrambling backward into the grass. Two shining eyes followed his movement, and he saw a long, slender mouth gape open to reveal rows of jagged teeth.

Terror pulsed through Gellion's veins. He had no weapon. He could not run. He could hardly even see.

The thing came at him again with astonishing speed, and Gellion tried to roll out of the way, but the stiff grass resisted him, and he moved as in slow motion. He saw the glisten of pearly teeth and felt a sharp pain in his leg as he pulled his knees up to his chest. With a gasp, he kicked out with his other leg and felt his foot crash onto a slippery head. The beast hissed in rage and lashed its tail, which was somehow still in the water two lengths away.

Gellion continued to scramble backward, trying to push himself to his feet as he did so, but everything around him was too soft and slippery. His hands sank behind him in the mud and his scrambling only seemed to bury him deeper. He saw the beast's eyes lock on him again, saw the impossibly long face open its maw, then there was another shape in the darkness—a gleam of silver.

The creature screamed, its mouth still gaping open. It twisted and lashed from side to side, but the figure above it just pushed the shining metal deeper into its back. The thing's struggles faded to twitches, then it was still.

Gellion lay in the mud, propped on his elbows with his heart beating out of his chest and his leg burning.

"I told you not to leave the platform at night." Eira heaved her sword out of the monster and looked at the black blood on it with distaste.

16

DINNER FOR THREE

Kyna took a deep breath and stared at the door in front of her. She longed to just turn around and leave.

It's for the greater good. The sooner the Council figures out this stupid prophecy, the sooner this can end.

Kyna balled her hand into a fist and knocked on the door. Muffled voices and footsteps answered immediately from within the house, and the door swung open to reveal a beaming Renyra.

Kyna grimaced in greeting.

"Great." Renyra motioned for Kyna to come inside. "The food is almost ready."

The apartment was pleasantly cool after the heat of the evening outside, with drawn curtains and dim lamps that cast a calming atmosphere over the room. Though she would still rather be in the Archives, Kyna could hardly keep her mouth from watering at the onslaught of aromas that assaulted her. Spices hung heavy in the air, undercut by the richer tones of oil and bread. Kyna had never smelled anything like it.

Renyra's willowy husband stood in the kitchen, stirring the contents of a pan that sizzled and spat with each stroke of the spoon.

He turned big eyes on Kyna and smiled, though the expression seemed to bear as much sadness as welcome. Was the Morcani elf ever happy?

"Please sit," Renrya said, taking a seat herself at the little table just outside the kitchen. It bore three wide plates and a pitcher of water, condensation frosting the outside of the glass.

Kyna drew out a chair and lowered herself stiffly. She glanced to the kitchen, wishing the elf—Firas was it?—would hurry with the food. Renyra was watching Kyna with those overly bright eyes. Kyna pretended to observe the apartment with what she hoped appeared polite interest.

Renyra poured water into the glasses on the table, then sat down heavily.

"I can't believe Kaelo killed those messenger birds," she said. "And what could he have done to the Rale line that all the experts in the city can't fix it? Then again, I shouldn't be surprised by that. Given what he can do to stone and vierstone, I suppose metal wouldn't be much harder." She sighed and leaned back in her chair, sipping her glass of water. Even when she relaxed, her shoulders remained square, her posture as upright as Liera's, but somehow lacking the tense judgment.

"What I can't understand is how he did it so quickly," she said. "Liera only told us hours before that she was going to send messages to the other Kindoms. How could Kaelo have learned about it so fast?"

"Maybe he was expecting it," said Kyna, relieved that Renyra had not tried to engage in small talk, but gone straight to more interesting matters. "You heard the Rale Master. She had been trying to find Liera for hours. The Rale could have been down since morning, and I doubt those birds are used often."

"They must have been fed in the morning, though," said Renyra. "You may be right about the Rale, but if you ask me, those birds must have died during late morning or early afternoon." She looked sharply at Kyna, the light of an idea in her eyes. "Do you think he could have a spy? Kaelo I mean."

Kyna smirked. "I find it unlikely that any elf in Tura would help Kaelo. I expect he moves about the city during the day, wearing his tunic or otherwise veiled from prying eyes. He must be keeping close tabs on Liera, though. Maybe he saw her writing letters after the meeting."

Renyra nodded, her brow furrowed. "He could have."

For a moment, the only sound was the sizzling from the kitchen. Firas remained silent, but was obviously listening to their conversation.

"What I want to know," Renyra said. "Is what Liera is going to do now."

"Probably hold another meeting." Kyna rolled her eyes. "Though I don't see the point. She listens to no one."

"She has to now!" Renyra's eyes blazed. "Everything she has suggested has failed. Surely she must listen to what we have to say?"

"That would imply Liera is a reasonable person," Kyna muttered.

"I'm sure she's a good leader," Renyra said. "I think it's just Kaelo that's making her so unreasonable. I can't imagine what it must be like, confronting her son after all these years."

Kyna thought of the look on Liera's face when she had seen her son that night in the street, and of what she had said to him.

"I can't imagine what it must be like having Liera as a mother," Kyna said.

Renyra's mouth twitched.

"The food is ready," Firas said.

Renyra jumped to her feet and took her own and Kyna's plates before Kyna had time to react.

"Stay there and I'll fill the plates," she said.

When Renyra set a pile of steaming food before her, Kyna observed it with wary interest. Half the plate was covered by a sort of spongy flatbread, with steamed vegetables on one side and what appeared to be bright orange mush on the other. The spicy smell made Kyna's eyes water.

"It's a Fieri dish," said Renyra. "One of my mother's favorites back home. Those are a type of bean we grow in the grasslands." She pointed to the orange mush. "It was no easy task, finding them in Tura, but Firas surprised me with them a few days ago." She cast a doe-eyed look at her husband. Kyna looked down at her food, a heat that had nothing to do with the spicy food spreading over her skin.

Cautiously she took a spoonful of the bean mixture and put it into her mouth. Her eyes widened. She had never tasted so much flavor in one mouthful of anything. The mix of strange spices was powerful, but not unpleasant, and Kyna took another bite, this time tearing off a piece of the spongy bread, which proved slightly sour, but was a nice contrast to the spice of the beans.

Kyna was shocked by how enjoyable the dinner was. The food was excellent, and she hardly had to speak a word the whole time. Renyra kept up a nearly ceaseless conversation all on her own, talking about everything from her home culture to the recent reunion of her Sira troupe. Kyna was grateful not to have to talk and found the conversation strangely comforting.

"Remsgraen is amazing," Renyra said after washing down the last of her bread. "An entire city built in the biggest trees you've ever seen, with vines as thick as two elves. Absolutely everything was run by magnets—the Remsgri invented almost all the technology to do with magnets, you know. Have you been outside of Tura? To other parts of Faeran?"

Kyna looked up, startled by the question. "Yes," she said hesitantly. "I am not from Tura, actually." She looked back to her plate, now cleared of food.

"Oh," Renyra said, clearly unperturbed by Kyna's unhelpful answer. "Have you been to Tura before?"

"I visited once before."

"It's one of my favorite cities, besides Telem Fier."

"And Remsgraen?" Firas asked with a gentle smile.

Renyra shot him a withering look with narrowed eyes, but there was a hint of a grin about her lips.

"They are called the Great Cities for a reason. It's not my fault I find all of them wonderful except the one in which I found you."

Kyna raised an eyebrow at the jab, but Firas took Renyra's retort in good stride, chuckling softly.

"We got him out of Morcanan as quickly as we could," Renyra explained to Kyna with a wink. "Living in cold caves surrounded by neutral colors will take its toll on anyone."

"Just because it is not to your taste does not make it any less impressive," Firas said. "Those caves are works of genius, with some of the best engineering in all of Faeran. There would be no indoor heating systems if not for those caves."

Renyra shrugged. "Live in the grasslands and you don't need indoor heating."

Firas rolled his eyes, but his soft smile remained.

Kyna watched the two with some confusion. They were complete opposites, and clearly had a fair share of differing opinions, yet even as they argued, each looked at the other as though the world revolved around each other. Kyna shifted in her chair, discomfited by a strange lurching in her chest. She shook her head and pressed her wrist to her thigh. The cold stone sent goosebumps up her arm, but the feeling in her chest remained. She frowned.

"I'm sorry," Renyra laughed. "I invited you for a nice dinner and a discussion about prophecies and here we are embarrassing you." She stood and bent over the table with outstretched hands. "I will take these plates away and we can get to business."

Kyna took a deep breath and pulled her copy of the prophecy from her pocket.

Finally, something practical.

Yet she was strangely reluctant to leave behind the dinner of casual conversation. The realization made her distinctly uncomfortable, and she slapped her piece of paper on the table with more force than she intended.

"Sorry," she muttered, glancing at Firas, who smiled. This only unsettled her more, and she fixed her eyes on the words before her until Renyra returned to the table.

"Here." Renyra took one of the copies she had made of the prophecy from the kitchen counter, then walked to a nearby shelf to retrieve a small notebook. She lay both on the table in front of herself and Firas.

"Now, I've been thinking over this a lot the last few days, and have made some notes, though it's much easier now that I have a copy of the actual words." She opened the notebook to some scribbled writings and skimmed them.

"I think the first half of the prophecy is fairly straightforward. It's only telling us what will happen—what is happening that is. 'The grounds will shake, the cities flood," she quoted. "'The life reversed will not come back. The source of darkness, lone and kin, will bring the monsters up again.' All of that makes sense. We've seen the monsters, and the earthquakes, and the 'flooding,'" she said the words in quotations, "of Daro. I'm thinking maybe the 'stone stained redder than their blood' might simply refer to death. Many elves died in the battle."

Firas had been listening to Renyra with a hand over his chin, deep in thought.

"But what about 'the life reversed?'"

Renyra puckered her brow, looking back at the words.

"The vierstone," Kyna said. "Don't the elves call it 'lifestone?' The reverse of life is death, right? So it must refer to the death of vierstone."

Renyra stared at her. "Yes," she said excitedly. "Of course. That must be it. See?" She turned a smug grin on Firas. "I told you this would work. We've already solved the first half of the prophecy."

Firas nodded obligingly.

"But then there's the second half." All smugness disappeared from Renyra's face. "The half that's more important—that could tell us how to stop Kaelo." She picked up the prophecy and read, word for word: "The stone that dies will not return, but safe from death is stone that burns. From which he hates his doom shall rise, a weapon forged from his despise. The swords that shape and cool too late, will drown in ash, bereaved their fate."

She looked between Firas and Kyna. "The first line is obvious, though hardly comforting. The vierstone that dies is gone forever. And the rest of the poem supposedly tells us how Kaelo can be stopped." Renrya fell silent then, frowning over her notes.

"We should go in order," said Kyna. "'Safe from death is stone that burns.' It sounds like vierstone that 'burns' cannot be destroyed."

"But what does that mean?" said Renyra in an exasperated voice. "Stone doesn't burn."

"Not as wood or cloth burns," Firas said. "But it does burn. Go to any forge and you will see stone, glass, and metal glowing red hot, sometimes with flames on the surface."

Renyra's eyes widened. "You think it means to literally place vierstone in fire?"

"Well that would certainly keep Kaelo from touching it," Kyna said with a snort.

"No, you're right!" Renyra said to Kyna's quip. "He has to *touch* vierstone to destroy it." She shook her head. "It's so simple. We keep him from touching it and he can't destroy it."

"But setting eternal flame to our cities hardly seems a reasonable solution," said Firas. His voice was serious, but Kyna could detect the flicker of a smile behind his eyes.

"Well." Renyra chewed her lip, clearly thinking hard. "It's too late for the city anyway. Maybe it refers to something else."

"There is plenty of vierstone not in the foundations of cities," Kyna said. "The earrings, but also stores in crafting workshops, and the odd item crafted of vierstone itself—statues, or religious objects."

Renyra was nodding. "That's true." Her face fell. "Do you think all the elves will have to take out their earrings to protect them?"

Kyna noticed that Renyra had not yet replaced her own vierstone earring. With the infrequency of elf births, Kyna imagined new earrings were not routinely available.

"No," Firas said. There was sympathy in his eyes and his arm moved below the table toward Renyra. "Kaelo was only able to destroy yours by touching you. He can't possibly do that to every elf in the city. I think the earrings are safest as they are."

Renyra nodded sadly.

"What about the next part?" Firas said when Renyra did not resume the subject. "It speaks of a weapon—a literal weapon from the sound of it, unless the swords it refers to later are metaphorical."

"Half the prophecies are metaphorical," Kyna said, raising her eyes to the ceiling. "But in this case, I think not. It seems straightforward to me—we must forge a sword from his 'despise.'"

"A sword?" Renyra said incredulously. "How could a sword stop Kaelo? We've already tried to stop him with javelins, arrows, and daggers. His armor deflects them all like toothpicks, and that's assuming we get a clear shot at him in the first place."

"What is Kaelo's despise?" Firas said.

No one spoke.

Kyna looked between the two, her foot starting to tap of its own accord. She didn't want to be *too* helpful. The elves had to come to their conclusions on their own. Did they have to be so maddeningly slow?

Renyra sighed. "We will come back to that," she said when the silence brought no answers. "What about the last bit?"

"Seems as straightforward as the beginning," Kyna said with a shrug. "If we don't make this weapon in time, it will be too late. Kaelo will go on to do worse things and we will have lost our chance."

A flicker of fear danced behind Renyra's eyes. "We've already waited so long. What if 'too late' refers to Kaelo destroying all the vierstone in Tura?"

"I do not think it prudent to dwell on that," said Firas. "For all we know, it could have referred to Daro's destruction, and we found the prophecy too late. We must proceed forward as though we still have time, or else all hope is lost." He paused. "According to this, that is."

"But Daro didn't drown in ash," Renrya said. "It can't have meant Daro."

"Whatever it means," said Kyna. "We had best avoid it. There are two important pieces to this—how to defeat Kaelo, and how to keep vierstone safe in the meantime."

Renyra let out a breath and nodded. "Right. I think we have a promising lead on the vierstone. I need more time to think on the sword. It would be helpful to have more opinions there." The hard sheen of resolve that Kyna was growing used to seeing in Renyra's eyes shone through. "We will bring this before the Council. Liera said herself that she would allow any elf with thoughts on the prophecy to share them. Hopefully Liera distributed the copies of the prophecy to the other members by now and they will have thought over it as well."

"If Liera hasn't called a meeting by late morning tomorrow, I will go to her myself," Renyra said. "Though I can't imagine she won't, with the messenger birds and the Rale today." She looked to Kyna, the fierce determination in her face fading to a smile. "I think we're making real progress on this. You have some good ideas. I'm glad you came."

Kyna clenched her jaw against the heat that threatened to rise in her face.

"The dinner was—good," she said awkwardly, then cleared her

throat. "If that is as far as we are getting with the prophecy tonight, I should be going on my way."

"Of course." Renyra stood to escort Kyna to the door. "You're welcome here any time," she said as Kyna stepped over the threshold.

The comfort Kyna had begun to feel with the little Fieri evaporated. She shifted uncomfortably and attempted a half smile before nodding and turning away.

"Good night."

She could feel Renyra's thoughtful eyes on her back until she reached the street.

Kyna did not go on her usual walk of the city that evening. Instead, she sat in her rooms, staring around at the unfamiliar furniture and artwork. The place reminded her of the temporary housing in which she had lived in Daro when the Domes of Rhelyon had collapsed from earthquake damage. Her original rooms in that city had been much nicer than either of the two accommodations that came after, with lofty ceilings and broad windows overlooking the sea. She had liked Daro. It had been hot, and there had been too many elves, but now that she was in Tura, those problems seemed laughable. An uncomfortable longing for the place welled within her. She had only been in Daro a few months, and had never meant to stay there. Why then, did she mourn for its loss? Why could she not stop thinking about it?

Spices lingered at the back of Kyna's throat so she smelled them each time she breathed in. She was pleasantly full, and pleased by how the prophecy discussion had gone, but she could not seem to settle into contentment. There was a strange tightness to her chest, almost an anxiety.

She was restless, but did not want to leave the apartment. She began to pace.

Things were moving too slowly. There was too much waiting. Too much uncertainty. What would Liera do now? Would she ever listen to the prophecy? What would happen if she didn't, and the Council never accepted it?

Kyna sighed in frustration and ran a hand through her hair. The hand froze at the back of her head as a painfully sharp image of Gellion performing the same gesture flashed into her mind. She clenched her fist at the roots of her hair, hoping the pain would overcome the memory, but it didn't work. She smashed her wrist against her leg, but the cool stone still only brought a slight chill to her skin.

What's wrong with it? What's wrong with me?

She began to pace again.

A broiling heat was beginning in her middle and spreading throughout her body. She wanted it all to be over. She had not meant to be pulled into this so deeply. She wished she had never come to Tura, that she had never met Renyra, never met Gellion.

The pain came again, this time deep in her chest. To her horror, she felt a sharp prickling at the back of her eyes.

No!

She kicked a chair and sent it sprawling away from the table with a satisfying crash, then stood still with eyes closed until her heartbeat slowed. Taking a breath, she pressed her wrist into her leg again. This time, the pain ebbed. Her mind cleared.

Relief washed through her body.

She wouldn't be in Tura much longer. For better or for worse, its fate would come soon, and then she would never see any of these elves again. She would make sure of it.

17

STONE THAT BURNS

Renyra glided along the Rale with a fluttering chest. It never seemed to stop fluttering these days. If she wasn't anxious over the fate of Tura and the elves as a whole, she was nervous about the next Turi Council meeting, worried about her vierstone earring, or remembering the all-consuming terror that had washed through her at Kaelo's touch. She had told no one but Firas the full extent of what had happened that night. Even telling her husband about the unreasonable fear and thoughts that had gone through her head had made her feel foolish. No matter how ridiculous it sounded, she knew Kaelo had caused all she had felt that night. He had somehow used her own mind against her, and though the fear she had felt at his touch may have been of Kaelo's fabrication, the fear that remained from the memories was very real.

Unexpected touches from other elves made her jump, nightmares haunted her rest, and her grief over lost home and friends grew all the more acute. Her life in Daro seemed absurdly simple now. How could her greatest worry have ever been whether aphids would infest the greenhouse tomatoes? And how much easier would opposing Kaelo be if Dulon or Gellion were here?

The latter thought had grown in Renyra's mind more and more as

Tura's situation became increasingly desperate. Whatever she had told Kyna, Renyra thought Liera was handling her job terribly, allowing pride and fear to rule her decisions at the expense of all the Turi. Would she have listened better to the experience and authority of Dulon or Gellion? What would they have thought of this prophecy?

Renyra's heart lurched. The prophecy. Even after all this time, she did not know how she felt about the ominous words and warnings Kyna had brought before them. Renyra had always had great respect for the elven prophets, though most were now dead, and those few still living had not reported visions or dreams for many centuries. All the same, Renyra could not shake the feelings of doubt that prickled at her conscience each time she read through this prophecy. Had it truly been forgotten until now—passed off as another relic of the Great War? Stranger still was that Kyna had been the one to find it. Renyra was growing to like the woman, even with her bluntness and penchant for sarcasm, but she did not strike her as a theological scholar.

Riu uses all in his own ways.

Unnamed doubt still lingered within her, but what else could the elves do? They had tried ambushing Kaelo, confronting him with a planned meeting, tracking him, shooting him, and capturing him. Nothing worked. Not only that, but nothing had come close to working, and now he had cut them off from the other Kindoms. The prophecy was the elves' only option, and despite its almost too perfect timing and unclear instructions, it may be what would save them all.

The Central Tower loomed before her as she dismounted her levit board and walked with her head held high across the square. As she and Kyna had predicted, Liera had called another meeting today, the morning after the destruction of the Rale. They would let her start the meeting her way, but whether the Lady of Tura wanted to or not, the Council would discuss the prophecy.

Renyra almost drew back when she walked into the meeting room. Liera looked terrible. Her colorless face seemed almost translucent—except for the dark circles under her eyes. She was dressed in silks as beautiful as ever, but her shoulders sagged under their weight, as though all of her troubles were woven into the fabric. The woman barely acknowledged Renyra's presence.

Kyna was already in the room and gave Renyra a subtle smile as she sat down. Renyra put as much confidence as she could into her reciprocation.

"You all know the situation," Liera said as Dorian wandered in just past the start time. "I doubt there is an elf in the city who doesn't know by now. We are cut off from the other Kindoms—from the rest of the Turi for that matter."

"If we had sent for help sooner, this wouldn't have happened," Tenille said in a cool voice, seeming unable to restrain herself from interrupting. Several nods met these words, but no one else spoke.

Liera looked at Tenille and flexed her fingers, but only said, "No, perhaps not." She looked to the rest of the Council again and continued. "We have no messenger birds and no Rale, but we are not walled into this city. I propose that we still send our messages."

Several eyebrows rose.

"We did not always have the Rale system. Throughout the Great War, we relied on boats and horses when birds were not available. We will resort to them again."

"You don't think Kaelo will be able to stop a ship leaving the harbor if he can shut down the entire Rale line?" Alos said.

"I am not proposing that we sail," said Liera.

Alos opened his mouth, then closed it again in confusion.

"I agree," Liera said. "Kaelo will try to stop any efforts we make to escape this city. There remains only a small portion of Tura with vierstone in the foundations, and when he has destroyed them, he will move on to whatever the next stage of his plan is. I very much doubt if he wants the interference of the other Kindoms just now."

Renyra noticed with a sinking stomach how Liera now spoke of Kaelo's plans as immanent fact, unstoppable and unchangeable.

"That is why we send elves by stealth," she continued. "The Fieri are not much further by river than they are by sea. We will send elves up the Orhiri by night. They will go to Rone on Lake Orhirion, and from there, messages can be sent to Telem Fier and further to Remsgraen. As for the Morcani, we will have to send elves by horse—at least until they find a section of working Rale line further north."

"It is not a bad plan," Reanan said slowly. "But even if it succeeds, it could take weeks for anyone from the other Kindoms to arrive in Tura. Their assistance could be moot by then."

A chill silence overtook the room.

"It is all we can do," said Liera. "At this point, I do not expect any aid from the other Kindoms to save Tura from what Kaelo has planned, but it is still vital the rest of the elves know."

"So what is it you are proposing we do in the meantime?" Tornac said. "Sit back with a glass of wine and watch what Kaelo will do next?"

"We will continue our efforts to capture him," said Liera.

Renyra saw Kyna sit up, purpose in her face. Renyra nodded, ready to pounce, but then Liera went on.

"And we will consider this prophecy." Both skepticism and resignation were evident in Liera's words, but Renyra raised her brows in surprise all the same. Kyna looked almost impressed by Liera's show of reason and nodded in approval.

"I believe," Kyna said. "We have some leads there." She looked to Renyra.

Every elf in the room turned to stare at them.

"Go on," said Liera.

After a glance at Kyna, Renyra began. "The prophecy is split into two parts more or less: the first half, which tells us what is already happening, and the second half, which tells us how to stop it."

"And the third part," Kyna said. "Which tells us we're all doomed if we don't follow the second."

"Yes," Renrya said. "Thank you, Kyna. There are two pieces of that last part that we need to focus on: 'safe from death is stone that burns,' and 'a weapon forged from his despise.' One tells us how to keep the remaining vierstone safe, the other how to defeat Kaelo."

The Council Members were watching Renyra with stunned expressions. Renyra had the suspicion that Kyna was right, and few of them had given the prophecy much thought.

"I agree," said Tenille unexpectedly. "And we should focus on saving the remaining vierstone first."

"By burning it?" Alos looked like she had suggested eating the vierstone.

"By melting it," Tenille said.

Renyra blinked in surprise. "Melting it?" she said.

"Kaelo must touch vierstone to destroy it," Tenille said. "So melting the stone renders Kaelo incapable of destroying it. There is little we can do for the foundations of the city at this point, but we should consolidate the rest of the vierstone from workshops, homes, anything that is left, into one place and melt it down."

Of course—melting.

"Yes," Renyra said. "That's it!"

"In the forges?" Liera said. "We would have to keep a constant fire, a constant guard." She frowned. "The elves we took the vierstone from wouldn't be happy about it. Still, it is not a bad idea." She sat up straighter. "I will speak to Alsena—tell her to alert the guilds and the forge masters. If we are to do this, it must be done as quickly as possible."

"I cannot see how it could hurt," said Reanan. "If it works, we have a safe supply of vierstone. If it doesn't—well, I expect Kaelo would have gotten to it anyway."

"I agree," said Tornac.

Alos, Saethir, and Dorian gave their approval. Kyna nodded.

"Very well," said Liera. "We will begin the process immediately. I will have Coren divert some guards to the task, and Alsena will have the forges prepared. Did you have anything further to add?"

Renyra started slightly when she realized Liera was talking to her.

"Oh, well we came to a similar conclusion as Tenille for the first part. As for the second, we are still uncertain. It sounds as though the elves must forge a weapon—a sword. But something forged 'from his despise' could mean anything. An elf or a principle."

"Or a substance," Kyna said.

"Or," Tornac said. "It could mean a weapon forged by Kaelo himself. Forged *from his despise*—from his hatred. Maybe we must use his own weapon against him."

"Which one?" Alos scoffed. "His impenetrable armor or his dark powers?"

"Tornac could be right," Dorian said. "It would not be the first time an enemy's own power brought his downfall."

"Are we to wait until Kaelo spells his own doom?" Tenille said. "If we had the ability to take any of Kaelo's power, we would have captured or killed him by now."

"We might be able to use his power against him," said Dorian. "Force him to bring a building or a cliffside down on himself."

"Kaelo is too intelligent to get into that kind of situation," Liera said softly. "Whatever he is doing, he has thought it through thoroughly. Every move is planned. Unless we can find the source of his power, I cannot see how to use it against him."

"So what does it mean?" Reanan said. "What does Kaelo hate? What does he despise?"

Kyna's eyes darted toward Liera.

Liera.

Renyra formed her next words carefully. "What if it refers to an elf? An elf who is destined to make the weapon that spells his downfall?"

"An elf whom he despises?" Reanan said with confusion.

But other elves around the table were beginning to turn their eyes to Liera.

"Me," Liera said in a deadpan voice.

"It is possible," Renyra said softly. "You are a highly skilled metalworker, and you have a ... a connection to Kaelo."

A painful silence followed these words.

Liera lowered her eyes to the table, the rest of her body still as stone.

"And what sort of sword am I to forge that would stop Kaelo where others have not?"

Renyra had no answer to that. She could not understand how any physical weapon could be the answer to Kaelo's demise, but it is what the prophecy said. Had Firas been right that the 'swords' were metaphors for something else?

"If there are no further suggestions," Liera said in an icy voice. "I suggest we continue to move forward with the practical plans we have already discussed."

Renyra left the meeting room with her heart still fluttering. She wished she had come with a more solid understanding of the last part of the prophecy. Would Liera listen to her suggestions—or to prophecy in general—now that her own involvement had been implied? If the weapon didn't refer to Kaelo's own power, or Liera, what else could it mean?

Ahead, Kyna was walking briskly to the lifts. Renyra called to her.

Kyna stiffened and slowed her pace for Renyra to catch up.

"That went better than expected," Renyra said.

Kyna snorted. "Better than expected but not as well as we could have hoped." She stepped into the lift and pulled the lever to descend.

"I shouldn't have brought up Liera," Renyra said in a low voice.

"Why?" said a deep voice behind her.

Renyra jumped. Tenille and Tornac had entered the lift with them.

"I think it is entirely possible the prophecy refers to Liera," said Tornac. "If so, she must face the truth."

Renyra pressed herself against the wall of the lift. Even after all this time, she found it disconcerting to talk to this imposing elf that looked so much like his lost brother.

"But how is a sword supposed to stop Kaelo?" she said.

Tornac shrugged. "Maybe it only matters who wields it."

Renyra knit her brows. Could she have been thinking about this all wrong? Liera had failed to talk sense into her son, failed even to extract the purpose of his actions, but could she succeed where others had failed in stopping Kaelo by force? Renyra shuddered to think of Liera killing her own son with any weapon. It was unimaginable. Riu surely could not mean for such a thing to be the only solution.

"I am still not satisfied with it," said Tenille. "I intend to think hard on this."

The lift opened to the ground floor. Tornac nodded to Renyra and Kyna before following his mother into the hallway.

"Wait," Renyra said, extending a hand to stop Kyna. "I am meeting Firas for lunch. Will you come with us?"

A flicker of doubt passed behind Kyna's eyes. Renyra knew the woman did not always relish the company of other elves, but something Renyra could not explain made her want to break through to the aloof elf. There was more to Kyna than met the eye, she was sure.

"I think we should discuss this weapon more before tomorrow's meeting," she added.

Kyna glanced away, as though some other task was calling her, but then she nodded.

"Alright."

The companionable buzz that typically filled the streets of Tura on a nice day was cut through by an undercurrent of apprehension. Elves walked quickly to get from one place to another, their voices lowered and their eyes glancing about. It had been so ever since Kaelo's attacks began, but now a new fear hung on the horizon. No one could get out of Tura, and Kaelo had almost succeeded in wiping out all the vierstone from the city. Any day now his task would be complete, and no elf knew what would happen next. Renyra hoped Liera could get the vierstone consolidation mobilized in time. One more night might be enough to foil all of their plans.

"Where are we going?" Kyna asked when they passed the market and continued toward the Archives.

"To the best fish in Tura." Renyra flashed a grin at her. "At least according to an inside source."

Kyna glanced warily back to the market, but followed Renyra.

"Where are you from if not Tura?" Renyra said.

"Ard Gael."

Renyra nodded, though the answer was about as vague as the woman could have been. The small mountain range made up most of the Turi lands except for a stretch of flatter land south of the Wildwood.

"Maramor?" she asked.

"No."

Renyra raised her eyebrows and looked at Kyna with a wry smile. This seemed to disarm the woman. She gave a soft snort and relaxed her face into a nearly straight smile.

"I'm from the mountains of north central Ard Gael—facing the Wildwood. It is a small village, hardly worth noting on a map."

"Do you want to return there?"

"Maybe."

"I'm from a small village too. In the middle of the grasslands—about as far from anything as you can imagine. It was a lovely place with lovely elves, but the taste of travel and the excitement of cities drew me away. I don't know if I could go back to a place so quiet now, though the elves that remain there are some of the happiest I have known in all my travels."

Kyna nodded absently, her eyes drifting to the Archives and the fountain beyond. She glanced back at Renyra.

"You," she cleared her throat and looked ahead again, "perform Sira?"

"Yes," Renyra said with a grin, pleased by this unusual show of loquaciousness. "A traveling Sira show came through my village when I was young, and I spent years afterward hanging from trees and learning to balance on my hands. It was much later that another troupe came through, but that time I went with them. They were some of the best years of my life, traveling around Faeran. And then there is Sira itself. Being in the air is like ... like being an ether spirit. Like being a step closer to Riu, out of reach of the worries that plague the ground."

A line creased Kyna's brow.

"You could try it if you like," Renyra said. "I've been going to the training halls here for weeks. Actually, most of my old troupe is here." A thread of excitement shot through Renyra. "We could go there after lunch!"

A note of alarm touched Kyna's eyes. Renyra drew back at once. Kyna reminded her of a wild cat. It would take a gentler touch to earn her trust.

"Or not." Renyra said quickly. "I know it's a stressful time. I feel guilty myself sometimes for going to the training halls while the city is under such a terrifying threat. But Firas says that is all the more reason to find joy where we can."

Kyna stared straight ahead with unfocused eyes, as though thinking. Finally, she shrugged.

"I wouldn't mind seeing the training halls. Some time."

Renyra nodded, trying to keep a calm demeanor despite the glow of her triumph.

"Come on, there's Firas." She walked faster toward a small booth along the river surrounded by shaded tables.

Firas lifted a hand, and three other elves turned around from the table: Caerlyn, Alura, and Raren. Renyra's spirits lifted at once, but Kyna looked like she had been led into an ambush.

"Looks like the troupe is joining us. Come on." She tried not to laugh at Kyna's face and failed. "You'll like them."

Caerlyn, Alura, and Raren greeted Renyra warmly and looked at Kyna with interest.

"This is Kyna," said Renyra. "She came with us from Daro and is on the Council with me."

"And how did the Council go today?" Caerlyn said dryly after introductions were exchanged. "After what happened yesterday, I expect Liera is getting desperate."

"She is," said Renyra. "Today she's consolidating all the vierstone in the city to melt down and guard. And she's sending elves to the other Kindoms by river and horseback." Renyra stopped at once, glancing around. Perhaps she should not have shared that particular piece of news. If Kaelo somehow found out about those plans, he would certainly try to put a stop to them.

"Don't say anything," she said quickly. "If we are going to get elves out of the city it has to be by stealth, and Kaelo clearly has a way of finding out information that is not public knowledge."

"These elves she is sending are asking the other Kindoms for aid?" Firas asked. He had left the table to retrieve two plates from the nearby booth. Each contained a slab of brilliantly red fish on top of thick bread. He set the plates down in front of Renyra and Kyna.

"Thank you." Renyra turned to Kyna. "It may look simple, but it's the best fish you'll ever eat. Caught straight from the harbor and brought up the river to cook within hours." She looked back at Firas. "It's more to warn the other Kindoms than to ask for their help. Liera doesn't think anyone could get here fast enough to help at this point, not if it takes days to reach the other Kindoms and the Rale lines into the city are down."

"So what is her plan for Tura?" Alura said, apprehension plain in her eyes.

"Well, gathering the vierstone first of all." Renyra took a moment to sink her teeth into the fish sandwich. The rich, oily meat momentarily cleared her mind of all else.

"She is just going to let Kaelo have his way with the rest of it?" Raren said. "And what about the city? She is still trying to stop Kaelo isn't she?"

"Of course," said Renrya. "But nothing is working." She exchanged a look with Kyna, who had already taken several bites of her sandwich. Kyna raised a shoulder and nodded. Heartened, Renyra turned back to the troupe. "There is something else," she said.

She told them about the prophecy, reciting its words from memory and giving an overview of the discussions between herself, Firas, Kyna, and the rest of the Council.

"We are still trying to figure the last part out," she concluded. "But I think Liera is taking the right course of action—now that is. In the next few days, things will move forward whether we will them or no, and hopefully the Council will be able to make a better plan against Kaelo."

"Did Liera say who she is sending to the other Kindoms?" Firas said.

"No." Renyra looked more closely at Firas. The light of an idea shone through his eyes. "Why do you ask?"

He looked around at the other elves. "You say Liera wants stealth. We have all been moving about the city at night undetected. We have experience traveling through Faeran with and without the Rale, and you two," he looked to Renyra and Caerlyn, "know Auralia and Cuvan, not to mention the best ways to travel and communicate in the grasslands."

"And Trali!" Alura said, catching on at once. "We could bring Liera's message to Remsgraen and see Trali."

A warm buzz of energy was beginning in Renyra's chest. Go to Telem Fier? Return to the Fieri and reunite with the sixth member of their troupe in Remsgraen? All while carrying a message that could save the elves. How had she not thought of it before?

"Firas, it's perfect." She slid toward him and kissed him on the side of the head. "You're a genius."

"It would be everyone's choice, of course," Firas said, brushing off Renyra's compliment.

"Of course we'll do it," said Raren without hesitation. He looked to his sister, who nodded her encouragement.

Caerlyn shrugged. "Sure."

Renyra could see pleasure simmering beneath Caerlyn's nonchalant exterior. She knew her friend would be as excited as she was to see their home again after all these centuries. Was it possible Renrya would be able to see her family? She shook her head. This was a mission, not a vacation. The Rale didn't even run through her village, and time would be of the utmost importance once they landed in Rone.

A sudden spark of anxiety tempered Renyra's excitement. Did Liera already have an elf in mind for the journey? Would she agree to a party of five where one or two would suffice?

She would be just as glad to be rid of me on her Council.

Renyra smiled to herself, but a new concern now came to her mind. Was she needed more in the city? She was determined to crack the code of the prophecy, and if she left, she may never know the answer. What if the Council didn't solve it in time?

And what about Kyna?

Renyra turned suddenly to the silent elf, who was looking between all of them with an unreadable expression. Guilt flickered at Renyra's conscience. She had brought Kyna here for a pleasant lunch to discuss the prophecy, and here they were with the whole troupe discussing a trip to the grasslands.

"I will talk to Liera this afternoon," Renyra said as calmly as she could. "She may already have someone in mind, but I'll ask if she will consider us."

The conversation turned to other things then and never circled back to the prophecy. Eventually the group disbanded.

"Will you stay and talk with Firas and me about the prophecy?" Renyra asked Kyna.

Kyna hesitated, then said, "I should be going." She glanced behind her. "But think over it more. We can meet just before the Council tomorrow morning if you want."

"That would be great," Renyra said. "I'm glad you came to lunch with us, even if we didn't talk about the prophecy." She gave Kyna a guilty look, and the woman's eyes softened slightly.

"It was—" She paused, as though trying to find the right word. "Good," she said, somewhat lamely. "The fish," she added. "And—" Her eyes swept over the shady tables.

And the location? And maybe even the elves?

Renyra smiled. "I'll see you in the morning, then."

Kyna strode off to whatever was calling her attention, and Renyra said a quick goodbye to Firas and made for the Guild Quarter. With any luck, Liera would be talking with Alsena about the forges and gathering vierstone.

18

NEGOTIATIONS

"What," Valder said, a look of supreme fascination on his face, "is this?" He held a small, spongy ball, mostly cream colored but for a few flecks of brown. The ball compressed when Valder squeezed his fingers, then slowly regained its shape as he released it.

"Water lily seeds," Talaith said. She lounged back in her chair sipping a glass of iced tea.

Valder raised an eyebrow incredulously.

"They fry them in oil," Talaith explained. "I don't know how it works, but the seeds explode in the heat and form those." She pointed at the bowl of spongy spheres. "They're not bad."

"You eat them?"

Talaith rolled her eyes. "Of course. They're not there for decoration."

An eyebrow still raised, Valder placed the ball into this mouth and chewed it experimentally. He seemed pleasantly surprised by the result and grabbed a handful more, shoving the bowl toward Gellion, who took a few of the puffs and ate them.

"Huh," he said. "They almost melt in your mouth." He passed the bowl on, his appetite long since satiated with a meal of duck breast, multicolored rice, and grilled cattail stalks. Gellion had never seen any of the cuisine before, but had relished the fresh food after a week of corn-meal and salt beef.

It was wonderful to sit in a chair sheltered from heat and insects. Gellion's injured leg still ached from the last two days of riding, and the wound was starting to itch. He shifted, wincing at the pull of stitched skin along his calf. The crocodile's teeth had left long cuts down his skin where Gellion had ripped his leg back out of the beast's clutches. Several of the gouges had needed stitches, which Eira had insisted on doing herself. Gellion had been surprised by the nimbleness of the woman's callused fingers.

Gellion's leg was not his only discomfort. He scratched at the linen covering his head. It was night, and most of the Aektar had removed their head coverings, but enough people still donned them that the elves were not questioned for keeping them on. Since arriving in Masar, the traders and elves had been subjects to many a stare, but the elves seemed to be no more a target than the Dierna. All six of them were taller and paler than the Aektar, and Gellion had seen enough of the city to know that outsiders were a rarity.

This first night in Masar had reminded Gellion of his first night in Tradira, centuries before. Everything had been so shockingly different, a world he could never have dreamed up. The people of Masar were small and dark, but held a beauty Gellion would not have expected to find in the middle of a marsh. Their thick hair and large eyes were striking and expressive. In appearance they reminded Gellion of the Remsgri elves, but in dress and society the comparison ended.

Gellion let his eyes roam over the lounge. Dim lamps hung throughout the space, and the air was thick with spices. Men and women crowded around low tables, talking rapidly in a language Gellion did not understand. Everyone he could see wore the same loose linen.

"Do they have a king?" Gellion asked.

"They have a Mushad," Eira said, cutting off a conversation she had been having with Haf, who scowled. "He is the head of the Aektar, and they believe him the link to their god. He resides in the palace with the rest of the spiritual leaders."

Gellion nodded, his brows furrowed. "Is there nobility?"

"There's not supposed to be." Talaith's eyes showed the skepticism behind her words. "The Aektar do not have classes. All commodities are meant to be public. It makes trading with them simple and fast, but not the most profitable, as there is no one to compete for our goods."

"Will we be able to see more of the city?" Veldon was clearly trying to keep the eagerness out of his voice, though it shone in his face.

Gellion hid a smile.

"You will remain in your rooms while we conduct business," Eira said severely. "I will not be held responsible for any incidents you may cause in the city, and your presence may hinder our trade agreements."

Veldon looked crestfallen.

"But," Eira's expression softened ever so slightly. Even her stout determination to dislike the elves had begun to erode where Veldon was concerned. "When we have concluded our negotiations, we will need to restock on provisions before leaving for the Falspires. You may accompany us then to help carry packs—*if* you keep your heads down and mouths shut."

Veldon bowed his head subserviently, a smile playing at his lips.

The company retired as soon as the last of the tea had drained from their glasses. Visitors to Masar were uncommon enough that there were no large inns in the city, but Eira had secured them a few rooms above the lounge. All were eager to sleep on a mattress in a space screened from insects.

⁂

"It's absurd," Eira said, eyes ablaze. "They won't see finer wool anywhere in Tala and they price it as common linen."

"Just let them sit on it," Talaith soothed. "They're testing us as they always do, but we will not take less than two thousand akams' worth for the lot."

"We could threaten to move on," said Haf. "The Kayda will give us fair prices."

Gellion's eyes followed the argument. Though he regretted the unfair treatment of the traders, this was as much excitement as he'd seen all day. Eira, Talaith, and Haf had gone into the city after breakfast to begin their negotiations with the Aektar board of traders, leaving Gellion and his brothers confined to their room until late afternoon. The room was nice enough—clean lines and minimal furniture with a single oil lamp hanging low from the center of the ceiling—but it offered little in the way of entertainment.

"They don't need wool," Eira snapped. "The Aektar aren't stupid. They know this is the only market we can sell that wool in for a decent price."

Gellion knit his brows. Trade was not his specialty, but he was no stranger to its rules and nuances.

"Tell them you plan to trade the wool to the elves if they will not take it," he said.

Eira raised her eyebrows. Valder and Veldon stared at Gellion as though he had suggested a collective field trip to Tura.

"To us," Gellion said with a grin, sweeping his arm to include Veldon and Valder in the mix.

Eira eyed him warily. "Go on."

"Say we are emissaries from the elves, here to trade fine goods—that we are prepared to pay competitive prices for Dierna wool. Name the price you want and see what they say."

Eira's expression shifted to mild interest.

Talaith was openly grinning.

"Force some competition on them," she said.

"What if they refuse, or call our bluff?" Haf said. "You aren't actually prepared to buy our wool." It was not a question. The elves had no money and no intention of returning to Tala, and the traders knew it as well as they did.

"No," Gellion said slowly. "But with us there to back you up, why should they doubt your word? *Our* word." He looked to his brothers. There was a spark of mischief in Valder's eyes. Veldon looked as though he would much rather stay shrouded as a human and slip out of Masar unnoticed, but he did not object.

Eira considered him for a long moment. "Why do you care?"

"You're taking us to Suri Ranta," Gellion said. "Against your wishes." He was gratified by a subtle spark of discomfort in Eira's eyes. "The least we can do is help with your trade endeavors. Among our people I am no stranger to negotiations."

Eira seemed to be warring with her reluctance to associate with the elves in public and her desire to land a profitable trade deal.

"Fine," she said at last. "You may as well earn your keep."

Gellion and Valder exchanged a grin. Even Veldon's eyes lit up at the prospect of venturing into Masar at last.

"Four thousand akams? I am very sorry, but that is absurd. No."

"It is the market price for Dierna wool," Eira said calmly, though a glint of steel touched her voice.

"Wool is everywhere," said the man. "We are surrounded by sheep on all sides."

"The Aektar have no trade relations with the Albaren," Eira said cooly, "and mountain wool is coarser than Dierna wool. Not to mention we produce ten times the number of sheep the Falspires can support. You will pay higher prices for lower quality wool with the Kayda."

All three of the Aektar traders were looking at Eira with controlled expressions. The man speaking was younger than the other two, with black hair undisturbed by grey and a clean shaven face the color of cinnamon. Eira had told Gellion that his name was Saladin.

"We have named our price at twelve hundred akams for the lot," Saladin said. "It is a fair price."

"That is far less than you offered last year," said Eira.

"It has been a difficult year. We do not have the same coin for wool that we once had."

"You have the same need."

"Need?" A corner of Saladin's mouth rose. "Dierna wool is a lovely thing, but I cannot say that we need it."

"No? I have seen Dierna wool furnishing every lounge and building in the city. In the winter more than half Masar is donned in it to keep out the cold rains."

A muscle twitched in Saladin's jaw, but confidence still dripped from his bearing. He knew he still had the upper hand.

"We will not pay more."

"Very well." The steel of Eira's voice was now in her eyes. "You will get no wool."

"Then you will sell none."

"We will."

The board of traders raised their eyebrows collectively.

"To whom?" said Saladin. "We have already established that the Albaren and Kayda have wool of their own. Do you expect they will pay top dollar for 'softer' wool from a foreign nation?"

"They might." Eira shrugged. "Foreign goods in themselves are considered fashionable by some."

"By some, but not by the Kayda, and given the history of your nations, I cannot see the Albaren fighting over anything Dierna made."

"I am not referring to the Kayda or the Albaren. There are other competitors on the market, and if you insist on ignoring our price points, we will turn to them instead."

Saladin let out a humorless laugh. "Other competitors?"

"Elves."

Saladin's smile froze on his face. He stared at Eira as though she had suggested trading with ghosts.

Gellion shifted uncomfortably behind the screen that shielded him and his brothers from the traders' view. Passersby milled to either side, paying no heed to the official negotiations occurring in their midst. Eira had said that trade in Masar was conducted in public to symbolize honesty and openness. The irony of their current situation gave Gellion a grim satisfaction.

"Elves?" said an older, stouter Aektar trader. He scoffed. "I would believe this of the Kayda, but I always thought the Dierna were a bit more solid in their grip on reality. You claim to have trade relations with a different *race*?"

"We do." Eira did not bat an eye.

"Where are these elves? Why have they traded with no other humans until now?"

"The elves have been trading with the Albaren for generations."

"So they say."

Anger flashed in Eira's eyes. "It is a verifiable fact! The Dierna may not like the Albaren, but we have had no small amount of contact with them over the years. The elves have resided in a city north of Albarad for hundreds of years. They keep to themselves mostly, but they do import goods from others."

"Goods such as Dierna wool?" The stout trader looked more than a little skeptical.

"Enough," said Saladin before Eira could respond. His face was serious, and a spark of anger had lit in his eyes. "I see that you are insulted by our offer, Trader Eira, but it is no reason to invent falsehoods."

"They will offer us four thousand akams' worth for the lot," Eira said, ignoring Saladin's accusation. "Match that and we will trade with you instead—in honor of our long-standing relationship. But if you cannot come close to their offer, it would be madness for us to accept."

Saladin shook his head, but held a touch of discomfort in his expression. He clearly needed this trade deal more than he was letting on. Eira had been correct in her calculations.

"How can we trust this claim?" he said. "I warn you, if we find these elves never existed it will taint our relationship with your clan forever."

Gellion had to give Eira credit; she did not look the least bit guilty or unsure of herself. It was no wonder Saladin was growing nervous.

"There will be no need to investigate," Eira said. "We are traveling with the very elves I speak of."

Some of the color drained from Saladin's face. His companions looked wildly around as though faeries would descend from the sky at any moment.

"What is this?" Saladin's voice was thin.

Eira shrugged. "The elves of Daro wished to explore trade options with the Dierna and the Kayda. We are escorting a few of their emissaries to Suri Ranta."

"Here? In Masar?" Saladin looked equal parts disbelieving and terrified. It was difficult to discern whether his words were those of skepticism or panic.

"Yes," Eira said. "Here. Talaith, bring Gellion."

Talaith and Haf had been silent throughout the meeting, letting

Eira carry out the act with her superior skills of manipulation. At Eira's words, however, Talaith stood and walked into the surrounding crowds, looping back around to where Gellion waited with his brothers.

"I think it best we only bring one of you," she whispered. "They're getting nervous, and I don't want to pull this off as a threat."

"I will be thoroughly charming," Gellion assured her.

Talaith snorted and led Gellion out from behind the screen. As Gellion entered the space before the board of traders, he removed his head covering. The eyes of each Aektar were large and round as dinner plates.

"This is Gellion," Eira said. "A respected trader among the elves."

Gellion pasted his most welcoming smile on his face and gave a small bow to the Aektar. The men stared at him, taking in his auburn hair, emerald eyes, and strange amalgamation of Dierna and Aektar attire. Gellion wished he could have put a little more effort into his appearance before appearing as a foreign emissary.

"It is good to meet you," Gellion said. "Masar is a beautiful city."

Saladin was at a complete loss for words. The color in his face had returned with interest, a dark flush spreading up from his neck. Gellion heard a faint, stifled laugh somewhere behind him and knew Valder was enjoying the scene immensely.

The remainder of the trade negotiations went quickly.

"Brilliant." Talaith stirred her glass of tea as people passed them to either side in the markets of Masar. "Did you see the look on their faces? You would have thought I dragged a leashed dragon into their midst." She laughed heartily. "Four thousand akams. Eurig will be thrilled. And if the Aektar ever bring up the elves again, we will truthfully tell them that the elves suddenly disappeared from Tala—that it was a one time deal. After your vouching," she indicated Gellion with a finger, "they will never be able to accuse us of falsehood. Of course, I doubt those three will bring up the elves at all before the Mushad."

"Keep your voice down," Eira snapped at Talaith, scanning the crowds around them. Despite her tone, there was obvious pleasure in her face, and she had been markedly civil to the elves as they walked through the colorful market stalls of Masar restocking on food and supplies.

The company now sat in the shaded pavilion of an outdoor lounge. Veldon was paying no attention to the conversation at hand. His eyes were roving over every inch of his surroundings. Gellion could hardly keep his own gaze from wandering over the remarkable city. Every surface was made of a shining black wood, built in sharp angles and clearly watertight. Wide bridges connected platforms and buildings, and canals wove between the paths. The city's foundation was formed from sturdy logs of the same black wood as everything else. The Aektar apparently harvested the wood from the dense forest abutting the northern borders of the marsh, floating the timber on rafts pulled by water buffalo.

"It was a good deal," Eira said. "But we should not talk over it any further. We will finish restocking our supplies and prepare to leave Masar quietly in the morning."

"Alright, alright." Talaith rolled her eyes and flashed a smile at Gellion, who pulled his attention back to the traders.

He agreed with Eira's desire to move on from Masar. The city had provided a temporary distraction from Gellion's greater problems, but it was time to set his sights to them once again. A twinge of anxiety twisted in his chest, and Kaelo's face hovered in his mind's eye.

"How long is the journey to Suri Ranta from here?" He carefully filtered the strain from his voice.

"A week," Eira said. "Maybe more if we run into weather."

"Surely not snow?" Valder looked shocked.

"No," said Eira. "It is the storms we should be wary of. They roll in off the sounds. Most don't make it past the mountains, but they can get nasty in the passes before breaking on the higher peaks."

"Sounds like the mountains are no joy to live in," Valder said.

Talaith snorted. Even Haf grimaced in agreement.

"They are dangerous," said Eira. "But the Kayda would not leave them for anything."

"What ties them to the mountains?" Gellion asked. He had been to Morcanan only once and had been impressed by the beauty of the mountain peaks, but even the Morcani restricted their dwellings to the southern borders of the Terulian Mountains. The harsh winters and stark landscape gave little in the way of foundation or food, except perhaps hunting.

"Spirits," Talaith said. "Ancestors."

"The soil is fertile," Haf said. "And the deep water sounds provide vast amounts of fish. Not to mention the Kayda have protection from any attacks by land. So far as I know, the Albaren have never turned their attention to the Falspires beyond grudging trade, but even they would be hard pressed to launch a naval attack through the narrow openings of the sounds."

Gellion nodded thoughtfully. The Albaren seemed to hold the real power in Tala and used it freely. He wondered that the elves had never thought to learn more about their neighbors of the last few centuries. If they had, they would never have agreed to ally themselves in battle.

Not even for vierstone?

Gellion looked away from the humans, clenching a fist.

"We should move on," Eira said.

They spent another half hour finishing out their supplies. By mid afternoon, the company was on its way back to the lounge. Haf left the group to see that the horses were being properly cared for in the stables that bordered the city. Veldon looked from one side to the other as they walked, drinking in the diversity of ages and faces around him.

Only when they came upon an elderly woman, coughing wetly and leaning against a young lady dressed in white, did the delight fade from Veldon's face.

"What is wrong with her?" he asked, concern in his eyes.

"She is sick," Gellion said.

Veldon watched the woman stumble into a building. It was long and flat compared to the towers surrounding it. The lady in white opened the door, and the sounds of more coughing and moaning wafted out into the air before muting again when the door closed.

"What is that place?" Veldon had stopped in the street, staring.

Eira answered. "It is a sick house. There are many in Masar." Her voice was matter of fact.

"A house of healing?" Veldon asked. Such buildings were not

uncommon among the elves, but were usually reserved for the largest cities, made to treat injuries most commonly incurred from accidents. Since the Great War they were seldom used and lightly staffed.

"Disease is rampant in the marsh," Eira said. "Insects. Moisture. Bad water. Aektar medicine is extensive, but the herbalists cannot save everyone."

Veldon looked deeply troubled, his brows drawn together as he continued to stare at the doors to the sick house.

"Come on." Gellion led Veldon away with a hand on his shoulder. Veldon followed, but his eyes lingered on the sick house until it was behind them.

Gellion had hoped for a restful evening and a quiet departure from Masar the next morning. He was anxious to be out of human cities again—away from the stress of constantly keeping up his guard and evaluating people's reactions to his every word and action. At first it seemed that he would get his wish. The traders and the elves returned to their rooms and stowed their purchases safely into their traveling packs. Haf returned within the hour with news that the horses were fed, watered, and well rested, ready to continue on the next day.

It was an afternoon of high spirits. Eager as everyone was to continue their journey, they were just as eager to enjoy their last day of comfort.

Owing to the success of the wool ruse, the humans offered to buy the elves a hearty dinner at one of the nicer lounges in the city center. While Gellion was reluctant to go out again, he could not bring himself to turn down the unusual hospitality of their companions, and found himself out in Masar again that evening.

"This is a *nicer* place than where we have been staying?" Valder said skeptically.

The interior of the lounge was certainly more lavish than anything they had yet seen in Masar, but Gellion had to agree with Valder that he much preferred the atmosphere of the other lounge.

He could hardly hear his brother's voice over the raucous laughter and din of shouting voices that seemed to bounce off of every surface in the room. As if the noise was not oppressive enough, smoke hung in the air so thickly, Gellion could hardly make out the facial features of anyone around him. His head was already spinning with the fumes by the time they reached the bar.

"We'll have to wait a while for space to open up," Talaith shouted at Gellion. "We can get a drink and wait here."

"Could we wait outside?" Gellion said, but Talaith indicated that she could not hear him. He motioned to the door and began to walk toward it before Talaith could answer. Valder and Veldon fell into step behind him.

"We help them more than double their profits and they reward us by taking us *here*?" Valder said after a few lungfuls of clean and blessedly quiet air.

"I expect it is considered a luxury here," Veldon said. "The fumes they smoke are likely expensive."

"And is volume of voice another symbol of wealth?"

Veldon smiled. "It could be, for all we know."

"I just want to be on our way to Suri Ranta," Gellion said. "Something tells me it will be a long and much more difficult journey from the marsh through the Falspires than it was from Arvain to here. The sooner we start, the sooner we get it over with."

"That's the spirit," Valder said.

"Have you had any more luck with the vierstone?" Gellion asked Veldon, ignoring Valder.

Some of the spirit seemed to fade from Veldon's eyes.

"No," he said glumly. "Not any more than we discussed before." He shook his head. "I fear it could take years to learn enough about vierstone to figure it out, and the elf that did this could have had centuries to do it. It's the vierstone masters back in Faeran that should be examining this. For all we know, they already are."

"I still say you're as good as any of them," said Gellion.

Veldon blushed.

"Besides," said Gellion. "If the elves in Faeran perceive no further threat beyond Daro, they may not be looking into it at all."

"I will keep trying," Veldon said, though there was little confidence in his eyes.

The distant sound of agitated voices drew Gellion's attention. He turned to an open expanse where a large group of people was milling around like a disturbed ant hill.

"What's going on there?" Valder followed Gellion's gaze.

"No idea." Gellion narrowed his eyes, trying to see more clearly. Everyone was facing the middle of the square, where a wooden beam stood like a sail mast out of a raised platform. The crowd's voices sounded angry, yet a buzz of excitement seemed to radiate from them. Men and women outside the lounge were starting to notice the action and flocked toward the square with all the others, calling to each other in Aektar.

"What are they saying?" Veldon asked Gellion, clearly forgetting that Gellion didn't speak Aektar.

"I don't know." Gellion's curiosity was piqued, but an undercurrent of anxiety was beginning to spread through his body. The scene unfolding in the square reminded him uncomfortably of his public trial in Tradira. The same collective emotion seemed to be afflicting these people. They were anticipating something, and Gellion very much doubted it was something good.

"Let's go back inside," he said.

"Why?" asked Valder.

Gellion looked harder toward the square, trying to discern what the post in the middle was. He could almost make out—

He stiffened.

"Come inside," he said, trying to keep his voice calm.

Valder looked at him sharply. "What is it?"

"Not something we want to watch."

"What are they doing?" The confusion in Veldon's eyes turned to concern.

Gellion was starting to back toward the lounge's doors.

"Just come on," he said.

But it was too late. In the square, the crowd was parting for two men in black leading a third man bound between them.

Gellion's heart pounded. He knew what was coming. It was a practice held in Tradira, but one he had always managed to avoid witnessing until now. Veldon and Valder had turned back to watch, ignoring Gellion's pleas to return to the lounge.

The two guards had led their charge to the post, and a man in official looking robes stepped onto a raised platform beside it. Silence spread through the square as his deep voice echoed off the surrounding buildings.

He spoke Aektar, but Gellion could tell by the cadence that the man was reading an official proclamation, probably followed by the crimes of the man that stood below him.

"Come on!" Gellion tried one more time. "This has nothing to do with us. We can't do anything about it. Eira and the others will be waiting."

"What are they doing Gellion?" Veldon's voice was soft.

Gellion opened his mouth and closed it.

"I think," he said. "It is an execution."

Valder looked down.

"What?" Veldon's eyes were wide. He looked back at the man cowering between the guards. The crowd was now shouting their anger at him. The robed man had finished speaking.

"They are going to ... to kill him? There? In front of everyone?"

"Yes."

The shock in Veldon's eyes was slowly transforming into anger.

"Why?" he said.

"I don't know," Gellion said quietly. "He may be a murderer himself, or else committed some other crime deemed worthy of death. It is not uncommon among the humans."

"Not uncommon?" A flush was rising up Veldon's face.

"It is a punishment." Gellion glanced around. People were starting to stare at Veldon's rising voice. "Veldon, there is nothing we can do. There are hundreds of people down there, and we are not Aektar, or human for that matter. Come inside."

Veldon stood his ground.

"He's right Veldon," Valder said. He looked sick. "We should go."

"No." Veldon did not take his eyes off the square. The prisoner was standing on the platform beneath the post now, and a rope was lowering behind him. The crowd's shouts grew louder.

"What do you plan to do?" Gellion said. "Run down there and save him? Bring him with us to Suri Ranta? Why not Faeran while we're at it?" Gellion could not keep the anger out of his voice. He knew what Veldon was feeling, but making a scene wouldn't help the man about to be hanged, and it could very well bring harm to all of them.

A look of pain crossed Veldon's face that made Gellion immediately regret his words.

"Veldon, I—"

But Veldon's eyes had locked on a man passing beside them. The man wore the same black shroud as those who now stood to either side of the prisoner in the square.

Gellion reached for Veldon as he stepped in front of the guard, but Veldon shrugged him off.

"Who is that man?" Veldon said in Albaren. He pointed to the square.

The guard looked taken aback. He glanced from Veldon to his brothers, and his eyes narrowed in suspicion.

"A criminal," he said gruffly.

"For what offense?"

"Veldon," Gellion said sharply, looking apologetically at the guard.

"What has he done?" Veldon said.

The guard was glaring at Veldon now, obviously irked that a foreigner would question him so.

"He is a blasphemer." The guard blew a forceful breath out his nose. "He spoke against the will of Al."

Veldon's eyes burned with indignation.

"He spoke? That's all?"

The guard drew himself up, his anger rising to meet Veldon's.

"Blasphemy is a crime punishable by death. All know this." His hand strayed to the hilt of a sword at his side. "And you would do well to remember it *alkar*."

Gellion did not know what the last word meant, but its connotation was plain by the way the guard spat it. Veldon opened his mouth to respond, but Valder spoke first.

"We will." Valder pulled Veldon back by the shoulders.

A dull clank and a roar of voices came from the square. Gellion reluctantly looked toward it.

The man accused of blasphemy was hanging by his neck, jerking and struggling at the end of the rope. A wave of cold spread from Gellion's head to his feet. He was suddenly glad he had not yet eaten dinner. He looked away from the gruesome sight, turning his eyes instead on Veldon.

Veldon's face was white, and his eyes held utter, disbelieving horror. He stood perfectly still, watching the man's struggles subside until he hung limply from the noose.

Gellion closed his eyes.

"What's going on?" Eira's voice came as a relief.

"Are you with them?" The guard pointed at Veldon.

Eira paused momentarily, glancing between the three brothers. A sudden fear prickled at Gellion's mind. Would she disown them now that they were causing trouble? At the beginning of this journey he would not have been surprised, but now—

"Yes," she said at last. "Is there a problem?"

"I want them out of the city. You will join them. And any others in your party."

Eira opened her mouth in shock for a moment before composing herself again.

"We are leaving in the morning," she said with cold dignity.

"You will leave tonight," the guard said. There was no room for argument in the look he gave her. His hand was still resting on the sword hilt.

Eira gave him a long look, clearly itching to stand up to the burly man, but then she nodded once. She waited until the guard had turned away before bringing her eyes to rest on the elves. Gellion could hardly meet her gaze. She looked at Veldon, whom the guard had pointed to in his anger.

But Veldon was paying no attention to Eira, or to the retreating back of the guard. Gellion doubted if he had even heard the guard's orders. He stood with slack posture, defeat in every inch of him. His eyes followed the gentle sway of the man who had just died.

19

TO FORGE A SWORD

Kyna wrapped her hands around the cool metal of a hoop, wondering how she had gotten here. Beside her, Renyra beamed encouragement.

"That's it, straighten your arms and pull your legs over your head. You can bend your knees if you need to. Then hook your knees over the hoop and you can let go."

With gritted teeth, Kyna followed Renyra's instructions. It was harder than she had thought. She did have to bend her knees, but an unexpected pleasure rippled through her muscles as she lifted herself off the ground.

"Good," Renyra said. "Hook your knees and let go."

Kyna did, lowering herself until she hung upside down. She fought the urge to grin like an idiot. She felt weightless.

Through her inverted peripheral vision, she saw elves moving in every direction, some on the ground, some much higher than she was. Where elves didn't move, objects did, flying and flipping through the air. Everything was in constant motion, the elves so concentrated on their tasks, Kyna couldn't imagine that they noticed the time passing.

"Now swing yourself up and grab the hoop, then you can pull your-self into a seat." Renyra's voice came from a direction in which Kyna had not expected. She shook her head, disoriented, but arched her back and swung forward to pull herself up into the hoop.

The world around her realigned into its proper place, but the sensation of weightlessness remained. A surge of adrenaline emanated from Kyna's chest as she looked down at the ground, but it was not from fear.

The hoop around her had begun to rotate lazily with her movements so that she got a sweeping view of the training halls. She watched an elf wrapped in a swath of fabric spin and plummet toward the ground, only to be caught in a knee bind just before she reached it.

Kyna rotated again.

Two elves did dizzying flips over each other off of a springy surface.

She spun further.

An elf pivoted on a taut wire on one foot.

There was so much to look at.

"It's great, isn't it?"

Kyna looked down with a start. She had almost forgotten Renyra was there. For the last few minutes, she had forgotten entirely about the Council meeting and Tura's fate. Kyna did not answer Renyra, but the perceptive Fieri seemed to know how she felt anyway; she smiled.

"You can come to the training halls whenever you want," Renyra said. "Although—" Her smile faded.

"What?" Kyna said, trying not to sound too concerned.

"Well, I spoke with Liera yesterday."

A slow sinking began in Kyna's stomach.

They're leaving.

"Liera agreed to send me and Firas—along with the rest of the troupe—to Telem Fier. She wasn't happy about it at first, but our suitability for the task leaves little room for argument."

Kyna was still rotating in the hoop ridiculously, but was grateful for the excuse to hide the disappointment in her face as she spun away from Renyra.

She chided herself. She was being absurd. Why should she care if Renyra left the city—if every elf in Tura left the city? She didn't need Renyra to complete her task, not now that the Council was finally showing openness to the prophecy. It would be better, even, without Renyra's pestering attempts at friendship and forced dinners.

"When do you leave?" Kyna said casually.

"Tonight."

So soon.

"Up the river?'

"Yes."

Renyra was watching Kyna as though deep in thought. Then a slow smile spread up her face.

Kyna knit her brows. "What?"

"Come with us."

Kyna's brows rose. "Excuse me?"

"Come with us," Renyra said excitedly. "We already have five, what's one more? You have as little reason to stay in Tura as I do, and it would be doing something good for the elves here. You could always come back afterward. I'm sure the Fieri will send some elves to Tura once they know what's happening."

Kyna stared at her.

Go with Renyra? Was she mad? Travel across half of Faeran with a troupe of Sira performers to enlist the aid of the Fieri and Remsgri against Kaelo? Kyna barely suppressed the sardonic laugh that threatened to pass her lips. She could think of little worse than spending days, even weeks, of travel trapped with five other elves—especially these five.

And yet.

Kyna's hands tightened on the metal hoop holding her in the air. The myriad of happenings around her continued uninterrupted, but seemed to take on a slower, skipping rhythm. What would happen if she did go? If she just left Tura behind? Left her responsibility behind? Her hand absently stroked the hoop.

The feeling of cool stone on her wrist made Kyna jump. Her cuff had pressed up against the hoop. It was like a veil lifting.

No.

"I can't," she said, disgusted by how difficult the words came.

Renyra's face fell. "Why?"

Kyna hesitated. "I have to stay on the Council. If both of us leave there will be no one left to bring reason to them."

The Council. That was why she was here. That was her purpose.

Liera had postponed the meeting scheduled for this morning until the afternoon, claiming that she needed more time to see to preparations before reporting on her efforts. She had not deigned to tell the Council Members this until just before the allotted time, however, and both Kyna and Renyra had come to an empty meeting room. It had not been easy for Renyra to convince Kyna to spend the extra time in the training halls, but in the end, Kyna had given in. Now she fervently wished she had not.

"The Council is on the right track now," said Renyra. "And we have one more meeting. We've told them all we can at this point."

"I am staying." The words came out icier than Kyna had intended, and a twist of guilt made her look away from the hurt on Renyra's face.

Grabbing the hoop to either side, Kyna lowered herself back to her knees and dismounted the same way she had gotten up. Her heart sank as her feet touched solid ground again. She was suddenly angry at Renyra for forcing her to come here, for taunting her with the possibility of a future that could never be.

But even in her anger, Kyna could not bring herself to release the scathing words that came to her lips.

"It is a—kind offer," she said instead. "But my place is here."

Renyra nodded. She was clearly still disappointed, but accepted Kyna's excuse with grace.

"Alright. You know your path better than I. But you will be missed."

The same lurching sensation that had assaulted Kyna in Renyra's kitchen gripped her chest again. She had to get out of these cursed training halls. She needed to go to the Council Meeting; she needed to reground herself in purpose. Renyra was proving a distraction she could not afford.

"I need to go to my apartment before the meeting," Kyna said.

She fixed her eyes to the floor as she walked out of the training hall, refusing to allow the feats around her to pull her attention. None of this was a distraction she could afford.

Yet as the door closed behind her and she walked into the hot street, she felt a part of herself remain stubbornly behind, calling her back.

"We have prepared a furnace in one of the metalworking shops in which to melt the vierstone," Liera said. "We have spread word as far as we can while remaining discrete, but the supply is woefully small. I am hoping we have simply not reached enough elves. If this is all the vierstone that remains in the city, I fear it is hardly worth guarding."

An anxious murmur spread through the room. Liera had postponed the meeting to tell them this?

"What is more," Liera said slowly. "I have confirmed that Kae—" she paused. "That the last of the vierstone in the city has been destroyed."

The murmuring gave way to shocked silence.

Kyna had to fight not to roll her eyes. They had all known this was coming. Had they expected Kaelo to leave the last bit of intact vierstone untouched as a memorial to the past? Yet every elf in the room looked as though a beloved family member had died unexpectedly.

"That's it then?" Reanan spoke softly, but his voice filled the room. "The only vierstone left in Tura is a small furnace full and our earrings?"

Liera did not answer.

All of the Council Members were watching her, waiting to see what she would do next, but for once Liera seemed to be at a loss.

"So we go to the next part of the prophecy," Kyna said when the Lady of Tura kept her silence. All eyes turned to her. "We did what we could to save the vierstone we had—though too late to be of much use." Kyna glanced at Liera. "But it is the last part that matters now. How to stop him."

"How do we know Kaelo is still in the city?" said Alos. "If he has succeeded in purging Tura of vierstone, who is to say he has not moved on already?"

"Why, then, did he go to such lengths to cut Tura off from the other Kindoms?" Tornac said. "If Kaelo had planned to finish his task in a couple of days, it would not have mattered that we sent birds to call for help. Even with an intact Rale system, no one could have come here in time to stop him. I say whatever comes next in his plan still involves Tura."

"I agree," said Tenille. "We must act as though Kaelo is still here and is still a threat not to be underestimated. Kyna is right. While we wait for elves to reach the other Kindoms, we must do all we can to decipher the last piece of the prophecy."

"The piece in which I single handedly forge a magic sword?" Liera said scathingly.

"Not magic," Tenille said calmly. "Vierstone."

Kyna raised her eyebrows. She looked around the table.

Every eye in the room had fixed on Tenille. Expressions ranged from wonder to incensed incredulity. Liera's face had drained of its prior cynicism, to be replaced by shock.

"What?" she said in half a whisper.

"Every word in a prophecy is significant," Tenille said. "You are reading it as though it is a simple rhyme with broad meaning. The prophecy says 'a weapon forged from his despise'. *From,* not *by.* A weapon is forged *by* an elf, it is forged *from* a substance. So therefore the sword—for I do think it means a literal sword—is made of something that Kaelo despises. Swords are traditionally forged from metal, but what metal would any elf hate?" She paused to let her words sink in.

"But," Tornac said. "There is a substance that Kaelo has been bent on destroying this whole time. What if his hate is not directed at the elves—not entirely at least—but at that which he is destroying?"

One side of Kyna's mouth curved upward.

"Can vierstone be forged?" Reanan said with a knitted brow. "You cannot forge a weapon of stone."

"Vierstone is not a normal stone," said Tornac.

"I do not believe it is truly a stone at all," Tenille said. "Certainly not a pure one." She looked to Liera and hesitated. A strange look came to her eye. "You remember the crafting competition—in Daro?" Her voice was halting. Kyna now recognized the look in her eyes as deep pain. "Veldon crafted a lamp of pure vierstone. He worked it like glass, but it was hard as iron."

Now Liera's eyes were widening as memory and understanding mingled.

"Yes," she said. "I had never seen vierstone crafted that way." She suddenly looked at Tenille with a hard, hungry gaze. "Do you know how he did it? Did you see him do it?"

"No," Tenille said. "But surely you have a master of vierstone here? Could they not try the same method, but to make a sword?"

Liera stared at the table and nodded. "I will talk to Alsena. She has worked vierstone, but it is likely the jewelers, or—" Her head snapped up. She looked at Reanan. "One of the Builders who have worked with it in the foundations?"

Reanan looked thoughtful. "Perhaps. I have worked vierstone into foundations but I cannot say I am anything resembling a master. A jeweler might be better suited to the task—with the aid of a metal-worker who is accustomed to sword craft."

"This is all very well," Alos said. "But how is a vierstone sword supposed to help us?"

The room went quiet, some of the excitement dwindling beneath the weight of Alos's practicality. It was Renyra who answered.

"His armor. However he has made it, nothing we assault him with penetrates it. Maybe vierstone would." Excitement shone in her eyes. "Maybe vierstone even negates whatever power he possesses, and that is why he is destroying it."

"That seems a bit far-fetched," said Alos. "But you may have a point with the first part. Arrows bounce off him as though he were made of stone."

"But how are we to make this sword?" said Dorian. "Even if we find a craftsman skilled enough to forge it, we've just established how little vierstone we have in the city." He looked to Liera. "Is there enough to make a sword?"

Liera's face fell. "I don't think so. Not unless we uncover a fair bit more in the next day, and even then there would be no room for error."

"We could melt down all the earrings," Alos said.

"No." Renyra said. "Even if the elves were willing to give up their earrings, it would raise a glaring sign to Kaelo."

"The earrings have never been an option," said Liera. "If we are to get more vierstone, it will not be from Tura."

"What about Maramor?" Tornac said. He glanced at his mother before continuing. "You said you are sending elves up the river to contact the Fieri. They will pass by Maramor. You could send another elf with them to bring vierstone back on one of our boats. It would be risky, getting back into Tura, but it could give us enough vierstone for what we need."

Tenille had looked momentarily affronted by her son offering vierstone from her own city, but she grudgingly nodded.

"It is a good idea. You are welcome to our vierstone if it will save Tura."

"It is the best we can hope for," Liera said. "If we keep quiet, Kaelo may never suspect."

"I will go," said Tornac.

"Alright," Liera said. "I—"

"And Kyna," Renyra interrupted.

Kyna started and stared at Renyra in disbelief. She could just detect a darkening of Renyra's cheeks.

"If she wants," Renyra added, then quickly continued before Kyna could respond. "The land around Tura is dangerous, just like it was around Daro before its fall. The rivers there were infested with foul beasts, and it is safe to assume that the same is true here. Two elves are better than one for a return journey. It would be a disaster if the vierstone was lost while defending the boat from river monsters."

Tornac had looked at Renyra with surprise at her initial outburst and now glanced at Kyna uncertainly, but was beginning to nod.

"Two elves might be wise."

Kyna was still too dumbfounded to speak.

"You have already convinced me to send five of you to the grasslands," Liera said. "Now you advocate for seven?"

"The number will not matter once we are out of the city," said Renyra. "And seven elves can be as quiet as five." She spoke with a casual confidence that would have made any argument by Liera seem petty.

"Very well," Liera said grudgingly.

Kyna looked between Renyra and Liera with a gaping mouth, furious that she had been volunteered for this journey and was now being spoken of as though she had happily accepted the offer.

"I—" Kyna began.

"Kyna is from Ard Gael," Renyra said. "She knows the area and has already seen the sorts of creatures we may deal with around Daro."

Renyra was obviously hiding a smile now. She had cornered Kyna, and she knew it.

"But—" Kyna stammered.

"Will you go, Kyna?" Liera asked.

Kyna's mouth was still open. The whole Council was watching her now, awaiting her reply.

It would be a relatively fast trip to Maramor with a motor boat. She would be back in Tura before anything important happened and could ensure that the vierstone made it safely to the forges. It was vital that vierstone made it to the forges.

It was the prospect of waiting several more days in utter boredom in Tura that made Kyna say, "Yes," with a sideways glare at Renrya.

"Good," said Liera. "You leave tonight."

20

STORMS IN THE MOUNTAINS

Gellion's departure from Masar was not how he had pictured it. The giddiness that had possessed the group earlier was entirely gone, replaced by grim silence on all parts. Strangely, Eira seemed the least upset of the traders by Veldon's behavior. She had merely given him a disapproving look when told of his reaction to the execution, then gathered the others in her typical militant and efficient way.

It was full dark by the time they rode their horses out the northern road of Masar. They would have to ride until they found a space wide enough to set up camp. This was the main reason for Gellion's guilt. Their premature departure from the city had done no real harm otherwise. The Aektar traders were unlikely to learn of the Diernas' association with a street disagreement, and the party would have left first thing the following morning anyway. But they were all tired, and a nighttime ride through the marsh was not anyone's idea of a decompressing evening.

"It is only a day's journey to the northern edge of the marsh from here," Eira said when the glowing lights of Masar were beginning to fade in the distance. "There is no waypoint in this direction, but the ground will become more solid soon. We should be able to make camp off the path."

Gellion was wary of this plan given his previous experience off the path, but Eira assured him that the crocodiles were not likely to attack a group this large, and they would set a guard to warn of any signs of approaching danger. Out of guilt, the elves took the first three watches, which brought them nearly to dawn. Gellion slept poorly even when not on guard and suspected Veldon had not slept at all. The bitterness had left Veldon's face now, leaving behind a sadness that was somehow worse in its quiet persistence. Gellion did not know what to say to him.

As the traders began to move about at first light, preparing to start the first full day of their resumed journey in earnest, Gellion went to Veldon.

Veldon did not look up at Gellion's approach, but his sudden stillness betrayed his notice. Gellion glanced at Valder, who stood nearby, clearly listening.

"Veldon?" Gellion said.

Veldon looked up slowly, his eyes fixing on the horizon past Gellion.

"I should not have stopped the guard," he said softly.

"I understand why you did."

"I endangered us all. You were right. There was nothing I could have done."

"That has never stopped you from trying before." Gellion smiled. It was one of the things he admired most about Veldon—he never abandoned hope. It was a trait that sometimes grated on Gellion's more practical nature, but he could not help respecting it.

Veldon grimaced. The haunted look returned to his eye.

"It was the crowds. Their reaction, their *cheers*."

"I know," Gellion said gently.

"And to decide a man's life should end based upon a choice he made —a word he said." He shook his head.

Gellion did not answer this time. A circular room of stone swam before his eyes, Liera at its head, calling for her own son's death sentence. Around the room, hands rose to support her proposal. Gellion's pulse quickened. He had felt the same as Veldon, then. He had chosen to keep life and death a matter for Riu's judgment. Now doubt flickered at the edges of his conscience.

To the side, Valder looked between Gellion and Veldon. Neither

Valder nor Veldon knew the full story of what had happened with Kaelo. Like most Turi elves, they knew who Kaelo was, but they had been born after his banishment. He doubted either of them knew how close the elves had come to holding an execution themselves.

"Try not to think about it," Gellion said. "There is nothing we can do to change the practices of the humans, but we can help our own people. We must move forward. Act on the things we can change."

Veldon sighed. "I know." But the deep sadness remained in his face.

The return of dry ground and woody plants was even more welcome than Gellion had imagined. He had not realized how the relentless beating of the sun had worn on him until he entered the shade of trees once more. His was not the only sigh of relief at the coolness, yet the sway of the Marsh Road seemed to stay in his head for hours after stepping onto solid ground. By evening, even that had passed, and Gellion felt reunited with familiar territory once more.

The forest north of the Great Marsh was of dense hardwoods. Grass turned to ferns and leaf litter, and moss covered rocks and tree trunks. The humidity was still oppressive in the trees, but breezes fluttered the leaves above their heads and occasionally touched the forest floor.

The horses seemed as glad as their riders to be free of the marsh. Synabra regained the bounce in her step and renewed her attempts to sabotage Gellion's leadership by nosing ahead of the other horses, or stepping off the path to grab mouthfuls of greenery.

As the path led further from the marsh, monotony returned to their days, bringing with it a kind of comfort and normality. The traders' annoyance at their forced departure from Masar faded into memory, and they looked ahead to the opportunities of the mountains. Pleasant conversation between the two races colored the hours of travel. Only the nearing dangers of the Falspires dampened Gellion's spirits.

Veldon had resumed his study of vierstone at night and acted more himself with each passing day, but he was clearly still troubled by what he had seen in Masar, and, Gellion suspected, what he had seen in Arvain as well. It was a shock, seeing poverty, sickness, and death when one had spent his whole life among the elves in Faeran. Gellion knew better than any how Veldon felt. But it was something he had grown to accept.

After their fourth day of travel, the land began to slope upward. The density of the forest did not thin, but the trees turned from thick, gnarled oaks to slender beeches. The path began to wind, following the easiest way through the steepening terrain. Synabra snorted her displeasure at the increased effort of climbing, but was less inclined to challenge Gellion's authority with her focus on her footing.

"The air is cooler," Valder said after the first day's climb into the Falspires. "But I haven't noticed anything strange yet."

"You will," Eira said. "We are not far enough into the mountains, and it is still daylight. We will have to start setting a guard at night now. Keep the fire alive and watch for signs of danger."

It was with an uneasy heart that Gellion took the first watch that night. He stared into the shadows of the trees as the others slept. The sounds of night overtook the landscape as the moon rose high enough to top the surrounding peaks, but no sound was unfamiliar or concerning. Mostly he heard insects, frogs, and owls. The occasional broken twig or rustling brought his attention in the jerk of the head or a twitch of the ears, but the disturbances rarely repeated, and their sources never came within sight of the glowing embers of the fire. Gellion's anxiety eased with each passing hour of peace, and by the time he woke from a restful sleep in the morning, the rumors of the Falspire's strangeness seemed a silly myth.

The elves broke their fast with palpable relief, but the humans seemed more on guard than ever.

"Today begins the more treacherous mountain roads," Eira said. "And the closer we come to Suri Ranta, the more we will have to worry. Keep your wits about you and do not do anything stupid." She glared at the elves, but Gellion could detect the hint of a smile about her lips.

<hr>

"What was that?" Veldon's was the first voice to sound any alarm.

Gellion tensed and followed his brother's gaze into the deepening shadows of the trees. He got the impression that something had moved just before his eyes focused, but now there was nothing. Veldon's sharp eyes darted back and forth.

"What did you see?" Gellion asked warily.

It was a moment before Veldon responded. He did not look away from the trees as he spoke.

"I saw a shift of the light. Like smoke but more substantial."

"An animal?"

"I don't know." He rubbed the back of his neck, as though flattening raised hairs on his skin.

"I didn't see anything," said Valder. "But I've felt we were being watched since the sun sank below the mountains."

"You may as well get used to that," said Haf over his shoulder. "It won't go away any time soon."

As usual, the elves followed behind the traders, mimicking their more experienced maneuvering as best as they could with their mounts. Eira had been as good as her word. The second day in the Falspires had been painfully slow going, and Gellion had kept a white knuckled grip on his reins the whole time. The road would twist precariously down steep precipices, only to laboriously climb the next incline half a mile on. It felt like they were walking at least three times the distance they covered, and though the path was reasonably well maintained, it gave little regard to railings. Gellion was not afraid of heights, but his trust in the lumbering animal beneath him was less than satisfactory when it came to stumbling next to rocky cliffs.

"If we stop for every strange thing we see or hear in the trees we will be weeks getting to Suri Ranta." There was an exasperated edge to Eira's voice. "Nothing will harm us while we are traveling on the road, not in a group as large as ours and not before dark."

Gellion had long since learned to trust Eira's word when it came to these things, but as twilight lengthened, he found it more and more difficult to ignore the increasing frequency of movements and sounds at the edge of his vision and hearing. No matter how quickly or subtly he moved to catch the phantoms, he could never seem to get a clear view of anything. Glowing eyes winked out of existence beneath a shrub, a wisp of smokey light dissipated in an unfelt breeze, strange calls blended and merged with the sounds of rustling leaves.

Was he imagining it? Were the stories of the mountains playing with his senses and imagination? The feeling of being watched had risen in Gellion now, and he could not seem to shake it.

When Eira called to make camp for the night, Gellion did not know if he was more relieved or wary of staying in one place.

"Are there not any towns we could stop in?" Valder's voice was a little too casual.

While they had not passed through anything Gellion would call a town, smatterings of small dwellings had appeared on neighboring mountainsides, and smaller paths sometimes led from the main road into the trees.

"Not convenient ones, and not here," said Eira. "There are villages in the heart of the mountains, but most Kayda cities lie on the banks of the sounds or along the southern edges of the Falspires bordering the lowland forests. To get to a village, we would have to take side roads, and even then we would find no inns or vacant stables. We would be an inconvenience to the locals."

"And they would be happy to do it," grumbled Talaith. "The Kayda love being hospitable as much as I love sleeping indoors. It's a win-win if you ask me."

Eira looked at her cooly. "It is faster to stay on the road. We have camped along it any number of times."

"And we have had unpleasant experiences many of those times."

"We do not know the local roads," Eira snapped. "Who knows how far they wind through dense forest before joining a village? For all we know, these roads could lead to an abandoned hunting cabin, or a recluse's hideaway as easily as to a welcoming village." She slid smoothly from her horse and stood with resolute finality. "We camp here and leave at first light. With any luck we will reach Suri Ranta the day after tomorrow. Two nights sleeping off the road won't kill you."

"I'll remember those words," Talaith muttered.

Eira ignored her and began to gather wood.

Though Gellion slept little while camping along the mountain road that night, the company met no more than lingering eyes and eerie noises at the edges of the fire.

The next day was grey and cool, and in the hope brought by daylight, Gellion's anxiety turned from the surrounding strangeness to what lay ahead. In less than two days, he would be asking the Kayda for passage across the Semestrial Sea. After all he had been through, arriving safely in Faeran in less than a week seemed an impossible fantasy. Yet the alternative was unthinkable. What would they do if the Kayda refused them? There was no possibility that any ships remained in Daro now, and with the landlocked Elder Clan as their only ally, they would be forced to steal a boat if they wanted any chance of arriving in Faeran before the autumn. The thought was repugnant, but Gellion knew he would do it in his present desperation.

These worries and many others plagued Gellion throughout another day of slow and steep progress through the mountains. The A'vaeri came to his restless mind and attempted to bring order and peace. He could almost feel the reassuring weight of a staff in his hands as he thought through spins and poses with as much precision as he could with open eyes. This worked for a while, but worry crept past his defenses. Even if he did arrive safely in Faeran, he would likely be coming to a situation just as bad, or worse, than his current predicament. It was unbearable not knowing what was happening, and even worse thinking of how his mother must feel amid it all, thinking three of her four sons dead. Tornac would blame Gellion for everything. Maybe he was right.

"Come on, cheer up."

Gellion jumped at the proximity of Valder's voice. He had ridden up beside Gellion.

"After tomorrow, you will never have to sit on a horse again." He grinned, and Gellion half heartedly returned the gesture. Veldon rode just ahead of Gellion, wearing a morose expression similar to what Gellion felt his face must have looked like moments before.

"Between the two of you, I feel we are on a funeral march."

"I was just thinking," Gellion said.

"About what we do if the Kayda refuse us?"

Gellion let his silence answer the question.

"And what we may be returning to if they don't?"

"Well, yes," Gellion admitted.

"It's on my mind, too, you know. But worrying about it won't change what happens, or make an unpleasant future any more bearable. It just ruins the peace of today."

"I agree, but that doesn't make it any easier to stop."

Valder laughed. "No, I suppose it doesn't." He looked past Gellion into the shadow of the trees. "It is a spooky place here, isn't it? It has a way of playing on the nerves, making fears seem worse and hope seem further away."

A shiver ran up Gellion's spine.

"Did you hear the growls last night?" said Valder.

"Yes."

Valder frowned. "I wonder what they were. It made my skin prickle. And the winking lights in the trees—sometimes I felt I could almost hear voices in the breeze."

"I know what you mean," Gellion said. "Everything seems so hostile, as though we are intruders, or being ... being ..."

"Hunted?"

Gellion closed his mouth and nodded. Both he and Valder were silent for a few moments, lost in their own dark thoughts.

"Well it's only one more night," Valder said with forced lightness in his voice. "How much worse can it be?"

The storm did not hit all at once, but Gellion knew something was wrong long before the first peal of thunder or drop of rain.

It started with the fire—an ordinary fire of beechwood that burned merrily in wait for the pot of water that would cook their dinner.

They had stopped to make camp just shy of dusk, and Haf had managed to shoot a couple of rabbits in the dying light. Fresh rabbit with wild rice sounded wonderful after another harrowing day of mountain passes. Gellion was staring into the fire with a rumbling belly, glad for something to look forward to, even if it was only dinner.

The flames licked the wood around the sides and crackled within its depths, shooting spirals of smoke into the air each time they swayed or popped. Gellion knit his brows, leaning closer. A flicker of blue was darting along the face of the fire, there one moment, gone the next, then back again in a new place. The color seemed to have a life of its own, following no pattern of breeze or heat.

Curious, Gellion reached for a stick and leaned toward the fire. Slowly, he reached forward, submerging the stick into the fire's base.

Without warning, a tongue of flame shot out like a whip and lashed across his hand. Gellion yelped and dropped the stick, scrambling backward.

Everyone in the company turned to stare at him. Their alarm turned to amusement when they saw Gellion crouching with a burned hand, but Gellion sat watching the fire in shock. Had there been a sudden gust of wind he hadn't noticed? Had the stick been exceptionally dry, causing the flames to engulf it instantaneously? But the fire had traveled through the air, not up the stick. It had lashed out directly at Gellion's hand and disappeared after it struck true.

Gellion rubbed the back of his hand where an angry welt was forming.

"Here, pour some water on it." Veldon held out his flask to Gellion.

"Thanks," Gellion muttered, letting out a breath of relief as the cool water took some of the sting from his hand.

"What happened?" Something in Veldon's face bespoke more than brotherly concern. He glanced at the fire warily.

"I don't know," said Gellion. "I saw blue flickers in the flames so I stuck a stick into them, and the fire just—lashed me. It jumped through the air and burned me. I know it sounds crazy."

"No." Veldon's eyes scanned the trees around them, then the sky. "There is something in the air tonight. An energy I do not like."

"What do you mean?"

Veldon did not get the chance to answer. A loud crash followed by a string of shouts and curses brought them both to their feet. A pot lay on the ground next to the fire, its contents soaking the surrounding soil and Haf's feet. Haf himself, who was evidently the source of the cursing, was bent double, holding one arm with a grimace of pain.

"Haf!" Talaith ran to him, coaxing his injured arm away from his side. It was bright red from wrist to elbow.

"It just flared up!" he said. "Doubled in size when I tried to set the pot over it."

Sure enough, the fire was noticeably larger now—too large for the amount of wood it burned.

"Everyone get back," Eira said sharply, not taking her eyes off the fire. Even as she watched, the flames reached higher still, blue sparks now lacing the orange like poison in veins.

"What is it?" Valder stepped beside Gellion and Veldon.

Eira didn't answer, but looked to the sky, where, even in the darkening blue of the evening, the outline of black clouds was evident above the mountains. The mass moved toward them with visible haste, a stain on the sky spreading like ink.

"Into the trees." Eira gathered her bag and two of the horses and made for the shelter of the forest.

Gellion glanced at his brothers. Veldon looked worried, Valder confused.

"Come on." Gellion moved to help Talaith with the unpacked sacks.

They hurried beneath the trees and piled their packs together. Just as Gellion looped Synabra's lead rope around a low branch, a gust of wind so strong it almost stung his skin roared up the slope, nearly knocking him to the ground. Synabra let out a shriek and pulled back against her restraint. The whites of her eyes showed even more than usual, and she pawed the ground wildly.

"Easy!" Gellion shouted, though he could barely hear his own voice over the thrashing branches above him. He grabbed the mare's rope and tried to pull her close enough to place a hand on her neck. Behind him, he heard the cacophony of similar struggles.

"Don't—escape!"

Gellion caught disjointed words on the air, though he could not tell who had shouted them. Synabra was standing still again, but her eyes rolled, and her nostrils flared.

A hand gripped Gellion's shoulder, and he wheeled around to see Veldon trying to lead him to their pile of belongings. The traders were huddled on top of the supplies, which were backed against a copse of trees.

"Stay low," Eira shouted over the roar of the wind. "And stay alert."

Gellion reached for the hunting knife at his hip, which the traders had blessedly returned to him after leaving Masar.

"What's happening?" he demanded. The wind whipped his hair in alternating directions, obscuring his vision.

"A storm," Eira said unhelpfully.

"The fire—"

"We told you the storms of the mountains were not normal storms," Talaith said.

The cold touch of rain brought goosebumps to Gellion's skin. He wished they had more cover than the trees, but nothing short of a building would shelter them from the rain in this twisting wind. He squinted and ducked as water cascaded through the leaves above and whipped into his face. It was as though someone were throwing the water directly at him.

A flash of silver illuminated the mountains, bringing millions of raindrops into a frozen moment of sharp relief before leaving the forest in darkness somehow infinitely blacker than before. A crash of thunder shook the ground beneath Gellion's feet, followed by a deep rumble reminiscent of a growling beast.

The horses screamed. Gellion was suddenly glad that all of the company's supplies were underneath them and not strapped to the panicked animals. He would be shocked if all eight of the beasts were still here after the storm ended. If it ended.

"It came so fast!" Valder's face shone wetly in another flash of lightning.

"Let's hope it ends as quickly." Gellion spat out the rainwater that had flooded into his mouth when he spoke. He could not have been wetter if he jumped in a lake, and with the wind, the temperature felt more like late autumn than summer. Wrapping his arms around himself, Gellion bent over and tried to shield himself from the relentless rain and freezing blasts of wind, simultaneously praying to Riu that they were not all obliterated by a bolt of lightning.

Even as the thought occurred to him, the air seemed to shimmer with electricity. Gellion could feel the hair on his arms fighting against the rain to stand on end.

Please. Make it stop.

This time Gellion heard the thunder before he saw the lightning. A crack sounded so loud he thought the world must be splitting apart, and then everything was drowned in white. Gellion threw his arms over his head instinctively through air so charged with electricity that it almost felt solid.

He waited for the pain, for the end. He waited to smell burning flesh and fall into darkness. But the blinding light died away, and he still felt the icy kiss of rain on his arms.

More cracks rent the air, and Gellion dared to peek through his arms. Lightning lit up the trees in nearly continuous flashes now, lending an air of slow motion to Gellion's surroundings. He saw a huge shape moving through the trees and heard branches splinter and crack.

Smoke and steam rose from the body of the tree as it fell, and as Gellion's eyes tracked its movement, he saw a huddled figure beneath it.

Gellion tried to shout a warning, but knew it was no use in the noise of the storm. Instead, he sprang from his crouch toward the figure, grabbed on to the first bit of clothes and skin he encountered, and staggered backward with all his might, pulling a body with him.

Though Gellion could not distinguish the tree's crash from the thunder, the ground shook with the weight of its trunk as it hit the soggy ground. Gellion twisted away from the onslaught of branches and dove forward so that he landed on top of who he now recognized as Haf. He gritted his teeth as branches slammed into his back and twigs bit through his clothes like needles. Following their initial impact, the branches swung back and slapped Gellion again. As the tree's momentum slowed, the wind continued to whip its branches.

"Crawl!" he shouted into Haf's ear, trying to shift enough of his weight off the man to allow him to move forward. With what sounded like a steady stream of cursing, Haf managed to extricate himself from under Gellion. Gellion pulled himself under the branches behind Haf, doing his best to shield his face from the twigs while keeping his limbs from sinking in the sticky mud.

After an agonizing minute, Haf grabbed Gellion's wrists and pulled him free of the mangled beech tree.

His brothers were at his side in a moment.

"I was sure it crushed you." There was a slight quaver to Valder's voice. "Over here."

The pile of supplies lay half buried beneath the fallen tree, but Eira and Talaith were crouched atop those that remained exposed.

"Is anyone hurt?" Eira called.

Haf grunted and slumped to the ground next to her. Seeming satisfied with this answer, Eira turned to Gellion.

Every inch of Gellion's skin stung from scrapes, but he shook his head and joined his brothers next to the humans.

"Should we go back to the road?" he asked.

"No," Eira said without hesitation. "We would be blown off the mountain, and trees can fall over the road as easily as here. We just have to wait. It can't last all night."

Another bolt of lightning exploded a tree in the distance, causing all of them to jump. Amid the flashes of lightning, Gellion thought he saw wisps of red and purple lights moving about the trees, reflecting off the rain drops.

Ether spirits.

Toward the road, a brighter light caught his attention.

Squinting through the rain and the trees, Gellion could just make out the glowing outline of their campfire, its red and blue flames still burning fiercely through the storm.

21

THROUGH THE WALLS

Renyra sat on her bed with her torn and stained wraps in her lap. Where she was going, there would be no shortage of brand new wraps in every color and pattern imaginable, yet she could not bring herself to dispose of these that had seen her through the destruction of Daro and a battle. She tucked them into her bag.

The nice thing about owning almost no belongings anymore was that she had very little to pack. An extra set of clothes and enough food for a few days was all she needed—that, and a javelin and dagger.

Leaving Tura was bittersweet. This apartment had never felt like home, but for a short while the city had given Renyra a foundation after her whole life had been flipped upside down. Training Sira, going to Council meetings, and walking the market strip of the Orhiri River had become a new normal—a reliable routine. But Renyra knew that staying in Tura would not guarantee the continuation of that routine. There was an ominous air about the city. Every elf waited with bated breath to see what Kaelo would do next, and there was little the Council could do about it until they received vierstone from Maramor. Renyra would do all she could to make sure that happened.

One last thing went into Renyra's bag. She had not worn her vierstone earring since it had turned black. It was a loss she did her best not to dwell on, for its implications were so anxiety inducing as to make her panic. She had tried to find a replacement earring, but vierstone earrings were typically commissioned, almost always for the birth of a child. As this was not a terribly common event, there were no vierstone jewelers by craft anymore, just those common jewelers here and there with the necessary skills.

Tura was probably the easiest place in all of Faeran to find such an elf, but everything had happened so fast after Renyra's confrontation with Kaelo. It seemed impossible that it had been less than a week since that traumatic night. Renyra shivered. She had gone to the Guild Quarter with Firas, but every elf they spoke to had said it would take weeks to create an earring. They did not have weeks, and now any vierstone they could have used was melted in a hidden furnace. Renyra could only hope that she would be able to obtain a replacement in Telem Fier.

Everything Firas had ever said about elves without vierstone ran through Renyra's mind each time she thought about her earring. How quickly would it take effect? Had she already grown more distant from Firas without noticing? She didn't care about losing crafting skill—she never crafted in the first place—but her connection to her family and friends was everything to her. She moved her fingers to her head, shoulder, and chest.

"Ready?" Firas walked into the room, dressed in dark traveling clothes.

"Yes."

"What's wrong?" he said immediately.

Renrya smiled and shook her head. "Nothing. I just hope I can get a new earring in Telem Fier."

"I am sure that you will." He put a hand on her shoulder. The pressure was comforting, but Renyra did not feel the usual thrill of awareness from him.

"You can wear mine until then," he said.

Renyra drew back. "I could never! Firas no, please keep your earring. It's my own fault mine is gone."

"Because you tried to stop Kaelo? How is that your fault?"

"I should have been more careful. I underestimated him."

"We have all underestimated him." He sat next to her on the bed. "Being without vierstone for a few weeks will not have any noticeable effect on you. It would take years."

Renyra nodded, but worry still clouded her mind.

"If you are that concerned," said Firas, "just ask for a small piece of vierstone when we get to Rone. You can carry it in your pocket, or strap it to your wrist until you can get a new earring."

Renyra lit up at once. "That's a great idea!"

Firas smiled.

Renyra collapsed against Firas and wound her arms around his waist.

"I can't believe that I'm going back to Telem Fier—that *we're* going back. It will be so wonderful to see the grasslands again. And the smells! And tastes."

"Mmm," said Firas with an exaggerated sigh. "I do look forward to the food."

Renyra snorted. "Stop teasing. I'm excited."

"I know," Firas chuckled. "It is good to see you so. I know how much this means to you."

"I only wish it were under better circumstances," Renyra said. "I can't imagine how Auralia and Cuvan will react when we tell them everything. I don't know what they can even do before hearing more from Liera."

"I think the best thing they can do is mobilize the Fieri and the Remsgri—to prepare for an attack like Daro and Tura, should the worst occur. Gather what vierstone they can collect and set guards."

"Yes." Renyra sighed. "By the time we get to Telem Fier, I expect Liera will have forged the sword of vierstone if everything goes to plan."

Firas nodded, but there was a line between his brows.

"What?" Renyra asked.

"I don't know. There is just something about all of this that doesn't seem right."

A chill crept along Renyra's spine. "You feel it too?"

Firas looked at her sharply.

"I don't know how to explain it," Renyra said. "Just—making a sword out of vierstone—*killing* an elf with vierstone. It seems wrong.

More wrong that just killing him in the first place, I mean. Do you think Tenille could be wrong about the vierstone?"

Firas was silent for a moment. He stared straight ahead, deep in thought. "Her interpretation does make sense with the words of the prophecy." He shook his head. "I can think of no better explanation."

Renyra was ashamed by the relief she felt that the happenings in Tura were about to be out of her hands. She was tired of making decisions that affected an entire city and more than happy to remove herself from a situation that could involve murder, but the very existence of these thoughts brought a nagging guilt to her conscience.

You cannot help everywhere all at once. You must choose where your strengths lie.

Forging swords was not her strength, nor was fighting other elves. Renyra was a skilled hunter and enjoyed her time tracking and throwing javelins in the wilderness, but she had felt a useless coward in the battle at Arvain. She had hated every moment of it and had been as afraid of killing as of dying. Not to mention, her two attempts at attacking Kaelo had ended in disaster. Her double failure still burned inside her chest.

It doesn't matter as long as he's stopped.

Sneaking out of cities and carrying important messages was much more to Renyra's abilities—and to her liking. She would do far more good on this journey than she would staying behind. She only hoped it would be enough.

It felt almost familiar to dress in black and slip out of the apartment at night, but this time Renyra did not know if she would ever return. It was not nerves, but excitement that charged through her blood as she stepped down the street, Firas in tow. They were not going far. Liera had prepared a boat for them in the river just south of the Central City.

Renyra did her best to walk casually. It was not yet so late that the streets were empty. They had decided that a boat moving upriver in the dead of night would be more suspicious than one posing as a barge for goods moving a late evening shipment. There would be nothing to suspect until they had passed the Central City, and even then, Kaelo would have to be holding constant watch on the river to notice them. Renyra thought it unlikely Kaelo was watching the river at all.

"We must assume he knows everything of our plan," Firas had said when Renyra voiced her doubts. "We do not yet know how he gets his information. I think it is wise to guess that he knows exactly what we are doing and when we are doing it, and prepare to escape despite him."

Renyra's hand strayed to her back, her fingers brushing the javelin secured there. She no longer had much confidence using the weapon against Kaelo, but it was better than nothing.

"There," Firas whispered, nudging Renyra toward a dark shape bobbing in the water ahead of them.

Renyra nodded silently and quickened her pace. She strained all of her senses to detect any sign of watching eyes or shifted shadows, but caught no trace of suspicious activity.

"I suppose we should wait in the boat?" she said as they approached the lapping shore of the river. Crates and bags were interspersed in the boat, some containing food supplies for their journey, some empty to provide shelter. All gave the illusion of simple purpose.

Renyra leaped over the side of the boat and landed on soft feet in its bowed belly. She nearly shouted in shock when a shape loomed from behind a box.

"It's me," Alura said quickly. "And Raren." A second shape rose beside her.

Renyra let out a shaky breath. "Are any others here yet?"

"I am."

Renyra nearly jumped again at the deep voice that came from her other side.

Tornac sat with his back against a crate, his legs stretched out to the edge of the boat.

Hopefully Kaelo will be as fooled by the emptiness of this boat as I was.

Across Tornac's lap lay the most beautiful sword Renyra had ever seen—all curves and engravings.

"Are the others with you?" he said, stopping the smooth motion of his sharpener.

"Just Firas," said Renyra. "I guess we're still waiting on Caerlyn and Kyna."

The rest of the troupe had not questioned Tornac's involvement in their plan or Renyra's decision to include Kyna. Of course, Renyra had made it sound as though Liera had suggested them both. Firas had raised a knowing eyebrow when she told him. Renyra didn't care what he thought of her insistence to include Kyna. She was convinced that Kyna did want to come with them, but was held to Tura by something Renyra did not know. This plan provided the perfect opportunity for Kyna to get out of the city and help without being away for too long. Besides, Renyra had seen Kyna's appreciative glances at Tornac. She should be thanking Renyra for putting the two of them on a boat together for days.

"There's Caerlyn," Alura said softly.

A tall and curvy form was gliding beside the river.

Definitely Caerlyn. But where's Kyna?

Renyra was afraid that Kyna would not show. She had reluctantly agreed to Renyra's plan, and it would be all too easy for her to simply not come to the boat. It had crossed Renyra's mind to go to the woman's apartment before coming tonight, but she thought she had pushed her luck as far as it would go with Kyna.

"We'll wait ten more minutes." Renyra tried to sound confident.

The minutes dragged by. Tornac had stopped sharpening his sword and sheathed the shining work of art so that the only sounds were those of the lapping water around them and the distant murmur of voices from passersby.

A soft rocking of the boat was the only indication that another elf had joined their number. Renyra wheeled around, and a wild panic possessed her as she saw a pale face framed by dark hair.

"Alright, I'm here."

A relief as powerful as her fear rippled through Renyra's body like electricity. It was Kyna. The look on her face left no doubt as to her feelings regarding Renyra's plan, but she had come.

Renyra smiled weakly. "I thought you were Kaelo, come to foil our escape before it began." She glanced toward the others. All were relaxing now that Renyra was talking to the new arrival. Several lowered the weapons they had drawn at Renyra's gasp.

"The night's still young," Kyna said.. "Are we all here then?" Her eyes drifted over the dark shapes in the boat, lingering for a moment on Tornac before quickly moving back to Renyra.

"Yes," said Renyra. "Raren, are you ready?"

Raren nodded and moved to the back of the boat to the motor. They would have to go against the current the whole way to Lake Orhirion, but the solar powered motor was well tested against long journeys up the river, at least according to Liera.

"You remember what to do if you see anything suspicious?" Renyra said.

"Tap the side of the boat twice," Raren said. "But it's more likely you'll all know as soon as I do if we're attacked."

"Well, hopefully we won't need any of these precautions," Renyra said.

Raren was right. If Kaelo tried to stop them, it was bound to be a sudden and targeted strike. If it was something other than Kaelo— Renyra shuddered at the memory of lindworms erupting from the water like writhing intestines. She rubbed her arm subconsciously and shook her head.

"Everyone get down and stay silent. Keep your weapons within easy reach."

The elves melted into the shadows.

Renyra moved between Firas and a crate and lowered herself to her knees, bending over until she was beneath the side of the boat. Firas had more trouble making himself small, but pulled his hood closer around his face. Renyra could see the glint of a knife in one hand.

"Off we go," Raren said softly.

The burr of the motor overrode the sounds of the river as they surged forward. Renyra reminded herself that a supply boat going up the river was nothing suspicious. A buzzing motor would not give them away. Even so, Renyra flinched when an elf greeted Raren from the shore.

"That's good," Firas whispered next to Renyra's ear. "It makes us seem more natural."

Renyra nodded, but still her pulse mounted.

The surrounding lights grew brighter, and she assumed they were nearing the Markets. After a few more minutes, the lights began to flicker as they passed beneath trees, then went dark for several moments.

That will be the central bridge.

They were halfway through the Central City, but it was the area beyond the Guild Quarter that made Renyra nervous.

The Archives passed to one side, dark but for a few illuminated windows on the upper floors. Then the forges loomed over them from the other side of the river—huge, open air kilns, furnaces, and basins, all covered by a high roof. Only the slack tub sat open to the skies. It nestled right against the river, uncovered to gather rainwater. Its shadow enveloped the boat as they made their way toward the northern bridge, beyond which were only neighborhoods and gardens until they reached the walls of the city.

Renyra listened hard, but as they passed under the northern bridge, even the distant sounds of voices faded until the boat's motor and the song of insects were all that remained. The two sounds mingled until Renyra's ears were filled with sonorous humming. She tried to extend her senses beyond the boat and the river. All seemed quiet.

Raren had not spoken since acknowledging the elf who had called his name. Renyra wished he would say something encouraging, tell them that all was clear and safe ahead, but she knew a lone boat driver talking to himself would draw attention if any were watching. She bowed her head and waited for the attack she hoped would never come.

"The walls are ahead." Firas's voice was barely above a breath.

Renyra's heart leaped. Would they make it? Could it truly be so easy?

The boat moved forward at a steady pace.

We're close enough now, Raren. Speed up. Just a little.

Renyra willed the boat to go faster, to slip past the walls unnoticed. She could see the walls now if she craned her neck up—two slabs of stone rising to the star flecked sky.

Firas went rigid.

"What?" Renyra whispered.

"Didn't you feel it?" Firas said, his big eyes darting to the side of the river.

"No, I—"

The snap of splitting stone sounded in the air. Renyra gasped and sat up so fast her head smacked against the crate behind her. She yelped and grabbed at the back of her head, but quickly forgot the pain when she saw the cracks in the wall to the right of the river.

"Go!" she shouted. "Go through!"

Raren had not needed prompting. Before Renyra's last word he had revved the motor, and the boat shot forward. The rest of the elves peeled away from the boat's shadows and drew their weapons, looking all around for any sign of an elf. Renyra saw nothing.

Ahead, the wall began to crumble. An ominous moaning emitted from the stone.

"Faster!" Renyra gripped the edge of the boat with white knuckles. She strained her eyes through the darkness to look for Kaelo. He must be touching the wall. If they could see him, they could shoot at him, and although the likelihood of incapacitating him was next to nothing, they might be able to distract him long enough to get through before he collapsed the walls on the river.

"Can you see him?" Renyra called to Alura, who had her bow drawn and an arrow nocked.

Alura shook her head furiously, moving her aim between the two walls, ready to release an arrow at any sign of movement.

Then the wall blew apart into huge chunks, collapsing into the river with a series of booming splashes. Many of the pieces sank, but the river was not deep, and hunks of stone stacked on top of one another and stuck out of the water. Only a narrow strip of open water remained on the left side of the river—where the southern wall still stood. Surely Kaelo would not be able to get across the river before they reached the wreckage?

"There!" Raren pointed to a shadow flitting over the rubble.

Renyra dropped her jaw in disbelief as she watched what must be Kaelo leap from rock to rock and take a flying jump to land on the far side of the river. Alura loosed an arrow, but it flew far behind Kaelo.

They were almost to the walls now.

"Don't go to the left," Kyna said.

Renyra stared at her in amazement.

"He'll collapse the southern wall any moment," Kyna continued.

"We'll be caught in the falling rubble if we keep going at this rate. There are gaps in the stone sticking out of the river. We have a better chance of maneuvering through those."

Renyra could no longer see Kaelo, but heard the familiar crack of rock. Her eyes darted to the rubble lying in the water. Kyna was right. The pieces were huge, but there might be enough space between them to slip through. But the boat was so close to the opening now. Surely Kaelo couldn't collapse the wall before they reached the gap?

The moment of indecision tore at Renyra's nerves. "Go to the right!" she called at last.

The boat swerved wildly, throwing its occupants against crates and nearly tossing Alura out of its belly altogether. Tornac grabbed her arm and pulled her back in just in time for the boat to swerve the other direction.

Renyra shouted as water sprayed her in the face. Thick slabs of rock seemed to be on all sides.

"Hold on!" Raren yelled.

A terrible grinding sound accompanied violent vibrations as the boat skidded over the surface of one of the hunks of stone. Through the screaming metal of the motor, Renyra thought she heard the sounds of the other wall collapsing. The boat tipped sideways, spilling several sacks and a crate over the side as its propellers grasped for purchase. Then they were falling forward and landed in deep water with a satisfying *plunk*.

They seemed to stay in place for an eternal moment while the motor drank thirstily. Then it shot them forward again.

Raren whooped.

Renyra turned back to see two huge bites out of Tura's walls. Water frothed at the blocked opening into the city.

Sweet Riu, we did it. We got out.

Kaelo had been waiting for them.

"Why did he wait until we were at the walls?" Renyra wondered aloud. "He could have stopped us getting in the boat in the first place."

"He probably expected Liera to send elves out of the city by river," Tornac said, helping Firas restack a crate that had tipped over. "But I doubt he knew our exact plan. He couldn't watch the whole river." He wiped his hands on his shirt and looked around. "Is everyone alright?"

General nods met his words.

"Well done, Raren," Firas said.

"And Kyna," Raren said. "I think she was right. We would have been crushed by that wall if we had tried to slip under it."

Renyra turned to grin at Kyna, but the woman wasn't listening. She stood with her back to the group, looking out at the outline of distant mountains in the west, where the sky still held the last faded streaks of the evening's blue.

Something about her stance stopped Renyra from going to her. Was she imagining her home on that horizon? She had said she was from the mountains of Ard Gael. Would it be hard for her, passing so near her past without stopping?

Renyra faced downriver, watching the twinkling lights of Tura recede behind them. She thought of her return to Daro after the battle —how the Icemelt River had cascaded off an empty cliffside into the sea. Would she meet the same sight the next time she came to Tura?

There will be no more Daros. Not if I have anything to do with it.

They were on their way to Maramor. They would send vierstone back to Tura.

And then Tura's fate rests with Riu.

2 2

SURI RANTA

Gellion never thought he would be so grateful for sore feet, nor for the sight of a goat. The shaggy animals lifted their heads from the grass to consider the newcomers, then bleated their acknowledgement and returned to their task, clearly deciding the company posed little enough threat to detract from their lunch.

The beasts were curious, different from any species of goat Gellion had ever seen. Their horns spiraled backward and their ears flopped below their cheeks. The hair on some brushed the ground and obscured all signs that legs were concealed beneath.

It was not the goats, however, that made Gellion's jaw drop.

The pastureland sloped down the mountains to a river that cut through the range as though someone had sliced its path with a knife. The road followed the winding course of the river, and as it curved around the next bend, the pastureland abruptly ended, replaced by the strangest geography Gellion had ever seen.

The slopes were almost entirely devoid of trees, but shone an emerald green in the noon sun. What at first appeared to be ripples ran along their surface, but as Gellion looked closer, he saw they were cuts in the mountain, giant stair steps like the tiers of Daro that descended from the highest tree line to the river bank. The lines flowed in perfect sequence, each level the same width as the last.

"Tea."

Gellion tore his eyes away from the slopes to look at Haf, who sat his horse next to Gellion.

"All tea." He indicated the ripples of land.

"They grow crops *on* the mountain?" Gellion asked.

"Have to. They don't have enough flat land to support fields like we have."

Gellion stared at the terraces in fascination, trying to imagine how the humans could have altered the landscape so drastically.

Flickers of movement within the rows of tea plants caught Gellion's eye. There were people among the terraces, tending the plants. Throughout the morning, the forests had been thinning, and the slope of the land gentling. The goats had given Gellion hope that humans could not be far off, and now these clear signs of civilization were more welcome than Gellion could express. They would arrive in Suri Ranta by the end of the day. Finally.

The company would have reached Suri Ranta the day before had it not been for the storm. In what Gellion was sure was the longest night of his life, the storm had raged for hours on end, never loosening its grip for an instant until it died out in the hours before dawn. Two of the horses had disappeared—a pack horse, and Valder's mount, Bresgian. Valder had not been terribly cut up over the loss, and Gellion had been quick to offer Synabra as a replacement pack horse, joining his brother on foot for the remainder of the journey. The healing cuts on his leg still bothered him after hours of walking, but it felt good to use his own two feet again.

The mountain path had been strewn with leaves and branches, even the occasional tree that they had to maneuver around or move, but all signs of the storm had mysteriously disappeared within a short distance of their campsite, and the path had remained unimpeded ever since. Still, their time moving trees for a morning and the loss of two mounts had slowed them.

Their extra night in the mountains had not been pleasant, though no more storms came. The closer the company got to Suri Ranta, the closer the glowing eyes in the shadows seemed to come to their fire at night. Wisps of light still flickered at the edges of Gellion's vision in the darkness. He was sure they were spirits now and was immeasurably grateful for the prospect of sleeping behind closed doors tonight, wherever they may be.

"We'll get to Suri Ranta by evening." Haf urged his mount forward again. "The road keeps sloping down till it meets with the Sielu Sound at the end of this river. The city's on the banks of the sound."

Haf had been uncharacteristically talkative with the elves since the night of the storm. Gellion met the man's gruff offer of companionship with relief. If dragging Haf away from a falling tree was the only way to earn his trust, Gellion supposed it had been worth it.

The tea plantations slowly transitioned to a mix of root crops and cabbages with strips of pastureland between. Small houses began to appear between fields, and the river below steadily widened. Just before evening, the mountains opened to the Sielu Sound. Golden light slanted onto a glassy surface of water that stretched to far shores. On two sides of the sound, mountains rose straight out of the water, reflecting on its surface in a perfect mirror. Even the clouds reflected on the water, their edges beginning to color with the sinking sun. Nestled on a piece of flat land that extended from the river's opening, sat Suri Ranta.

It was not as large as Gellion had expected, for the traders had claimed the city was the center of the Kayda people. The winding rows of brown buildings would have fit snugly into the second tier of Daro, though Gellion saw houses extending up the slopes into the mountains. Unlike Masar, Suri Ranta was not a city of straight lines, but artful arcs and circles. The streets ribboned through houses that from a distance formed patterns reminiscent of the terraced tea fields. Each building was made of brown wood, with steep roofs and stone chimneys.

Gellion took a deep breath as he looked beyond the city to the docks that extended into the water. Narrow ships dotted the sound, some anchored next to the docks, some floating in its deep middle. One ship was making steady progress for the far end of the sound that disappeared around a mountain in the distance. The water would keep going until it merged with the Semestrial Sea—until it broke on the shores of Faeran.

Talaith had said the Kayda were a hospitable people, but after his treatment in the last three human nations, Gellion was still taken aback by the quiet eagerness with which the Kayda welcomed the company into their town.

Upon the company's arrival, several young men, following the stern direction of a middle-aged woman, took all of the horses to a low roofed stable on the outskirts of the city. There was much bowing during this interaction, to which Gellion smiled uncertainly, trying to show his thanks.

"You will have dinner with us?" asked the woman who had directed the care of their horses. She smiled, bringing about a web of laugh lines around her eyes and mouth. A few strands of grey shot through her black hair, which was swept on top of her head with painted pins.

"Certainly," said Eira. "It is good to see you again, Ruta."

Ruta's grin widened. "And you Miss Eira." She had a motherly, round face, and skin as smooth and golden as honey. She spoke the trade language with a subtle accent that lent a much more musical lilt to the words compared with the Albaren or the Dierna.

She turned her eyes on the rest of the company.

"You know Talaith from our last stay," Eira said. Talaith smiled and bowed to Ruta, who returned the gesture in kind. "You have not met Haf?"

"I have not had the honor." Ruta bowed to Haf, then looked to the elves. She saw Gellion first, and made no change in her pleasant expression, but as her gaze moved to Valder and Veldon, apprehension flitted across her eyes. Her smile strained.

"We have brought some friends," Eira said with only the slightest hesitation before the last word. "Elves, from the coast north of Albarad."

Gellion held his breath, watching Ruta for her reaction. Everything depended on the Kayda's reception of the elves.

Ruta nodded slowly, seeming to evaluate the elves. Again, her eyes lingered on Valder and Veldon. Gellion tried to assume a pleased and open expression, hoping his brothers were doing the same. Finally, Ruta's face split again into a smile, though Gellion could still sense wariness behind it.

"They too are welcome in our home." She bowed to Gellion and his brothers. "Come, rest and change while I make dinner." Ruta turned away and began to walk into the streets of Suri Ranta, clearly assuming the company would follow on her heels.

Gellion hesitated. He had wanted to go straight to the city's leader, to present Eurig's letter immediately. Eira seemed to read his thoughts on his face.

"We will see the Sovereign soon," she said in a low voice. "Perhaps even tonight. But it would be unmentionably rude to refuse an offer of dinner from our hosts."

"You have stayed with this family before?" Gellion asked. As they walked, many interested stares followed them through the streets, though they bore an essence of curiosity rather than suspicion.

"A few times. When we have larger trading parties, everyone is scattered among houses. I stayed with Ruta and her family once, and she has insisted on claiming me for every visit since." Eira rolled her eyes, but there was unmistakable fondness in her voice. "The boys who took our horses are her nephews."

"She was expecting us?"

"She often lingers near the city gates in the evening. She is the spirit guide for the city and wards the gates each night."

Gellion fought the urge to glance over his shoulder toward the path that led from the mountains.

"Is it safe to walk the streets at night?" he asked with what he hoped was a light voice.

Eira shrugged. "I've never had any trouble, but then I rarely walk the streets of Suri Ranta at night."

Gellion eyed the deepening colors of the sky, unsure if he was reassured or not.

Ruta's home was square and dark with paneled sides and a pointed roof. There was no grass outside the house, but rocks, arranged in artful formations with wooden sculptures and fences interspersed in a simple but tasteful display. Ruta removed her shoes before opening the front door, and Gellion did likewise. He noticed a dried bunch of flowers and leaves nailed to the top of the door frame.

"Manu!" a high voice called the moment Ruta entered her home. A small boy who barely came to Gellion's knees stumbled to a stop in the middle of the front room. He had the same golden skin as his mother with black fringe nearly covering a pair of wide eyes that stared with something between fierce interest and uncertainty at the group of strangers.

"Shh," Ruta said softly to the child, muttering several words that Gellion did not understand.

Gellion nudged Veldon, who was staring at the boy with an expression as shocked as the child's. At Gellion's prompting, Veldon wrestled his features into a more neutral expression, though his eyes still drew inexorably to the small boy.

"We have guests, Aku," Ruta called. "We serve six more tonight."

"Six?" a man's voice answered from the neighboring room. The man called Aku stepped into the room wiping his hands on a towel. He was the same height as Ruta, with a thin mustache and long goatee.

"Ah," he said with a jolly grin after a glance at his guests. "Dierna traders, then. I will double the menu. Half an hour." With that, he bounced back into what Gellion assumed was the kitchen.

"I will help with the meal," Ruta said. "Please, make yourselves comfortable. Come, Hakan." The little boy followed his mother into the kitchen, but stared at the company over his shoulder until he was pulled out of sight.

Gellion looked around. The room had polished wooden floors and walls, with sliding doors leading to adjoining rooms. The space was simply decorated with low furniture, candles, and furs. The atmosphere was strangely calming, but Gellion's mind still could not rest. A glance at Veldon and Valder told him they felt the same. Though each sat on a low couch with hands clasped before them, both were exchanging glances and fidgeting.

Gellion sat next to them.

"Eira says we will speak with the Sovereign tonight if possible," he said softly.

They nodded, but anxiety showed plain in their eyes. This breach in their composure did nothing for Gellion's own nerves. He tried to take heart that the Kayda had been welcoming thus far, but showing politeness to strangers did not equate to gifting them with a boat. The elves had no way to repay the Kayda, no way to earn their trust or respect.

Gellion fingered Eurig's folded letter in his pocket. He had carried the note on his person ever since the night of the storm, terrified that it would be damaged or lost before their arrival in Suri Ranta.

Now they were here. Perhaps just a few blocks away from the person who could enable the elves' return to their kin. Would they be back in Tura within the week? How long had it been since the battle at Arvain, since the refugees of Daro returned to Faeran? Gellion had lost track of time completely, but was sure it had been at least a month since the battle. Kaelo could accomplish a lot in a month.

In the precarious mountain passes, Gellion had expected to be distracted from his usual thoughts and dreams of his old mentor, but the eyes that surrounded the campfires at night had reminded him too vividly of the creatures that had converged upon Daro in the last weeks before its downfall. Something about the mountains felt *wrong*. Wrong in a similar way to the earthquakes and the dying vierstone and the monsters.

He was sure it was all in his head. The mountains were a strange place, but there was no reason to allow them to disturb him, not when he hoped to leave as quickly as possible.

Gellion's musings were cut short by shuffling footsteps behind one of the sliding doors. A shadow appeared in the frosted panels, and the door slid smoothly to the side to reveal a stooped woman. Everyone in the room stood automatically.

A strange tightness seized Gellion's chest. The woman's face was a net of wrinkles, her hair steely gray and thin. She was tiny, and moved with obvious difficulty into the room. Gellion was both seized by a desire to help the woman and shamefully repelled by her advanced age.

"Heleena." Eira bowed to the old woman.

Heleena peered at Eira for a moment, and Gellion wondered if her eyesight was poor. The wrinkles around her eyes certainly seemed to be squeezing and obscuring them. After a moment, however, the old woman smiled and nodded, stepping forward to grasp Eira's hands in her own knobbed and wrinkled fingers.

"This is Aku's grandmother," Eira said.

Gellion's eyebrows rose before he could stop them. This was the grandmother of the stout man he had just seen, which meant she was the *great*-grandmother of the little boy. Though such relations were incredibly common among the elves, he had never met anyone in Tradira with a great-grand anything. He wondered how old this woman was.

Eira introduced Heleena to each member of the company. Again, Gellion braced himself for the old woman's reaction to meeting elves, but again the information that creatures of legend stood in her living room seemed to bring her no great surprise—until she saw Veldon and Valder.

Her eyes traveled shrewdly between the brothers, and a strange light seemed to glow in her gaze. Valder and Veldon clearly noticed the reaction as well, and their smiles faded slightly under the woman's scrutiny. Gellion knit his brows. Why them? The Kayda seemed to have no issue with elves in general, or with Gellion, but something about Valder and Veldon gave them pause. The only noticeable difference Gellion could conceive between himself and his brothers was his hair color, but all the Kayda seemed to have black hair, just like Valder and Veldon. Did they find the look strange on a foreign race?

"It is an honor to meet you," Veldon said.

Gellion could tell Veldon was fighting not to stare at Heleena the same way he had stared at Hakan. He was sure Veldon had never seen a being so outwardly old in all his life.

"You have a lovely home," Veldon continued.

Heleena considered Veldon with what Gellion thought might be narrowed eyes, though it was hard to tell. She tilted her head back to see him more clearly. Veldon retained his polite smile. If he was uncomfortable, he did an excellent job concealing it.

Whatever Heleena saw in Veldon seemed to satisfy her, for her expression softened.

"You are kind." Her voice was deeper than Gellion had expected and held a soft quaver. She turned back to Eira. "How was your journey through the mountains?"

Eira told Heleena of the storm, describing the fire, the lights, and the fallen tree. Heleena's face grew troubled as she listened.

"A spirit storm," she said when Eira had finished.

"A what?" Veldon asked.

"The spirits of the mountains are twisted and dark," Heleena said. "They revel in destruction and chaos."

"You think the spirits caused the storm on purpose?" Gellion asked.

"Oh yes," Heleena said in a matter of fact voice.

Talaith looked skeptical, but kept her mouth shut. Even Haf looked uncomfortable. Eira was watching her hands with focused interest.

"Do these storms happen often?" Gellion said.

"Often? No, I wouldn't say that. They did not happen at all in my mother's time. But they do happen now, and only to people."

"What do you mean?"

"A spirit storm rarely affects an area beyond human presence. It may attack a village, or a band of travelers," she nodded to the company at large. "The storms do not follow a path, but appear and disappear where they please."

An uncomfortable chill was spreading along Gellion's skin. Eira had not described the sudden start and stop of the storm in her story, nor had she mentioned the abrupt end to its path of destruction beyond their camp. Despite Talaith's rolled eyes, Gellion could all too easily believe the storm had been more than a natural meteorological event. Normal storms did not stoke fires, contain flashing colors, or fell trees precisely where the only people for miles crouched in terror.

Heleena watched Gellion carefully. "None of you have been to the mountains before?" She indicated him and his brothers.

"No," said Gellion. "We had never been east of the Falspires until recently."

Heleena looked at him for several more moments, as though trying to ascertain the truth of his words.

"I see," said Heleena at last. "It would seem the spirits arranged a special welcome for your visit." She glanced at Valder and Veldon again, and there was more to her smile than simple humor.

Gellion exchanged a wary look with Veldon and Valder. Of all the scenarios he had imagined, the reality of meeting the Kayda was turning out to be much stranger than any of his musings. Both Ruta and Heleena acted as though they *knew* something about Gellion and his brothers, as though they had seen elves before. But that was impossible. No other elves had ever come to Tala before Daro was founded, and Gellion would have known if any of those elves crossed the Falspires, or sailed east along the coast.

Heleena returned to her conversation with Eira, speaking pleasantly about the summer's favorable weather and the upcoming marriage of one of her nephews. She smiled as she talked, but every once in a while, her eyes still wandered to the elves, and the bright intelligence of her gaze showed something more than interest. If Gellion had to place it, he would say it was recognition.

23

THE SOVEREIGN

"Show exaggerated respect," Eira said. "Bow before first meeting her eyes and be as humble as you can." She passed a skeptical look over Gellion, who did his best not to bristle at her tone. He was no barbarian, and he had far more to lose than Eira should this first meeting with the Sovereign of the Kayda go poorly.

Gellion had been surprised to learn the Sovereign was a woman, not because he found women incapable of leading, but because everything he had seen of the humans thus far suggested that they did. Then again, the Kayda were already proving themselves to be vastly different than any other nation of humans Gellion had yet met. He could only hope this would work in his favor.

Valder gave Gellion an encouraging nod. Veldon stood stoically, staring at the closed door in front of them. All three of them had changed out of their traveling clothes after dinner, but their selection had still been limited and wrinkled.

At least humility will be easy to achieve.

Dinner at Ruta's had been a pleasant affair, with saltwater fish, beans, sweet potatoes, and greens. The fare had reminded Gellion of Daro and awakened a sudden and profound homesickness within him.

Now, he waited to speak with the only person who could send him home, and he wore wrinkled linen and cracked boots.

With a deep breath, he ran a hand through his hair, taking comfort from the familiar brush of vierstone against his fingers.

"Let's go," he said, and Eira pushed the doors open.

The room was no less simplistic than Ruta's sitting room, except for a single wall of blurred screens on which a breathtaking image of eagles in flight was backlit from an adjoining space. Candles and lanterns glowed in the corners, and at the far end of the room, a woman sat at a low table.

She was not so old as Heleena, but her face still bore a web of lines, and the hair that twisted into an intricate knot atop her head was silver. Despite her age, she sat with a straight back and a lifted chin.

At Eira's urging, Gellion walked forward, careful to keep his eyes politely lowered until he stood before the Sovereign, then he bowed.

Out of the corner of his eye, Gellion saw the woman bow in turn, and he rose to face her.

"Sovereign Esteri," Eira said from behind him. "I have come on behalf of Lawgiver Eurig to continue our relations of trade and friendship. But first," she looked to the elves. "There is a matter with which we would ask your help."

Sovereign Esteri lifted her brows. Her almond shaped eyes were rich brown and entirely unreadable, though intelligence was evident in their depths. She looked over the elves. Gellion watched her as closely as he could without openly staring, but saw no evidence of the same reaction to Valder and Veldon that Ruta or Heleena had shown. Was Sovereign Esteri simply better at masking her thoughts, or did Ruta's family have their own reasons for being suspicious of his brothers?

The woman spread her hands in front of her with an inclination of her head. Taking this as an invitation to speak, Gellion began.

"Sovereign Esteri." He lowered his head once more. "It is an honor to meet you. I am Gellion, and these are my brothers, Valder and Veldon. We are elves from Daro—a city on the coastline west of here."

"I know of Daro," Sovereign Esteri said.

Surprised, Gellion paused with his mouth open.

"Our ships regularly travel the coast," she continued. "We have seen the white city on the cliffs, and heard its name, along with tales of those that dwell there."

"Oh. Yes," Gellion said, his heart sinking. He hoped the Kayda had not taken any Albaren slander to heart. He suddenly felt foolish not to have realized the Kayda may have passed Daro by sea before. The elves had seen plenty of unknown ships on the horizon over the last two centuries, but few came close enough to distinguish, and none had ever caused any problems, so the elves largely ignored them, assuming them to be Albaren trading vessels.

"That city is the reason we are here," Gellion said. "It has been destroyed."

A twitch of an eyebrow showed the woman's surprise at the news.

"I am sorry to hear that," she said, and to Gellion's surprise, she sounded genuine. "I heard it was beautiful."

"It was." Gellion did not try to hide the pain in his voice.

He hesitated, then pulled Eurig's letter from his pocket. Not for the first time, he wondered at the letter's contents. Eurig had said the letter explained the elves' situation and asked for the Kayda's aid on his authority. Gellion's doubts of the man's sincerity had lessened as he got to know the Dierna traders, but he had never been able to entirely banish his suspicion. What if the letter condemned the elves as the demons so many humans seemed to think them? What if it described the death and destruction the elven army had caused?

Why would he send you across the continent only to condemn you? He could have done that easily enough in his own city.

But why send us across the continent to help us?

The doubts were as useless as they were too late. Gellion had no choice but to present the letter to Sovereign Esteri and accept whatever came after. He took a deep breath.

"I have a letter here, from Lawgiver Eurig." He held out the folded paper, its wax bent and cracked, but still intact.

Sovereign Esteri raised a thin eyebrow, then took the letter and carefully broke its seal. She unfolded the paper. Her eyes skimmed back and forth, making slow progress down the page. Gellion watched her hungrily, trying to see some hint of her reaction, but she gave none. Finally, she lowered the paper.

"You have not read this?"

A jolt of adrenaline moved through Gellion.

"No."

She looked back at the letter, then handed it to Gellion. With a pounding heart, he read.

Honored Sovereign,

I write this letter in my own hand, hoping it finds you and your people well and its couriers unharmed. This visit has long been planned, and I intend to keep every trade arrangement agreed upon before now, but a strange circumstance has added another purpose to this journey. Before you stand three elves—a legend scarce believed by my people until now, though long since accepted by you and yours, I am sure.

Of the elves, I have heard tales fit for adventure stories and nightmares alike, from faerie wings to fangs, and magics both wondrous and terrible. Whether any of these claims are true, I do not know, but despite the unfortunate circumstances of our races' first encounter, I believe that these elves follow a moral code as good as any Kayda's. Once my prisoners, they have convinced me by both word and action that their hearts are just, and their need to return to their people as true as any.

Were it within my power to grant them passage to their homeland, I would do it, but this is a task beyond my abilities, though very much within yours. As you once did for me, I now do for these. I have no right to ask more of you than you have already done for me, but I hope that in some way this request may bring justification to your kindness. I ask that you give these elves passage across the sea. There will be no return of their vessel, but rest assured its cost will be atoned for.

May your summer be bountiful, and your path long and peaceful.

Eurig of the Elder Clan

Gellion closed his eyes. He handed the letter to Valder.

"Will you leave us for a moment, Eira?" Sovereign Esteri said.

Though clearly not happy with the request, Eira bowed and left the room.

Sovereign Esteri watched the door until it closed, then slowly turned back to face the elves.

"Eurig is a trustworthy man," she said. "That he speaks so of one for which he once held prejudice means more than you know."

"You know him well?" Gellion said.

She gave a small smile. "Eurig did not tell you of the time he spent among the Kayda?"

Gellion glanced at his brothers and shook his head.

Sovereign Esteri nodded. "Over the centuries, the Kayda's relations with the Dierna have been more turbulent even than those with the Albaren. The Dierna can be a violent people with harsh laws and unstable politics. The Elder Clan is no exception. Eurig was the nephew of the Lawgiver, and was thrown alone into our lands as a punishment for cowardice in battle." She shook her head. "He was barely eleven. Somehow he made his way through our passes, though he barely survived the journey, still wounded from the battle he had fled and attacked by the spirits of the mountains. We took him in, as is the way of our people, though the only Dierna to cross our borders for decades had been raiding parties and spies. He recovered in Suri Ranta and remained with the Kayda until his clan stabilized."

"For many years, he learned of our culture—our trade and our government. When he left as a young man to return to his people, he promised he would return to us with the friendship of his clan to pay for his life. And so he did. Within ten years he had ascended to Lawgiver. The Elder Clan is the only faction of Dierna with which we now hold prosperous and friendly trade. Though Lawgiver Eurig has not eradicated all the harsh ways of his people, you will find a stark difference between the running of Arvain and the large cities of the other Dierna clans."

Sovereign Esteri smiled. "I have not seen Eurig in some time. It is good to know he has not abandoned our ways."

Gellion stared at the ground. He hardly knew what to feel, let alone say. Eurig's generosity had been genuine. All the aid the elves had received had not been a trap, but a kindness payed forward from the woman now sitting in front of him.

Could Sovereign Esteri's story explain more than just Eurig's decisions? Gellion thought of the disparity between the Albaren view of the Dierna and his own experience in Arvain. Maybe the Albaren ire against the Dierna had not been completely unfounded if the relative civility under Eurig's rule had been in place for only a few decades. Not that any of this justified the Albaren's underhanded actions. Doubtless, they had embellished their stories and lied about the more recent infractions of their neighbor. Still, Gellion found himself grateful he had fallen prisoner to the Elder Clan and not any of the other Dierna factions.

A cautious hope was beginning to fill Gellion. If Kayda values were what gave the Elder Clan its softened edges and willingness to help a stranger, perhaps there was a real chance of finding unrequited aid among these people. He looked up at Sovereign Esteri and found her regarding him thoughtfully with her golden eyes.

"You are welcome in Suri Ranta," she said. "The spirit of The One inhabits all things."

Gellion ignored the obvious grins from his brothers and bowed his head in thanks. It was a promising start, but they were not out of this yet.

"Tell me," Sovereign Esteri continued. "Are there any elves remaining in these lands but you?"

"No," said Gellion. "We were separated in chaos and unable to search for the rest of our kin until our chances of finding them were nearly impossible. We believe they have all sailed across the sea, assuming us dead."

Sovereign Esteri nodded, her eyes downcast. "It is a terrible thing, to be separated from one's connections. Am I correct in assuming the Albaren to be the root of your troubles?"

Gellion glanced at his brothers, caught off guard by the woman's perception.

"They were, yes." There was no point explaining the elven source of their problems. It was best that all involved assume the Albaren had destroyed Daro.

She nodded. "And so obtaining a ship from them is quite out of the question. Yes. I see. And any elven ships were destroyed with the city or presumably taken by the kin who left you behind."

Gellion exchanged another look with his brothers. They showed the same surprise at the woman's deductions.

"Yes," Sovereign Esteri said again, still nodding and considering the elves. She looked down at Eurig's letter, then said, "I will do what I can for you."

A burst of hope radiated from Gellion's chest. He hardly dared believe her words. Could it be this simple, after all they had been through?

"This is not my decision alone," she added with a raised finger. "I will speak with the mariners on your behalf. Eurig says the vessel you require will not be returned. You intend to sail alone?"

"Yes," said Gellion.

"That is more difficult. We do not keep more boats than we use, and it would take weeks or months to build a replacement for any of them."

A splash of water tempered Gellion's burning hope.

"Would it not be better for one of our ships to sail you there and back with a crew?" the Sovereign said. "Is it a far journey?"

"It is a journey best undertaken by elves," Gellion said carefully. He had been prepared for this question, and given the mystique of the elves held by the humans, hoped this answer would be adequate. To his relief, Sovereign Esteri did not question him.

"Very well. I will relay your request," she said. "If it is within our ability to help you, we will."

It was the best Gellion could hope for. His smile was mirrored in the faces of his brothers.

"Thank you," he said. "Truly."

Sovereign Esteri shook her head. "My people believe a generous heart is the foundation of a true life. I would be a poor leader indeed if I did not reflect the heart of our ways. I will send for you when I have an answer from the mariners." She turned a skeptical eye over them. "You are mariners yourselves?"

"If you can provide a boat," Gellion said. "We can get it across the sea."

Sovereign Esteri did not get back to the elves quickly. Eira only smirked at the elves' impatience, saying haste was not a trait valued by the Kayda. This was becoming increasingly evident in the daily life of Ruta's home. Meals were as slowly eaten as they were prepared, and much of the day was devoted to calming repetitive tasks or meditation. Aku owned a herd of goats just outside the city and left each day to tend to them. Ruta often left the home as well, visiting sick villagers and prescribing herbs for every purpose imaginable. When she was home, she bustled through the house doing tasks Gellion could hardly keep up with. The traders and elves often insisted on helping with meals. At first, Ruta was scandalized by this insistence, but after a while she accepted their offer with thanks, conceding that cooking for six extra mouths was more than enough work to warrant their help.

Six extra mouths became three after a few days. The Dierna traders had accomplished their trade negotiations and had no further reason to stay in the Falspires. Gellion could not imagine restarting the journey they had just taken so soon, but supposed the traders were used to travel; they had chosen this as a life, after all. It was a strangely sad parting, but, to the abounding amusement of Gellion and Valder, Talaith kissed Veldon on the cheek before marching out of Ruta's house, leaving the poor elf scarlet and unable to make eye contact with anyone for nearly an hour. Haf gave a gruff nod to each elf before following her. Eira came to stand in front of Gellion.

"How's the leg?"

"Mostly healed."

She raised her eyebrows.

"We heal quickly." Gellion shrugged.

"Hmm. Well." She extended a hand. "I wish you luck. Sounds like you'll not be returning to a peaceful life if all works out."

Gellion smiled and took her hand. "Not exactly. But the sooner a threat is faced, the sooner peace can return. Thank you for bringing us this far."

Eira rolled her eyes. "We did nothing, just allowed you to follow us. I've had worse cargo." She allowed a hint of smile to tug at her mouth before dropping her hand. Nodding to Valder and Veldon, she turned and walked out.

"Told you she liked us." Valder beamed as the door shut behind her.

The house became quieter after the traders' departure. Though Aku and Ruta were often out, Heleena was almost always in the sitting room reading and writing, or telling stories to Hakan. Her eyes followed the elves constantly when they pretended not to look, though she was nothing but civil to them in word or action. Ruta continued to give Valder and Veldon apprehensive glances almost every time she saw them, and Gellion's curiosity was growing beyond his politeness.

"Why do they look at you that way?" he asked Valder and Veldon, sitting in the privacy of Ruta's yard.

"I have no idea," Valder said. "Maybe it's our devilish good looks." He gave Gellion an apologetic look that suggested he lacked this particular family feature.

Gellion rolled his eyes. "I'm serious. They watch you as though they recognize something in you, something they do not trust."

"I agree," Veldon said. "But I can think of no reason for it. We have not behaved or spoken any differently than you, and it is an impression they both had the moment they set eyes on us."

"What does it matter?" asked Valder. "The Sovereign didn't seem to mind us any more than she did you," he looked to Gellion. "And it's her we need on our side. Ruta and Heleena's looks are odd, I'll grant you that, but they're not hostile to us. They're probably just disconcerted by having elves in their home."

"But only certain elves?" Gellion raised a brow.

Valder shrugged. "What do you intend to do, ask them?"

"I think I might."

Both Valder and Veldon stared at him.

"Why not?" Gellion said. "I can't come up with any valid reason for their suspicion, and I want to know."

"Things are going well for us here, Gellion," Valder said. "Don't bring up something that will get us kicked out again. Just let it go."

"I won't upset Ruta. I'll ask indirectly—ease into the subject."

Valder looked doubtful.

"They act as though they have seen elves before!" said Gellion. "I want to know why. And all that in the mountains—the creatures, the spirits."

"You really think that was a 'spirit storm?'" Valder said.

"Heleena's description was close enough to our experience to convince me it was more than a lightning storm. And did you hear what she said about the storms? They didn't happen in her mother's time. It's exactly what Eurig told us. The mountains were not always as they are now. They used to be safe—or as safe as any wild mountains can be—with no monstrous animals or strange occurrences. Is it not familiar to either of you, what we passed through in these mountains?"

Valder looked skeptical, but Veldon stared into the distance.

"Veldon?" Gellion prompted.

"I know what you mean," Veldon said. "Eurig described animals just like Renyra found in the wilds outside Daro. Unnatural creatures that only come out after dark and watch from the shadows. The very air in those passes seemed to hold something wrong, especially during the storm. It was almost similar—" he trailed off.

"To the feeling during the earthquakes in Daro," Gellion finished.

"What are you saying?" Valder looked between the two. "You think whatever is affecting these mountains is the same as what was in Daro?"

"I'm saying," said Gellion. "That there are questions about this place that I want more answers to, and I think Ruta and Heleena are more likely to have those answers than most in Suri Ranta. We have nothing else to do while we wait on the mariners anyway."

"Just be careful," Valder said.

"When am I ever otherwise?" Gellion said with a grin.

Veldon scoffed.

"Can I help you with that?" Gellion took the other end of a tray that Ruta had been struggling to heave on top of a cabinet.

"Thank you," she said brusquely, seeming annoyed at needing help but grateful for it all the same.

"The least I could do given your hospitality." Gellion smiled.

"It is a great honor to host guests," she said with dignity.

"All the same. You have been very kind. It is a lovely place." He looked out the window toward the distant waterfalls. "I'm glad to have seen it before returning to the elves."

Ruta's hands paused for a fraction of a second on the dishes she was cleaning.

"Sovereign Esteri said the Kayda have known of the elves for a long time," Gellion continued in a light tone. "And seen our city on the coast."

Ruta nodded. "We have heard of the elves for generations."

"Did you never see any of us until now?"

Ruta paused again, glancing at him.

"No, we have never seen the elves with our own eyes, though we have heard Albaren descriptions."

Gellion chuckled. "I can hardly imagine what those must have been like."

Ruta looked back down at her dishes. "They say your eyes shine like gems, and your hair is like silk. That your skin ranges every color under the sun," she glanced at Gellion's arms. "And that you can make metal float in the air and move faster than a horse."

"Oh," said Gellion, a little awkwardly. He had not expected anything so favorable from the Albaren. But then the Albaren's animosity to the elves had not spanned generations. It was possible these descriptions were centuries old.

"Your eyes are like gems," Ruta said quietly. She was peering at Gellion strangely. He shifted, unsure how to respond. Ruta seemed to be thinking to herself, trying to decide on something. Resolve flowed down her face.

"You *are* elves? All three of you?" The words were bold, but she immediately looked frightened by her forwardness.

"Yes," Gellion said, taken aback. "Of course."

Ruta's posture relaxed a bit, but there was still hesitance in her gaze.

"What else would we be?" Gellion asked.

Ruta hesitated, then shook her head.

"Please," said Gellion. "I see how you look at my brothers. What is it you fear?"

After another moment's hesitation, Ruta looked Gellion square in the face, her expression one of defiance.

"We have not seen elves in the mountains, but we have seen many things. Many beings. Creatures, spirits, shapeshifters, faeries."

Faeries.

Gellion had heard the term attributed to the elves in Albarad, and not in kindness.

"There are tales of one who walked among us once, veiled in human appearance. A selkie. A shapeshifter. One of the seal folk. He was pale of skin with shining black hair and eyes the color of a reef. Green. Emerald."

Gellion's interest sharpened. "You saw this selkie?"

"I never did. The selkies come to shore—in storms, at the solstice, when they are lonely, we do not know why—and shed their seal skins, walking as humans. They are beautiful, and they are seductive. They seek those who are unhappy with their lives, who are not at peace, and lure them from their homes. Sometimes they leave children. Sometimes they take children." Her eyes strayed to the door that led to the sitting room.

Pale skin and black hair. Sea green eyes. Of course. She feared for the safety of her child. She feared that Valder and Veldon—maybe even Gellion by association—were selkies.

"I promise you, Ruta, my brothers and I hold nothing but gratitude for you and your family. We are elves, not selkies, and would never dream of harming any of you." He paused. "But, you said one of them —the selkies—walked among you for a time. That he had green eyes and pale skin?"

"The tales of the selkies are as old as the Kayda. Stories of children born with webbed fingers, pointed ears, or other deformities and strangeness. But believing in the faeries is different than encountering them. There was a selkie in this village. Before my time, but in my mother's, and by all accounts he looked a good deal like your brothers."

Gellion's heart raced. Had there truly been a selkie in this village? Or could it have been an elf? Ruta's mother would have been alive during the time that the mountains' 'strangeness' had allegedly begun. Could it have been caused by something, by some*one* who came to the mountains during that time? An elf who looked like Veldon and Valder. A Turi—with black hair, pale skin, and green eyes. Gellion could hardly comprehend the meaning of it all. Was it possible? Was it merely coincidence? Or was Ruta wrong? Had the Kayda, in fact, seen an elf before? Had Kaelo been to Suri Ranta?

PART III

24

A JOURNEY UNFORESEEN

Kyna had thought traveling in absurdly close quarters with six other elves would be miserable, and she had been perfectly right. At least the supply crates allowed for some privacy if you fancied edging yourself between them and the rim of the boat. Kyna did this as frequently as social grace would allow, though she didn't know why she cared what the others thought of her. In all likelihood, she would never see Renyra and her troupe again after today, and Tornac—well, he was no social butterfly himself. Mostly he gazed upriver with a look of grim determination. When he did speak, however, Tornac had surprised Kyna with a wit and dark humor that contrasted pleasantly with his scowling seriousness in Council meetings. He smiled about as much as Kyna did herself, but he got on well with the troupe when he applied himself and had been a great help getting them up the river.

The Orhiri River was swift and deep, though narrow as far as rivers went. Here, in the heart of Ard Gael, it banked between steep gorges of sleek shale, tossing froth against the shining rocks at every bend. It was an entirely different beast than the lazy stream that wound through Tura. The further the company traveled upriver, the more their little boat fought to slice against the current, but so too did the conversation and spirits of the group become lighter.

The night of their escape had been tense, then frantic, then possessed of a giddy relief tainted by anxiety. They had met no further trouble after slipping past the walls of the city, but glowing eyes had watched them from the riverbank for miles beyond Tura. Once, Raren had spotted a glimmering body weaving through the water beside the boat, after which the rest of the company had lit torches to deter any attacks. Either the flames had worked, or they had all been lucky.

That had been two days ago. The boat made good progress considering the current, but it was still too slow for Kyna's liking. She hoped Maramor's legendary spires would peak over the edge of the gorges before the sun set on another day.

Kyna leaned back against the side of the boat and stretched her legs to almost full extension. Renyra and Alura were entertaining the group doing acrobatics on the crates. Kyna tried not to show too much interest, but her mingled admiration and jealousy drew her eyes inexorably to the flexing of their bodies.

Renyra had been circling Kyna the whole trip—looking for opportunities to talk with her, telling her about the grasslands, being overly smiley. Kyna expected she was trying to make up for forcing Kyna into this trip.

"There should be a flat bank around the next bend," Tornac said.

Alura and Renyra drew themselves upright from back bends and sat down on the crates to listen.

"We can stop there for a few moments if anyone needs to," Tornac continued. "If I am right, we will arrive at Maramor in a few hours."

Kyna sighed in relief. She was sick of being damp from the spray of the river, sick of trying to sleep on a curved metal surface that bobbed offshore, and sick of the boredom that had quickly overtaken the initial interest of the passing landscapes. The sooner they got to Maramor, the sooner they could return to Tura, and with vierstone in tow, events were bound to move quickly upon their return. A flutter that could have been excitement or fear beat against Kyna's chest at the thought. Would it work? Would the Council follow the prophecy as it was meant?

The boat veered around a bend, sending a sheet of water against the cliff face to their left. There was, indeed, a flat bank of rocks ahead.

Firas was steering the boat today and eased the craft's nose toward the rocky shore.

Solid ground was a blessing. If Kyna closed her eyes she could still feel the rhythmic motion of the boat, still see water rushing past her, but the feeling began to fade after a few minutes. Raren pulled some food out of one of the crates and passed it around: oatcakes and nut paste with a handful of wrinkled apples. Kyna chewed blissfully and lay back on the rocks while the rest of the company stretched and moved about the space.

"Will the five of you stop in Maramor before continuing to the grasslands?" Tornac said.

Kyna perked up, listening for the answer.

"I don't think so," said Renyra. "It would be nice to restock, but Rone isn't far from Maramor. We might be able to get there before dark if we go straight on."

Tornac nodded. "Probably. The river starts to widen beyond Maramor, and the current slows. Once you reach the mouth of Lake Orhirion you will go faster."

"If we can get to Rone by this evening," said Caerlyn, "we should be able to reach Telem Fier tomorrow. The Rale through the grasslands is fast."

A weight of tension settled over the group. No one had mentioned Tura, or Kaelo, or anything about their purpose since the day before. It was all too easy to forget the looming danger in the wilderness of Ard Gael. More than once, Kyna had wondered what would happen if she simply jumped ship and lived in the mountains until all of this was over. Each time, she gritted her teeth and pressed the stone in her cuff against her wrist. She would not abandon her duty. She could not shy away now. She had come too far.

No one else spoke after the sobering reminder of their destination and purpose. After their food was eaten and their muscles stretched, the group filed reluctantly back into the boat.

A few hours should have seemed like nothing compared to two and a half days, but somehow the afternoon wore on more tediously than Kyna could have imagined, inexorably slowed by the nearness of their goal. Kyna searched for the outline of spires and buildings around every curve of the gorge, but was consistently disappointed by the silhouettes of trees.

The first herald of approaching civilization was not spires at all, but another boat anchored in the water ahead. Shading her eyes against the glint of the water, Kyna saw two elves working a net in the river. They straightened and looked around when they noticed the boat coming toward them, and smiled and waved when Tornac greeted them.

The current had noticeably slowed, and the cliffsides began to fall away to either side. Above the sheer rock, silvery green leaves shimmered in the wind that blew through the chasm, and birds soared and swooped from one side to the other in the playful draft. Smears of pink interspersed the green and became more numerous. The redbud trees of Maramor.

They rounded another bend, this one gentler than the last, and Kyna nearly gasped. What she at first took to be massive boulders sticking out of the water extended upward seven stories to the top of the gorge. The columns were thick and rough hewn at the bottom, but gained shape and intricacy as they grew, until they met each other at the top to form a huge bridge, the sides of which were carved in flowing patterns.

Firas guided the boat easily between the pillars, and Maramor opened before them.

Kyna did not know what she had been expecting, but the reality of the city nearly took her breath away.

Rock still framed the river, but it eased its edges and height, rounding and tapering to form ledges on which massive buildings rose as though from the rock itself. The architecture was similar to that of Tura, yet unique, with flowing lines of metal, stone, and glass that always ended in a tower or a spire. In the shadow of the sun, it looked like the mountains had grown teeth.

Pathways and bridges linked the buildings, and redbud trees grew everywhere the soil allowed. The river had widened enough that islands began to appear in its middle. Some were only bare formations of stone, others bore a tower, or sculpture.

Then, on the right, the cliffside gave way entirely, like a bite in the mountains. There was a rocky shoreline that sloped upward, then rose in jagged steps to rejoin the mountains behind. The heart of Maramor climbed the steps.

Kyna stared. Spired buildings clung to the cliffs, with spiraling staircases and lifts linking the jumping terrain. From the buildings and pathways, round platforms extended into thin air, like floating lily pads with tapered bases. Every bit of stone was carved, every bit of metal polished, and throughout it all were the shimmering pink leaves.

Kyna's face flushed as she realized she was the only one gaping. Everyone else in the group had been to Maramor before, yet wonder still shone in most of their eyes.

"I know haste is important, but I wish we could just stay one night," Alura said wistfully. "The lights are so lovely."

For a moment, Kyna thought Renyra was going to give in. The longing in her face was unmistakable, but the little Fieri shook her head.

"We have to move on," she said regretfully. "After we've gathered Trali in Remsgraen and passed on our messages, we can come back."

The docks of Maramor were a patchwork of floating wood that extended from the tapered shore. There were no large vessels—not like the ships in Daro or Tura—but flat barges and small to midsized boats like the one they had come in. Firas eased the boat to an empty space at the docks, and Raren jumped onto the platform to help tie the boat to a cleat.

Everyone leaped to the docks, grateful for another opportunity to stretch their legs. Kyna let out a sigh. Surely she, at least, would be spending the night here. A few hours' head start down the river was not worth the sacrifice of a bed, and Tornac would have to gather the vier-stone before they left. Her insides twinged at the thought of being alone with Tornac. She had tried not to overthink the situation. In all likelihood, Tornac would be steering the boat the whole time and they would each keep to themselves until Tura. So what if he was Gellion's brother? Tornac didn't even know that Kyna had known Gellion, and his resemblance to his brother meant nothing to Kyna. It should mean nothing.

Kyna was pulled from her thoughts to find Renyra standing in front of her.

"Well," Renyra said, a smile pulling at her lips. "This is goodbye. For a while."

Kyna nodded and shifted her feet.

"I'm glad you came with us." A hint of guilt colored Renyra's smile, and she glanced at Tornac. "And I'm sure Tornac will appreciate the help getting back."

Kyna nearly flushed at Renyra's raised eyebrow.

"At least the trip back will be faster, going downriver," Kyna said. "We should have the vierstone in Tura in two days."

"Right," Renyra said, her conspiratorial look replaced by one of worry. "I hope you don't meet any trouble getting back. Hopefully Liera will set guards to watch for you after seeing what Kaelo did to the walls."

"Assuming she thinks we survived the attack," Kyna said.

"We left no signs of the boat."

"Except a crushed crate."

"Oh." Renyra knit her brows. "Well, I can't imagine she thinks us dead from that. Anyway, I would go in daylight this time. Looking back, I wish we had left during the day ourselves." She sighed. "I wish I could see the sword forged—see what happens next. I'm afraid for Tura. What if we interpreted the prophecy wrong? What if it doesn't work?" Her bright eyes turned to Kyna. "I wish you were coming with us to Telem Fier, but I'm glad you will be in Tura. You will be a help to the Council."

Kyna let out a soft snort and grimaced.

"You will," Renyra insisted. "And you will have to tell me everything that happens."

Firas had appeared beside Renyra. "We should go," he said softly, putting a hand on Renyra's shoulder.

Renyra reached up to squeeze his hand and nodded. She turned back to Kyna.

"Good luck," she said. "May Riu be with you." She reached out a tattooed hand, and Kyna took it.

"Good luck to you too," she said, and was surprised by how much she meant it.

Renyra smiled, then followed Firas back into the boat.

The troupe waved a final greeting as they pulled out, and the boat shrank away until the purr of its motor mingled with the wind.

"Shall we go?"

Kyna tore her eyes away from the river. Tornac was watching her with a raised eyebrow and a ghost of a smile. For a moment, he looked so much like Gellion, Kyna's throat seemed to close.

She swallowed and nodded.

Maramor was even more intricate up close. There was no Rale line—Kyna imagined it would be useless with the constant change in elevation—but lifts flowed seamlessly with both terrain and architecture to transport elves to the lofty buildings with little effort.

Tornac walked with purpose, giving courteous but quick greetings to the elves they passed. Everyone seemed to know him, but then, his family had run Maramor for centuries according to Gellion. Kyna clenched her hands. She could all too easily imagine Gellion here, surrounded by beauty, known by all. Gellion had never told her why he left. It now seemed an odd omission, given everything else he had told her. Kyna shook her head and lengthened her stride to keep up with Tornac.

"We will go to the crafting halls first," he said when they had reached the first series of suspended platforms. The ground was solid, but Kyna still felt strange knowing there was nothing below them.

"It may take a while to gather the vierstone, and we should plan to leave first thing tomorrow morning. I will give our instructions to Bredan, one of our most skilled stoneworkers. He's most likely to know where to find vierstone. There is some vierstone in my family's halls as well. I will get that."

"What should I do?" Kyna said.

"Come with me. You may be able to help Bredan gather vierstone. I can secure us a boat for the return." He made a sharp turn and began to climb a winding stair. Kyna followed him up the steps with a sigh. She hated stairs.

"You could also help pack some food for the next couple of days. You'll stay in our halls tonight, and the kitchens are easy to find."

The stairs ended at an arching set of doors rimmed in glass. Their surface was inlaid with marble, and their handles were of swirling metal.

And I thought Tura was frivolous.

The crafting halls were open and bright. Tornac's boots clicked on the shining floor as he turned down the second hall on the left. Kyna could have gotten lost in the place. There were doors everywhere. Tornac chose one of the them and held it open for Kyna, who bowed through with a mumble of thanks.

The metallic smell of stone greeted Kyna. The room was huge, with workbenches and shelving lining the walls and half finished sculptures and bricks neatly arranged in the center. Towering windows overlooked the gorge and let in streams of light that showed a haze of white particles in the air.

"Bredan."

Kyna turned to Tornac's voice and saw him clasping hands with an elf standing at one of the workbenches.

The stoneworker had the kind of smile that never seems to leave a face once it arrives, toothy and broad. A dusty apron hung over his solid build, and his hair was grey, though upon closer inspection Kyna realized it was just more stone dust.

"You took your time in Tura," Bredan said to Tornac, winking at Kyna as she approached. "And who might this be?"

Tornac glanced at Kyna, and a hint of color crept up his neck. Kyna felt her own surge of heat when she realized the implication of Bredan's teasing.

"This is Kyna," Tornac said in a slightly too formal tone. "And both of us have to return to Tura tomorrow. We were sent by the Turi Council. I need your help."

Bredan's eyes sobered at that, though his smile remained. "What can I do?"

"We need vierstone. All the vierstone in Maramor that is not built into the foundations. And we need it tonight."

That wiped the smile off Bredan's face. "What?" His expression was slack with shock.

"Exactly as I said," Tornac said. "I will take care of the vierstone in the high halls, but we also need to secure a boat and provisions, so I'm trusting you can gather the rest."

Bredan was at a loss for words. He looked between Tornac and Kyna, as though expecting the joke to break any moment. When neither spoke, he said, "Why?"

A flicker of annoyance passed over Tornac's face.

"It is a long explanation that we don't have time for now. Know only that all of the vierstone in Tura is destroyed, and Kaelo is behind it."

Bredan's jaw dropped. "Kaelo? What do you mean destroyed? Tornac—"

"He is killing the vierstone. Turning it black. We don't know how, and we don't know why, but we have a way that might stop him, and we need vierstone to do it. As there is none left in Tura, this is our only option." His face softened. "Please, Bredan. I wish I could explain further, but we must hurry. If we gather all the vierstone by tonight, I will tell you the full story then."

Bredan stood for a moment more with his mouth open, then slowly closed it and nodded.

"I will do it."

"Thank you. Tell anyone who asks what I told you. It is no secret. Kyna can come with you if you need help."

Bredan looked at Kyna, wrinkled his brow in thought, then shook his head.

"No, I know where to look. But there is a fair amount. Do you really need all—"

"All of it."

Bredan bowed his head. "Very well. I will bring it to the high halls by this evening."

If the morning and early afternoon had dragged by, the evening came with startling swiftness. Since Bredan had needed no help with his task, Kyna followed Tornac around all of Maramor. Every part of the city was as beautiful as the crafting halls, and Kyna realized only after walking for over an hour that she was not sweating. The mountains cooled the air and brought a sweet scent of earth and fresh water. It was a comforting scent.

Together, she and Tornac ensured they would have a suitable boat for the morning and gathered supplies with as short of explanations as they could get away with for the elves they encountered. They decided to transport the vierstone in sacks, which they would nail into a crate to secure to the boat. Now they only needed the vierstone.

Tornac led the way to the high halls—the center of Maramor and home to his family, though Kyna realized with a twinge there may not be many of them left. With Tenille in Tura and all three of Tornac's brothers gone—Kyna ground her jaw against the uncomfortable feeling that assaulted her stomach. Gellion's father had died at the end of the war. Was Tornac the last of his kin?

Out of the corner of her eye, Kyna watched Tornac as they rose in a lift to the platforms extending from the high halls. There was a line between his brows that seemed to deepen as they grew closer to the halls. He had not spoken for a while.

No wonder he never smiles.

The high halls were aptly named. Hallways upon hallways, indoor, outdoor, lined with columns and windows—Kyna was grateful to have a guide and hoped Tornac did not send her on any errands.

"There is a dining hall in the central chamber near the kitchens. We'll go there in an hour to eat, and you can pack tomorrow's food afterward while I find Bredan to see how he is getting on with the vierstone. The guest chambers are this way."

He led her to a small room with a southern wall of pure glass. There was a bed, a dresser, a thick rug, and sheer curtains pulled to the side of the window. Kyna stepped forward to see the view. The sun had disappeared behind the mountains an hour before, and lights were beginning to twinkle into existence throughout the city. Kyna could see why Alura had wanted to see them. Strings of silver and blue hung from the platforms and lined the bridges and stairs. Kyna imagined that in the black of night they would look like stars suspended in the gorge.

"It is a beautiful city," said Tornac.

Kyna nearly jumped to hear him right beside her. He was looking out over the city below, an expression of fondness in his eyes, but there was something more. Sadness? Pain? Kyna looked away.

"It is a pity you must leave so soon, and visit under these circumstances."

"Yes," Kyna said, watching a heron wing its way to the far side of the river from the docks.

"Renyra said you are from Ard Gael."

"Mmm." Kyna glanced at Tornac, but his eyes were still fixed out the window on the distant mountains.

"Where?" he said. "You do not look familiar."

"A village on the northern side of the mountains," Kyna said. "I have not often left. And I am—young."

Tornac nodded. "Born after the war?"

"Yes."

"You are lucky." The pain came back to his eyes.

"I have been in a battle," Kyna said, almost indignantly.

Tornac knit his brows and looked at her, then understanding seemed to break through whatever trance had held him.

"Oh. Of course. Liera said you were in Daro." Then his eyes widened, and he looked at Kyna as though he had never properly seen her before.

"You were there," he said softly. "In that battle."

Kyna nodded. She could practically see the storm of emotions battling behind Tornac's eyes. He held his mouth open for several seconds before any words came out.

"Did you—" he trailed off.

Know your brothers? See them die?

Tornac clamped his mouth shut again and shook his head, clearly thinking better of asking the question.

"I am sorry," he said. "I'm sure you do not want to talk about that." Tornac attempted a smile, but it came out a grimace. "I will let you relax before dinner. I don't know about you, but I'm covered in enough river sand to polish a diamond."

Kyna snorted. "A necklace of diamonds."

Tornac's grimace softened to a real smile. Kyna's chest constricted at how it transformed his face. His eyes shone in the reflected lights from the window, and with the blue tint, his hair could have been any color. Kyna barely stifled a gasp of pain and turned her eyes back to the window.

"I'll come get you in an hour," Tornac said as he walked out. "I know this place can seem a labyrinth to newcomers."

He closed the door behind him.

Kyna curled the fingers of her shaking hand and pressed her wrist against her chest. The cold stone lay flat against her skin, but still the unbearable pressure in her chest remained. It grew. She felt like she was unraveling from the inside, and there was nothing she could do to stop it.

A sudden fit of rage coursed through her body. She ripped the cuff off her wrist and threw it on the ground, fighting against the sobs that threatened to rise in her throat. Flattening her palms against the glass, she bowed her head between her shoulders and took deep, shuddering breaths.

"It wasn't my fault," she breathed through her teeth. She closed her eyes, but Gellion's face seemed to burn against her lids. She opened them with a gasp.

"He could never have been mine. It is better this way." Still the pain came, and her vision blurred.

"He should never have been mine. It is better this way."

THE LEGEND OF THE SELKIE

Valder's eyes lit with a fire Gellion had not seen for weeks.

"I've never seen one like her," he said, his eyes roving back and forth over the small vessel bobbing in the water. "All wood."

"She is called *Brasa*," Sovereign Esteri said, "and has made many safe trips to Albarad."

The Sovereign wore layers of silk in rich colors and elaborate designs, her hair pinned ornately to the top of her head, yet somehow she did not seem out of place on the docks that extended into the Sielu Sound. She smiled with pride at the vessels that surrounded them, from large trading ships to humble fishing boats. The boat in question was about thirty feet long, with smooth wood painted white and brown and wrapped sails. It was perfect. Easily sailable by three people and large enough to withstand the waves of the open sea.

"And the mariners have agreed to part with her?" asked Valder with some awe.

"*Brasa* has served her time well. She is still strong, but her final voyage is within sight. We build in a different style now." Sovereign Esteri indicated several boats anchored further into the water. Their bodies were noticeably narrower—more angular. "It will be at least a few days before she is ready to sail. Perhaps a week. Her last voyage was not kind, and the mariners will need to make repairs before she is seaworthy for a journey like yours."

"We will wait," Gellion assured her. "Thank you, Sovereign. I wish we could repay you for this."

"Your gratitude is payment enough." She raised an eyebrow and gave him a sly smile. "Besides, our friend Eurig has agreed to fund a replacement."

Gellion chuckled. "Right."

The sight of *Brasa* filled Gellion with a wild longing he could hardly bear. Before him was a way home, a way back to the elves. It was real. Somehow he still could not let himself embrace hope in full, not until he and his brothers were on the water—on the shores of Faeran for that matter. But all the same, it was more possible than he could have imagined weeks ago. Even a week's delay did not dismay him as it once would have.

Part of Gellion was relieved at the excuse to stay in Suri Ranta a bit longer. Ever since his conversation with Ruta, Gellion had been trying to convince his brothers that an elf had been in Suri Ranta before, and that it could have been the same elf who had destroyed Daro. Valder and Veldon had not reacted with as much enthusiasm as Gellion had hoped.

"I suppose it's possible," Veldon had said when Gellion finished recounting Ruta's descriptions. "But why would an elf have come to the Falspires? That would have been around the time Daro was finished being built, right?"

"Exactly," Gellion said. "It probably would have been a few decades later, which means elves were on Tala already. It would have been easy for one to cross the Falspires, or even sail to the Sielu Sound."

"But why?" Valder asked. "What would an elf want to do in Suri Ranta?"

"I don't know, but if it was around the time the mountains began to ... to corrupt, or whatever happened to them—don't you think he could have caused this? The same elf that destroyed Daro? You've agreed yourselves that the monsters, the *feel* of this place, is similar to how Daro was the last month we were there."

"Veldon agreed," Valder said.

"Well it is," Gellion said resolutely. I'm only saying that it is worth learning more. If there was an elf here, and if his story is connected to Daro, knowing what happened could help us. We might even find out the cause, the purpose of all that happened, and get a clue as to what will happen next and how to stop it." Gellion's voice had grown more excited as he spoke. He was sure this was important, and his brothers' skepticism grated on him.

Gellion wanted to find out more before they sailed to Faeran. He had to at least try. Even if his brothers did not share his suspicions, they would surely go along with him if they were stuck here another week. What else was there to do?

"We would be happy to help with the repairs," Valder said to Sovereign Esteri.

Gellion snapped back to the present and looked at his brother sharply.

"No," Sovereign Esteri said. "I will not have my guests working."

"I build ships among our own people," Valder pressed. "I would enjoy seeing the craft of a different style."

Sovereign Esteri looked at him for a long moment. "If it will interest you, you may offer your help to the mariners themselves, but respect their wishes if they choose to work alone."

"Of course," Valder said, unable to hide his excitement at the possibility.

After promising to send one of the mariners to speak with Valder, Sovereign Esteri left them.

"I think we should use this time to learn all we can of what happened here," Gellion said in a low voice when they were alone.

Valder sighed. "You can play at detective all you want. I will not stop you. But I'm bored out of my mind sitting in Ruta's house all day. It'll be great to be on a ship again, and I want to know all I can of the boat we are relying on to carry us across the Semestrial Sea in a week." He looked at Gellion significantly, as though to remind him of the importance of the task that lay ahead.

Gellion had to admit that Valder had a point. They knew how to sail, but it had been centuries since Gellion had to navigate a full journey without a motor, and the wooden vessels of the Kayda would undoubtedly move and respond differently than the metal boats he was used to. Their safety could rely on a working knowledge of the *Brasa*.

"Alright," he said grudgingly. "But I still say Ruta's legend is important. I want to talk to Heleena. She's ancient—for a human. She must have been alive when the 'selkie' was here. She may even know more about how the mountains became as they are now. She said the changes began in her mother's time."

"She certainly appears to hold the same suspicions of us as Ruta," Veldon said. "Just be careful. Ruta was reassured by your frankness, but you can't know how Heleena will react. She may be old, but she is sharp."

"I will be careful," Gellion said. "And I want you two to come with me."

"Doesn't that seem a bit intimidating?" Veldon asked. "Three of us interrogating her?"

"We're not interrogating her," Gellion said. "We're just asking if she knows anything that could help us." He shook his head. "It *must* have been an elf. Ruta's description fit perfectly. Black hair, pale skin, green eyes, Ruta said herself he looked like you two, like a Turi."

"Ruta never saw the selkie," Veldon pointed out. "She is only describing the appearance legend has told her. She said he was a seal man. Naturally he would have black hair and eyes like the sea. It could just be coincidence."

"I wish we were selkies," Valder muttered. "Turning into seals would make getting back to Faeran a lot easier."

Gellion ignored him. "The elf who destroyed Daro was Turi," he said stubbornly.

Valder rubbed his face in frustration. "But this was over a century ago. You think the elf was planning his attack for that long?"

"Why not? Whatever he did to vierstone must have taken him years to learn. Veldon still hasn't come anywhere near figuring out what it was. What if he hid away here, away from the elves, while he worked it out?"

Valder did not look convinced.

"Will you come with me to talk to Heleena?" Gellion said. "That's all I ask. If nothing comes of it, you can play with the sailboat the rest of the week, and I won't bother you about it again."

Valder's mouth twitched. "Fine. I'll come. But if your prying causes the Kayda to chase us away as shape shifting seals, *you* are responsible for building us a new boat."

Heleena was in the back garden of Ruta's home. Unlike the front of the house, the space was overflowing with flowers and herbs. Narrow paths wound between the plants, and in the center of the yard was a round pond full of colorful fish. Low benches surrounded the pond, and Heleena sat on one of them. Her hands were clasped on her knees, her face tilted toward the weak mountain sun. Her eyes were closed.

"Maybe we should come back later," Veldon whispered.

"You may speak now," Heleena said. Veldon jumped in surprise. "You have already interrupted."

Veldon's face flushed. Heleena opened her eyes and looked at the elves. As usual, Gellion could make no guess at her thoughts.

"We did not mean to disturb you." Gellion bowed his head. "We only wished to ask you about something."

Heleena nodded slowly, turning her gaze on each elf in turn. "Ask, then."

Gellion glanced at his brothers before he began. "I spoke with Ruta the other day."

"I am aware," Heleena said before Gellion could continue.

Gellion paused. "She told you—"

"Of her suspicion, yes. A suspicion I share."

Gellion noted her use of present tense with unease.

"She also told me what you said," Heleena continued. "And of your —interest in the selkies." She raised an eyebrow.

"We are interested," Gellion said. "May we sit?" He indicated the benches curving to either side of Heleena. She gave a barely perceptible nod.

Gellion sat and leaned forward with his elbows on his knees.

"I will make the same promise to you, Heleena. My brothers and I mean no harm to your people. We are who we say we are and are indebted to the Kayda for helping us. I hate to ask for more, but there is one other thing you can help us with."

Heleena's face remained impassive. Gellion took the lack of reaction as permission to continue.

"We have heard the story of the mountains from many people. How the Falspires used to be clean and safe, how they only became as they are now in the last centuries. We passed through the mountains to get here. You know what we experienced."

Gellion hesitated, wondering how much he should tell this woman. Veldon had cautioned him against her sharp mind, and Gellion could see shrewd suspicion in the faded brown of her eyes. If Heleena knew anything, she would not give up that knowledge casually.

She's no Chiara, Gellion thought bitterly. The Albaren woman had practically forced information on him, but of course that had all been part of her game. If Gellion wanted Heleena to be honest with them, the only way was to be honest with her.

"The things we have seen and felt here are not unfamiliar," Gellion said. Valder and Veldon looked at him with barely hidden alarm, but made no move to stop him. "Our city was destroyed, but it was not by the Albaren. It was by a force from within. One we do not understand, and one that we think may be tied to what happened here, two hundred years ago. Please, can you tell us what happened? If I am right, it could help save our own people."

Heleena did not answer at once. Her eyes passed from the elves to the lazily swimming fish.

"The world moves in patterns," she said, tracking the winding progress of the fish. "Movement, nature, history—it repeats, different each time but still the same underneath." She looked out to the mountains. "The spirits in these mountains were once pure. Those spirits have been growing stronger again for many years. The corruption is receding. In another generation, the mountains will again be what they were before, though new souls will walk their shadows and till their soil."

Gellion tried to make sense of Heleena's words, but found himself struggling to find meaning. He remained silent, hoping she would go on.

"The corruption began slowly," Heleena said. "Before I was born. The animals grew more bold, more vicious, and became twisted and obscene. Their eyes haunted the shadows, and the air of the mountains grew heavy with hostility." She looked directly at Gellion, a sudden fire in her eyes.

"You ask me about the selkie. What do you want to know that Ruta has not said? He came to the village when I was a child, after the corruption began. He was a part of it. Drawn to it or part of the cause, I do not know, but the sea walkers never come with honorable intentions. He did as his kind is wont, then disappeared—from sight that is. He returned at least once." Her eyes were distant with bitter memory.

Gellion watched Heleena closely. Had she seen the selkie? Was she holding something back? But Heleena continued with no further explanation, and Gellion did not dare interrupt her.

"Then came the earthquakes."

It was like an electric shock. All three brothers visibly jerked. Even Valder looked entirely interested now, all traces of doubt banished from his face.

"Earthquakes?" Gellion asked in a hoarse whisper.

Heleena nodded. "They came slowly at first, and grew more powerful over time. Eventually, whole mountainsides collapsed. And all the time the spirits grew more angry, the storms came, the monsters drew nearer and more numerous. I was a young woman then, raising my family with horrors all around."

Gellion could hardly make sense of the onslaught of thoughts and emotions crowding his mind. Earthquakes. Monsters. Selkies.

It had been Kaelo. It had to have been. The selkie had been seen just after the corruption began. Whatever Kaelo did with vierstone had started here, in Suri Ranta, and if Gellion was right, the process affected far more than vierstone itself. How long had Kaelo been here, and what had he been doing in all that time?

Gellion took a steadying breath. He had to talk to his brothers. The time had come at last to tell them about Kaelo. All of it. The evidence was too strong now, and if Kaelo had been here, he might have left something behind—clues to his purpose or his plans.

But first they needed more information. They needed to know where to start, where to look. They needed to know everything about what Kaelo had done in this town.

"Heleena." Gellion tried to keep his voice controlled. "Do you know any more about this selkie? Can you tell me what he did while he was here, or if there is anyone in this town who might have seen him?"

Heleena's lips pressed tightly together. Her eyes seemed to bore into Gellion's soul. A sort of resolve settled over her features.

"I never saw him myself. I was only a child." She sighed. "But there are none in Suri Ranta who can tell you more than I."

Gellion held his breath, waiting for her to continue.

All suspicion and pride had left Heleena's eyes now, and she looked at Gellion with sadness.

"It was my mother's sister the selkie took."

"Took?" Gellion said.

Heleena nodded.

"What do you mean?" Gellion said. "Would you tell us what happened?"

Heleena took a slow breath. "My aunt was called Isla. She was younger than my mother and was never content with the simple life my family led. She saw Albaren trading ships and Dierna caravans—saw what wealth could buy and what nobility looked like. She had a good heart, but she was restless." Heleena sighed and looked around at the beautiful garden, as though lamenting that anyone should desire more. Then her eyes hardened.

"The selkie was one of the many hauntings drawn to Suri Ranta in that time. He began to walk among us in shadow. None saw him clearly, but rumors spread that a faerie, a nightwalker, was visiting the village." She grimaced. "Anyone enjoys a good ghost story. I do not know how many people actually saw the selkie, or how many pretended they did. I doubt many truly believed there was a faerie at all." A shadow fell over Heleena's face.

"That is when Isla began to act strangely. I was five at the time, maybe six. I remember only vaguely, but though my mother did not like to talk about it after, she told me the full story when I was older. Isla began to disappear for hours at a time, always at dusk, or before dawn. At first she would not say where she had been, but she smiled as she said it, and her eyes were distant and wild."

"Isla was a pretty girl, twenty years old and not yet married. She was proud, and wanted adventure and luxury. The village boys bored her. She wanted more. Selkies are drawn to those who long for what they cannot have. The dissatisfied are willing victims, and Isla's beauty alone would have drawn the attention of any selkie. After a while, Isla started to tell stories about her disappearances, claiming that she was being visited by a faerie. At first everyone thought she was making up stories for attention, or to add excitement to her life, or that she was taking the rumors in the village and running with them. My grandmother tried to keep a watch on Isla, but the girl always managed to slip away, and as time wore on, people began to think she was going soft in the head. She seemed to believe everything she said and walked through the days distracted and bleary eyed."

Heleena shook her head. "None believed her then, but now we know it was true. Isla was being lured away from her family by a sea walker, charmed and seduced. Then the charm broke. The selkie disappeared—they always do—and Isla came home broken hearted and disgraced. She was pregnant."

"Pregnant?" Gellion said in disbelief. Until now he had been following Heleena's story with Kaelo planted firmly in place of the selkie, but this? An affair with a village girl, a *human* girl? It couldn't be.

"With child," Heleena said, apparently thinking Gellion had not understood the word. "It was impossible to believe that everything had been in Isla's head then, but still, most thought she had been secretly seeing a man in the town, or met someone from a neighboring village. Some even thought she had been taken advantage of in her state. But as Isla's term lengthened, she began to come back to herself. She was depressed and heartbroken, but she was very much sane, and slowly her pain turned to anger, then determination to raise the child. But when the child was born, there were none who could doubt the truth in Isla's story, however impossible it seemed. It was a fae child, there was no doubt about that."

Gellion cocked his head. "A fae child?"

Heleena nodded sagely. "Had pointed ears, skin the color of pearl, eyes the same shining green as the selkie Isla had described."

Gellion drew in a sharp breath and exchanged a look with his brothers. They were both wide-eyed and pale.

A fae child indeed.

"Many urged Isla to throw the changeling into the sea to be reclaimed by the faeries. She wouldn't hear of it. But faeries do not let their offspring live among humans forever. They always reclaim them eventually, as we warned Isla, but it was still a shock when the child disappeared."

Gellion raised his eyebrows.

"The selkie reclaimed his changeling, as is their way. Isla never saw the selkie again, though rumors of sightings still appeared now and then over the years. The corruption of the mountains grew stronger, and over time, the story of the selkie and his changeling was forgotten, or exaggerated to the point that it became legend. Isla eventually married, her wild spirit tamed for good after her ordeal."

Gellion stared at his hands, his mind once again whirring with the unbelievable information. There was no doubt in his mind now. The child Heleena described had been an elf—or half elf he supposed. He shook his head. Was it possible? He had never even considered if elves and humans could reproduce. The more important question was *why*. Why would Kaelo have sired a son or daughter in the Falspires? Could he have been in love with the Kayda girl? But why would he have disappeared and then taken the baby? Could the child's conception have been a mistake? If so, Kaelo would not have wanted a half elf being wandering the human world.

One thing Gellion knew for certain was that Kaelo had not gone back to the sea after the child's disappearance. He had remained in Suri Ranta—or near it—and caused the earthquakes Heleena described. Had he been experimenting? Planning the destruction of Daro and whatever came after?

"Heleena," Gellion said. "This selkie. He must have stayed in the area. I think he had something to do with the corruption and earthquakes. Do you have any idea where he could have been? Where he could have hidden? Did your aunt ever say where the selkie took her? An abandoned building, for example, or a cave—a place that no one ever goes?"

"Stayed in Suri Ranta?" Heleena looked incredulous. "I don't think so. Selkies always return to the sea. He may have come upon the land again, but he would not have stayed in the mountains all that time."

Gellion tried to restrain his frustration. "I think this one was different. Please, can you think of any place like I described?"

Heleena narrowed her eyes in thought. "There are ruins above the city—an old grain mill that was never repurposed. But children play up there. And there are caves all over these parts."

"What about your aunt?" he persisted. "Did she ever say where she went to meet the selkie?"

Heleena hesitated. "Isla tried to bring my mother to the place she had met the selkie, after her child was taken. She must have thought he would take the changeling back there. But they never got to the place. She could not find it again, and the spirits drove them away."

"The spirits?" Gellion said, another idea forming in his mind. "Are there places they are more concentrated? A place your people consider haunted, or dangerous?"

Gellion immediately knew he had hit on something. A dark look passed behind Heleena's eyes.

"There are places we do not go," she said. "Places heavy with anger and fear, where those that venture do not return."

Excitement was growing in Gellion's chest. "And wherever Isla took your mother—it was one of those places?"

"Yes."

"Can you take us there?"

Heleena drew her brows together, some of her old suspicion coloring her eyes.

"What do you hope to find?"

"Answers."

"I doubt you will find anything in the mountains."

"We have to try."

"It has been years since the selkie was seen."

"He is not here anymore. He is attacking our people, probably across the sea by now. That's why we have to get back. But first we must find out anything we can about him."

Veldon and Valder were looking at Gellion curiously. Gellion was sure they now suspected an elf had been here, but they still did not know what Gellion knew. They did not know *who* had been here.

Heleena clasped and unclasped her hands, looking between the elves. Finally she said, "I will not go with you. But if you seek to risk your own lives, I will not stop you. Ruta is better with the spirits than I. She can take you as far as our people go. Then, you will be on your own."

KAELO

"I knew it," Gellion said breathlessly, closing the bedroom door behind him. "I knew it was an elf."

"It does seem to fit," Veldon said slowly.

"Of course it does!" Gellion said. "Earthquakes. There were *earthquakes*. Ones that came suddenly and brought down mountainsides. That doesn't sound like natural earthquakes to me. And the monsters, the corruption. It's all the same, don't you see?" Gellion began to pace. The cushions they slept on at night were rolled away in cabinets during the day, leaving the room surprisingly spacious.

"It's all what happened in Daro, but drawn out over years—decades. Whatever he did in Daro he had to test, to perfect, and this is where he did it. Maybe even where he learned it. He must have landed here in the mountains when he sailed from Faeran. What better place to hide than mountains?"

"Gellion."

Gellion stopped his pacing to look at Valder, who was staring at him as though he were mad.

"What are you talking about? Who is 'he?' This mysterious elf we've been talking circles around for weeks and months?"

Gellion paused. "Yes."

Valder cocked an eyebrow and looked at Veldon.

"We know you are not saying all that you know," Veldon said to Gellion. "Even in prison in Arvain I knew you were holding something back when you described the elf. You said Renyra had seen him, and you had glimpsed him, but you spoke with a certainty beyond your proof. You have never been one to make wild assumptions without good cause."

Gellion shifted, his mouth suddenly dry.

Valder drew his brows together. "What is it? Is it someone we know? Someone you're protecting?"

Panic was rising in Gellion's throat. He had been planning on telling his brothers about Kaelo, but now that the moment had come, he could not seem to form the words.

Valder and Veldon exchanged another glance.

"Please, Gellion," Veldon said. "You can tell us. What is it you know?"

Gellion took a deep breath through his nose.

"It is a long story," he said softly. "One that few know."

Running a hand through his hair, Gellion tried to decide where to begin. Did they really need to know everything?

They deserve to know everything.

The knowledge did not make his decision easier. He had hardly spoken of Kaelo since the man had disappeared from his life nearly seven centuries before. His chest tightened, but he took a breath, and began.

"You know that our family lived in Tura, before either of you were born."

They both nodded, clearly confused by the direction Gellion's story was beginning.

"Mother was a metalworker in the city. I was fascinated by her work from the time I was old enough to understand it. She handled metal with the familiarity and knowledge of a lover—confident but gentle, coaxing, full of admiration." Gellion smiled at the memory despite himself. "She began to teach me, slowly, carefully over the years, but as I grew in maturity and skill, she decided that I should be apprenticed to someone outside of the family, a mentor who could teach me with impartiality, one with greater skill than even she. The metalworkers of Tura were the greatest craftsmen in all of Faeran, and the mentor she chose was the best of them."

Gellion looked away from the entranced stares of his brothers.

"Kaelo," he said.

Even from the corner of his eyes he could see Veldon and Valder's reaction to the infamous name. Veldon's eyes widened, and Valder straightened.

"He made beautiful things," Gellion continued before they could say anything. "Elegant, curving lyres that produced music to haunt the soul. Shirts of metal rings so fine and delicate they felt like cool liquid flowing through your hands and lay on your shoulders like your own skin." Gellion closed his eyes and shook his head.

"I do not know why he agreed to teach me. Perhaps he was a friend of mother or father, or maybe he was simply eager to pass on his knowledge. I don't know, and likely never will. But teach me he did. I owe most of my skill to him, though I only studied under him for five years."

Silence filled the room. Gellion did not know where to go from here.

"Kaelo," Veldon said in an almost awed voice, but understanding was beginning to show in his face. "That's who this is? The elf who caused the earthquakes, who destroyed the vierstone? Who came here, to Suri Ranta?" He raised his head sharply. "Mother told us about him, but she spoke as though he were dead, and she never mentioned you." He looked at Gellion as though seeing him differently than ever before.

"How do you know this is Kaelo?" Valder looked almost affronted by the secret Gellion had kept all these years. "How long have you known? In Daro?"

Gellion shook his head. "I should have known. I should have guessed before we left the city, but I didn't see it. Not in time. I glimpsed his face when I chased him through the city that night before we left. I knew he was familiar, but his was a face I had not seen for centuries, and one that I don't think I wanted to believe. All the same, the familiarity had been bothering me for a while when Renyra came to me during the battle and described him. It all fell into place then. I could picture his face as though the years between had never happened.

I knew he had stolen my tunic—the one I made for the competition in the same style he had taught me. I knew I had seen him in the city before, always before an earthquake. He attacked around me, but never me directly. He ran from me."

Gellion remembered how the ground had opened beneath him when he had ventured too close to Kaelo the night before the Kindom Council's parting—stopped, but not seriously harmed him. He remembered how the buildings around him had fallen the night he chased Kaelo, leaving him and his workshop perfectly safe between.

"He remembered you?" Veldon said.

"I think so," said Gellion.

"What was he like?" asked Valder. "In Tura I mean." He seemed to have gotten over his annoyance at Gellion's secret keeping and was now leaning forward in his eagerness.

Gellion sighed and looked past Valder at the swaying trees beyond the window.

"He was quiet. Serious." He shook his head. "But that does not describe him accurately. He was serious about his work, but he was patient with me. He was brilliant. A good teacher. And despite his contemplating and serious nature, he could be charismatic. He was slow to laugh but also slow to anger, and when he did laugh, it carried such joy you could not help but join." Gellion started to smile at the memory, but it quickly faded.

"I expect to see him truly angry, to see him lose control, would have been terrifying. I never did. There were times when I could sense anger rising just below the surface, a presence that seemed to change the consistency of the very air in the room. His eyes would appear to darken, to go—opaque, and you could feel the strength of the control he exerted to master himself. But mostly, he was a gentle and patient master. I admired him more than I can say."

Gellion clenched his jaw at the sudden prickle behind his eyes.

"Then of course you know what happened, though perhaps not all. Even I do not know the full truth. During my apprenticeship, Kaelo fell in love with a woman named Arela. They were wed, and from what I could see, he loved her deeply. Those were the best years of my apprenticeship. Kaelo was advancing metallurgy beyond what any could have imagined with an energy and joy that bled into my own work."

"But despite his skill and prestige, Kaelo was not the High Metal-worker of Tura. That title belonged to an elf named Bardan, who himself had been Kaelo's mentor many years before." Gellion grimaced. "I did not like Bardan. I was still barely more than a boy at the time, but he was never kind to me. I think he was jealous of Kaelo—of his skill and his esteem, maybe even his mentorship to me. Bardan looked on Arela with envy, and began to flatter her."

"I watched from the outside, a boy who did not fully understand what was happening. Kaelo grew quiet, brooding. I cannot say all that happened between those three, but I could feel the anger simmering beneath Kaelo's skin."

"Then one day, wild rumors flew through the streets of Tura. An elf was dead—two elves were dead—killed by another elf. It was impossible, unthinkable. It had never been done in living memory. I was afraid and confused, and when I heard Kaelo's name, I was devastated. I would not believe that my master had done such a thing. But Kaelo would speak no word for himself. The evidence was overwhelming. Kaelo had been found kneeling next to Bardan's stabbed corpse, Arela dead on the rocks below the cliffs. His wife and the man who had tried to steal her away."

"It affected me deeply." Gellion spoke in a whisper now. "There was no trial. Kaelo would not speak, so what was the point? There were no living witnesses. I watched Liera publicly banish him, while I silently begged him to defend himself, to say *something*. But he did not. He left the city with a face as impassive and unreadable as wood."

Gellion clenched his fists. The memory still brought heat to his chest. Why had Kaelo kept his silence? He had left the city without saying a word to Gellion, or to anyone else. Had he felt no remorse for his actions? No loss at the death of the wife he had loved so dearly? Did he not owe an explanation to his family and the apprentice who admired him above all others?

Veldon was pale, his eyes shimmering with shock and sympathy. Valder's mouth was hanging open, but his expression was as serious as Gellion had ever seen it.

"Did you ever see him again?" Valder asked.

Gellion closed his eyes and raked a hand through his hair. This was the part of his story he had hoped to avoid. There was no good in telling it. It held no ramifications for their current predicament. But to answer Valder any differently would be a lie. His brothers deserved better than that.

"Yes," he said heavily. "My apprenticeship and Kaelo's banishment were all before the elves knew of the power of vierstone's touch. A little more than a century into Kaelo's exile, vierstone earrings were becoming common—distributed to all Kindoms. After a while, Kaelo came back to Tura. He broke his exile and went to Liera in secret. I was on the Turi Council by then, highly ranked among the metalworkers of the city. I don't know what happened between Kaelo and his mother in private, but she brought him before the Council the next day. He had asked for a vierstone earring—claiming it his right as an elf to be given one. But Liera refused him, instead turning the meeting into a trial for broken exile, punishable by death."

Veldon gasped, incredulity clear on his darkening face. Valder looked outraged.

"She tried to have him *killed*?" Veldon said. "Her own son?"

Gellion nodded, his own anger at the situation long since cooled to numb sadness.

"She put him on trial before the Council, naming his past guilt grounds enough for a death sentence, claiming that his exile had been an act of mercy now betrayed. There were ten of us on the Council then. We agreed that the vote must be unanimous to carry out Liera's justice. Eight voted for Kaelo's death." Gellion looked down. "I voted against," he said quietly. "One other voted against as well, but I have since wondered if Liera would have gone ahead anyway if there had only been one opposition, or if the other elf would have voted the same if I had not been the first to oppose Liera. As it was, Liera was forced to release Kaelo, though still under banishment. He was not to enter Tura again on pain of death, and the other Councils across Faeran were warned against him—against giving him sanctuary or any vierstone."

Gellion took a deep breath. "That was the last time I saw him. Until recently."

No one spoke. Valder was staring at the ground, apparently deep in thought. To Gellion's surprise, something very much like anger was beginning to spread over Veldon's face. The whites of his knuckles showed against his fists.

"Veldon?" Gellion said uncertainly.

Veldon looked up. His eyes were hard, burning with a fire Gellion had seldom seen in their kind depths.

"How can they do it?" Cool anger laced his words.

"Do what?" Gellion glanced at Valder, who was watching Veldon warily.

"Kill!" Veldon spat. "Hate. Disown. Threaten. How can any of it exist?" There was pain in his eyes now. "The Albaren, the Dierna, the Masar—it was all shocking, but they are different races. They are not us. But the *elves*?"

"Veldon, what are you saying?" said Valder.

Veldon took a breath. He seemed to be trying to form more coherent words.

"In the Great War, there was death, pain, and suffering, but it came from the phoenix. It came from evil, from Olcon himself. But this—it comes from us."

Gellion could feel his heart starting to beat faster again. He wished he had never brought up the trial. He didn't want to talk about this, to think about this. It was no good, it couldn't be changed.

"The humans allow their own people to live in squalor and hunger," Veldon said. "They punish with imprisonment and death. But the elves are no better, punishing by banishment and exclusion, threatening death."

"It isn't that simple." Gellion's own frustration and anger were rising, try as he might to quench them. Veldon didn't understand. He had never been a leader. He had never had to make decisions for a city, or a nation. There was so much more to it. It was so much harder.

"It is wrong!" Veldon's eyes blazed.

"Of course it's wrong!" Heat burned in Gellion's core. He turned his eyes on Veldon with an intensity that made his brother draw back. "The justice you speak of is as broken as the world it serves! It has to be. It deals with things that were never meant to be." Gellion ran a hand through his hair and took a calming breath. "And so it results in things that were never meant to be. But that doesn't make the decisions to enact justice wrong. It can't make them wrong." He shook his head, trying to convince himself as much as Veldon. "It just makes them harder."

Veldon's rising shoulders had gone slack. There was still pain in his eyes, but much of the fire was extinguished.

"Whatever happened in the past—" Gellion began, then took a breath and started over. "We cannot change these things, Veldon. We can only do the best we can with the decisions we can make. For whatever reason, and by whatever means, Kaelo is in Faeran. Now. Threatening our family and friends. I know it. I don't know what will happen when we stop him, but I don't want to find out what will happen if we don't. If we had taken Kaelo from this world sooner, we might all be safe with our families now. No elves would have died in that battle, or in Daro. It was my own foolish mercy that landed us here."

Gellion lowered his head into his hands. After several long moments, he felt a hand on his shoulder.

"You cannot know what would have happened." The anger had gone from Veldon's voice. "Maybe you are right about all of this, but I do not think taking Kaelo's life in Tura would have been right. It should not have been Liera's decision to dictate his life or death then, any more than it was within your ability to decide Dulon's fate in that battle."

Gellion winced.

"I do think you're right about one thing," Valder said. "I think there is more to Kaelo's story than we know. Centuries' worth. And any answers we can get from this place before we return to Faeran are worth finding out."

DEPARTURES AND ARRIVALS

Lights still dripped from the floating platforms like trails of liquid luminescence. It would be hours before the sun crested the mountains of Ard Gael and painted the silvery essence of Maramor in gold. Kyna wondered how many hours a day the city spent in twilight. Not that she minded the soft light, nor the darkness. In Kyna's opinion, night was the best time to be alive, but she did not like early mornings. She had only gone along with Tornac's punctuality for the promise of an earlier arrival in Tura if they left before the sun's cresting.

The crate of vierstone was sealed and secured to the center of a shallow boat. Kyna had looked on the barge with suspicion, but Tornac said it would be more stable in the current, and they no longer needed the edge of speed. The current alone would carry them to Tura as quickly as they had arrived in Maramor, but a charged motor still lay waiting at the back of the craft.

Tornac had disappeared back toward the city, leaving Kyna waiting on the docks. She tried to enjoy her last moments of solid ground before taking back to the water.

Her heart had developed an annoying habit of speeding its pulse at random intervals, as though to remind her what lay ahead these next two days, and beyond in Tura. Considering the direction of conversation in her room the previous night, Kyna worried what Tornac would bring up in two days of bored solitude. He was clearly not as taciturn as she had first hoped.

By the time Tornac had returned to her room the night before, Kyna had been clean and changed, presenting a face both normal and poised. Dinner had been a quiet affair—for Kyna at least. Tornac had spoken with members of the Council of Maramor most of the time, including Bredan the stoneworker. Kyna had been impressed by the amount of vierstone the elf had managed to collect in an evening, and Tornac's family hoard had not been small either. The crate now bobbing in the lap of the shore was heavy. It was also priceless. Kyna thought of the more spirited parts of the Orhiri River, and apprehension rose in her belly. Speed would be important, but safe passage was vital.

What is he doing?

Tornac had not specified why he ran back up the docks, only said he would be back within ten minutes. Kyna walked in a circle, then looked upriver. Had the others arrived in Rone last night? Would they be crossing the grasslands today? Kyna had never seen the grasslands and could hardly imagine what they must be like from Renyra's stories. She pictured something akin to the rolling hills of Diernas, but with larger and stranger animals.

"Sorry." The docks creaked with Tornac's steps. His eyes were bright with exercise and his hair a glorious tangle from the wind. A bow was slung over one shoulder. "I forgot weapons."

Kyna noticed the same beautiful sword he had carried from Tura strapped to his hip.

"I thought a ranged weapon might be useful as well. Can you shoot?"

"No," Kyna said. "But I can throw my knives."

"Good." He tossed the bow and a quiver of arrows into the boat. "Ready?"

Kyna was only half listening. Movement beyond the docks had caught her eye, and she was watching the progress of a woman running down a staircase with the grace of a deer.

"Do you know her?" Kyna asked warily.

"Who?" Tornac furrowed his brow, then followed Kyna's nod toward the woman who was now stepping onto the docks. His brow relaxed, but he looked down with an expression Kyna could not read. "Oh," he said.

The woman approached the boat with a flushed face and springing step.

"I thought I had missed you again." She was carrying a wrapped object and stopped in front of Tornac gripping it in front of her.

She was pretty, in the way that a fire is pretty. Her eyes bore an intensity that nearly made Kyna step back.

"Again?" Tornac cocked his head.

"I meant to give this to you before you left for Tura weeks ago. But —" She trailed off, and her fingers gripped the wrappings harder.

Tornac nodded, his expression softening to a kindness that made Kyna feel an intruder on their conversation.

"Things happened quickly," he said.

The anxiety in the woman's eyes transformed all at once to an equally powerful sorrow. Kyna thought the woman would surely break whatever object she was holding, but then she relaxed her hands.

"Here." She held the bundle out to Tornac. "I—he would want you to have it." Her voice was halting, but not quavering.

Tornac did not reach for the gift at once. He was staring at it with a look of anguish that made Kyna avert her eyes. She wished she had waited in the boat. Yet curiosity raised Kyna's gaze again as Tornac gingerly took the package and began to unwrap it from the top. It was the hilt of a dagger, curved and etched like the sword at his hip. He gripped the hilt and pulled the blade partway out of its sheath. The metal was nearly white and edged on one side.

Tornac closed his eyes. "I don't know why people always give me weapons," he said with a humorless laugh that was almost a sob. Despite his words, Tornac opened his eyes and looked at the dagger as though it was the most valuable thing in the world.

"I can't." He pressed the knife back in its sheath and held it out to the woman. "You should have it."

"I have plenty of his things. You will take it." Her words left no room for argument, and her eyes burned with determination.

Tornac just shook his head.

"I will never escape the stubbornness of your family." An edge of fondness colored the force of the woman's voice. "I am not taking it back. You may bring it with you or throw it into the river."

Tornac looked as though she had asked him to throw his own soul into the river. He lowered the dagger and carefully rewrapped it.

"Thank you," he said.

"Do not thank me. It is not mine to give, only to pass on." Then she turned to Kyna. "Keep this one safe, will you?" Her eyes glanced back to Tornac.

At a loss of what to say, Kyna nodded.

Gratified, the woman took a step back and gestured to the boat behind them.

"Go on, then. I will untie the boat."

By the time Kyna collected the will to ask Tornac about the woman, the sun had almost risen above the mountains to the east. She had not thought her own voice would be the first to break the silence of the trip, but the wild musings of her mind were becoming unbearable. Had the woman been Tornac's wife? But it sounded like the dagger had belonged to someone now gone—one of his brothers? Why would the woman have had it if she were Tornac's wife? The hilt had looked like something Gellion would make.

Tornac sat at the back of the boat, absently adjusting the rudder to follow the path of the river. The wrapped dagger lay beside him. Kyna made as though to check the security of the vierstone crate, then sat with her back against it, facing Tornac. She studied her fingernails for a while, then said as casually as she could manage, "So, who was she?"

Tornac looked at her blankly, then seemed to realize what she was talking about. Even sitting, Kyna could see him stiffen. He moved his eyes back to the river.

"Farra."

The name sounded familiar. Hadn't Gellion mentioned a Farra?

Tornac took a breath. "My brother's wife."

"Oh!" Kyna said before she could stop herself, shamefully relieved by the woman's identity. "Veldon's wife."

Tornac's eyes locked onto her.

Kyna immediately clamped her mouth shut, but the damage was done.

"How—You knew Veldon?"

Idiot. Why did you even bring up Farra?

There was no getting out of it now. Kyna nodded slowly.

"And Valder. But *knew* is a strong word." She paused, then plowed on. "I knew Gellion better."

Kyna did not know what had made her say it. Had it been the crushing disappointment in Tornac's face, or some insidious desire within herself to talk about the object of her own pain? Either way, she had not expected the flash of anger that crossed Tornac's eyes. He must have seen her surprise at his reaction, for he drew a mask of neutrality over his emotions a moment later. He took a slow breath.

"Gellion." Tornac nodded, a peculiar smile touching his lips that was devoid of humor. He looked down at the dagger beside him and began to finger its wrappings. "Have you known all this time that I am his brother?"

Kyna hesitated. "Yes."

"I am surprised."

"I didn't want to—"

Tornac held up a hand. "Not that you said nothing, but that Gellion ever mentioned me to you." He gave Kyna a searching look. "You must have known him well."

"Oh." Kyna looked down. "Well."

Tornac picked up the dagger and began to unwind and rewind its wrappings. "And you ... were you ... with them? In the battle?"

Pressure was building in Kyna's chest again. She fought the panic that licked at her nerves, acutely aware that the stone at her wrist would do little to save her if she lost control now.

It wasn't your fault. He didn't matter. It wasn't your fault.

The mantra played in Kyna's head like a chant against evil.

"No," she said. "It was chaos when the Albaren turned on us. I ... I never saw them. Any of them. Not after the fighting started."

Kyna did not know what she wished she could tell him. That his brothers had died quickly? Painlessly? Heroically? What did it matter? They were dead nonetheless.

Tornac clenched his jaw and swallowed, but did not cease the rhythm of his winding.

"How many died?"

"I don't know." Guilt rose in Kyna's throat.

'We never would have made it this far without you.'

She hadn't known the Albaren would betray them. How could she have known?

"At least a few hundred," she said.

Tornac's hands stilled. "So many." His voice barely breached the hum of the boat's motor. He was staring at the dagger, its exposed hilt gleaming in the sunlight. "And Gellion led them there."

Heat shot up Kyna's spine at the accusation in his tone. Much as she tried to convince herself the massacre had not been her fault, she knew it wasn't Gellion's, either. Yet he had died for it.

He didn't matter.

Then why did she care about the honor of his memory?

"All the elves decided to go to that battle." Kyna looked straight at Tornac until he met her eyes. "It was not Gellion's fault."

The anger in Tornac's glare was palpable. For a moment, Kyna could see Gellion behind his rage.

"Not his fault?" he said through gritted teeth. "My mother told me what happened at that Kindom Council. What Gellion did. The alliance would have fallen through without him."

"He couldn't have known how it would end." Kyna matched Tornac's glare. "All the elves were fooled by the Albaren."

"It doesn't matter what he did or did not know about the humans. He knows what battle is. He knows what it does—" Tornac's voice broke on the last word. When he spoke again, it was softer, almost to himself. "But it never affected him before. Why should it now?"

Kyna narrowed her eyes, thinking of Gellion's disturbed recollections of the Great War.

"What do you mean?" she said.

Tornac didn't seem to hear her. He was staring at the dagger in his lap.

"None of them would have been there if it weren't for him. They shouldn't have been in Daro in the first place. Veldon—" He broke off, and the anger bled from his face as suddenly as it had come, revealing the grief laid bare beneath. He bowed his head over the dagger and ran his hands over his face. "They shouldn't have been there," he said.

The pressure within Kyna was threatening to break. She could almost feel Tornac's pain in the air. She could feel her own eyes beginning to burn. She clenched her jaw. It wasn't supposed to be like this. She wasn't supposed to feel this way—this great weakness of the elves. Why couldn't she stop it? She wished she had never met Gellion. She wished she had never set foot in Daro.

Suddenly, Tornac's horribly familiar features were too much to bear. Kyna could still feel the grief and anger radiating off of him like heat waves, which fed the panic growing inside her. She stood and moved to the other side of the crate, sitting down with enough force to rock the boat. Taking deep breaths, Kyna concentrated on the cool spray of the river.

Just a few more days. Then you never have to see these elves again. No brothers of Gellion, no friends of Gellion, nothing at all to ever remind you of Daro or Tura. You will forget him in time. Just a few more days.

She leaned her head back and closed her eyes, trying to empty herself of emotion. After a while, she felt her skin cool around the stone pressed into her wrist, and her inner turmoil turned cold.

It could have been ten minutes or a few hours that Kyna sat like that, but a grumbling stomach eventually forced her to abandon her cover. Tornac had not moved from the motor or said anything, but he watched her as she approached the supply bags. Kyna pulled a hunk of bread from the bag.

"I'm sorry," said Tornac.

Kyna looked up at him. His face was calm now, but still bore the traces of his earlier temper.

"It is—fresh, still," he continued. "And with all that has happened in Tura, it has been easy to distract myself. But whatever happened in Daro, it was by no fault of yours. I should not have let my temper get the best of me." He held out a pear to her and his lips twitched in an attempted smile. "A family trait you may be familiar with."

Kyna snorted and took the pear. "Quite."

***

The rest of the day was spent in companionable silence cracked by the occasional conversation, though topics steered well away from Daro. Tornac was intelligent and surprisingly easy to talk to once he shed his sullen exterior, though he still had a tendency to be blunt and harsh. Kyna liked him all the more for it.

Like Gellion, Tornac was a metalworker, though he seemed much less defined by his craft than his younger brother. He had the mind of an engineer and preferred writing and drawing plans to working with his hands. Kyna listened with one ear and tried to enjoy the features of Tornac's face without seeing Gellion in them. His nose was ridged and his face longer. It was easy at times to see him objectively, but then he would run a hand through his hair, or turn his face so the light caught it at just the right angle. Kyna started to keep her eyes on the landscape when they talked.

All in all, it was a far superior day of travel than any of the days previous, with the added benefit of riding the river's current. Going downriver was even faster than Kyna had imagined. By nightfall, the northern range of the mountains had shed their height, giving way to hills and flat shoreline.

Kyna slept poorly that night. The closer she grew to Tura, the harder it was to ignore the momentous events she would have to confront when she returned. She wished she had never let Renyra coerce her into this trip. It had been nice, getting away for a while, but it made facing what came next so much harder. What had happened in Tura while they were away? Would the forges be ready for the vierstone? Had Liera found a suitable smith to forge a vier-stone sword?

What dreams came to her troubled rest were filled with melted stone, rushing water, and ash.

She woke tired and anxious. With any luck, they would reach Tura before nightfall, but it would still be a long day on the river, with plenty of time to think.

Tornac's contemplative scowl crept back onto his face as the day progressed, and his conversations grew further apart and more serious. His mood bled into Kyna, and she fidgeted with anything that passed through her hands while watching the horizon for the silhouette of a distant city.

"Do you think Kaelo will try to stop us?" Tornac sat at the motor, his hand resting on the rudder control even though the river had calmed and now guided them of its own accord.

"He might," Kyna said with a shrug. "If Liera has any sense, she'll have taken measures to prevent his interference after what happened when we escaped."

Tornac blew air out of his nose in a way that told Kyna he had as much confidence in the Lady of Tura as she did.

"We will approach the walls long before dark," Tornac said. "Kaelo would have had to station himself at the river's entrance every day and night since our departure to catch our return." He furrowed his brow. "Surely the elves will have cleared a path through the rubble in the river by now."

"I expect so," Kyna said absently. She was growing bored with this speculation.

"Are we doing the right thing?"

This made Kyna look up. "What?"

"This prophecy. What if we got it wrong? If all of this was for nothing and we have just doomed Maramor's supply of vierstone?"

Kyna sighed. "We haven't got it wrong."

Tornac narrowed his eyes. "How can you know that?"

"Because it makes sense."

"But what happens once we make the sword and Liera has it? Is she to track Kaelo down? That tactic has not worked well thus far."

"Prophecies don't always tell you how a thing happens." Kyna tried to keep the exasperation from her voice, but did not entirely succeed. "They just tell you that it happens. When Liera has the sword, Kaelo may come to her for all you know."

"That didn't work out well last time either," Tornac muttered, skepticism plain on his face. "I just hope the messengers reach the other Kindoms as quickly as possible. If this sword doesn't work, we will need all of them to stop this."

Kyna made no comment. The other Kindoms would never get to Tura in time. Even if Renyra and the troupe reached Telem Fier tomorrow, it would take days to mobilize elves on a ship, and days more to sail to Tura. As for Morcanan and Remsgraen, word may not reach them for another week. Tura would be alone until the sword was forged. After that, help from the other Kindoms wouldn't matter anyway.

"What is that?"

At first Kyna thought Tornac meant the outline that had just appeared on the horizon. Tura. Within sight at last.

Tornac, however, was not looking at the distant city, he was looking in the water. His eyes were wide.

Kyna gripped the side of the boat and peered over its edge. The water was clear, though not shallow enough to grant a view to the bottom. Just under the surface swam a group of creatures as mesmerizing as they were alarming. Sinuous and rhythmic, they undulated their bodies in rapid frequency. Trails of black liquid streamed behind them to create moving patterns that intertwined with each other in the current. There were at least a dozen of the things on this side of the boat, and all of them had their bulbous eyes turned toward it.

Their blank stares made Kyna's skin crawl. She wanted to back away from the water, but she couldn't seem to take her eyes off the creatures. Ridiculous as it sounded, she was sure they were staring at *her*.

"They don't look like they can get out of the water." Tornac looked to the other side of the boat. "And they are too small to do damage to the boat. I've never seen anything like them here though." He twisted to check the motor. "We have plenty of power, still, and we are not far now. If I crank the motor we should be back in Tura in about an hour."

"Do it," Kyna said without hesitation. She wanted to get rid of these things, whatever they were. Would they follow the boat into the city if given the chance?

The hum of the motor rose in pitch, and the boat surged forward. For a moment, the horrific eels began to lag behind, then their undulating became more frantic, and they came level with the boat again, their eyes still fixed upward. A cloud of black was trailing behind the boat. What on Riure were these things?

Kyna's heart raced, and her skin grew cold. She pressed her wrist against her thigh.

The bulbous eyes expanded, and wild splashing erupted all around the boat as the creatures twisted in arcs out of the water.

Past her scream, Kyna heard the whisper of metal as Tornac drew his blade. She reached for her daggers.

"What happened?" Tornac shouted, slashing his sword as black bodies started to flip into the boat.

"I don't know!" Kyna backed against the crate of vierstone, her legs in a crouch and her hands in front of her wielding her blades. Where the eels landed, residue smeared over the metal of the boat, thick and sticky. The things made no sound except their wet flopping, but the silence was somehow worse than any shriek they could have uttered.

"Cut off their heads!" Tornac had abandoned the motor and was hacking away at the horrid creatures.

Kyna sliced and stabbed, but her knives kept slipping over the mucus-laden skin of the things. Then one of the eels made a targeted leap straight at Kyna, opening a round mouth of stubby teeth. Kyna screamed and slashed her knife, but the thing slipped past and latched onto her arm. Its teeth may have been stubby, but they were sharp as needles. Kyna screamed again and smashed her arm and its passenger against the crate, but that only increased the pain in her flesh. The eel hung on like a leech.

More of them were flipping into the boat. Kyna stabbed with her other hand, tears running down her face as she tried to ignore the pain and horror of the eel on her arm.

She heard a shout of pain from Tornac, followed by a stream of cursing. Then the engine roared, and the boat flew forward so suddenly its front lifted out of the water. Kyna was sure the flat craft was not meant for such sudden speed and clung to the crate behind her while stomping on the still thrashing bodies around her feet.

Slowly, the thrashing stilled. Water sprayed past the edge of the boat, but no more eels came with it.

"We can't keep this up for long," Tornac yelled over the motor. "But maybe it will lose them."

Kyna wanted to hack at the creature still embedded in her skin, but was afraid she would fall out of the boat if she loosened her grip on the crate. The thought of being in the water with a pack of those things nearly made her vomit. She tightened her grip.

By the time Tornac slowed the boat, Tura was a definable shape on the horizon. Kyna could recognize the Central Tower and even the Archives. She was beginning to feel dizzy and stumbled when she took a step away from the crate.

Tornac faced upriver, watching the water for any signs of renewed attack. None came.

An eel was attached to the back of his shoulder, and he swayed slightly as he turned back to face her. His face was pale.

"Here." He stepped toward her. "Put your arm on the crate."

Kyna did so, trying not to wince at the pain or look at the horrid creature. Black slime oozed over her arm where its body touched. Tornac took his sword and sawed through the thing's neck. Its body spasmed, then slid off the crate and landed among its brothers below with a sickening squelch.

The jaws did not release, but Tornac gingerly grabbed the eel's lips with his fingers and pried them open. A perfect circle of crimson punctures outlined Kyna's arm. The surrounding skin was red and inflamed.

"Wash the black stuff off in the river," Tornac said. "The wound itself looks fairly clean."

Kyna moved to the side of the boat on shaking limbs and clasped one hand over the bite mark while she washed the goo from her skin. She felt weak and lightheaded.

Tornac sat down heavily. His eyes were unfocused, and his color even more drained than minutes before.

Kyna's stomach knotted. She should have removed his eel before washing her arm.

"Lean forward." Kyna wiped off one of her knives and approached Tornac, trying to still the shaking in her hands. He did as she said without comment.

Grimacing, Kyna sliced through the eel's neck, being careful not to cut Tornac.

"I need to cut away your shirt here." The thing had latched on straight through the fabric. She cut his shirt in a circle around the dripping head, then pried its mouth open as Tornac had done.

"Thank you."

"I can rinse it if you want, but there isn't any black slime. Your shirt saved you that at least."

Tornac shook his head. "Let's just get to Tura. Are you alright?"

Kyna nearly laughed, though that may have been from shock. She was weak and horrified, but Tornac looked a lot worse, as though half his blood had been drained—

Kyna made a disgusted sound.

"What?" Tornac said.

"Leeches. They were like giant, slimy leeches. They sucked our blood, don't you see? I feel like I haven't eaten in days. Your leech was bigger than mine, and you can barely stand."

Tornac nodded with a grimace. As though to test the theory, he tried to stand, then thought better of it and half crawled to the motor. He glanced backward.

"They don't seem to be following." He looked at the sea of slime in the boat with revulsion. "Though I'm not sure how many more there could have been. At least the vierstone is alright."

The crate was covered in black goo, but otherwise unharmed.

"We will be a sight getting into Tura." He snorted. "At least nothing Kaelo throws at us can be as bad as that."

They pulled through the walls of Tura without incident. As Kyna had expected, half an army of elves was stationed at the remains of the collapsed wall, and no trace of rubble remained in the water. They attracted stares and exclamations, but Tornac steered the boat steadily onward until they reached the forges.

A narrow dock extended into the water next to the slack tub of the forges. Before Tornac had brought the boat abreast of the platform, several elves had run onto the docks to greet them. Behind them was Liera.

She froze when she saw the slime-filled boat and its shaken occupants, but she quickly overcame her shock and looked at them with a grim expression.

"Thank Riu you've come."

2 8

THE GRASSLANDS

I t had been a long time since Renyra had boarded a Rale. The station was small. Though Rone was a fairly large city, it bordered Lake Orhirion to the north with nothing to the east but the mountains of Ard Gael. It was an important port city for Turi trade, but had little use for the Rale except to ferry goods to and from Telem Fier, far to the southwest.

Two sets of tracks led to the city—one inbound and one outbound. A few smaller tracks branched like a fan to hold Rale cars not in use or under repair. Renyra felt the buzz of excitement within her as she approached the sliding doors of the outbound Rale. This was the last segment of the train, which extended to the south like a metal caterpillar. The sides of the Rale were sleek, with polished windows and silver sheets of metal flowing seamlessly from tip to tail. Sunlight reflected off its surface.

Renyra had always loved the movement and anticipation that saturated the atmosphere of Rale yards. There was something fresh about arrivals and departures that set the mind to imaging: journeys across land and sea, new experiences, passing landscapes. She had missed this. And she had missed the grasslands.

Caerlyn's eyes glowed with the same fervor, and she grinned at

Renyra. Both of them had exchanged their Turi garb for wraps as soon as they had arrived in Rone. It felt wonderful to move in the loose fabric, to feel the breeze cut through the heat trapped around her body. For the first time since leaving Daro, Renyra almost felt herself again. She reached into a pouch in her wraps, where a coarse hunk of vierstone no larger than the end of her finger met her touch with a tingling welcome. Never again did she want to go so long without its presence. She had felt separated. Isolated. When Auralia had placed the small stone into her palm, Renyra had nearly cried.

Renyra turned to see Auralia hurrying toward her with a cage of birds.

"Take these to Telem Fier in case something happens to the Rale," Auralia said. "As soon as you have spoken to Cuvan, have him write to me." Worry colored the woman's features. As Lady of Rone, she could not leave her city while such a colossal threat lingered downriver, but Renyra could tell how much she wanted to speak with Cuvan herself. The two elves were the Kindom Council representatives for the Fieri and had been in Daro just months before.

Auralia had reacted to Renyra's news of Tura much as expected. At first, she had doubted Renyra entirely, insisting that no elf could destroy vierstone or collapse streets and buildings, let alone an elf centuries gone and exiled from the Kindoms. She had been appalled by the destruction of Daro, of course, but surely it had been a freak natural disaster?

It was the word of four other witnesses that convinced her in the end.

"We will watch." Auralia's eyes hardened against her worry. "Anything unusual or concerning will reach Cuvan's ears as quickly as possible."

Renyra did her best to look confident. She had always admired Auralia. The Lady of Rone was capable and fierce, but also showed a compassion for her people as strong as any family bond.

Auralia took a breath and smiled at Renyra, then walked back up the platform toward her city.

Renyra looked down at the cage. There were four birds perched on wooden pegs. They were grey, with white bellies and scarlet splotches over their eyes and tails. White outlined their eyes.

The birds looked up at Renyra with unblinking eyes and swiveling heads. Renyra smiled. Of all the animals she had cared for in Daro, birds were the biggest mystery to her, but that made them all the more enticing.

"Let's go!" A voice turned Renyra's attention back to the Rale. She was alone on the platform. Raren was waving from the door of a Rale car.

A burst of excitement radiated from Renyra. For a moment, she forgot all about Kaelo. She handed the bird cage to Raren and stepped onto the Rale.

An hour into their journey, the Rale had passed the ring of civilization that radiated from Lake Orhirion. Only hunters and wanderers ventured into the wild landscape that now stretched to the horizon.

The grass seemed to have absorbed the sun's essence, glowing a brilliant gold and throwing light about in shimmering waves each time the wind blew. The tips of the grass would have reached the windows of the Rale, but the golden blades lay nearly flat in the stream of wind next to the tracks.

"Look!" Alura's face was plastered to the window.

Renyra followed her gaze to a small herd of buval. The bulky animals had their flat noses lowered in the grass. Horns as thick as Renyra's legs flowed back from their heads over massive shoulders. Their back legs were deceptively small for their weight. Renyra had always thought the beasts funny looking, but the brindled stripes that ran from their shoulders to their tails reminded her of marble. They were beautiful in their own way, with gentle eyes nearly obscured by wrinkles of skin. One might think impaired vision would make the buval easy targets for predators, but hardly any animal would attack a herd of the giant animals unless it was desperate. The beasts had incredible hearing, and those horns could be deadly.

The Rale hurtled past the herd, but the animals merely lifted their heads to watch its progress.

"Have you read Liera's note to Cuvan?" Caerlyn said.

Renyra blinked and pulled the envelope in question from her bag. "It's sealed," she said.

Caerlyn snorted.

"What do you think Cuvan will do?" asked Raren.

"Go to Tura?" Alura said.

"It would do no good." Firas's brow was creased in thought. "By the time Cuvan arrived, Liera would have enacted her plan for better or for worse. By then, either Kaelo will be defeated, or all the vierstone in Tura will be gone. There will be nothing left to protect and no one left to fight."

"What if he destroys the city?" Renyra shuddered. If Tura fell into the sea like Daro, it would take thousands of elves with it.

"If he does, I doubt a ship full of Fieri will make much of a difference," Caerlyn said. "Firas is right. Sending elves will do no good no matter what happens in Tura. We are here to give warning, not plead for aid. Cuvan needs to guard Telem Fier, to be aware of the threat."

Renyra looked down at her hands. There were so many possibilities for what would happen next, each more terrible than the last. In the best of cases, an elf would die at the hands of his mother. At the worst? She clenched her fists. The tattoo of the three-pointed star on her right hand expanded against her stretched skin.

It was more than fear and uncertainty that gnawed at Renyra. Every time she thought of the night she had ambushed Kaelo, a fire of shame lit within her. What had he done to make her lose all reason and rational thought? Had she merely lost her nerve at his touch? She had vowed to make him fear her, to make him pay for his disregard of her threat, but instead she had cowered on the stone at his feet. There was a part of her —a small part, but one that refused to be quenched—that hoped Liera's plan did not work. She wanted another chance at Kaelo.

"Kyna and Tornac will be in Tura soon," Renyra said. "Riu willing, this will be over in a few days, and this journey will be for nothing."

Riu willing.

Had Riu's will stopped anything bad from happening so far? Renyra wanted to believe that some good would come out of all of this, but she could not imagine what it might be.

The wilderness beyond the window faded back to crops, then to scattered villages. Renyra smiled at the familiar square buildings. Flowers and shrubs overflowed from the windows and yards of every home, and brightly painted doors made a rainbow of color through the streets. It filled her soul with more hope than she had felt in months to see towns untouched by fear and destruction. She doubted these elves even knew what had happened in Daro, or if they did, it was a distant tale of a faraway place. Little did they know the message that could change their lives was speeding past them by Rale. Even if Kaelo was defeated, the elves had still lost two entire cities' worth of vierstone, plus the quarry at Daro. Would there be more expeditions? Was there any more vierstone on Riure?

Renyra tried to focus on the present. Worrying would do her no good.

The landscape grew more lush as the Rale drew nearer to the Braided River in the east. Each shade of green fed Renyra's excitement. Telem Fier couldn't be far now.

"There it is."

Renyra looked up to see Caerlyn pointing out the window. Sure enough, a brown rectangle had appeared on the horizon, stretching to either side as far as the eye could see.

The walls of Telem Fier.

29

PAINT IN THE MOUNTAINS

"It is over this ridge." Ruta's expression was dark, and her eyes were narrowed. She pointed at a winding dirt path that continued to climb up from the valley of the sound below.

A sheen of sweat slicked Gellion's brow. It was much cooler in the mountains than in Diernas or the marsh, but the steep inclines were just as sweat inducing. Ruta tackled the vertical paths with steady legs and barely a huff. She moved among the rocks and hills like a goat, and her golden skin looked more rejuvenated than taxed by the shine of her sweat.

The further they climbed, the more breathtaking the view behind them became. Though beech trees largely obscured the Sielu Sound, occasional breaks in the trees revealed the sparkling water far below, stretching into the distance between the mountains with glittering waterfalls dotting its sides. Gellion wondered how high they would have to climb to glimpse where the sound met the sea beyond.

With a sigh, he turned his back on the promise of escape and continued his ascent toward the ridge Ruta had indicated. The woman had spoken little of where they were going. If anything, she seemed more superstitious of the location than Heleena had been, and had made no shortage of comments about the elves' foolishness for seeking it out. All the same, Gellion was grateful for her cooperation.

"Ruta." Gellion increased the length of his stride to catch up to her. "Can you tell us any more about this place? Why the Kayda do not come here?"

"The Kayda do not come here because we are smart," she said with a sharp glance, clearly indicating that Gellion and his brothers lacked this particular trait. "We know not to trifle with dark spirits and the things they corrupt and twist." A look of fear flitted across her face.

"Have you been here before?" Gellion asked.

"No," Ruta said, a little too quickly.

Gellion let the silence stretch the obvious lie until it grew too uncomfortable for Ruta to bear.

She bowed her head. "I tried to come once. When I was a girl. I have always had a high affinity for the spirits, and I thought I could understand the place better than others—find out why it was so hostile. I did not get far. The air grew heavy; the wind seemed to carry its own voice. I saw eyes and heard growls and grew more and more frightened until a screeching bat flew right at my face." Ruta shuddered. "Its eyes were red. To this day I am sure of it. And its call was like nothing I have heard since. I ran all the way back to Suri Ranta and never came again."

"Heleena said the corruption has been ebbing these last years," Gellion said. "It may not be so hostile here anymore."

Ruta was clearly not convinced. She did not speak again until they reached the top of the ridge. There she stopped so suddenly Gellion nearly ran into her.

"This is as far as I go," she said.

Gellion looked around. The land flattened over the ridge. Trees had taken advantage of the stable ground to thicken in both girth and density, with a mat of moss and ferns beneath. The path they had been following continued, but it was overgrown and seemed to peter out altogether a short way beyond.

"The slope continues further into the trees," Ruta said. "It is there that I went before." Her eyes went hard. "It is there that Heleena's aunt searched for the changeling." She glanced back toward Suri Ranta. "Will you be long?"

Gellion caught a hint of worry in her voice. He wondered if it were for herself or for them.

"We might." He hefted the bag of food he had brought. "I think we can find our way back."

There was clear relief in Ruta's face. "You are sure?"

"Of course," Gellion said. "You have done enough in bringing us here. Thank you."

Ruta bowed her head. When she straightened again, she shot a wary glance into the trees.

"Be careful." With that, she shuffled back down the path.

"Talaith didn't exaggerate about the Kayda's superstitions," Valder said as he watched Ruta's head sink below the ridge.

"Can you blame them?" Gellion said. "Think what it was like in Daro with the earthquakes and monsters. If that was normal life for generations, I can only imagine what sorts of legends and fears would arise."

Valder raised an eyebrow and tilted his head in agreement.

"Fair enough," he said. "So, where do we start?"

"I suppose we just follow the direction of the path until we get to the slope Ruta mentioned," Gellion said. "Then we look around for some sign of habitation—a building or a cave maybe."

"You really think Kaelo would have lived in a cave for centuries?" Veldon said.

"He may not have had a choice," said Gellion. "Or he may have built a house away from prying eyes. Clearly something kept the humans from this place, whether it was by Kaelo's own doing or not."

The brothers waded into the underbrush.

In the warm light of midmorning, nothing about the forest seemed odd or daunting. Gellion began to wonder if all of this was just Kayda superstition after all. The birds that perched along their path all seemed perfectly normal, and the air was warm and clean.

By the time the ground began to slope upward again, there was no more visible sign of a path, but the tall trees and moss made for a thin underbrush, and the ferns never reached above Gellion's knees.

"Start looking," Gellion said. "There are faces of rock where the mountain starts to rise again." He indicated the moss covered cliffs that wrapped around the mountain to their right. "There might be caves in there. Or Kaelo may have built a dwelling along their shelter."

The brothers spread out, searching for any sign of something out of place in the wild landscape. As Gellion approached the cliffs, he began to notice fewer ferns and less moss on the ground and trees. He thought nothing of it at first, assuming that less light must penetrate the ground near the cliffs, or that the slope lessened the amount of rainfall the plants received. The plants that remained, however, looked sorrier and sorrier the further he walked. Brown spots dotted fern fronds, and the moss turned a sickly yellow. Even the trees began to lose their girth and the fullness of their leaves.

Gellion stopped and looked around. He could see what now seemed a splash of brilliant green back where the slope had begun. The beginnings of a chill started up Gellion's spine.

It's just a disease—a natural fungus. It has nothing to do with angry spirits.

Shaking his head, Gellion continued to the cliff face. A thick layer of moss encased the sheer stone, though patches of it were the same yellow as the moss on the nearby ground. Gellion ran his hand along the stone, wincing when his hand brushed a mushy bit of moss. It certainly seemed the type of cliff that would house a cave. Even on the hike from Suri Ranta, Gellion had seen dark and gaping cracks in the mountainside.

Gellion walked along the cliff face until it abruptly ended in what seemed to be an old rock slide that cascaded to the ground a hundred feet below. Frowning, Gellion retraced his steps. There had been no sign of a cave entrance along the wall, and no sign of any dwelling. Disappointment ate at Gellion, but he refused to admit defeat yet. It was a big mountainside, and if the Kayda never went past that ridge, the place he was looking for may be further up the mountain.

In the distance, Gellion could see Valder and Veldon walking through the trees.

"Any luck?" Valder called.

"No," Gellion said. "The cliffs end a short way behind me. Did you search them in the other direction?"

Veldon nodded. "Nothing. It does seem a strange place, though. Even in the sunlight there is something off about it."

Gellion nodded. The further he had walked, the more he had begun to notice a strange stillness. The persistent breeze that had followed them up the mountain was now weak and intermittent. The birds had thinned and quieted.

"The plants don't seem—healthy." Gellion eyed the yellow moss beneath his feet.

"I know." Worry creased Veldon's brow.

"I know there is something here," Gellion let out a frustrated breath. "I'm going to check this way again. Maybe I missed something —didn't look high enough or at the bases of the cliff. Why don't you two try to find a way further up the mountain? There must be a break in the cliffs somewhere."

Valder and Veldon nodded and turned back the way they had come. Gellion faced the cliff and put his hands on his hips. Could the moss be hiding a gap in the stone? Maybe if he kept his hand on the wall, he would feel a give where no stone stood behind it.

With a grimace, Gellion placed his hand back on the sickly moss and pressed slightly, then walked along the cliff once again. Several times he paused in excitement, only to realize there had only been a hole in the cliff, or a patch of thicker moss. As he walked, he looked above and below him, trying to find any sign of a cave entrance, but the minutes dragged on, and soon he could see the end of the cliffs ahead. He kept going. He would check every inch of this cliff, and do it again on the way back. He wanted to be absolutely sure he had not missed anything.

But there was nothing.

How could there be nothing? The stories all fit. Kaelo must have been here. Had he destroyed all evidence of his life here? Built a house and then burned it down?

Gellion let out a growl of frustration and began to walk back toward his brothers again. Maybe there was another cliff face further up, or even a house in plain sight. Still, Gellion kept his eyes on the cliff.

He stopped dead. His eyes darted to the place where he had seen the glare, but now he saw nothing but dull rock. There had been a light, he was sure of it. Sunlight reflecting off metal? Very slowly, Gellion took a step back, keeping his eyes exactly where he had seen the glint.

Nothing.

Gellion puckered his brows. Had he imagined it? Had sunlight reflected off a drop of water—moisture from the moss or a bit of persistent dew?

A short burst of breeze came, and Gellion nearly jumped.

A dancing shadow of leaves fell over the rock face, and a faint streak of blue appeared as if ignited by magic. The breeze died away again, and sunlight bathed the rock once more, obscuring whatever glow there had been.

Heart fluttering, Gellion moved backward until his own shadow fell across the rock where he had seen the blue stripe.

A grin spread over his face.

***

"Stand here." Gellion positioned his brothers so that their shadows fell over the bit of rock he had marked with a broken branch.

With a pair of incredulous looks that were almost laughable, Valder and Veldon stood where they were directed.

"Now look at the rock," Gellion said.

Both gasped. Where the three elves' shadows fell, a fine network of blue lines showed faintly on the rock.

Gellion flashed a grin as his brothers turned to stare at him.

"It's glow paint, or ink. The darker the shadow, the stronger it glows." He approached the wall and cupped his hands over a piece of the markings. Through a slit in his fingers, the inside of his hands turned blue.

Veldon's eyes widened. "It looks like—"

"Fieri paint," Gellion said triumphantly. "*Elf made* paint."

Valder looked at him doubtfully. "The humans could have invented something similar."

"But could they impregnate it into stone?" Gellion said with a raised eyebrow.

"What?" Valder put a hand against the rock where the paint colored it. He closed his eyes for a moment, then they flew open. "Sweet Riu, you're right."

"That's why it's still here," Gellion said in increasing excitement. "Even Fieri made paint can't last centuries on exposed rock unless it's been incorporated into the stone itself. And this has been."

"And an elf must have done it," said Veldon faintly.

"Stand back where you were," Gellion ordered.

The markings appeared again.

"I wish it were night." Gellion frowned as he peered at the patterns. "I'll bet this is as bright as a lamp then." He brushed away moss where it had grown over the paint strokes. "Move to your right a bit."

The shadows shifted, revealing more marks.

"I think they are leading to something," Gellion said. "They all converge." He tore away at a patch of moss. "Here!"

Beneath the moss, where the glowing lines converged, was a perfectly square impression in the stone. In its center was a small hole. Valder and Veldon stepped up behind Gellion, looking over his shoulder.

"What is it?" said Valder.

Gellion placed a hand over the hole and concentrated. Just beneath the surface of the stone, he could sense several thin openings in the rock —perfectly straight and cylindrical.

"Hand me a twig," he said. "Something thin and strong."

After a few moments, Veldon handed him a sliver of wood from a beech tree.

Gellion fit the sliver into the hole in the stone and slid it into the first opening, catching the lever within. The other two openings had their own levers, and when switched in the right directions, the three fit together to trigger a mechanism deeper within the stone. A human might have picked the lock for hours trying to find the right combination, but for an elf who could see stone as Gellion—or as Kaelo—the lock was simple, obvious.

A resonant *crack* echoed from within the cliff, followed by a series of scraping sounds. Gellion jumped back from the rock with a pounding heart. A puff of dust dissipated into the air, and some of the hanging moss shifted.

Cautiously, Gellion approached the cliff again and placed his palm over the square impression.

He pushed.

The rock moved inward.

A slow smile crawled up Gellion's face. He turned back to his brothers.

"I believe we found him."

Valder let out a bark of a laugh. Veldon smiled in wide-eyed amazement.

"You, my brother, are a talent," Valder said. "I am sorry I ever doubted your skills of detection."

"A mistake I'm sure you will not make again." Gellion bowed. "Now." He stood aside to reveal the dark gap in the stone. "Who's first?"

Two things struck Gellion about the cave. First, it was dark compared to the brilliant sunshine outside, but by no means pitch black. In fact, once his eyes adjusted, he thought he would be able to see fairly well without any other source of light. Two, from what he could see, this place was as like to a cave as a palace was to a warehouse.

Veldon and Valder's gasps echoed Gellion's thoughts.

The ceilings of the cave were high and arched, like the inside of an Albaren cathedral. Light filtered into the space from several points in the ceiling, sending scattered beams to rest on the floor and walls. Gellion squinted toward one of the sources of light and saw a round opening in the ceiling, sealed by what appeared to be dusty glass.

What the light illuminated was more shocking still. Had Gellion not seen the moss covered cliff outside for himself, he would have thought himself in the grand suite of a castle. All surfaces were stone, but a smooth stone, finely cut at the corners as though crafted by an expert stonemason. Gellion wiped a layer of dust away from the stone with a foot. It was polished.

A large fireplace sat on one side of the room. There was a wooden table and chairs, a cupboard, and a couch. Several twisting shapes that

Gellion recognized as elf made solar lamps hung from the walls and sat on side tables. Two arching doorways flanked the fireplace, leading into other rooms.

"To answer your question, Veldon," Gellion said in an awed whisper. "Yes, I think Kaelo could have lived in a cave for centuries."

Veldon gave a weak snort as his wide eyes took in the beautiful room.

"How in all of Riure?" Valder said.

Gellion nearly laughed. "He can break stone with a touch. I suppose that means he can also craft stone with a touch."

Gellion stepped into the room and looked back at the door they had come through. It was a thick slab of rock, carved as smoothly as the inside of the cave. On the inner side, there was a metal handle. Gellion tested that the handle worked, then closed the door behind them.

"Well," he said. "Let's see what we can find."

A cursory search of the main room revealed little of interest. Aside from the furnishings, there was nothing but a few pots, pans, and cooking utensils. A little disappointed, Gellion led his brothers into the first archway. It opened onto a smaller room, though still with vaulted ceilings and skylights. A bed sat in one corner, its base of stone, with thick silks and furs on its mattress. There was a chest against a wall, and a small desk that was bare except for a solar lamp. Gellion opened the dusty chest and reached inside, but only felt more silks and furs.

His frustration grew. Had he and his brothers gone to all this trouble only to find an abandoned dwelling cleared of all evidence of its owner? Had Kaelo taken everything with him? Destroyed it? With a sigh, Gellion went back into the main room.

He paused in front of the second archway. Veldon had crossed his arms as though cold, and was casting wary glances around the room.

"What?" Gellion said.

"I don't know," Veldon said. "It just feels—oppressive, in here. Don't you think?"

Gellion looked around the beautiful cave. "No."

"It's a bit dusty." Valder patted the back of a red couch to demonstrate. "But otherwise pretty homey. I wouldn't mind living in a place like this."

The wariness did not leave Veldon's eyes, but he dropped his arms and let a small smile touch his lips.

Gellion clapped Veldon on the back of the shoulder.

"It's a cave. It's bound to feel stuffy. Come on, let's look in the next room." He held his breath as he passed through the second archway, afraid the room beyond would prove as unhelpful as the first.

His jaw dropped.

Like the first side room, this room contained a stone bed and a chest, with a much larger desk, but where the walls of the first bedroom had been smooth, this room had deep shelves cut into the stone on one side, and every one of them was filled with tomes and scrolls.

Gellion approached the shelves. They were meticulously organized, without a paper skewed out of place. Several of the stacks were bound in leather, and one shelf held titled books.

"An avid reader?" Valder suggested.

Gellion snorted.

Veldon's eyes lit with excited interest. He ran his hands over the pages and pulled out a thin, leather bound tome. He flipped through its contents, eyes skimming.

"This one is all handwritten notes on—" He squinted to make out the words in the low light. "Chemistry, I think."

"Ah of course," Valder said. "Not an avid reader in his exile, but an avid scientist."

"An obsessive scientist," Gellion muttered, fingering through several piles of notes on what looked like geology.

A startled cry from Veldon made Gellion and Valder jump.

"What is it?" Gellion said sharply.

Veldon was holding a book with an expression of awe. He held it open to a page that showed a colored sketch of a smooth, green stone.

"These books." He indicated the shelf of titled tomes. "They're all on vierstone." He flipped through the pages gently, but excitedly. "They're ancient. But—" He shook his head. "I couldn't find anything like this in Daro. I searched the whole Archives when Dulon asked me to look into the black vierstone. Aryn had found some relevant books that mentioned vierstone in their descriptions, but there weren't whole *volumes* on it."

"He must have taken them from the Archives in Tura." Gellion took one of the books from the shelf. This one seemed more recently written than the decrepit book Veldon held. It was printed in strong ink with printed pictures rather than hand drawn sketches.

"This is it," Gellion said breathlessly, closing the book and looking over the shelves. "This is Kaelo's work. There is no doubt. I can't believe he left it all here—but of course he couldn't have taken it with him to Daro. He must have been accumulating this the whole time he was here. But these notes." His eyes lit with an almost manic gleam. "They must say what he did—somewhere. They must give clues to how he destroyed vierstone, how he learned to affect stone as he does. Maybe even why." Gellion felt almost faint with the sudden weight of the work that lay ahead of them. "We have to look through it all. Every bit of it. Even if we have to delay our journey by a week or more."

He began to pace.

"Veldon," he said. "Read those books on vierstone. Valder and I can start on his notes, a shelf at a time."

Gellion had not known time to pass so quickly since he had left Daro. The dim light of the skylights made reading difficult, so the brothers took their work outside and brought several of the solar lamps with them to charge in the sunlight.

So absorbed was Gellion in his work, he was surprised to hear his stomach growl and find the sun well past its zenith in the sky. He nibbled at the food in their pack and continued on, moving their work inside once the solar lamps proved bright enough to read by.

The first two shelves of notes and scrolls ranged in topic from physics, to chemistry, to the structure of rocks and glass. It seemed as though Kaelo had sought to master all of the physical sciences in his exile, and based on the complexity of his notes, he very well may have succeeded. Gellion found the information interesting, when comprehensible, but it gave no hint to what Kaelo had planned to do with it. The notes were simple, rote facts and diagrams.

Veldon remained glued to the books on vierstone, often raising a hand to his earring and twisting it absently as he read. Valder quickly grew bored with his task and took to searching the rest of the room. He went to the desk and began to sift through its drawers.

"Here," he said excitedly.

Gellion and Veldon dropped their studies and came to look over Valder's shoulder. He held a stone in his palm, small and smooth. It was black as pitch, seeming to absorb all light the solar lamp threw at it.

Valder looked up at them, eyes sparkling. "Is it?"

Veldon reached forward and took the stone in his fingers. Even in the bluish glow of the lamp, Gellion could see the color drain from his face.

"Vierstone," he whispered. He handed it to Gellion.

Gellion's stomach clenched as his hand wrapped around the small rock. It had been vierstone alright, but like the stone in Daro, it held no trace of the life that had once flowed through it. It was cold and black. Dead.

Gellion had already been sure that this cave was Kaelo's, but here was a piece of entirely incontrovertible evidence.

"He really was here," Valder said.

Gellion rolled the blackened stone in his palm and looked at the mountain of pages contained in the shelves. Did the answer to this stone lie before him? Might he discover what Kaelo had done to make himself so powerful? Could Gellion do the same thing? Gellion squared his shoulders against the shiver that threatened to move up his spine. If he could do the same, would he?

"It's getting dark," Veldon said.

Gellion looked up, surprised to see the lamps were now the only source of light in the room.

"Maybe we should stay," Valder said. "I don't fancy that climb down the mountain in the dark."

From the worry on Valder's face, Gellion suspected the hike was the least of his worries. They could bring the lamps with them to light the path. But they were no longer in the protection of Suri Ranta. Gellion had little doubt that eyes and flickering lights would appear in the darkness here as they had on their journey through the mountains, only this time they had no fire and little path. Ruta's story of the corrupted bat was fresh in Gellion's mind. There could be much worse than that waiting in the darkness.

"We didn't bring much food," Gellion said reluctantly. "And I want a full day up here tomorrow. It wasn't too long of a hike. Going back down will be even faster, and we have lamps. And knives. Besides, there's still a bit of light out I think. We can't have been here that long."

Valder and Veldon nodded, though both looked nervous.

"Come on," Gellion said. He was as loath to leave his work as he was to venture into the darkness outside, but he couldn't deny the weariness of his mind, nor the returned grumbling of his stomach. It would be best to come again tomorrow, well rested and alert.

"Let's go back now, and we can bring enough food tomorrow to last us a few days."

He picked up the solar lamp from Kaelo's desk. It was already dimmer than it had been when they first brought it in from the sunlight hours before. He hoped the light would last them down the mountain.

Gellion had expected the walk back into fresh air to be a relief, but when he stepped out of the cave, he began to understand what Veldon had meant about the air feeling oppressive. The sky was still a dull indigo to the west, but it was darker out than Gellion had thought, and he could feel an irrational anxiety forming in the pit of his stomach. He drew a hunting knife from his belt and gripped the lamp tighter.

"Put that branch back over the entrance," he said to Valder, indicating the branch he had used to mark the cave earlier. "I didn't latch the door all the way, but it could still be hard to find in the daylight."

In the gloaming, the blue paint glowed ominously against the stone. Gellion shivered. That sight alone would have been enough to scare off any curious Kayda past dark.

"Do you remember where the path was?" Valder leaned the beech branch against the glowing markings.

Gellion did not answer at once. He knew the direction of the path, but his confidence in finding it was much lower now that he was looking into the dark trees.

"We follow the cliff face a bit further and then walk down the slope until it levels out. The ridge should be obvious then, and we can find the path." Before his brothers could answer, he started off against the cliffs, his lamp held before him.

But with every step away from the cave, his anxiety grew. The feeling of being watched that had plagued them throughout the Falspires came back with a vengeance, and the hair on the back of Gellion's neck began to prickle. He jumped at every sound: a hooting owl, a snapped twig, a gentle rustling.

"Stop." Veldon's voice was unnaturally calm. It turned Gellion's blood colder than if he had shouted. "Come back."

Gellion stood frozen, the hand holding his lamp shaking slightly. They had only walked a few minutes, but it felt like much longer.

"What?" Gellion said through gritted teeth.

"Back to the cave." Now there was a quaver in Veldon's voice.

Gellion's eyes darted around, trying to find the source of Veldon's fear, but he saw nothing.

Valder was already backing up, but Gellion stood his ground.

"What do you see?" he whispered.

"I don't know what it is," Veldon said. "But we don't want to meet it. Come slowly."

Gellion hesitated a moment longer, then joined his brothers in retreat, keeping his back to the cliff and walking sideways.

A low growl rumbled from the trees. It was deep and purring, and it raised every hair on Gellion's body. He gripped his knife harder and lengthened his stride.

The soft swish of leaves followed their progress, like something large brushing through the ferns. Gellion heard no footsteps, but the thick moss was sure to muffle any.

Then came the eyes.

Gellion had been watching for them, but they were no less horrifying for his expecting them. Almond shaped and crimson, they seemed to glow with a light of their own in the deepening darkness of the forest. Try as he might, Gellion could make out no outline of the beast. It was as though its body were blacker than the surroundings.

The growl came again.

"You're sure you left the door unlocked?" Valder's eyes were fixed on the hovering red dots in the trees as he sidestepped along the cliff.

"Yes," said Gellion. "We just have to push in."

"And close the door in time," Valder said.

Gellion swallowed past the growing knot in his throat. He did not understand the depth of his fear. He had faced wild animals before. Three armed elves with a cliff at their back should make easy work of a wolf, but this didn't sound like any wolf Gellion had ever seen.

"Should we shout at it?" Valder suggested. "Try to scare it off?"

"I don't think so," Veldon said.

For some reason, Gellion agreed. This animal did not seem like the kind easily deterred by intimidation. Any show of aggression was more likely to provoke an attack. Gellion almost wished the thing would attack. Surely the terror of being stalked was worse than any fight.

"I see the branch ahead," Valder whispered.

The trees were thinning now, affected by whatever disease plagued this place. In the lightening shadows, Gellion saw a shape moving, closer than he had thought. He could feel its presence in the air. His heart pounded.

Just a little further.

Another low growl.

Then, a hair-raising yowl split the night.

"Go!" Gellion shoved his brothers toward the branch still forty feet away.

The shape lunged. Gellion spun sideways along the cliff, lashing out with his knife. It missed, and something heavy hit the stone beside him. He ran backward in a crouch, both lamp and knife raised in front of him.

The creature slunk to the ground. Powerful shoulders rose and fell as it stalked forward on huge paws with claws as long as Gellion's fingers. It snarled and spat, its teeth as black as its hide. Gellion recoiled. He had seen cats like this before, attacking from the shadows of the Wildwood, or in battles led by the phoenix. What was it doing here?

The cat twitched its tail, then lunged at Gellion again. Gellion ducked and leaped sideways, the fur of the beast brushing his arm as it passed. The thing sank its claws into the soft ground and spun wildly back to face Gellion. It was just about to lunge at him again when it twitched sideways and screamed.

"Here!" Valder called from behind the cat. He was standing outside the entrance to the cave, waving the beech branch.

The hilt of a knife extended from the cat's haunches. The beast recovered quickly, however, and looked all the more angry for its injury.

"Come on!" Valder shook the branch in challenge at the cat. It stood with its feet splayed, unsure for a moment who to attack, then it lunged at Valder. Gellion threw his own knife and ran toward the cave. The blade stuck in the beast's shoulder, bringing another shrieking yowl, but it did not slow the creature's attack.

Valder wielded the beech branch like a sword, spinning out of the way as he kept the woody weapon between himself and the cat. His defense saved him from the beast's teeth, but he still slammed against the cliff with the force of the attack. Gellion ran forward, looking around frantically for anything else he could use against the cat.

Then a bright light appeared.

"Get back!" Veldon shouted. He had leaped out of the cave wielding a torch, its flames nearly blinding after the soft glow of the lamps. He advanced on the cat, swinging the fire at it. The beast snarled and spat, but stepped backward, limping from its injuries.

"Ah!" Veldon snarled back at the animal, an angry gleam in his eyes. "Inside!" he shouted to Valder and Gellion. They did not need further encouragement. Gellion ran into the cave's entrance, Valder close on his heels.

"Get the door ready to close," Veldon said.

Valder and Gellion positioned themselves behind the stone door.

In a flourish of flames, Veldon ran backward and jumped into the cave. Gellion and Valder slammed the door behind him.

They all stood panting for a moment, listening for any sounds outside, but either the cave was well insulated, or the cat had given up its hunt.

"Are you alright?" Gellion asked Valder, who was rubbing his shoulder.

Valder nodded. "Just a bruise. It didn't get a good hold on me."

Gellion took a deep breath and tried to still his shaking hands.

"Where did you get that torch?" he asked Veldon.

"By the fireplace. There were still a few matches and some cooking oil around."

Gellion shook his head and ran a hand through his hair.

"You may have saved us all."

In the flickering flames of the torch, Veldon flushed, then grinned slyly.

"I don't think so. You were holding your own with that branch." He nodded to Valder, who laughed.

"The A'vaeri can translate to any weapon," said Valder. "I'll have to consider the use of branches in the next tournament." He dropped his hand from his shoulder and looked around. "Well, looks like this is home for the night after all, unless either of you want to try getting down the mountain again. I, for one, will be sleeping in silks and furs tonight." He walked toward the first bedroom.

"I hope the furs are from a panther," he muttered.

30

REDDER THAN BLOOD

"It's no good." Veldon stacked the fourth and final volume on top of the rest. "Most of this is just speculation and theory. It's all fascinating, but these are only enforcing what I already knew about vierstone. There is a current from an unknown source that carries through the stone on constant loop. Elves can tap into that current at a touch and channel it through their bodies to direct at stone, or metal, or glass. It allows us to see into the elements, as it were."

"Like bats." Valder was leaning back in Kaelo's desk chair, eating an apple and flipping through notes on metamorphic rocks.

"What?" Gellion looked up from his own pile of notes with raised eyebrows.

"Echolocation," Valder said. "Using sound waves to see objects around you." He shrugged. "Only this is using some mysterious rock wave and looks inside objects rather than into space."

Veldon stared at him. "Well, yes. It is something like that, I suppose." He blinked and looked down at the piece of blackened vierstone in his hand. "And that current's been stopped in this. But we already knew that. We knew that even in Daro. I'm still no closer to understanding *how*. Whatever Kaelo did, he must have invented it himself."

"Well, he had plenty of information to pull from." Gellion indicated the meticulously organized notes surrounding them.

They had spent days in Kaelo's study, steadily going through every pile of notes and every book. After the attack by the cat, the three of them had spent an uncomfortable and dark night in Kaelo's cave, the light of the solar lamps quickly spent. Ruta had been amazed by the elves' reappearance in the village the next morning, thinking them taken by the spirits as so many before them. The elves were vague in their description of their work, saying only that they had found what they were looking for and required some time to study it. Both Ruta and Heleena had watched them suspiciously through their explanation, but they helped prepare several days' provisions for the elves anyway.

Since then, Gellion and Veldon had not left the cave. They charged the solar lamps in shifts, so there was always a source of readable light inside, and spent most of the day shifting back and forth between reading and speculating. Valder joined them in the afternoons and nights, spending his mornings working with the Kayda mariners on the *Brasa*. The boat was coming along more quickly than expected, and would likely be ready to sail by the next day, but Gellion was determined not to leave until they had learned all they could from Kaelo's cave. Once they left Tala, Gellion did not expect to ever return, and there was no way they could transport all of Kaelo's notes and books down the mountain and onto the little craft to weather the sea. They would stay as long as it took.

"We just have to keep looking," Gellion said. "So far we've only found objective information—facts. Kaelo must have written down notes of his progress somewhere. Maybe he had a journal, or at least made personal notes on the most relevant pages." He shuffled through the diagrams in front of him.

Valder groaned. "I've been reading about physics for days. I don't know how much more of this forced education I can take."

Heat rose to Gellion's face. "And what if that 'forced education' saves lives back in Faeran? What if one of the concepts you're so loath to read about for a few days holds the answer to how Kaelo is destroying vierstone and collapsing entire cities?"

"I was only joking," Valder muttered.

Gellion sighed and ran his hands over his face. The constant reading was wearing him down too, but they couldn't stop.

"Why don't you keep searching through his desk?" Gellion said in a calmer tone. "You didn't look through every drawer the other night did you?"

Valder shook his head. "No. But it was just more notes mostly, with some stone working tools. I stopped looking through them when I found the piece of vierstone." He sat up in his chair and opened the top left drawer, emptying another stack of papers onto the desk. With a sigh, he picked up the first page.

The afternoon wore on. Gellion's anxiety grew with every tome he put back on the shelf. What if they didn't find anything in all of this? What if this was nothing more than a personal library, a hobby?

That doesn't explain the earthquakes and the spirits that flock to the cave like moths to a flame. Nor does it explain the black vierstone in the drawer.

Gellion's determination flagged and strengthened in turn, his general mood following suit. Valder and Veldon had learned not to interrupt him except with promising information, so when Valder stood up brandishing a handful of folded papers, Gellion perked up at once.

Valder was grinning. "Oho!" He held up the papers as though they contained incriminating evidence.

"What?" Gellion's heart started to beat faster.

"You'll never guess what these are." Valder bounced from heel to heel.

Gellion could see the papers contained handwritten words with what looked like lines of address at the bottom. Letters?

Valder was still grinning and had made no move to give Gellion his prize.

"Are you going to tell us what they are or just invent a dance with them?" Gellion said.

Valder raised an eyebrow. "I could do both, if you'd like."

He laughed aloud at Gellion's expression.

"Alright, alright. These." He smiled at the papers mischievously. "Are letters. Correspondence with none other than—" He paused for emphasis. Gellion was forcibly reminded of Dulon. "One Commander Vensure."

"No," Gellion exclaimed.

"Oh yes," said Valder.

Gellion reached for the letters, and Valder gave them to him, but not before swiping them away once for good measure. Gellion read hungrily, barely taking in the words the first time through in his eagerness to get through them. There were only three letters, each shorter than the last.

The king is ready to mobilize should your insights prove true. We have received reports of raids on the borders, but I have written to our Marchons in Nescari to confirm. As to the other that we discussed, the king believes we have force enough to move against the Dierna without aid. I am still convincing him of the wisdom of your proposal. I am confident he will agree in time. I will notify you if we move forward, contingent upon the truth of your claims.

Raids are confirmed. Report how many outposts are in the Pass. The King is ready to agree. I need one more week.

All is ready. We will dispatch an envoy in two weeks. Do not forget your end.

"Riu above," Gellion said.

"What do they say?" Veldon said, abandoning his vierstone books. Both he and Valder leaned over Gellion's shoulders to read.

Gellion shook his head, mind spinning from what he had just read. The letters introduced as many questions as they answered. They were clearly a continuation of a conversation started long before, but what they did reveal sent sparks of adrenaline through Gellion's blood.

"He really did it," he said, strangely disappointed. "He betrayed us all to the Albaren."

Veldon was frowning. "It does sound that way."

"What do you mean sound?" Gellion stared at Veldon in disbelief. "He was in contact with Commander Vensure! From the sound of these, they met in person at least once before this correspondence." He stood and began to pace. "Are there any more?" He rounded on Valder.

"Not in that drawer."

Gellion cursed. "I wish we had Kaelo's responses. These hardly answer anything." He stopped his pacing and stood still, trying to think. "He clearly reported Dierna raids to the Albaren, and from the second letter it seems he worked as a sort of spy for them. But what was his 'proposal' that Vensure references? What did Kaelo promise them?"

"Vierstone?" Veldon suggested. "He must have told them about it to give them a way to bribe the elves to their cause. Or maybe the help of the elves was what he promised them."

Gellion shook his head. "Vensure said the king thought they didn't need help. He had to convince him."

"But Vensure clearly thought it was a good idea," said Veldon.

"I still don't think that's it. Nor do I think Kaelo would have promised them vierstone. As far as I know, vierstone is useless to humans."

"He could have lied," Valder said.

"Maybe." Gellion was not convinced. The letters made it sound like Kaelo had forged some kind of deal with Vensure contingent upon the Albaren allying with the elves.

"There must be more letters." Gellion walked to the desk.

"I don't think so," Veldon said. "Kaelo was in Daro by the time Amadeo came to you and Dulon—assuming Amadeo was the emissary referenced in the letter. Kaelo probably left for Daro as soon as he received this, and any further correspondence would have been from there."

Gellion snorted in frustration.

"I think this merely confirms the theory we have discussed before," said Veldon. "Kaelo used the Albaren to lure the elves out of Daro so he would have an empty city to destroy. He promised the Albaren something in return, maybe just help in their war, maybe something else."

"But there we hit the same issue," Gellion said. "They *didn't* need help in the war. It was all a ruse. They betrayed us and tried to kill us if you don't remember. Was that Kaelo's plan? Why not just collapse the city while everyone was still in it?"

"A city of hundreds of elves?" said Valder. "We would have caught him before he could finish the job. He couldn't have gotten through the whole city."

Gellion was silent for a few moments, thoughts racing.

"Maybe he didn't know," Gellion said.

"Know what?" Valder said.

"Maybe the Albaren betrayed him too."

Valder raised an eyebrow. "I know he was your mentor, Gellion, but from what we've seen, his turning the elves over to the Albaren would not be too shocking."

"But it doesn't make sense," Gellion said. "If he just wanted to kill everyone in Daro, what was the point of destroying all the vierstone first, or going to the Albaren? I still think he could have managed to collapse the city with the elves in it if he had wanted to."

"Gellion's right," Veldon said. Gellion and Valder looked at him, both surprised. "The letters sound like Kaelo was trying to convince Vensure to ally with the elves, not eliminate them. Maybe he did just want the elves distracted, and made an empty promise, or a promise of alliance, to get it."

Valder let out a deep breath. "So this really doesn't help us at all. He wanted Daro abandoned to achieve the goal we still don't know the purpose of in a way we still don't understand."

Some of Gellion's excitement drained away. "Yes."

"It's still valuable information," Veldon said. "The more we know, the more we have to draw from to make guesses at Kaelo's plans." He furrowed his brow. "But this still doesn't explain the woman who talked to the Dierna."

Valder frowned seriously. "Does Kaelo have a particularly high voice?" he asked Gellion.

Gellion glared at him. "I think it's safe to assume Kaelo did not go to Arvain."

"It must have been an outside job then." Valder shrugged. "Miyela trying to sabotage Dulon's decision to bring the elves to battle."

"What about Kaelo's child?" said Veldon quietly.

Gellion stiffened. It was a subject they had all avoided discussing these last few days. Gellion had found the idea of Kaelo's having sired a son or daughter on a human girl so ludicrous that he had nearly forgotten that part of the selkie's tale. But Ruta's description of the child had been too close for comfort, and then there had been the second bedroom in the cave. Unless Kaelo had often entertained guests in his haunted mountain cave, the bedroom must have been for someone.

"I know it is strange to think about," Veldon said when neither Valder nor Gellion answered. "But I think there *was* an elven child here, and all evidence points to it having been Kaelo's. If he had a daughter, he could have sent her to the Dierna."

"To sabotage the alliance he had forged with the Albaren?" Gellion put his face in his hands and groaned. "Unless we find more to go on, I don't see how any of this will help us stop Kaelo. What we need to focus on is how he is managing to destroy vierstone and collapse buildings. Let's just get back to his notes."

Veldon clearly wanted to pursue the subject of Kaelo's alleged child further, but let the matter rest for the time being, walking back to his books with thin lips.

The evening found the three brothers still at their work after a short dinner of sweet potatoes, nuts, and dried fish. After Valder's discovery of the Albaren letters, excitement had dwindled once more to painful monotony. Valder had abandoned his search of Kaelo's desk to recharge the lamps and make their dinner, then grudgingly resumed the task as the skylights began to darken.

Gellion absently watched his brother's progress while he perused diagrams of mineral composition. The remaining desk drawers did not seem to contain any more notes, but piles of rocks and stone-working implements. Valder observed the items with a bored air. He had arrayed the tools on top of the desk and was beginning to pick up rocks. Many appeared to be common stones from the mountains, but as Valder continued to pull them out, some were carved into shapes. Valder paused over what looked like the most intricate carving of a flower Gellion had ever seen.

"Not a bad hand at stone working." Valder looked back into the drawer and reached for a back corner.

He recoiled so quickly he caught his hand on the drawer and sent it crashing to the ground. Stones scattered everywhere, and Valder leaped backward with a startled shout, staring at the drawer's spilled contents as though they had attacked him.

"What?" Gellion and Veldon said at the same time. Both were on their feet.

Valder stood holding one hand as though burned, his eyes wide in shock. He opened his mouth, closed it, then shook his head and took a step backward.

"Valder?" Gellion's skin was going cold at the look on his brother's face.

Still, Valder did not answer. He let go of his hand and looked down at it, then back to the rocks on the floor. Had he touched a sharp rock? But Gellion saw no trace of injury on Valder's hand.

"Use words Valder," he said, alarm in his voice now. "Did something hurt you?"

Valder shook his head. "No. I ... I don't know. It was—"

Gellion exchanged a look with Veldon, who was clearly as flabbergasted by Valder's behavior as he was.

Valder kneeled down next to the drawer and slowly reached for one of the rocks. When his fingers closed around it, he stiffened, but did not recoil again. He stood and held the stone out in his palm.

The stone was hard to make out in the dim light. It was dark, and looked roughly cut, but was smooth as glass. Gellion frowned.

"Obsidian?" he said.

"No." It was Veldon's voice, so soft Gellion barely heard him. "It's vierstone."

"Really?" Gellion knit his brows. He could see the resemblance, but there was something different about this rock.

"It's not vierstone." Valder was looking at the rock like it was a repulsive creature. "But I think it is the answer to Kaelo's power."

"What?" Gellion breathed, leaning closer to the stone.

Veldon hurried to bring one of the lamps closer and held it over the stone. In the light, Gellion could now see that its surface and shape were identical in every way to vierstone, except for one glaring difference.

Cold flushed over Gellion's limbs. His throat seemed to close entirely.

No.

Gellion's breathing came faster, and he drew back from the rock as Kaelo's soft voice played in his head. '*That is not for you.*'

Gellion had seen a stone like this before, but only in his dreams.

The stone in Valder's hand was red as fresh blood.

31

TELEM FIER

Cuvan took a long time to look up from Liera's letter. The paper looked small in his hands, and he handled it with exaggerated care.

"This is confirmed?" Cuvan's voice was rich and slow. "It is Liera's son?"

"Yes." Renyra had already told Cuvan everything that had happened from the time he had left Daro until now. She hoped the letter explained anything she had forgotten.

Folding the letter, Cuvan bowed his head. His hair was short and inky, with the whirled pattern of Telem Fier shaved into one side.

"How long ago was this written?"

"Nearly four days," said Renyra. "We sent two elves back to Tura with vierstone."

"With vierstone?" Cuvan's brows knit.

"Yes, I—" Renyra hesitated. Had Liera's letter said nothing of the sword? "The Turi are going to forge a sword of vierstone to wield against Kaelo. No other weapon pierces his armor and—there is a prophecy."

Cuvan lifted his chin. "What prophecy is this?"

Renyra recited the words. It was all too easy by now.

"I have never heard this prophecy," Cuvan said.

"It was found in the Archives of Tura."

"Hmm." Cuvan looked doubtful. The Fieri placed more stock in prophecies than any other Kindom, and Telem Fier's archives were bound to hold extensive records. Could this prophecy have been over-looked among such vast stocks? Or maybe Kyna was right, and its words had been written off as another prelude to the Great War.

"And Liera thinks this will stop her son?" Cuvan seemed more confused than skeptical.

Renyra did not know how to answer. 'Yes' seemed too confident, too hopeful, almost a curse to the luck of the feat the Turi were about to attempt.

"There is hope," Renyra said.

"Then why warn me?"

"Because if the prophecy is wrong," Firas said. "Or if Liera does not fulfill it, there may be no chance to warn you. We have done all we can in Tura, but if this plan fails, we do not know what Kaelo will do next, or where he will go. He tried to prevent Liera from warning the other Kindoms. Clearly he does not want his threat known or his plans compromised. We can all hope that this warning is in vain, that Kaelo's threat will stop in Tura, but we must behave as though it will not."

Cuvan gave Firas a long look, then nodded slowly.

"I see."

I see? Is that all he has to say?

Renyra had never had any interaction with Cuvan until now, only seen him from afar and heard stories of him. She supposed his slow speech and consideration of his decisions were good qualities in a leader, but they were getting on her nerves.

"Why do you think he will move beyond Tura?" Cuvan said.

"He didn't stop at Daro," Renyra said. "Why should he stop at Tura?"

Cuvan took a deep breath and looked between them all. He seemed to be debating his next words.

"It seems to me as though Kaelo is enacting revenge upon the Kindom that exiled him," he said. "Upon the mother that exiled him."

"We cannot know that for sure," Firas said.

There was sadness in Cuvan's face. He shook his head.

"I grieve for Tura, and for the elves who have suffered because of this, but I cannot see this as any concern of the Fieri."

Renyra's jaw nearly dropped. "Not our concern?"

"Liera brought this upon herself."

A cold silence met these words.

"You defended her." Firas's eyes flashed with a rare spark of anger. "In Daro, when Miyela was attacking Liera."

"I put an end to a malicious comment aimed at a Council Member in public," Cuvan said. "An accusation that had nothing to do with the matters being discussed. It does not mean I disagreed with Miyela."

"It is not only Liera that Kaelo has hurt," Renyra said. "There were Fieri in Daro. We were two of them." She indicated herself and Caerlyn with a harsh gesture.

"Daro was an unfortunate tragedy, but—"

"But what!? It was on a different continent? It was the fault of the elves of Daro, not Kaelo? No. It was Kaelo. All of it. He has already destroyed a good portion of the elves' vierstone. He has killed! You would leave the Turi to their fate because of the mistakes of their leader?"

A slow anger was building in Cuvan's face.

"I would not risk the lives of my Kindom to come to the aid of a city already fallen."

"We are not asking you to." Firas's expression was hard. "We are asking you to prepare. For all we know, Kaelo is moving against all of the Great Cities. Telem Fier could be a target."

"No elf will destroy our vierstone while I draw breath."

"The same sentiment was shared by Liera, I am sure," said Caerlyn. "This is not simple, Cuvan. He does not attack by force but by stealth, and when he is forced to attack head on, he calls the very stones to his aid."

"He escaped an armed force of at least a dozen, probably twice that," Renyra said. "Even using stealth of our own has backfired every time. You need to post guards. You should start identifying the sources of vierstone in the city. Kaelo can only destroy what he touches. Gather all the vierstone you can, and if he does come, melt it down and guard it."

Cuvan considered her. "I believe what you have told me, and I thank you for this warning. An elf destroying lifestone is a tragedy beyond comprehension, and the Fieri will be a part of any ensuing justice and decisions as they affect the elves at large in the aftermath of that tragedy. But," he sighed, "I cannot disrupt the running of this city on the chance of a possibility that Kaelo will come here." He held up a hand when Renyra opened her mouth. "I will speak with my Council about all of this. And I will write to Auralia as you requested. If the other Fieri leaders disagree with me, I will listen to their council."

There was nothing more to be said. Alura and Raren were glaring at Cuvan. Renyra was about to turn and leave when she remembered the request she had to ask. Asking Cuvan for anything more rankled her, but they could not leave their task incomplete because of the stubbornness of one man.

"We will need passage to Remsgraen," she said in a clipped tone. "We have a message for Rhosti as well."

"I can arrange a Rale for you," Cuvan said. "But I would not expect Rhosti to take any further action than I."

Renyra raised her eyebrows. "I think that is for Rhosti to decide."

She walked away from the Lord of Telem Fier without a backward glance.

***

Renyra fumed as she walked through the streets of Telem Fier. Even the excitement of the sprawling city around her could not take her mind off Cuvan's refusal to see reason. Was it so much effort to post guards and gather vierstone? It would do no harm if Kaelo never came and could save Telem Fier the fate of Tura if he did.

"We should have brought Auralia with us," Renyra said. "She would have talked sense into him."

Caerlyn gave her a sideways glance, then looked pointedly at a passing stall selling rugs.

"What?" Renyra said.

Caerlyn shook her head. "I just—I think he has a point."

Renyra stared at her. "You said just this morning that he should guard the city."

"I know, but hearing it all said like that."

"Said like what?"

"Maybe Kaelo is only seeking revenge on the Turi. Maybe it would be prudent to wait and see what happens in Tura before taking any drastic steps."

"Setting guards is not a drastic step!"

"It can be. For a city as large as Telem Fier. Cuvan said he would help in the aftermath if Kaelo is stopped."

"And if he's not?"

"You were the biggest supporter of that prophecy! Now you have so little hope in its success?"

Renyra bit her lip.

Caerlyn let out a forceful breath. "I'm only saying that Cuvan is trying to protect his people—*our* people—in the best way he can. We did what we came here to do. Cuvan knows what's happening in Tura, and he will tell the leaders of the Fieri. It was never our job to rally our Kindom to the aid of Tura. We should carry on to Remsgraen and finish our task, then let the leaders handle things."

The rest of the troupe was standing awkwardly around Renyra and Caerlyn, looking from one to the other. The fight drained out of Renyra. She did not agree with Caerlyn, but she didn't want to fight with her either. Caerlyn's argument did carry some sense. They had done all they could to convince Cuvan of Liera's warning. There was no reason to let his reaction spoil the only day they had in Telem Fier.

Grinding her teeth, Renyra nodded and continued to walk up the street.

After a few minutes, the joy of being back among the Fieri overcame Renyra's dark mood. Color swirled around her on all sides as elves dressed in wraps came in and out of shops and glided by on levit boards. For once, it was her companions who stood out with their straight-cut clothing and pale skin.

Telem Fier held more life than Tura. Laughter was louder, smiles were broader, and doors hung open to the streets. There was always the echo of song in the air, and the smell of spice was so heavy Renyra could almost taste it. There were no tall buildings, and sunlight bathed the stone streets, reflecting off of painted doors and dyed fabrics that hung from walls and awnings. Solar panels glinted on every roof.

Renyra smiled as they passed a group of women dancing on a corner. Their tattooed arms were raised to the sky, and they sang as they moved. She laughed at Firas, who looked profoundly taken aback. Color rose in his cheeks.

"We should find a place to stay," Caerlyn said. "I know some inns ahead."

Just then, Renyra caught sight of a jeweler's shop.

"I'll meet you there," she said to Caerlyn, and squeezed Firas's hand before dodging through the crowds to the open door.

The inside of the shop was cool. Renyra blinked as her eyes adjusted to the low lighting. Glass displays showed necklaces, bracelets, rings, and jewels in every shape and color. Renyra had to pull her attention away from the beautiful adornments to look for the shopkeeper. There was a workbench in the back of the store, littered with tools and bits of stone and glass. A woman in orange and blue wraps was bent over the bench with her back to Renyra. Renyra cleared her throat.

"Oh!" The woman straightened and looked around, then smiled. "I apologize. When I am at my work I notice nothing else." She put down her tools and brushed her hands on her clothes. "What can I do for you?"

"I need a vierstone earring," Renyra said without preamble.

The jeweler's eyebrows shot up and her gaze fell at once to Renyra's middle.

"You will have a child?" There was confusion in her voice.

"No." Renyra shifted her feet. "No, it is for me."

The jeweler's eyes shot from Renyra's stomach to her ears.

"For you? What happened to yours?"

"It's a long story. But it is gone."

The woman tutted. "Of course you will need a new one then, and as soon as you can get one I imagine." She crossed the small room and began to shuffle through drawers. "I don't routinely keep vierstone in the shop. I will need to find some."

"I have some here." Renyra drew the uncut stone from her pocket.

The woman raised her brows again and reached for the rock, examining it with practiced eyes.

"Is there a style you prefer?"

"Anything you can make by tomorrow morning."

The woman paused, then looked at Renyra like she had told an amusing joke. Renyra did not know when Cuvan would secure a Rale line for them, but it was best to play it safe.

"All I need is a shard of vierstone attached to an earring backing," Renyra said. "I must leave tomorrow, and there may not be time for me to commission a proper earring. I came from Tura, and the jewelers there said it could not be done." She smiled at the jeweler. "But you know how the Turi are."

The jeweler raised an eyebrow. "A vierstone earring by tomorrow morning?"

Renyra nodded.

A slow smile spread up the woman's face. "I will show the Master Crafters what can be done in an afternoon."

STONE BREAKS

Gellion tried to concentrate on the words in front of him, but it was like ignoring someone calling his name. With another effort of will, he forced his eyes to focus on the page. His heart had pumped with adrenaline when he found these notes on volcanoes and the Great War. Not only had he been going cross-eyed reading about scientific principles, this new subject seemed more likely to give possible insight into Kaelo's plans. A brief flip through the pages had shown several sections of handwritten notes in the margins. Gellion had forced himself to be patient and start at the beginning.

But even the prospect of this new subject matter couldn't keep his eyes from drifting to Veldon. The chunk of red vierstone—if that's what it was—lay in the palm of Veldon's hand. He was running his fingers over the smooth surface with a grimace on his face. On the desk before him sat the piece of black vierstone Valder had found days before, and next to it, Veldon's own vierstone earring.

It had been only the night before that Valder had discovered the red stone. Not knowing how else to refer to the mysterious substance, they had simply been calling it 'redstone.' Veldon had been studying the rock intensely for hours, but had said little. Gellion longed to know what

Veldon was thinking, if he had learned anything, but he didn't dare disturb his brother's concentration.

Valder had come to the cave midmorning with news that the *Brasa* was ready for departure. As soon as Gellion deemed Kaelo's notes and belongings properly inspected, they could begin their journey back to Faeran. It was a maddening situation. After all this time, home could be only a week away, and it was Gellion's own decision keeping them from it. They had already learned more here than Gellion had dared to hope. Kaelo was unequivocally responsible for the doomed alliance with the Albaren and had spent centuries in this cave developing his plans to destroy vierstone. The discovery of redstone was crucial, Gellion knew it. They just had to find out what it was. He hoped the answer was somewhere in the pages they had yet to read.

"What do you think?" Valder asked Veldon.

Gellion's eyes shot up to watch Veldon.

Veldon took several moments to answer. He placed the redstone on the desk and some of the tension of his shoulders seemed to melt away.

"It is—wrong," he said. "It makes my skin crawl, yet there is something fascinating about it too."

Gellion knew what Veldon meant. He too had handled the stone. His vierstone earring had seemed to grow cold as he turned the hunk of rock over in his hand, and he had felt exactly as Veldon now described.

Then he had tried what had made Valder recoil in shock the night before; he had tried to use his connection with vierstone to look *into* the redstone. It had been like an electric shock, sending waves through his body reminiscent of those felt during Kaelo's earthquakes. He had not touched the stone again. There was no doubt this was the key to Kaelo's power, but Gellion was no longer sure he wanted to know how it worked.

Veldon was faring better than either of his brothers in his attempts to observe the inner mechanisms of the redstone. He winced when he tried to look inside it, but kept his hold and his wits.

"I think I am beginning to understand," Veldon said softly. He touched the vierstone earring on the desk. "Vierstone's current runs at a constant rate in a constant direction." He touched the black stone next. "There is no current at all in this stone—the 'dead vierstone' as it were."

His fingers moved to hover above the redstone. "There is a current in this one, constant and similar to the one in vierstone, but—" He reached for the vierstone earring again and allowed the fingers of his other hand to touch the red rock. He shuddered, then nodded. "But I think it runs in the opposite direction."

A loud slam made both Veldon and Gellion jump. Valder, standing next to Kaelo's desk, had slapped his hand on the wooden surface, a gleam in his eye. Without a word, he jumped to the nearest shelf and started sifting through pages.

"What?" Gellion's heart was still racing from Valder's outburst.

Valder did not answer, but seemed to be muttering to himself as he excitedly rifled through papers.

"Here!" He pulled out a stack. "Move over." He put the pages on the desk next to Veldon's array of rocks and thumbed through their contents. When he had found the page he was looking for, he smashed a finger over the words and looked up with a wild grin. "Frequency!"

Veldon and Gellion looked at each other as though fearing for Valder's sanity.

"Excuse me?" said Gellion.

Valder rolled his eyes, clearly annoyed at his brothers' lack of instant comprehension.

"Currents run at certain frequencies—waves that have amplitude *and direction.*"

"Yes," Gellion said slowly. "So?"

"So! Those waves can interact with each other. If two waves have frequencies of opposing direction, the frequencies will clash, cancelling the waves entirely." He pointed at the redstone. "If that holds a current identical to vierstone, but in the opposite direction—"

Gellion's eyes widened as he imagined himself extending the current of vierstone out of his fingers and into metal or stone.

"It would stop the current in vierstone," he said.

Veldon looked at the redstone with new horror. "So you can use this stone like vierstone?"

"You must be able to," Gellion said, his excitement growing. "That's how he did it—he extended the current of this stone through his body and into the vierstone of Daro."

Valder furrowed his brow. "But how does it explain how he caused earthquakes and collapsed buildings?"

"Maybe the very act of destroying the vierstone within the foundations caused it to split apart?" Veldon said.

Gellion shook his head. "No, I don't think so. When I chased him, he cracked the street and made the stone break out into a pillar to throw me off my feet. That was more than just breaking, that was controlling." His eyes moved to the redstone, a sudden chill spreading over his skin. "You say this has the opposite frequency of vierstone. What do you think that would do to the nature of the redstone itself?"

Veldon cocked his head. "Reverse it?" His eyes widened. "You think Kaelo created an opposite of vierstone?"

"An anti-vierstone," Valder said gravely.

"He could have." Gellion eyed the redstone. He dreaded touching it again, yet longed to test his theory.

"Well, what does vierstone do? What is its nature?" said Valder.

Gellion thought, trying to imagine himself using vierstone, then shook his head and opened the drawer in Kaelo's desk containing rocks. He held one of the simple mountain rocks and closed his eyes, feeling the warmth of his earring, noticing more than ever the gentle waves that flowed through his body to his fingertips, extending into the rock.

"It allows us to see," he said. "To feel." He felt the structure of the rock—the knowledge. "It allows us to understand."

"Both rock and each other," Veldon said softly.

Gellion opened his eyes.

"You know what happened to the elves who left the Great Cities before vierstone became widespread," Veldon said.

"Their skill faded," Gellion said. "They couldn't craft the same, or keep their cities in repair."

"Nor did they bear any love for one another," Veldon said. "These books," he indicated the tomes on vierstone, "only attempt to explain it, but something about vierstone connects us to other elves—allows us to see and understand each other as much as rock, or metal."

"So what does that mean for vierstone's opposite?" Valder said. "It would cut us off from each other?"

"Maybe," said Gellion. "But for Kaelo's purposes, I think we should focus on how vierstone allows us to interact with stone and metal. What is the opposite of understanding?"

"Ignorance?" Valder said.

"That wouldn't enable Kaelo to control rock."

"That's it," said Veldon quickly, a light of understanding in his eyes.

"What?"

"Control," he said. "That is the opposite of understanding—of empathy. Mindless control."

Gellion ran his thumb over the tips of his fingers, thinking. With vierstone, he could understand metal well enough to work it, blend it, shape it. With his level of skill he could even coax it to behave as he wished, but he could not control it. It was more of a gentle suggestion that the metal took on willingly.

"It would allow its user to move and alter the elements to his will," Gellion said, staring at the redstone with a mixture of longing and horror. There was only one way to be sure of their theory.

Valder and Veldon seemed to share Gellion's thoughts. They looked from him to the stone. Gellion was the most skilled crafter—the most accustomed to using vierstone to accomplish his goals.

Heart thumping, Gellion picked up the mountain rock again. With his other hand, he reached for the redstone, but paused before touching it. He remembered how the vierstone in his ear had gone cold, and what Valder had said about the opposing frequencies.

Putting down the mountain stone, Gellion unfastened the vierstone from his ear and placed it on the desk. He took a steadying breath and grabbed the hunk of mountain rock in one hand and the redstone in the other. He closed his eyes.

The redstone did not warm in his hand as vierstone often did, but he could feel its energy moving beneath his skin. It raised the hair on his arms.

The silence in the room was charged. Even with his eyes closed, Gellion could sense Valder and Veldon watching him. He took another breath and tried to forget them, to focus only on the piece of mountain rock in his right hand.

He could not sense it.

He frowned as he tried to see the structure within, but he may as well have been holding a hunk of wood. He could still feel the current of the redstone against his fingers, however. He pulled on it, directing it through his body and into the stone.

The sensation nearly made him open his eyes and drop the rock. It was so foreign to anything he had ever felt with vierstone. It was cold. It made his skin crawl, yet it pumped adrenaline through his veins.

What was he supposed to do now? If he couldn't sense the rock's structure, how could he influence it?

The current was at his right fingertips now. Not knowing what else to do, he extended the current from his fingers as he unconsciously would with vierstone, and thought, '*Break,*' as hard as he could.

The current rushed through him like an icy blast of air, carrying an incredible sense of power. Gellion could not see into the mountain rock any more than he had before, but suddenly he knew he could do whatever he wanted to the stone—tell it anything, and it would obey.

The rock split apart in his hands.

Gellion's eyes flew open.

Both Valder and Veldon had gasped and were staring at the remains of the rock with wide eyes.

A slow grin spread over Valder's face. "You did it."

Still clutching the redstone, Gellion let the rock pieces fall to the desk. The memory of the feeling that had rushed through him upon using the stone lingered like the cold after brushing skin against snow. He wanted to try again, and he never wanted to do it again.

"Are you alright?" Veldon said, eyeing Gellion.

Gellion nodded. Carefully, he placed the redstone back on the desk.

"That's it then," Valder said triumphantly. "This is how he's done it all. If we can get that redstone off him, he'll be powerless."

"Yes." Gellion was still staring at the stone. "He would be." He blinked. "But I don't think that will be as easy as we think. I can't imagine he will have just stuck a piece of rock like this in his pocket to grab whenever he wants to use it."

"It still means he can be stopped," said Valder. "He isn't possessed by some dark spirit we have to exorcise. It's just a piece of physical rock." He stood, an excited gleam in his eye. "We can leave tomorrow.

We have that stone. We know how to stop Kaelo. We have to get back to Tura and tell the elves what we—"

"No," Gellion said.

Annoyance flickered on Valder's face. "Why? You want to finished reading this entire shelf of notes first?"

"Yes. Valder, we know how he's doing it, but we don't know why. We don't know the full extent of his plan. We might find the answer here somewhere, and that's worth a delay."

"He wants to get revenge on his mother, the Turi, the elves as a whole for all we know," Valder said. "Sounds like plenty of motivation to me."

"I don't know," Veldon said. "You may be right, but where does it end? Destroying Daro may have been an act against the elves, but it didn't affect the Turi specifically and had no effect on Liera."

"Maybe it was just practice," said Valder. "He could be in Tura now, doing the same."

Gellion's stomach dropped. "If he destroyed all the vierstone in Tura, it would ruin the city—" A new and more terrible thought entered his head. "Or he could destroy the entire city. Riu above, we could never rebuild it. We don't have any other sources of vierstone."

"But why not start in Tura if that was his only aim?" said Veldon. "He seems to have gone to a lot of trouble to destroy Daro, and it raised a huge alarm to the elves in Tura. Surely the survivors of the battle have gone back and warned the Turi by now. They'll have had the city on lockdown against Kaelo."

"Not if they don't know it's Kaelo," said Gellion. "Renyra was the only one besides me who knew, and I don't know if she—" He hesitated. "Got there. Maybe Kaelo didn't expect anyone to find out it was him."

"His identity would be less important than what he's done," said Veldon. "The elves can still take precautions against an unknown attacker if they know he's there."

"It fits, though," said Valder. "Destroying the city that ruined his life—the people that ruined his life. Taking all of their vierstone when they denied it to him."

"It's not big enough," said Gellion.

"Destroying a Great City isn't big enough?" Valder raised his eyebrows.

Gellion shook his head. "Not for what he's done. Veldon's right. What he did to Daro took centuries of planning. He could have spent half his exile discovering this." He indicated the red and black stones on the desk. "All of that just to take down the city he blames for his downfall? It's not like him. It's too petty."

"He has lived centuries without vierstone," Veldon said. "I think the Kaelo you once knew is a very different man now. He could have become obsessed with revenge." He sighed. "But I'm still not sure it's enough."

"This is why we need to keep looking," said Gellion. "There is more to this than we know. We know how he is accomplishing his goal, but without knowing the full extent of that goal, we're still blind. There may be nothing else here, but we have to try." He smirked at Valder. "Besides, those hours of agony studying physics bore some fruit after all, didn't they?"

Veldon laughed. Valder rolled his eyes with a lopsided grin.

The discovery of redstone was both motivating and distracting. Gellion was more determined than ever to fit more pieces into the puzzle of Kaelo's story, but the significance of what he had learned from the redstone made reading about volcanoes dull work.

The notes on volcanoes slowly transitioned into the eruption over Morcanan that had sparked the beginning of the Great War. The mountainside had been buried in ash, out of which the great phoenix had risen to reign its terror over the elves for two centuries. Gellion knew as well as any what had happened in those years.

Had Kaelo been in Faeran all the years of the war? That had been after his second exile. Had he sat by and watched his kin fight for their lives, hoping, perhaps, that the phoenix would enact the revenge he now sought to carry out himself? Despite Valder's and Veldon's doubts, Gellion could still not believe that simple, destructive revenge could be Kaelo's driving motive in all of this. Many elves had died in the battle at

Arvain, but if Kaelo had not known about the awaiting betrayal, the only victim of his attacks on Daro had been Aryn, and she had been hot on the heels of the secret to his power.

Whatever his brothers said, Gellion was convinced that Kaelo could have found a way to take down Daro and all those in it without being caught. Any doubts Gellion had carried on that matter disappeared with his first use of redstone. Gellion fought a shudder. As strong as the sense of power had been, so too had been the sense of wrongness. Yet still, part of him longed to try the stone again. If he could match Kaelo in strength, he could stop him, whatever his motive.

Gellion shook his head and refocused on the words in front of him. They were in Kaelo's handwriting.

Phoenixes rise from ash, but why has there only ever been one? Volcanic eruptions have occurred since the beginning of time, but none ever produced a monster until the war. Is it a question of volume? Did it take a full mountainside of ash to form sufficient conditions to raise a phoenix? Does the magma have to form and cool under specific conditions? Or was there only one phoenix, and Olcon simply used the eruption that best coincided with his timing?

Gellion knit his brows, his interest at last pulled away from the redstone. He had never considered the scientific origins of the phoenix before. The thing had been a demon—a dark spirit raised by Olcon, the fallen rival of Riu. Surely the laws of nature did not matter in a case of divine intervention? But Kaelo's musings made Gellion think. Olcon could not create out of nothing. Maybe the phoenix had risen under significant physical circumstances.

With a sigh, Gellion turned the page. This was all interesting, but it had nothing to do with Kaelo's plans to destroy vierstone and fell cities.

"I think we should learn more about the child," Veldon said.

Gellion looked up, taken aback by the sudden change of subject.

A tinge of pink touched Veldon's cheeks.

"It is just so strange. An elf having a child with a human? And it seems so out of Kaelo's character, so out of line with what he was trying to accomplish here. He might have been in Suri Ranta working on all of this long before the child was born for all we know, but for the better part of a century he would have had another elf here with him, a child for part of the time, but an adult for much of it."

Valder was frowning. "I hadn't thought of it that way. That is assuming Kaelo *did* take the child, though. It could have disappeared another way—lost in the woods, taken by one of those giant monster cats. It sounds to me like this Isla was not entirely right in the head. For all we know, she could have done something to the child and passed it off as faerie magic. The Kayda would certainly be prone to believing it."

"What I don't understand," said Gellion, reluctant to have this discussion, but seeing that there was no way out of it, "is why the child was born at all. Either Kaelo fell in love with the human girl and the birth of a half elven baby was an accident, or he," Gellion shifted uncomfortably, "planned it."

Valder raised his eyebrows. "You mean intentionally seduced a human girl to take the resulting child?"

"Either option seems far-fetched," Gellion said. "But there is the second bedroom, and Heleena said the child had green eyes and 'faerie ears.' I can't see any way around it. And trust me, I've tried."

Veldon was nodding, running his fingers absently along the side of his jaw.

"I think it is safe to assume that by whatever means and for whatever reason, Kaelo did sire a son or a daughter here, and in all likelihood, they grew up in this cave, working with Kaelo on his plans."

Gellion felt an uncomfortable pang in the pit of his stomach. He suddenly felt foolish for having passed Kaelo's child off as a strange but insignificant fact. Veldon was right. A child did not remain a child long, even as an elf, and a fully grown elf raised under Kaelo's careful guidance and armed with redstone could prove a powerful weapon.

"Kaelo was alone when I saw him," Gellion said. "And when Renyra saw him. If he has an accomplice in this, where are they?"

"You think he has a spy," Valder said.

"No elf would have seen Kaelo's child before," said Gellion. "They would go completely unrecognized in a crowd." A chill spread through his blood. "Especially during a Kindom Council."

The three brothers stared at each other for several moments, each absorbing the magnitude of this theory.

"They were probably in Daro all the time," said Veldon. "Passing information to Kaelo as the alliance, and eventually the search for Kaelo, progressed."

"What about the Dierna?" Gellion said.

"I still think that was unrelated," said Valder. "But," he shrugged. "If Kaelo had a daughter, I suppose it could have been her who went to Eurig. Though I still don't see why he would sabotage his own plan."

"I think we need to ask Heleena more about Isla's child," said Veldon.

Gellion nodded reluctantly. "I say we try to get through the rest of these notes tonight and go back to Suri Ranta in the morning. We're running out of food anyway."

"Then we can leave?" said Valder, brightening.

"Then we can leave. But we had better read fast."

Valder's face fell again.

Gellion returned to Kaelo's notes on phoenixes and volcanoes even more distracted than before. He could not think about the possibility of Kaelo's child as a spy among the elves. He could not think about redstone, how it was made, or how it worked. He had to finish these notes. He had to make sure there was no further evidence pointing to Kaelo's goal. Only then could he set his mind loose to make sense of all the pieces.

Following Kaelo's musings on the origins of the phoenix, the notes turned to explanations of ash—notably, volcanic ash. He had written chemical and geological explanations for the changes stone underwent from magma to ash or to volcanic glass or other igneous rocks.

Then the notes turned again to the phoenix. Was the beast autonomous or controlled entirely by that which raised it? How had Olcon raised the phoenix? Had it been Olcon at all?

Gellion sighed, tempted to skim through the rest of this section and move on. These were just ramblings of Kaelo's interest and curiosity—

scientific and philosophical musings that no doubt had helped fill his long years of solitude. Gellion didn't have time for this. He needed to get through the rest of these notes tonight.

He turned to the next page, increasing the speed of his skimming.

More notes on ash. More notes on phoenixes. Kaelo's mind seemed to have flitted from one subject to the next and back again.

Gellion flipped another page. He was just about to pick up this stack of papers and put it back, when he saw a bold circle of blotted ink around two words.

Gellion paused, staring at the uncharacteristic mess with a sudden increase of pulse. His thoughts raced over one another, trying to form too many connections at once.

Yes, that could explain it. It was a theory Gellion had never heard of before. But why had it meant so much to Kaelo? Had he merely been excited by his probable discovery in his boredom, or had all of these notes been more than idle curiosity?

"Look at this," Gellion said, picking up the notes and bringing them to the desk.

Valder and Veldon gathered around the pages, and Gellion pointed to the thickly inked words, repeatedly outlined and blotted as though Kaelo hadn't been able to control his hand anymore in his excitement.

'Vierstone ash.'

ASHES OF STONE

Kyna's skin prickled with sweat. The air was saturated with moisture and bore the tang of minerals. Despite this, Kyna felt cold. Even as waves of heat distorted her vision, she clasped her arms about her body.

She told herself the cold was from loss of blood, but it had been two days since she and Tornac had floated into the city aboard a boat filled with slime and dead leeches. Kyna closed her eyes. Sleep had not come easily since her return, but two days of regular food and water had replenished her strength. No, the cold was from no physical weakness.

"Where is he?" The usual control was absent from Liera's voice. Her hair stuck out of its braid in the humidity, and her eyes were wide. She glanced at the sun hovering above the buildings to the west.

"It's been seven hours," she said.

"He will come." Alsena's gaze flitted among the elves gathered around the forges. In all, there were nearly twenty of them—more than Kyna thought necessary, but Liera had insisted on Coren bringing seven guards. The armed elves were interspersed among the full Turi Council.

The tension in the air was as palpable as the heat. Behind Liera, a towering furnace smoked and sizzled, a set of bellows automatically stoking its fire every few minutes. Above it was a stone basin. Kyna couldn't see the molten material within, but a glow of green shone off the basin's upper lip. It was filled with liquid vierstone.

Kyna kept her distance from the furnace, not just because of the unbearable heat, but because the vierstone within seemed to give off waves of awareness, as though the excited atoms within the burning stone were projecting their very existence to any elf near enough to feel it. Kyna's thoughts were inexorably drawn to the vierstone quarry in Daro. Standing next to an entire wall of uncut vierstone had affected her far more than she had imagined. Then there had been an earthquake. Gellion had fallen against the cliffside.

Kyna blinked and pulled herself back to the present. It would not do to think of Gellion now. The only thing that mattered was this furnace of vierstone. For better or worse, Tura's fate would change today, perhaps within the hour. Her job would be done. She glanced at the slack tub below the furnace. Her heart pounded.

"Finally." Liera straightened and strode toward an elf who was strolling in from the street. He was slight for a Turi, with brown hair swept back in a tail. A leather satchel hung from his shoulder. He raised his eyebrows.

"I am not late, am I?"

Liera went red. She could not honestly say, 'Yes,' so settled on waving a hand dismissively.

"Are you ready?" she said.

The elf nodded and walked to the furnace, dropping his bag on the ground.

This was Maelom, the jeweler and vierstone worker Liera had recruited to forge her sword. Kyna watched him. He exhibited none of the nerves that wracked most of those in attendance and began to set up his workspace with patience.

Upon her return to Tura, Kyna had been surprised by how much Liera had accomplished in less than a week. Not only had she secured the forges and kept her own meager supply of vierstone melted, she had found an elf able to work vierstone and had him train under a sword smith for days. No elf had ever tried to cast or forge vierstone, but Liera said they had run promising experiments.

Less promising had been the likelihood of Kyna's and Tornac's return with any vierstone to work with. Liera had been as surprised as she was relieved to see them show up at the forges five days after their disappearance.

"Thank Riu you've come," she had said. "We thought ... the others ... the riders to Morcanan—they didn't make it."

"What?" Tornac had stood at the news, but swayed and sat back down with a dazed expression.

"We sent three elves on horseback at the same time as you left. The next day, they wandered back to Tura on foot, disoriented, with confused memories of an ambush."

Only a collapsed wall and blocked river had shown any trace of the company bound for Maramor, and Liera had feared the worst, but she had carried on with her plan regardless. Kyna had to admit herself impressed with the woman's determination.

The last two days had been a scramble of preparations and rushed Council meetings. Despite her exhaustion and the twisting of her stomach that seemed to get worse by the day, Kyna had attended every meeting and helped stand guard at the forges while Alsena's stoneworkers and metalworkers melted and managed the vierstone.

Last night, Maelom had begun.

Kyna had expected the sword making process to take a few hours, maybe half a day, but had been surprised to learn how long the elves would have to guard the forges while Maelom completed his task. After dark, she had watched with wary fascination as he poured molten vierstone into a mold. It had looked like liquid emerald, impossibly green with shifting shades that shimmered with their own light. The mold had been simple—a long bar the length of a sword.

The night that followed had been long and tense. Guards had patrolled the forges while the bar of vierstone cooled in preparation for its fate. There had been no disturbance. No one had seen any sign of Kaelo since the night of Liera's planned escapes, and the Council was getting nervous.

So was Kyna.

The day had been torture, nothing but endless waiting and silence. Maelom had begun to forge the sword at dawn, hammering, heating, then hammering again until the bar resembled a sword—wide and straight. He had then plunged the heated blade into a tub of sand to cool slowly throughout the day. Seven hours. It had felt like seven days.

But now it was time. The Council was here, Maelom was beginning the last steps of the forging, and Kyna's stomach was in knots.

Maelom reached into the tub of sand and brought out the blade, then lay it on a bench. A handheld machine sat beside it, wired into the wall with a handle and a sand belt. Maelom wrapped his fingers around the handle's grip and flipped a switch that made the sand belt whir into motion with a loud *whooshing*.

Kyna flinched as Maelom began grinding the blade. The sound was high-pitched and piercing. Surely all of Tura could hear. Liera seemed to be thinking the same thing. She was watching not the sword, but the nearby streets, ears pricked for any sign of danger.

The grinding went on.

And on.

Kyna quickly grew bored and began to fidget with a nearby file in her agitation. The blade looked like a sword to her, why couldn't Maelom just stick it in a hilt now and be done with it?

"Tedious isn't it?"

Kyna's eyes shot sideways to see Tornac leaning against a pillar next to her.

"Have you ever seen a sword forged?" he said.

"No." Kyna cocked an eyebrow. "Have you ever forged a sword?"

"Many." He sighed. "Though not by choice. It is a long process, and a difficult one to perfect. I cannot say I ever perfected it, but I made passable weapons for their purpose." He nodded toward Maelom. "It could take a few hours to finish the grinding and filing."

Kyna let out a long breath. "Hours? And is that the last step?"

"No. Right now the metal—the vierstone—will be too soft. It would never hold up to a beating. He will need to reheat the blade and cool it quickly to harden the material, then temper it to prevent brittle-ness." Tornac shrugged. "At least, that is what one would do with metal. This is all new territory."

"Liera seems confident it will work."

"Vierstone holds properties similar to metal—but also to stone and glass. My father always said that the skill of a vierstone worker lay in bringing out the right properties. Maelom is good at what he does. If he can manage it, this blade will have the flexibility of metal, the strength of stone, and the razor edge of glass." His eyes shone at the prospect, a rare demonstration of excitement.

"Then let us hope he can manage it," Kyna said.

Another hour crawled by before Maelom finally picked up the blade with a pair of tongs. It was noticeably slimmer, with a sharper edge, but hardly looked worth the hours of grinding. He moved to the forge and thrust the vierstone into the fire. It glowed an ethereal green as Maelom carried it to the slack tub and submerged it in the cool water with a loud sizzle and a pillar of steam.

Kyna began to shift her weight from one foot to the other. Maelom went back to the forge and started to heat the blade again.

Oh come on. Hurry.

This would be the tempering, the last step.

Liera was watching the sword like a mouse watches a hawk, her eyes wide and intense. Was she afraid of what would happen when the sword was finished? Afraid that she would have to confront her son, with a weapon this time, rather than words?

Kyna's pulse quickened.

Maelom was quenching the blade in the slack tub again. Now he was taking it back to the bench.

Heaven help us, he's picking up the grinder again.

This time the screeches only lasted a few minutes. Maelom polished the sword with a cloth, then brought a hilt out of a drawer to set the blade into.

Every eye was fixed on the sword as Maelom held it up.

It was incredible.

The blade was brilliant green, with swirls and folds of contrasting shades weaving over its angles like a polished abalone. Even from her distance, Kyna could tell its edge was razor sharp on both sides, its tip a needle.

Pride shone in Maelom's face, and he stepped toward Liera, presenting the sword hilt first. He visibly shivered as he held the bare vierstone in his palms.

Liera's hand was steady, but hesitant. She took the weight of the weapon gracefully and held the blade up to examine it more closely. There was a hunger in her eyes—an almost wild joy—as she stared at the physical embodiment of a prophecy.

Despite herself, Kyna felt a chill spread along her skin at the sight. She had done it. She had brought the prophecy to the elves and seen it followed through. Now all she could do was wait.

Every elf in the room seemed entranced. Council Members and guards alike stared at Liera, their breaths held for what would happen next.

Then Liera lowered the blade and turned to regard her onlookers. The spell broke. Liera was standing in a hot forge, holding a sword that was beautiful, but only a sword. The wonder faded from her eyes. The Lady of Tura turned to Kyna. Her expression seemed to say, "What now?"

Kyna swallowed. She glanced back at the street, then across the river. This was as far as she knew. The rest had never been up to her. The basin of liquid vierstone drew her eyes again. She had helped secure the basin above the forge with a system of pulleys. Chains tethered the set-up to the ground on either side.

Liera kept her gaze on Kyna.

What do you expect me to do now, Kyna thought, *bring you to Kaelo?* There was no need.

A collective intake of breath made Kyna turn to face the street.

There, in broad daylight, stood Kaelo.

Every muscle in Kyna's body tensed.

Kaelo carried no weapon, but wore the same red and black material as he had the night he confronted Liera. No arrow or sword would pierce the interwoven metal—no normal weapon that is. Could a vierstone sword do what metal could not? Kyna bit her lip.

The guards had raised their weapons, but no one made any move to approach or attack the lone elf before them. Liera looked as though she had been slapped in the face.

Well, you got what you wanted. Something happened.

Kaelo had his eyes fixed on Liera. He stood still, ignoring the guards, ignoring all other elves crowding the forges.

Liera raised the vierstone sword in both hands, its tip wavering.

"It is too late." Her voice was steadier than her hands, but there was fear in her eyes—fear, and hatred. "You did not stop the elves we sent to the Fieri and the Remsgri, and you cannot destroy the vierstone in these forges." She pulled her eyes away from him for an instant to look at the glimmering blade in front of her. "And here, I hold your downfall in my hands."

Kaelo made no answer. His eyes drank in the sword, but his expression remained unreadable as wood. He took several steps toward Liera.

Liera's hands tightened on the hilt of the sword, and one leg jerked as though to step backward, but she stood her ground.

"You were a fool to come here," Liera said. "To Tura, and to these forges. Is it revenge you sought? Revenge for the justice you received?"

A corner of Kaelo's mouth turned up.

"Justice." He almost chuckled at the word. "There is no justice among the Turi." His gaze roamed over the elves around him. "There is no justice among the elves."

"Why then? Is your cause so noble that none may know it but yourself?"

"My cause is no secret. You say I seek revenge for justice? No. I seek justice itself. True justice. Not for myself, but for all elves. Justice is based upon fact—reason. But there can be no reason in a world of passions and fear—of corruption and anger." He raised his head and narrowed his eyes at Liera. "In a world of love and hate."

No elf moved. Each Council Member and guard hung on Kaelo's every word. Kyna watched the sword in Liera's hands like it was a living viper. She clenched her fists.

"I intend to alter that world," Kaelo said. "To fix it." He cocked his head and turned his attention to the sword. "I did not know if it was possible to forge a blade of vierstone." He spoke quietly, as though talking to himself. "It seemed plausible enough. I am delighted that it worked."

Liera drew her brows together, confusion replacing the anger in her eyes, joined by a note of panic.

"You're mad. Everything you have said. It doesn't matter why you've done these things. There is no sense in it. And there is no reasoning with you." She set her jaw. "It is time to end this."

Kaelo raised an eyebrow, then stepped forward.

Liera's eyes widened, then she lunged.

Kyna stifled a shout as the blade drove toward Kaelo's chest.

There was a clink of metal, and Kaelo jerked backward with a grunt. Kyna gasped, her throat seeming to close in on itself.

Then Kaelo looked down. The tip of the sword had not even dented his armor.

Kyna let out her breath.

Horror spread over Liera's face. Kyna could not tell if it was from the prophecy's failure, or from what the woman had just tried to do. Liera still held the sword in both hands, her arms extended straight in front of her, the sword's tip resting against her son's chest.

Kaelo slowly raised his gaze from the sword to his mother, a cold fury in his eyes. But there was more than anger in his face. There was shock. He stared at Liera as though he had never truly seen her.

The same shock and anger coursed through Kyna's blood. Liera would have killed him. She had *tried* to kill him. In front of the whole Council—an unarmed man. Her son. Kyna looked around her. No one else seemed appalled by Liera's attempted murder, only that it had not worked.

Hypocrites. The hypocrites.

Resolve flowed into Kyna's fingertips. She had become weak. She had almost begun to believe she was mistaken, that there was something to these elves she might have missed. But even Tornac was glaring at Kaelo with hate in his eyes. Would Renyra have felt the same? Would she have done anything even if she hadn't?

Why does it matter? She is as blind as the rest.

A loud clanging made Kyna jump. Liera had dropped the sword on the floor. Her hands remained open where she had gripped the hilt. Her fingers shook.

Kaelo dragged his eyes away from Liera and looked down at the sword, then bent toward it.

A rush of movement came from all sides as guards and Council Members alike made to stop Kaelo.

"Do not move." Kaelo's hand was on the stone floor. All movement froze.

Kaelo leaned forward and picked the sword up by the hilt. He stood, and his eyes roved the blade.

"Who is the murderer now?" he said softly.

No one made to attack Kaelo again, though his hands were free of the stone floor. Liera blanched.

"I did not need the sword," Kaelo said. "But it will be useful, I am sure."

He laid his palm flat against the sword, and his face contorted as though in pain, but then black began to spread from his fingers like ink over a page. The stain overtook the blade until the sword seemed a deep shadow amid the dimly lit forges. Then a new color began to seep into the blade. It looked as though Kaelo had cut his hand—that blood was spilling over the blade. The swirls of the sword's surface reappeared from the black, but what had once been shades of green, jade, and emerald turned to crimson, ruby, and scarlet. A smile curved Kaelo's lips.

Liera's mouth was hanging open.

"Stone stained redder than their blood." Tenille's whisper floated to Kyna's ears.

Hushed murmurs filled the forges, but the elves seemed transfixed by the scene before them. Even Coren made no move to order his guards.

Liera was trying to find her voice. She gaped like a fish before summoning a semblance of confidence and saying hoarsely, "You cannot escape. You are surrounded by the whole city, and armed elves who will knock the sword from your hands and bind you before you can work your black magic. Drop the sword, Kaelo. It is over."

Kaelo looked up, surprised. "No, mother. It is only beginning. I said you would all thank me. And so you shall. But there is much work to be done before that day. Daro was nothing—a test, an initial cleansing of vierstone, a way to get the elves back on Faeran where they belong. Tura was the true beginning, but it is far from the end." He glanced at the basin of vierstone above the forge. "That vierstone is no safer than this sword. No safer than all the vierstone in Faeran. It is a weakness and a curse. A curse of which I will rid the elves."

Liera had backed up almost to the forges now, and Kaelo was only a few steps in front of her. He gave her one last look, then raised the crimson sword over his head.

"No!" several elves cried.

"Shoot!"

Kaelo slashed his sword. Liera barely had time to raise her arms over her face before the blow fell, but the blade did not hit the Lady of Tura. A metallic crack split the air, followed by a series of slithering clangs. Kaelo had severed the chains that held up the right side of the vierstone basin.

The chains whipped back through the pulleys, snapping them with the force of their acceleration. The basin jerked, then tipped.

Kyna watched with wide eyes as shimmering vierstone poured through the air in seeming slow motion. Then it landed directly in the center of the slack tub.

Molten stone met water. The air exploded.

Kyna had been expecting it, but was still shocked by the violence of the reaction. Steam and shouts filled the forges. She could hear the fall of footsteps as elves scattered, trying to escape the stifling steam and the ash that had begun to rain.

Kyna covered her mouth with her shirt and squinted her eyes against the particles in the air, but remained where she was, holding on to the pillar behind her.

Coren was yelling at his guards, but it would be madness to shoot or stab in such low visibility. It was the street in front of Liera's house all over again.

Amid the chaos, the ash began to settle.

There were still a handful of elves under the roof of the forges, but they were far from the site of the explosion. Most elves had taken shelter in the streets. The ground around the slack tub was a blanket of greenish grey. Motes of ash still hung in the air, but Kyna could make out the faces of elves again.

"Where is he?" Liera was a picture of grey, the whites of her eyes standing out to make her look half crazed.

Movement near the slack tub caught Kyna's eye. In the center of the heaps of ash, stood Kaelo. His hair was dusted grey, and his eyes were bright. Through the haze, he looked straight at Kyna, and smiled.

Kyna's lips twitched into an answering grin.

Kaelo kneeled in the ash and buried both of his hands.

By now, several of the other elves had seen him, and those who had fled the forges were making their way back into the aftermath of the explosion.

"Stop him!" Coren shouted.

Arrows flew; they ricocheted off Kaelo's armor like twigs. Elves ran at him; pillars of stone threw them back.

"Enough!" Kaelo's voice rang through the forges and stopped every elf in their tracks like a spell. Kyna could feel the essence of fear flowing through the stone beneath her feet from Kaelo's touch, but it did not extend into her. Every other elf cowered as though facing their own personal demons.

Hands still buried in ash, Kaelo bowed his head.

Kyna's heart was making a supreme effort to escape her chest. She gripped the pillar behind her with white knuckles and held her breath in anticipation. Would it work?

A moment passed in hanging silence, then the ash surrounding Kaelo began to glow green. It glowed like coals, like the dust of starlight. Smoke rose in tendrils from the heap, and emerald flames began to ignite over the surface of the shimmering ash. Kaelo tensed in effort, then he gasped and staggered backward.

A moment later, an enormous pillar of scarlet flame engulfed the vierstone remains.

Kyna screamed as a wave of scorching heat passed over her and fell to her knees with her arms over her head. Wild flashes of light painted the insides of her eyelids, and she squinted through her arms to see what was happening.

The flames had begun to swirl in a hypnotizing spiral. They morphed and bulged and began to take on shape. A hair-raising screech made Kyna clap her hands over her ears.

Now elves were fleeing in earnest. She could see Alos running for the river, followed by several guards.

Another shriek rent the air.

The crimson flames swirled faster and grew in size. They had reached the roof of the forges now. They swelled, then condensed, then soared upward with a roar. The roof splintered and launched into the air. Kyna dived beneath a nearby table to avoid the falling debris.

She craned her neck up from beneath her shelter to see the shape within the flames solidifying into what looked like embers. They clumped together to form a chest, then a head, then a body. Flames extended from the body and lashed out into a tail. The creature burned white hot for a moment, then fanned out huge wings with a clap like thunder and let out a piercing cry.

Bits of slate and burning wood still fell around her, but Kyna ducked out from under the table and crouched in the remains of the forges, looking up at a creature she had heard about her whole life.

It was bigger than she had imagined it, the size of a small ship with a wingspan many times larger. Shades of crimson, orange, and black mottled its feathers—or were they scales? Whatever they were, they glowed at the edges, like bits of solid metal covering burning embers beneath.

A phoenix.

The great bird beat its wings—curving sails of metallic feathers that trailed flames. Its tail lashed in a cascade of fire, then it descended in a flurry of fiery wings to land where minutes before had sat a pile of ash.

Kyna rose on trembling legs. The bird swung its head to regard her with molten eyes that seemed to move like liquid even when they stilled on Kyna's face. Its beak looked like swirling obsidian, curved to a wicked point.

All the blood drained from Kyna's face as she stared at the beast. It was as gorgeous as it was terrifying, and its gaze seemed to bore into her soul.

A shape moved from behind the overturned slack tub. Kaelo stepped in front of the phoenix. He looked at the bird as though it were Riu himself, a treasure beyond all comprehension. The beast turned its head to regard him. A smile spread over Kaelo's face.

Those elves who had not run for their lives were beginning to rise from the wreckage. Liera was on her knees, looking as though she might faint. Tornac was helping Tenille to her feet, but his eyes never left the great bird. He looked far worse than he had after the eel-leach attack—

pale, ash smeared, and with a look of hatred so profound it chilled Kyna's bones.

Kaelo extended a hand to the phoenix, and it lowered its head until its beak was level with Kaelo's head. Kaelo placed his palm on its glassy surface. The phoenix's eyes seemed to glow brighter, and its feathers ruffled with a sound of sizzling steam.

His hand still on the beast's beak, Kaelo turned to look at Kyna. His eyes were wild, fierce. He extended his other hand toward her.

The reality of the phoenix had at first given strength to Kyna's doubts. How could any elf hope to control such a beast? But now, as the phoenix once again turned its molten eyes on her, she saw that Kaelo had known what he was doing. He had raised a monster of legend, a monster that was loyal to him, its creator.

Adrenaline coursed through every nerve in Kyna's body. She had done it. Weeks, months, years of work had not come to nothing. It had taken more coercion than she had anticipated. The elves were not as easily manipulated as she had hoped. But they had accepted the prophecy in time—the prophecy that set up the perfect conditions for Kaelo's plans to unfold, the prophecy Kyna had written.

Kyna had doubted, she had feared, but she had succeeded. And now it was all over. Her role was complete.

She stepped through the smoldering rubble toward the phoenix, toward Kaelo, toward her father.

Pride burned in his eyes, though Kyna could not tell if any of it was for her. He grasped her hand and stepped to the side of the phoenix, which bowed its head and extended one wing to the ground. Kaelo leaped onto the beast's back, pulling Kyna up with him.

The phoenix was warm, but not painfully so. Its feathers were slippery and felt almost like glass.

Elves were flooding in from the streets now. Kyna looked down from the phoenix's back and saw Tornac staring at her with slack shoulders. Betrayal was written in every inch of his face. Gellion's spirit seemed to emanate from his accusation.

Kyna's triumph wavered. Doubts flitted back into her conscience.

Daro's destruction had taken far more skill and cunning than she had anticipated, as well. Dulon had been ready to believe anything that would bring glory, and later salvation, to his precious city, but Gellion—

Guilt stabbed at Kyna's middle.

No. Do not think of him.

Kaelo had managed all the arrangements with the Albaren, while Kyna dealt with the Dierna. Neither had gone to plan. The Albaren had betrayed Kaelo as readily as Kaelo had betrayed them. Even the Dierna had lied to Kyna about their numbers. What should have been a simple stalemate between human kingdoms, the elves sandwiched harmlessly in between, had become a slaughter. The elves weren't supposed to have died. Gellion wasn't supposed to have died.

Kyna stopped her thoughts abruptly. It didn't matter. The plan had worked regardless. Daro's vierstone had been destroyed, and the elves had left Tala with no threat of human pursuit. She would not allow Gellion to ruin this moment. He was gone. He was nothing—a casualty in the fight for a better world. A world that would come to fruition now.

Kyna pried her gaze away from Tornac.

Cries issued from the streets, and Kyna saw the first volleys of arrows and javelins coming toward them. The phoenix screeched and swirled its tail in an arc, clearing all in its path, then it lifted its wings and beat down with a force that vaulted them high into the air. Kyna gripped Kaelo's sides, but his armor was as slick as the phoenix. A moment of panic seized her as the bird rose higher into the air and began to bank to the side. She flung her arms around Kaelo's waist and locked her wrists together. Against his back, she could feel the rhythm of laughter deep in his chest.

Kyna glanced back once to see Tura falling away below her, then the flames of the phoenix's tail obscured her vision. She turned away, pressing her face into her father's back as they soared toward a new future.

3 4

THE CHANGELING

Heleena watched the elves with expressionless eyes as they walked toward her. She was sitting in the back garden of Ruta's house again, fish circling each other in the pond at her feet.

Tension pulled at Gellion's shoulders. This was the last piece. If Heleena could tell them more about Kaelo's child, they might be able to put together a semblance of a story of Kaelo's last years.

All but his ultimate goal.

The night before, Gellion and his brothers had stayed up the better part of the night reading through the last of Kaelo's notes. Aside from the wildly circled 'vierstone ash,' they had found little of interest in the remaining pages. Valder and Veldon had found Kaelo's theories about the origins of the phoenix intriguing, but were unconvinced that they had anything to do with his current actions. Gellion was less sure.

Kaelo had always been calm and even-tempered. A simple revelation about a monster long dead would not have caused him to repeatedly circle, rewrite, and blot his discovery.

Vierstone ash. Morcanan was one of the original four Great Cities. Its vierstone deposits were located in the mountain into which the city extended. What if that vierstone had extended up the whole mountain, or deep within its base where magma had churned and burned it?

Vierstone—lifestone.

Maybe a phoenix could only rise from life-giving ash.

But why had the possibility so interested Kaelo? The phoenix had died over three centuries ago.

Had Kaelo written these notes during the war? Could he have been researching ways to kill the phoenix? Gellion cringed at the onset of pain long cooled but still sharp. It had been Gellion's own father who had killed the phoenix in the end. None knew how he had accomplished what so many before had failed. His father had died in the final explosion caused by the great bird's destruction. No living elf knew what had finished off the beast.

But the ink of Kaelo's notes had seemed too fresh to be four or five hundred years old. The notes had contained no date, but Gellion would estimate they couldn't be older than two centuries, probably less than that.

Valder cleared his throat, snapping Gellion's attention back to the task at hand. Heleena was watching him, one eyebrow raised.

"Did you find what you sought?" she said.

"Yes," said Gellion.

Heleena nodded. "You must have, to be gone so long. I admit myself surprised to see you back alive."

Gellion could not tell if the woman was pleased or not by the unexpected outcome.

"We found more than we could have hoped for," Gellion said. "Enough to help us apprehend the threat that awaits us in our homeland. But there is one more thing we would like to ask you about before we leave."

Heleena extended a wrinkled hand to her side in invitation.

"Isla's child. Can you tell us more about them? Anything you remember, or were told?"

Heleena looked down and sighed, as though the memory tired her.

"Of course I remember the child. I was only a child myself, but I think that has sharpened my memory more than faded it. My grandparents shunned Isla's baby, but my mother was protective of her sister, even if she did not approve of her ways. She helped Isla, and in my young ignorance, I grew to love her babe." She let out another breath, sadness clouding her eyes.

"Her—daughter?" Gellion said when Heleena did not go on.

Heleena nodded. Out of the corner of his eye, Gellion saw Veldon look at him sharply.

"The changeling was a beautiful thing," Heleena said. "Like a porcelain doll. Skin smooth and pale—impossibly soft to my callused little hands. She was born with a head of glossy black hair, and it had grown half to her waist by the time she disappeared, though she was only a year old. She could run like a liltie before then, too, her feet barely seeming to touch the ground. She was fae, but I thought it made her all the more beautiful. I cried for weeks when she disappeared. I always hoped she would visit again—shed her sealskin and come to me in the night. I even dreamed she would take me back to the sea with her." Heleena shook her head. "I was foolish and young. I never saw her again."

Gellion had been squeezing his hands together with increasing force throughout Heleena's description.

"Thank you," Gellion said as calmly as he could. "You have helped us immensely, Heleena. I am sorry for the sorrow this has caused you."

A sudden spark of fire came to Heleena's eyes. "If you find that selkie, put an end to his power. He has brought naught but trouble to our people, and it seems he is doing as much or worse to yours. It is only his nature, but he should see justice all the same."

Gellion bowed his head.

"And," Heleena said softly, the merest hint of wistfulness coloring her voice. "If you see his daughter—" She trailed off, at a loss of what to say.

"I will," said Gellion.

"Well, that's that," said Valder, sitting with folded legs on the spongy floor of their bedroom. "I guess it was Kaelo's daughter who went to the Dierna.

"There's no way to be sure," Gellion said. "But it does seem likely."

"So who is it?" said Veldon.

"What, Kaelo's daughter?" said Valder. "What makes you think we would know her? She must have been here with Kaelo until recently, right? Maybe she was helping coordinate things in the outside world while Kaelo was focused on Daro."

"Maybe," Veldon said. "But Gellion's right. The Kindom Council would have been a perfect opportunity for an unknown elf to make an appearance with no questions asked. Kaelo must have been getting information on how his plans were progressing somehow, and he would have risked being recognized if he made appearances himself."

"He had Gellion's magic tunic," Valder said. "Maybe that's how he was spying."

"No," Gellion said. "He had to have someone on the inside. He was always a step ahead of us." Gellion had begun to pace. He was racking his brain to recall all that had happened in the last weeks he had been in Daro. "I had wondered how Kaelo knew to silence Aryn. According to Dulon, almost no one knew that she was researching vierstone, and Kaelo got to her within an hour of her alleged discovery—before she could tell anyone."

Valder sighed. "So we're looking for a Turi woman less than a century old who no one had ever seen before the—" Valder trailed off at the look on Gellion's face.

Gellion felt as though he had been submerged in ice water.

A pale woman with black hair. A woman who appeared with the Kindom Council ships but could have come from anywhere. A woman born after the Great War, who had not returned with the Kindom Council. A woman with a straight nose.

"Kyna." The name barely sounded past his lips. The icy water around him was making it hard to draw breath.

Valder stared at him, confusion turning to stark comprehension in a moment. Veldon's face had drained of all color.

Gellion put his face in his hands and let his fingers run through his hair. The cold in his body was turning hot as shame and anger took turns battering his insides. He had been such a fool.

"She told me herself she was born after the Great War," said Gellion. "I didn't see her on the ship from Faeran, but mixed in the crowds after the Sira performance. When I asked where she was from, she said north of Tura, but I never saw her with any of the Turi visitors."

His stomach twisted painfully.

"Sweet Riu, it was her all along. How did I not see it? She tried to convince me to vote in favor of the alliance." He groaned. "And after we accepted, she worked with Dulon to get the elves on his side. She had no real reason to stay in Daro." Another painful stab, this time in his chest. He laughed dryly.

"She was one of the night patrols. I bet she staged the whole thing when she 'caught sight' of Kaelo."

Closing his eyes, Gellion thought back to every moment he had spent in Daro with Kyna. She had never cared for him. In their first conversation she had found out he was on the Kindom Council. She must have latched onto him then and kept up the ruse until the elves were safely out of Daro.

My tunic. My knife.

Gellion buried his head further into his hands.

Had it been Kyna herself who had taken his possessions to give to her father, or had she merely told Kaelo about them? Riu above, had she known about Gellion's connection to her father all the time? Gellion had confided in her. How she must have laughed at him.

And then there was Dulon. Kyna had worked closely with the Lord of Daro in the end. Had she given him and Gellion false information to ensure they never caught Kaelo? Try as he might, Gellion couldn't remember the conversations with Kyna and Dulon well enough to know. And what about Aryn? Kyna must have known Dulon had her on Kaelo's trail. Had Kyna known the woman would die for her work? Gellion's breath caught in his throat. Had she known of the Albaren betrayal? Had she led Dulon to his death knowingly? Had she led Gellion to his death without caring?

Veldon was looking at Gellion with more sympathy than Gellion could stomach. He stood and turned his back to his brothers.

"She used us all," he said.

His fingernails bit so hard into his palms, he was almost able to blame the pain for the sudden sheen in his eyes. His skin was hot, his arms nearly shaking from the rage simmering within him. This is what he got for opening himself to someone. He had gone against his better judgment, and he had paid dearly for it. All of Daro had paid.

No.

Gellion released his hands, his anger wavering in a sudden spark of hope. But she had cared. He had seen it, dammit. That night in Nescari she had opened to him for just a moment, and he had seen it.

But then she turned you away.

The rage came back in greater force than before. Maybe some part of Kyna had grown to care for Gellion, but it was clearly not big enough to interfere with the plans of her father. She had used Gellion. Manipulated him. Just like Chiara. But this one hurt so much more.

Veldon and Valder were silent. Gellion knew they were looking at each other behind his back—their poor brother whose love had betrayed him. The pangs in his chest came again.

I didn't love her.

"I'm sorry, Gellion," Veldon said gently. "Really, I am."

Gellion turned to face his brothers. Veldon looked afraid to go on, but took a breath.

"But now that we know, we can draw everything together—everything we have learned. That is what really matters. Stopping Kaelo. And now we can get back to the elves and help them."

Gellion took a slow breath. Was Kyna in Faeran now? Was she moving among the elves, spinning lies and deceit to help her father?

"Kaelo convinced the Albaren to draw out the elves from Daro," Veldon said. "We don't know how, but we know Vensure worked with him. Whether or not Kaelo knew of the Albaren's planned betrayal, he sent his daughter to warn the Dierna about the attack."

"But why?" Valder said in an exasperated voice.

"To play them off each other," Gellion said softly. Every part of him still hurt, still burned, but he went on. "He just wanted the elves out of the city, not sucked into a war on a different continent. Maybe he didn't trust the Albaren to keep their end of the bargain. If so, he was right. But he couldn't have meant for the elves of Daro to be destroyed. That would have been too easy with an inside contact so close to Dulon. He didn't need to go to all that trouble just to get the elves killed. He just wanted us out of the way, and it worked."

Thanks to Kyna.

"We don't know enough to guess at his full plan," Gellion said. "But we have enough information to bring to Tura—enough to make a serious dent in Kaelo's plans. Anything could have happened in Faeran by now, but we have to warn the elves about redstone." He winced. "And Kyna. We will bring all we know before Liera. Hopefully we're not too late."

35

LETTERS

I t was high noon, but Renyra sat in twilight. The canopy of Riverseep Forest was tall and thick. She stared at the twisting branches without seeing them, heard the calls of birds without registering their source.

The letter was still in her hand. She had read it at least a dozen times now—read it to herself, read it to Firas, read it to Riu with raised fists.

She twisted the vierstone in her ear, and the familiar comfort warmed her fingers and seeped into her soul. At least she had this back.

Renyra had been in Remsgraen for nearly a week now. Rhosti had been as reluctant to act on the troupe's warning as Cuvan had said he would be, but it didn't matter now. None of it mattered.

A phoenix.

The letter from Cuvan had come first. The Fieri were mobilizing, setting up an intensive guard not only in Telem Fier but in every city in the grasslands, and reforming an army that had not been seen for three centuries. Rhosti was following suit. The Remsgri were a peaceful Kindom, but defended their own with a ferocity unmatched by any other when cornered.

Tornac's letter had come second, this one for Renyra herself. He had described everything that had happened in the forges of Tura: the sword, Kaelo's words, the phoenix, and Kyna.

Kyna.

Renyra had been afraid when she heard a monster from legends had returned to the world. She had been afraid when she heard that Kaelo was not only undefeated, but prepared to destroy all the vierstone in Faeran. But it had been Tornac's letter that shattered her.

The prophecy had been a fake. No, it had been worse—step-by-step instructions to fall into Kaelo's hands and enable his goals. Everything the Turi Council had done since Renyra's arrival had been part of his plan. They had followed it to a tee.

Kyna had convinced Renyra to support the prophecy and voice her interpretations of its words as her own ideas.

To take suspicion away from herself.

Kyna had helped them escape Tura and bring vierstone back from Maramor.

So Kaelo would have enough vierstone to raise a phoenix.

Had Kyna told Kaelo everything the Council was doing? Had she laughed at Renyra's blind trust? Her foolish attempts at friendship?

How Kaelo had appealed to Kyna, Renyra did not know. Bribery? Persuasion? Threat? It didn't really matter, she supposed, but some sentimental part of Renyra hoped it was not entirely Kyna's free will that had brought her to lie to and betray all of the elves.

A monkey swung from a branch to Renyra's left. She watched it land ten feet below her and scurry up the trunk of a tree. Twigs fell to the forest floor another three stories down. The elves there did not look up. They must be used to foliage falling from the sky. Lifts glowed against the trunks of the bigger trees, and pathways wound and stretched between buildings and platforms, which hugged the thick trunks.

It was a sight as enchanting as the first time she had seen it, but it brought her little joy now.

Renyra had always been jealous of the elves that had weathered the Great War together. She had always felt left out of an event that defined the life of almost every elf she had ever known. In Daro, she had been forced to taste battle, and it had been a bitter reality she wished had never come to pass. Now she would get her foolish wish in full. There would be war again.

But this time things will be different.

The elves had fought and defeated a phoenix before. They would again, and this time their enemy was one they could understand—an elf.

"There you are." Caerlyn stepped onto Renyra's branch and sat down next to her. She looked at the letters crumpled in Renyra's hands and raised an eyebrow.

"Reading them again?"

"Just thinking."

"About what?"

"Finding Kaelo."

Caerlyn's brows reached higher up her forehead.

"I've tracked him in two cities now, why not all of Faeran?" Renyra let a weak smile touch her lips.

"Hmm." Caerlyn frowned, then began to nod. "Alright then, why not?"

Renyra looked at her. "What?"

"Tracking Kaelo. The troupe."

"Oh. I meant—"

"To go alone? Don't be an idiot."

Renyra snorted. "Thanks."

"No offense, but your first two attempts didn't turn out so well."

Renyra gritted her teeth. "That's why I have to try again."

"Sure." Caerlyn nodded.

"You really think they'll all want to come?"

"Obviously." Caerlyn swung her legs and cocked her head at the dizzying drop below her. "We've traveled across Faeran together before. We just did it again." She shrugged. "We'll have to figure out how to kill a phoenix, though."

Renyra's skin chilled. She hadn't even thought about the phoenix.

Caerlyn's right. You are an idiot.

"It wasn't an army who killed the last one anyway, was it?" Caerlyn said. "It was one elf."

"And no one knows how he did it."

"Well, whatever he did, he did it all by himself. Why not us?"

Renyra couldn't keep the grin from her face. It seemed so absurd. Tracking a demon bird and its power-possessed master across the continent, defeating the biggest threat the elves had known in centuries? It would never work, but somehow the idea of trying gave Renyra more hope than anything she had heard from Rhosti or Cuvan.

She let her fingers brush her vierstone earring again. The jeweler had done a remarkable job in a day. The stone was polished and pure and sat against her skin like living hope. She would get her chance to prove herself again. She would find Kaelo, have a few words with Kyna, and face the phoenix with her troupe behind her.

This time, she wouldn't underestimate Kaelo. This time, she would be ready.

If you enjoyed

ASHES
OF
STONE

Look out for Book III of the
Lifestone Trilogy:

SHAPING
OF
STONE

Sneak peak of chapter one follows...

SHAPING OF STONE PREVIEW
CHAPTER 1: CLOSED GATES

The gates of Tura were guarded. Gellion's steps faltered when he saw the teeth of spears outlined against the sky. It had been centuries since the Turi guarded their gates. Just seeing the city still standing was a relief of which Gellion had not dared to hope, but the spears sent shivers of cold over his skin. Was this merely a precaution against what had happened in Daro, or had Kaelo already begun to enact his plans here? Gellion glanced at his brothers. Valder and Veldon had seen the guards, too, and were watching them warily.

"How long do you think it's been?" Valder said.

"Nearly two months, I think." Veldon's eyes were fixed on the gates, as though trying to see what lay beyond them.

Gellion couldn't find his voice. Every day of those two months away from the elves, he had imaged what could be happening in Tura, wondering what his family must be feeling at his presumed death, wondering which of his friends had survived the battle at Arvain. The answers awaited him at last.

The cold over his skin spread to his lungs, constricting his breath. There was only one death he was certain of—the one he had witnessed with his own eyes. The sharp pain that had once accompanied any thought of Dulon was beginning to dull, but Gellion knew from his experience in the Great War that it would never leave him entirely. He was not prepared to begin the process anew if he found Firas had died, or Renyra, or—

His chest gave a sickening lurch. Could Kyna be behind these walls? So close after all this time? After all he now knew? It was possible she had died at Arvain. It would be better for the elves as a whole if she had. Yet the thought of the possibility still broke something inside Gellion.

She betrayed you. She betrayed all the elves. She never loved you.

A thousand times, Gellion had agonized over what he would do if he found Kyna alive in Tura, still in the confidence of the elves. Could the Turi have discovered for themselves that Kyna was Kaelo's accomplice?

Not accomplice. Daughter.

Gellion could still not comprehend the fact. Would anyone believe him? A part of him still doubted the revelation, but the evidence he and his brothers had found in Suri Ranta was too perfect. The spy had to be her. She had to be Kaelo's daughter. Gellion had decided to go directly to Liera as soon as he arrived. He would tell her everything. If all went well, he wouldn't even have to see Kyna, though what may happen to her when the rest of the elves knew of her treachery sent a chill through his bones.

It was useless to speculate, especially when the reality of all his imaginings was mere minutes away, but the habit had become so ingrained in Gellion, he could hardly seem to stop himself. He closed his eyes, trying to escape the turmoil and focus on the present. He turned inward. In his mind, he ran through the first steps of the A'vaeri, picturing his own body moving with precision and balance. His jumbled thoughts narrowed, aligned. The memories and worries were still present, but they bent to the immediacy of the now. Gellion sighed.

"Let's go." He spoke more to himself than to his brothers. Opening his eyes, he strode toward the gates.

The guards peered down at them as they drew closer, then one of them exclaimed and disappeared behind the gates. A few moments later, the thick sheets of metal that shaped the gates of Tura opened before them.

"Gellion!"

The voice sounded familiar, but it wasn't until the elf was nearly upon him that Gellion recognized Reanan, the Master Builder of Tura. Gellion had not seen Reanan since leaving the Turi Council two hundred years before, when he had sailed for Daro.

"Riu above," Reanan breathed. He stopped in front of Gellion with wide eyes. His skin was a deep tan—Gellion had always assumed he held some Remsgri or Fieri blood—but now his face was nearly as pale as Gellion's own.

"They said—" Reanan faltered, shaking his head as his eyes took in Valder and Veldon standing behind Gellion. "They said you were dead. All of you. Tenille—" The look of pain on Reanan's face made Gellion's throat constrict.

His mother.

So she has mourned us.

Gellion had known his mother would assume he and his brothers were dead when the rest of the elves of Daro returned without them, but somehow hearing it confirmed made the situation seem immeasurably worse. Had his mother blamed him for the deaths of Valder and Veldon? She had every right to. Tenille had been perplexed by Gellion's decision to accept the infamous Albaren alliance that had led to a near massacre of the elven army, but she had honored his choice at the time. Now he had brought her incomprehensible pain.

"Is our mother here?" Veldon asked.

Gellion's eyes locked on Reanan, his pulse racing.

"Yes," Reanan said. "All the Turi Council is." He was still staring at Gellion and his brothers as though expecting them to blow away in the breeze at any moment. "Tenille has been in Tura for weeks. So has Tornac."

Gellion stiffened. In all his visions of his homecoming, his older brother had always been safely back in Maramor, seeing to the running of their family's city. His mother had been there too for that matter, though Gellion had considered the possibility of her presence in Tura if Kaelo's return had become public knowledge. The heat in Gellion's blood began to drain until he could feel his face paling. The full Turi Council was in Tura. The gates were closed and guarded. Clearly something had happened to cause alarm. Was it more than simple precaution?

"But ... but how?" Reanan still seemed to be having trouble forming his thoughts into words. "How are you here? How did you get across the sea?"

Gellion disregarded Reanan's questions with the wave of a hand.

"It's a long story, and one I intend to tell in full before the Turi Council, but not now. Reanan, what has been happening? Why is the Turi Council here? And the gates—"

Reanan's mouth had been hanging open, but now he slowly closed it, the shock in his face turning to what Gellion could only interpret as dread.

"I fear you will not believe me if I tell you," Reanan's voice was weighted with weariness.

Valder snorted. "We'll believe your story if you believe ours." A corner of his mouth twitched up. "I think you will find us a less skeptical audience than you imagine."

Reanan did not smile. "It is not a story you will want to believe in any case." He glanced behind them, then back to the gates. "Come inside. It will be easier to show you."

Every step Gellion took behind Reanan increased the tension in his muscles until his heart was hammering with the stress, yet when he walked through the gates of Tura, the Great City looked exactly as he remembered it. A swell of affection rose in his chest at the familiarity of the flower lined streets and beautiful buildings. Above the homes and shops, Gellion could see the Central Tower gleaming alabaster in the sunlight. Elves passed through the streets around him. No beards, no beggars, no children, no backs bent to age. Gellion nearly laughed with the joy of being among his own kind once more.

It had not been an easy journey from Suri Ranta to Faeran. Gellion and his brothers had spent nearly two weeks in the mountain village across the Semestrial Sea. The Kayda people had been undeservedly accommodating to the small company of elves, but even among the Kayda, there had been suspicion, and Suri Ranta was far from a peaceful oasis.

Some of Gellion's joy at being back in Tura melted away as he thought back to the mountain cave west of the human town, where he and his brothers had spent sleepless nights uncovering the past and plans of the foe that now threatened Tura—if Reanan's responses were any indication. His joy dimmed further when he looked more closely at the elves walking with quick strides through the streets. The elves were nervous, many of them glancing toward the sky at regular intervals, or else keeping their heads lowered as they moved to their destinations.

Gellion looked at his brothers. Valder was beaming. He clearly hadn't noticed the air of solemnity in the city. Gellion didn't think Valder had given much thought at all to the dark knowledge they had learned since their departure from Suri Ranta.

Valder alone had immensely enjoyed the long days of sailing across the Semestrial Sea with nothing but sailcloth and a rudder. Gellion had sorely missed a motor at the back of the boat and had never crossed the sea with so few hands on deck. It had been a wet and slow journey, each moment more agonizing than the last as they made their painstaking way back to Faeran. More painstaking still had been their trek along the coastline for days until they arrived in Tura. Gellion was exhausted and salt crusted, and his nerves were wound tight as harp strings, but Valder seemed to feel none of these discomforts. Not for the first time, Gellion longed for his brother's easy resilience.

Pleasure was evident in Veldon's face as well, his eyes taking in all around him with an analyzing gleam, but a line creased his brow as his gaze locked on several spears and halberds latched to the back of elves who walked in a clear cadence of patrol. His eyes dropped to the ground. He stopped in his tracks with a sharp intake of breath.

A part of Gellion knew what Veldon's reaction meant before he followed his brother's gaze. Why else would a stone street procure such dismay? The suspicion did not soften the blow when Gellion lowered his eyes to the ground. The street was smooth—unbroken and grey— but through the grain of the stone, a latticework of ebony spread in every direction. Gellion lowered to his knees and brushed the stone with the tips of his fingers.

Dead. Lifeless.

He harbored no doubts that the rest of the city was the same. Every street, every building. His hand balled into a fist against the stone.

Gellion had been expecting this. Of course Kaelo had come to Tura, Gellion had always known he would, yet like his mother's grief, this confirmation of his worst fears brought more dread than he had anticipated.

He took slow breaths against his mounting anxiety. It was gone. All the vierstone in Tura. He knew it in his bones. They had arrived too late. Their warnings would fall on deaf ears. Their explanations would be useless. Gritting his teeth, Gellion rose to his feet and faced Reanan. The Master Builder was watching him.

"You know what it means, then," Reanan said softly.

"He destroyed it all?" Gellion said.

Reanan nodded. "The elves from Daro warned us, but it did no good. We couldn't stop him." He closed his eyes as though in pain. "We were such fools."

"What happened?" Gellion tried to control his voice, to keep frustration and panic from coloring his words. "What did he do? Please, Reanan, tell us plainly."

"I will, though I hardly think I am the best elf to do it." He glanced back at the closing gates. "But first let us go to the forges. We can speak there and you can see for yourself how the tale ends."

Gellion exchanged a look with his brothers. They were clearly as perplexed by Reanan's words as he was, but they followed Reanan to a pile of levit boards without further questions.

The boards were stacked next to a smooth metal path. Reanan stepped onto one of the boards and activated it with the press of his heel. The board rose off the ground with a barely audible hum. Gellion mounted his own board and felt his weight lift off of the path. He smiled despite himself. The levit boards seemed such a normal thing—a comforting thing. He had gravely missed Remsgri technology in his months crossing Tala.

A breeze swept Gellion's hair from his face as his levit board glided forward. He followed Reanan into the Scholar Quarter of Tura, his brothers close behind. Gellion forced himself to focus. Everywhere he looked, he saw black lacing the streets and buildings, but nowhere did he see other signs of damage. He frowned. In Daro, blackened vierstone had always accompanied earthquakes that had cracked the foundations of the city. Buildings had crumbled and split, roofs had caved in, Rale paths had broken. But Tura looked exactly as it always had.

They passed the glittering glass of the Archives and crossed a bridge into the Guild Quarter. Where was Reanan taking them? How could he show them what Kaelo had done when there seemed to be no damage to the city? Gellion longed to shower Reanan with questions and refuse to move another foot until the Master Builder answered them, but he bit his tongue and followed in silence. The forges were not far by Rale path.

Reanan banked his board right to follow a street running north along the Orhiri River. After a few blocks, he began to slow.

With Reanan in front of him, Gellion did not immediately see the forges. Hearing Veldon's gasp, he leaped off his levit board and stood to face the source of his brother's dismay. His stomach dropped. The forges of Tura were one of the Great City's wonders—huge and open to the air, with a sturdy roof to keep out rain and sun.

The roof was gone. A massive slack tub lay on its side next to the river. Some of the furnaces still stood, but their sides were scorched and pieces of stone crumbled from their edges. Several furnaces were nothing but heaps of rubble, surrounded by splintered planks of wood, twisted metal, and ash. It looked as though there had been an explosion.

Gellion swallowed past his tightening throat. He had spent years working metal in those forges. Had Kaelo done this?

"What happened?" Gellion's voice was a hoarse whisper. He felt Valder and Veldon step up on either side of him, but he could not seem to pull his eyes from the wreckage to see their expressions.

"What remained of the elves of Daro sailed into our harbor nearly two months ago," Reanan said. "Two days later, Kaelo made his presence known in Tura."

Every nerve in Gellion's body seized at the name. By now, he had no doubts whatsoever that his old mentor was behind these attacks, but he had been unsure whether the elves of Tura would have discovered the culprit's identity in his absence. A glimmer of hope lit in his chest. Had Renyra survived the battle, then? Had she carried Gellion's message to the elves?

"It began with an earthquake," Reanan continued. "But there was no more shaking after that. He just silently drained the city of vierstone until there was nothing left. We tried to catch him, threaten him, track him. Liera confronted him once, and it ended in a whole street's destruction when Coren launched an ambush against him. But nothing we did ever had a chance of succeeding. We were playing into his hands the entire time. Following the prophecy." Reanan nearly spat the last word. His face darkened, but there was something else in his eyes. Shame?

"Prophecy?" Veldon said sharply. "What are you talking about?"

Reanan hesitated. "There was an elf—from Daro. A Turi woman."

Gellion could feel his skin starting to chill.

"Kyna," Reanan said.

It was like a punch in the gut. Gellion struggled to keep his face under control. He could feel the eyes of his brothers boring into him, but ignored them.

"What did she do?" he said softly.

Reanan narrowed his eyes. "Did you know her?" he asked.

"What did she do?" Gellion repeated, enunciating each word. He was not about to explain his relationship with Kyna now.

"Liera brought her on the Council," Reanan said slowly. "Along with a Fieri elf from Daro—Renyra. They told us all that occurred in Daro. The earthquakes, the vierstone, and the alliance. Renyra warned us about Kaelo, though it was not until Liera saw him with her own eyes that anyone believed it. Anyway, Kyna brought a prophecy to the attention of the Council. She said she found it in the Archives." He shook his head. "It was perfect. Too perfect. We should have seen there was something wrong with it from the beginning, but we were desperate, and Kyna played her part well."

The pain in Gellion's stomach was starting to twist and transform. So the elves already knew Kyna was a spy. That gave Gellion a strange relief. Kyna must surely have left Tura by now if her secret had been revealed. He wouldn't have to speak with Liera after all. Not about this. But what had Kyna done? By Reanan's tone, the elves had learned of her treachery too late.

"The prophecy spoke of all that had been happening in Daro and in Tura," Reanan said. "It led us to melt what vierstone remained to us in a furnace. Kaelo couldn't destroy vierstone he couldn't touch. It made sense. But the prophecy went further. It spoke of a weapon—something forged 'from his despise.' We eventually interpreted it to mean a sword of vierstone. Kaelo wore armor that no arrow could penetrate, so we assumed a vierstone sword may succeed where no other weapon could. Kyna urged us along all the while, and we ate it up like sweet bread. It was all part of Kaelo's plan."

Gellion looked back at the destroyed forges. The Council must have made the vierstone sword here. His eyes moved to the overturned slack tub, then to the crumbling furnaces. An idea was forming in his mind. Memories of a lamp-lit study swam before his eyes. Two words, traced over and over and circled. Pages of notes on phoenixes and volcanoes.

"Vierstone ash." Gellion whispered the words. His mind whirled. Melted vierstone in the furnaces—meant to protect from Kaelo. Cold water from the river—a slack tub to cool the metal of a forged blade. He thought back to Kaelo's notes on volcanoes. There had been stacks of books on geology in those shelves, and Kaelo had pulled from them, written pages of his research on magma and ash.

Reanan stared at him. "How do you—"

Gellion cut him off. "What did he do with it, Reanan? What did he do with the vierstone ash?"

Reanan had gone pale again. He looked between Gellion and his brothers.

"He raised a phoenix."

Ice poured through Gellion's body and solidified in his veins. He stared at Reanan, willing the man to to take back his words, to say it was a joke, but the despair in his eyes was unmistakable.

A phoenix.

Gellion clenched his fists and closed his eyes. They were too late, and it was worse than they could have ever imagined.

"We need to go to Liera," Valder said again.

Gellion had refused Reanan's offer to bring them to the Lady of Tura. He wanted to think first, to process all that Reanan had told them, but how could he process the reality that a monster from his deepest nightmares had come to ravage his world once more, this time controlled by an elf he had once admired more than anyone in the world? It was ridiculous. It was impossible.

"We need to put this in perspective first." Gellion ran a hand through his hair. He was standing on a side street in the Guild Quarter, where Gellion had dragged his brothers after speaking with Reanan. Tura was a big city, but Gellion had once known many of the elves who lived here. He did not want the story of his or his brothers' return circulating the streets just yet. Not if their mother was here.

He shook his head.

One thing at a time.

But where to begin?

Veldon's voice cut through Gellion's thoughts.

"What did we learn in the Falspires that the rest of elves do not yet know?"

Gellion could feel his anxiety easing at the calm in his brother's eyes. He took a breath.

"We know how Kaelo played the Albaren and the Dierna, though that will offer little help to the elves now." He sighed and reached into an inner pocket of his shirt. "And we have this." He held out a roughly cut piece of stone, crimson and smooth with ripples like glass where it had cleaved. The stone cooled the tips of his fingers. He could feel his heartbeat slow and his anxiety dampen. The vierstone in his ear flared with heat, as though in protest.

Gellion had experimented with the redstone during their long hours of sailing. The stone both repelled him and drew him. He had begun to understand some of its workings, though he had not yet allowed himself to use its true power again. Well did he remember the rushing current that had flowed through his body when he used the stone as Kaelo had. He had ordered a rock to break in his hand and the rock had obeyed without a moment's hesitation. It had been a heady feeling, a powerful feeling, but so too had there been something *wrong* about it. Was it only because Gellion had seen Kaelo use that power to destroy his home?

Veldon eyed the redstone warily. He didn't like it when Gellion brought it out so casually. Of the three of them, Veldon seemed to be most sensitive to the mysterious substance. Gellion assumed it had something to do with Veldon's affinity to vierstone. All his life, Gellion had thought himself well attuned to the workings of vierstone. He could use its channel to make incredible works of craftsmanship and could influence the very properties of metallic elements under its influence, but Veldon understood lifestone itself in a way that Gellion could never hope to emulate—the same way their father had.

"I wish you would keep that hidden." Veldon pulled his eyes away from the stone to glance around the street.

Gellion shrugged. "No one here knows what it is."

"I still think we should be careful with it—both the stone itself and our knowledge of it. We still do not know where it comes from, or fully understand what it does. It could be dangerous, and not just in the hands of an elf using it for destruction."

"I am being careful," said Gellion. "I've brought it safely this far haven't I? Do you think I plan to start exploding rocks throughout the city? Challenging Kaelo to a duel at the top of my lungs?"

Veldon said nothing. He looked away.

Gellion sighed and slipped the stone back in his shirt.

"Veldon, I am taking it seriously, alright? I just don't see the harm in looking at the thing, or trying to figure out how it works. The better we know this stone, the better we can understand Kaelo's power."

"I'm not sure Kaelo's breaking stones is the power we need to worry about now." Valder raised an eyebrow. "He has a *phoenix*, and from what Reanan says, Kaelo can destroy all the vierstone in a city without causing any further damage or drawing attention to himself. It sounds to me like his use of redstone just paved the way for whatever he's doing now. It's nice to know how he did it, but I can't see how that," he motioned to Gellion's chest, "is going to help us against the same flying fire beast that kept the elves at war for two hundred years."

Gellion fell silent. Valder was right. Having access to Kaelo's weapon had offered a perfect solution to fighting him one on one, but Kaelo was not their only enemy now. What good was controlling the stones of a city when combatting an armored bird the size of a ship that could reign fire and fly? Gellion might be able to use his command of stone to trap the beast if it landed near him, but it was an unlikely hope.

"So we have nothing," Gellion said. "We can tell the elves why the army of Daro came to be massacred between two human armies, but not until months after the threat has passed. We can tell them that Kyna is Kaelo's daughter, but not until she has succeeded in leading the elves on a false chase and ensured the success of her father. We can tell them how Kaelo sent Daro into the sea and destroyed all the vierstone in Tura, but not until after he has raised a weapon far more powerful." A laugh escaped Gellion's lips, though he had never seen a situation less humorous. "The elves would have been just as well if we'd never escaped Tala."

"That's not true," said Veldon. "Any information about Kaelo could be valuable in stopping him. We don't know what he will do next. If he still intends to use redstone to enable his plans, our knowledge could still prove instrumental in his undoing. We may not have returned to the elves as saviors with all the answers, but we have returned with information that warrants hope, and we have returned to help."

"What makes you think anyone here wants my help?" Gellion said. "I just led a thousand elves into the worst disaster since the Battle at Mathtier and let my city fall into the sea without recognizing its destroyer was my old mentor who is—oh, yes—is only alive today because I spoke in favor of his life centuries ago!" Gellion's voice came faster and rose in pitch with each word. He could feel his emotions starting to pull him under again, his hands starting to shake. He had the sudden urge to take the redstone out of his shirt again.

"Gellion." From the gentleness of the voice, Gellion assumed it was Veldon who had spoken, but he was surprised to see Valder looking him in the eye. "You have to stop doing this to yourself. You constantly live in the past, torturing yourself with your failures and every decision you wish you had made differently. It does no good. You have the power to do something about what is happening *now*, and if you let the consequences of your past experience stop you from doing that, it will only add to your regrets and lessen the chances of the elves getting out of this."

Heat prickled up Gellion's neck. Was he so easy to read?

"He's right," said Veldon. "I have told you this before, Gellion, though you have done little since then to heed the advice." A sad smile curved his lips. "We can still tell Liera all we know and get a more complete story of what is happening among the Kindoms. I very much doubt this is an issue only afflicting the Turi now. We will learn what we can and go from there, making the best decisions we can with what we are dealt. It is all we can do."

Veldon's smile became more genuine. "Besides, you're forgetting the best benefit of our return that has nothing to do with what information we've gathered or what problems we have solved." His eyes lit with the innate joy Gellion had always envied in his brother. "We get to show mother we're still alive."

The thought only brought a fraction of the same joy to Gellion. Of course he was looking forward to seeing his mother again, but how quickly would her relief and happiness wear off after the initial reunion? How soon would that joy turn to anger, that relief to blame? He couldn't bear to see either emotion in his mother's eyes, not when he deserved them both so thoroughly.

As for his reunion with Tornac, Gellion felt only dread—deep and gnawing. There was so much more between Gellion and his eldest brother than this latest fault. Gellion could never do anything right in Tornac's eyes, and the last few months would have only proved Tornac's assertions of Gellion's irresponsibility and selfishness correct. Gellion wouldn't be surprised if Tornac was disappointed by the revelation of Gellion's continued existence. At least he would be happy to see Valder and Veldon, though Valder had likely earned some of his own enmity by following in Gellion's footsteps.

The excited spark remained in Veldon's eyes, though it was tempered by sympathy when he saw Gellion's face. Gellion did his best to appear pleased.

Valder hadn't noticed his elder brother's discomfiture. A wicked smile stretched across his face.

"We can 'show' mother however you want, but I say we scare Tornac witless with our resurrection."

ACKNOWLEDGMENTS

Writing a book is the most amazing and frustrating and wonderful thing. While most of the long hours are spent in solitude, it is astounding how many people it takes to turn an idea and some words into a novel.

There were those who helped shape the book itself—the words, the art, and the story. Equally important were those who supported me through the years of creating—the writing, the editing, the laughing and crying and fist shaking and celebrating. Thank you all. I couldn't have done it without you.

To Pamela, thank you for supporting this project and every project I have ever endeavored to pursue. To David, thank you for sharing your love of literature with me the last twenty-eight years and for being my first reader and reviser when my story was still a mess to behold.

Thank you Emma, for your words of encouragement each time I realized anew how hard writing a book was. You are an inspiration and a true friend.

Thank you Jake, for everything. For sharing me with my characters and my computer screen and supporting me in everything I do with undeserved confidence.

To my editor, Al, thank you for your hours of work and attention to detail, and your ability to see the art beyond grammar. To Emily, thank you for your beautiful illustrations that captured the characters and world in my head more perfectly than I could have imagined.

Last, but certainly dear to my heart, I want to thank the authors of every fantasy book I have ever read for showing me the beauty, magic, and power of stories. There are too many to name, but your influence shaped my world.

ABOUT THE AUTHOR

Haley Rylander is an author living in Denver, Colorado. It is her goal to write inspiring stories set in other worlds that reflect our own world in ways that can only be achieved through the magic and power of words. This is her first novel.

haleyrylander.com